END OF THE END

An Abaddon Books™ Publication
www.abaddonbooks.com
abaddon@rebellion.co.uk

This omnibus published in 2016 by Abaddon Books™,
Rebellion Publishing Ltd, Riverside House,
Osney Mead, Oxford, OX2 0ES, UK.

10 9 8 7 6 5 4 3 2 1

Editor-in Chief: Jonathan Oliver
Commissioning Editor: David Moore
Cover Art: Sam Gretton
Original Series Cover Art: Sam Gretton
Design: Sam Gretton and Oz Osborne
Marketing and PR: Rob Power
Head of Books and Comic Publishing: Ben Smith
Creative Director and CEO: Jason Kingsley
Chief Technical Officer: Chris Kingsley
The Afterblight Chronicles™ created by
Simon Spurrier & Andy Boot

ISBN (UK): 978-1-78108-469-4
ISBN (US): 978-1-78108-470-0

Printed in Denmark.

A POST-APOCALYPTIC OMNIBUS

END OF THE END

PAUL KANE • CAVAN SCOTT • SIMON GUERRIER

WWW.ABADDONBOOKS.COM

The Afterblight Chronicles

The Culled
Simon Spurrier

Kill Or Cure
Rebecca Levene

Dawn Over Doomsday
Jasper Bark

Death Got No Mercy
Al Ewing

Blood Ocean
Weston Ochse

Arrowhead
Broken Arrow
Arrowland
Paul Kane

School's Out
Operation Motherland
Children's Crusade
Scott K. Andrews

Journal of the Plague Year
Malcolm Cross, CB Harvey and Adrian Tchaikovsky

End of the End
Paul Kane, Cavan Scott and Simon Guerrier

OMNIBUS EDITIONS
America
School's Out Forever
Hooded Man

INTRODUCTION

ON REFLECTION, PERHAPS I should have called it *Beginning of the End of the End*.

It's been a long old journey thus far. *The Culled* was Abaddon Books' very first title, hitting the shelves back in the summer of 2006, after a dizzying year of setting up the imprint, finding talent, commissioning work, marketing, setting up distribution links and all the thousand small tasks that go into starting a new publishing imprint. Yr hmbl crspndnt wasn't even a gleam in Jonathan Oliver's eye at that point, still wrestling as I was with an unsatisfying back office job in London's financial district.

Si Spurrier was a *2000 AD* writer at the time, with several years and a great many mad, brilliant stories under his belt, along with a number of tie-in novels for Black Flame. His pitch for the first book for Jon's *Afterblight Chronicles* series of post-apocalypse thrillers was simple and stark: a British spec-ops soldier, hiding away from the horrors of the Cull, receives evidence that his girlfriend is still alive and makes his way to America to try and find her, killing everyone in his way and almost incidentally toppling an exploitative, child-snatching pseudo-Christian cult on the way.

It was a brilliant book: breathlessly fast, savagely violent, witty and tough, with an unexpected spiritualism, and themes of defiance and duty, faith and skepticism, civilisation and barbarism that have informed the series ever since. Amid the guns and the gangs and the push to survive, it also provided moments of absurdity: odd characters, peculiar practices and bizarre beliefs that provided stark relief for the book's darker moments. It showed us what the series—and to an extent, our whole imprint—should look like, and following Si's example, *Afterblight* has gone on to be one of our longest-running, most successful worlds.

The Culled's sequel, Rebecca Levene's *Kill or Cure*, came next, in 2007, turning Si's story over and following the soldier's girlfriend, Jasmine, as she desperately searched for a cure to the Cull and discovered too late the terrible cost of using it. Haunted by the Cure—by the voice in her head, driving her to callous, brutal selfishness—she became caught up in the schemes of others, reacting and adapting and turning people's manipulations to her advantage. The tension between the compassionate person she once was and the monster she was becoming provided a complexity and danger to the book, and the final showdown with her old colleague, who had thrown himself into the darkness Jasmine struggled against, was ultimately a battle for her own soul as much as for the lives of the innocents around her.

Scott K. Andrews' *School's Out* was the third *Afterblight* book, coming out of our very first open-submissions period, and hugely expanded the political and philosophical underpinnings of the world. Heavily inspired by William Golding's *Lord of the Flies*, it looks at the challenges facing children in an apocalyptic world, the many people who seek to exploit, abuse or hurt them and what it costs them to fight back. The story invoked child soldiers in bush conflicts in the real world and addressed intergenerational tension and the loss of innocence. The *School's Out* books are probably my favourite in the *Afterblight* universe: punky, defiant and bleak.

Paul Kane's *Arrowhead*, kicking off the *Hooded Man* series, was the fifth *Afterblight* book, and brought the spirituality hinted at in Si's book out into the forefront of the story. A post-apocalyptic retelling of the Robin Hood legend, with a full complement of merry men (and women), the story brings its hooded hero into communion with the spirit of Sherwood Forest, which appears to choose—and perhaps create—champions like him, to act as defenders both of the Forest and of England itself. Painted in the (relatively, for the *Afterblight* world) clean tones of myth and archetype, Paul's books were weird, mystical and atmospheric.

IT'S BEEN TEN years. On the way, we've published around a hundred novels in a score of worlds, added the Solaris and Ravenstone imprints to our publishing stable, and made a name for ourselves as one of the publishing world's pulpiest, smartest and most risk-taking newcomers. We've even picked up an award or two. And, of course, I came along, picking up the reins while Jon turned his focus exclusively to Solaris.

And *Afterblight*'s been with us all the way. Fully twelve authors have taken up the mantle, both new talents and established favourites, to tell stories of survival, suffering and—above all—courage in the face of horror. We've visited Central Europe, Australia, the Pacific Ocean and even the International Space Station, in stories ranging from the outrageously brutal to the nailbitingly tense.

Two years ago I commissioned *Journal of the Plague Year*, exploring the first few months of the Cull with three novellas telling of the chaos, confusion and violence of the early days. Last year I suggested we bookend the series, revisiting three of the longest-running and most-loved stories in the setting years later, and revisiting old characters. Where are they now? What trials have they met and overcome on the way, and what new problems have arisen to challenge them?

Scott asked me to get the brilliant Simon Guerrier in to pick up the story of St. Mark's. In *Fall Out*, Jack Bedford, the young King of England, is ready to take up his mantle, but there's a long way to go before he'll be accepted by the men and women who've established themselves as the leaders of Britain since the dust settled. And there are challenges in restoring the old, abandoned infrastructure of the twenty-first century that most people have never imagined (the clue's in the name).

Cavan Scott approached me for a gig, and I asked him to put together an outline finally bringing together Si Spurrier's nameless soldier and Rebecca Levene's tortured Jasmine; and he delivered beautifully. *Children of the Cull* is a dark, intense story building up to their reunion—after all these years—with a sort of horrifying inevitability as you gradually realise the happy ending they once dreamed of is almost certainly going to elude them.

Finally, Paul Kane was only too happy to return to the hero of the *Hooded Man* books. *Flaming Arrow* passes on the baton; Rob's getting old and looking to settle down, and wants to hand over his duties to his protegé, Mark. But there's tension in England, as power blocs are gradually forming and settling in place, and there are still enemies overseas. And there's a glimpse of a future darker even than the bloodthirsty present of the *Afterblight* world.

ULTIMATELY, IT'S NOT the end of the end. There are still questions unanswered; how does the future *Flaming Arrow* shows us come about? How, if at all, are *Fall Out*'s engineers, *Children of the Cull*'s biologists and *Flaming Arrow*'s sinister Schaefer linked? There are stories yet to come, of course. But for now, perhaps, *End of the End* is offering a little closure, a glimpse of futures our earlier books hinted at but never delivered on. Something for you to enjoy until we turn our attention back to the world of the Cull again.

Cheers!

David Thomas Moore
Oxford
April 2016

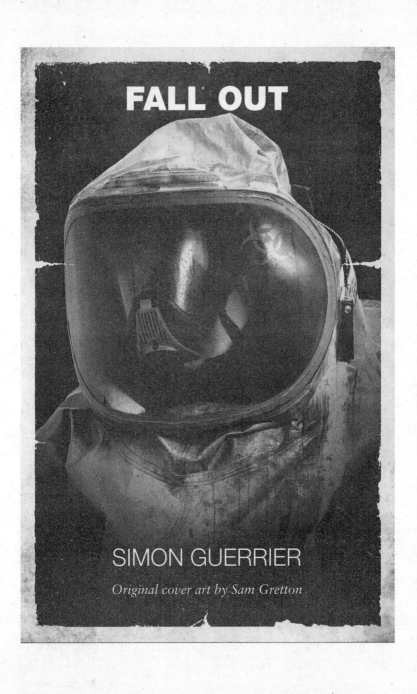

FALL OUT

SIMON GUERRIER

Original cover art by Sam Gretton

To Scott,
Who I've killed more than anyone else,
With gratitude

PART ONE

CHAPTER ONE

THE SURVIVORS TRUDGED up the old A683 towards her. They were a sorry lot, bent and broken by the long march and the horror they fled. Some didn't even have shoes, their bare feet bloodied from the ancient grey tarmac. They were a motley collection, a mix of the old and very young. Some carried snivelling children or helped prop up those more wretched than themselves. They stank, too, of blood and sweat and fear.

Even in their misfortune, they showed deference to the woman on horseback, stumbling off the roadside to allow her to pass. Her hood, her cloak, the bow on her back were all symbols of a power greater than one woman. Even in their plight, they knew not to get in the way of a Ranger.

"Who was it?" Aamna called down to them, keeping her voice low and stern the way she had been trained. "How many of them?" No one answered her, so she chose a gaunt looking man clinging to a baby. Livid purple bruises clustered round his eyes and on one side of his face. The hands that cradled the baby were dark with bruises, too.

"Anything you tell me can help," she told him, kindly.

"We'll sort them out, and we'll get you all home. You want to go home, don't you?" He only stared back at her. "They came in from the sea, yes?" she went on. "How many boats? What weapons did they have? Fuck's sake, give me something. Do it for the baby."

His lips trembled. "Fire," he managed to say. He lifted the baby towards her, to better show what had been done to his hands. Not bruises, but burns. And the baby... What flesh Aamna could see was purple and swollen. It didn't appear to be breathing.

Aamna glanced round. The old road cut through wild meadow which had probably been fields and farms in the days before The Cull. There was no sign of burning, or of whoever had attacked these sorry people. The pirates—if that's what they were—had not dared venture this far inland. But there was something else, too: something wrong. No birds wheeled in the air, no animals stirred the long grass.

West, towards the coast, clouds hung low and dark. The pirates would not risk putting out to sea again until the storm had passed—they'd still be in the town.

"Whoever they are," Aamna told the man, "they're gonna pay." The words took a moment to reach through his despair, then he only shook his head—whatever Aamna did, it was too late for him anyway. "Lancaster isn't far up the road," she told him, raising her voice for the others to hear. "Get them to send word to my lot. I'm gonna see what we're up against, and they better get down here quick. All right, get on before it chucks it down."

The man glanced back at the clouds churning low in the sky. Then, clinging tight to the dead bundle in his arms, he and the others shuffled away up the road.

Aamna set her horse in the other direction, riding into the storm.

SHE MET MORE survivors on the road, with worse burns. There were bodies, too; people who'd succumbed to their injuries. Flies buzzed around open sores. Aamna's stomach turned. She resisted the urge to stop, to check for signs of life, to help them if she could; the priority was to learn the strength of the enemy.

She sweated under her cloak, and it was more than apprehension. The air was warm and itchy, eager for the storm to break. Still the rain didn't come. A bald, scarred woman waved her arms feebly at Aamna and the horse, warning them not to go any further. Aamna had to urge her horse to go on. If she'd not been so thoroughly trained, she would have lifted the bow from her shoulder and had an arrow ready. But it was better not to present a threat until she knew exactly what she was dealing with. Besides, shooting the longbow would only throw her from the horse.

They crossed a roundabout, and the road passed between the ruined houses on the outskirts of the town. There were no more people now, not living ones. From the gaping window of one terrace sprouted the branches of a tree, nature reclaiming the long-abandoned buildings.

She rode on, not seeing any signs of life. Surely the pirates had scouts hidden somewhere, watching the road. Her horse's hooves echoed loudly all around, but still no one came to meet her. They were cowards, burning people with no means to fight back but not daring to step out in front of a Ranger.

Or letting her walk into a trap.

At the end of the terrace, the road turned, allowing her a first look down on the harbour. Banks of cloud hung low and oppressive, obscuring the view. No, not cloud—the buildings on the seafront billowed thick black smoke.

There was no sign of anything Aamna could take for pirates. Perhaps they had already gone back out to sea, hoping to outrun the storm. Or perhaps they were concealed behind the burning buildings. There was only one way to be sure.

When she prodded her horse, it only snorted. She tried again and this time it bucked, almost throwing her off. "Hey, big lad. You'll do what you're told if you want a Polo."

The horse—she didn't know its name, it was just the one she'd been given at the last post house—immediately settled. Aamna couldn't remember what Polos had been like, but the horses all obviously did. "Just you remember who's boss, eh? Now..." But the horse still wouldn't walk on.

With a sigh, Aamna jumped down to the ground and tethered the horse to a railing. "So," she said, "you guard our escape route. If you see pirates, try not to let them eat you."

SHE KEPT HER bow on her shoulder and walked with her arms slightly out from her sides, making it clear she had nothing in her hands. Still nothing stirred around her.

The houses were in better condition as Aamna made her way down the hill towards the sea. Some homes had been painted, recently, in bright colours. The gutters and brickwork were all well tended. In front of each house stood a tall, grey wheeled bin. This community had weathered The Cull and put itself back together, bringing back some of the old ways. Several of the houses had immaculate front gardens, though the flowers looked wilted and sickly.

Her ears rang as she strained to hear anything in the silence. The only sounds were her own footsteps and the beating of her heart. Any moment, she was sure, a pirate would step out in front of her, or open fire from hiding. But she went on, and still no one stopped her.

It started to rain—no, dust and small fragments drifted softly down from the smoke overhead. She couldn't help but breathe it in, and it felt hot and prickly. Her eyes and nose started to run.

Now she could hear fire. Another street, and the coloured houses gave way to a terrace all in black, the windows cracked and yellow from the heat. A splash of vivid blue paint on a wall in the middle. As Aamna got closer she made sense of the shape—the outline of a woman, cowering against the door, her arms raised to protect her face.

There was no sign of the woman whose body had shielded the paintwork. Perhaps she had been removed, taken by the pirates. Aamna didn't want to think what for.

Another street on and the damage was worse. The fronts of a few of the houses had come down. She looked in on charred remains: traces of furnishings, a scrap of curtain at a soot-black window. She thought she saw the contorted remains of a family but she didn't linger.

Now Aamna had to pick her way over the rubble in the road. There were chunks of brick and panelling, roof tiles and who knew what else. She listened for the sounds of anyone alive who might be trapped under the wreckage. There was nothing. Just the distant roar of fire—and the sea.

She made her way to the end of the street and out onto the harbour, a wide open space of concrete, covered in debris. Thick smoke reaching almost to the ground made it hard to see where the concrete ended and the sea began. Wait—she could see waves crashing against what had once been the smooth line of the harbour wall. Great chunks had been torn from the concrete.

What could have done this? Her first thought was some kind of bomb. It would have had to be pretty big to create such devastation. Perhaps the pirates had all been killed in the blast. But then, if you had such a weapon, why use it on a defenceless target like this? Perhaps it had been an accident. A ship, carrying a weapon, smashed into shore by the storm...

She had to know one way or the other. Up on the hill, her view of the harbour had been obscured by a large, wrecked building, billowing black smoke from a huge rent down one entire wall. She still couldn't see beyond it and would have to go round.

Aamna looked around herself as she made her way over the treacherous ground, feeling exposed. Her eyes and nose were streaming. Suddenly there was a pain like a fist in her stomach and she doubled over.

But she hadn't been shot; she needed to be sick. Half-digested pie spattered her boots. "Fuck," she muttered, wiping her mouth on the back of her sleeve. She prayed no one was watching.

A few more steps and she had to stop again to retch up bile. She felt dizzy and shivery, not fit for battle with pirates. But surely the smoke would affect anyone else just the same? She'd be evenly matched, unless the pirates had protective suits...

The thought sent a chill through her. She'd seen people in protective suits before. The Rangers who'd been sent down to assess Salisbury Plain, five years after the bomb had gone off there. One man, his suit hadn't been quite right and Aamna had heard the ghoulish tales about how the poisoned air had got him. Vomiting and shitting blood, purple sores all over his body.

Fuck.

But it couldn't be, not here. There wasn't an Army base anywhere for miles, and this wasn't the kind of place to keep a nuclear bomb. She turned to look at the huge building that billowed smoke. Was it her imagination, or was the fire inside it throbbing amber, perfectly in time with the beating inside her own head? Then her eye caught something else: the remains of a chain-link fence, now warped and twisted. The wind buffeted something fixed to it, a panel—no, a sign, black letters on yellow so the words would be clear from a distance:

THIS IS A LICENSED NUCLEAR SITE

Slowly, stiffly, Aamna walked away from the fire and the sea, back the way she'd come. She didn't feel shocked or sad or angry. Her only thought was to stop the other Rangers from ever getting this far.

CHAPTER TWO

THE REMAINS OF a man hung in a gibbet over Magdalen Bridge. Doleful sockets stared down at the snaking queue of people hoping to get into Oxford, but by and large no one spared the dead man a glance. They were mostly traders and local farmers, the regular ebb and flow through the gates of the city, and apparently well used to bodies in cages hanging at the gate. Yet one woman in the queue couldn't tear her eyes from the grim spectacle.

"It's fucking barbaric," said Jane Crowther. She was a lean, muscular woman in her mid thirties, with close-cropped hair that showed her many scars. The top of one ear was missing.

"Language," said her companion. Jack Bedford was twenty-three, cursed with acne and terrible, greasy hair that meant people often overlooked his piercing, watchful eyes. "Besides, we don't know what he did."

"And what would justify that?"

"Murder," said Jack. "Public drunkenness. Carrying arms within the city walls. It goes on." He nodded to the sign on the wall beside the gate, listing Capital Offences. "Look," he said. "Wilful damage to books."

"Well," said Jane, after a moment. "I can understand that one."

They had been in the queue for more than two hours. It started to rain, but they didn't move any more quickly. Now they were wet as well as cold and weary, and soon it would be dark. They'd been warned that the gates shut at nightfall.

"You sure you don't want to say something?" said Jane. "The Council said it was urgent."

Jack shook his head. "We're no more important than anyone else."

"But you're the—" She was about to say *King of England*, but a look from Jack cut her short. Instead she mouthed, "the you-know-what."

"Maybe. But we play it cool."

She snorted.

"You know what I mean," he went on. "Casual. Easy. I'm just an ordinary bloke."

"They asked you here by name. They used your title."

"Then why not offer us an escort? Anything could have happened to us on the way here."

Jane nodded. Since leaving the safety of St Mark's, they'd had run-ins with bandits on the road—but it could have been much worse. "Then what are they playing at?"

Jack smiled. "Politics."

At last the group in front of them reached the table, where a bored-looking guard took his time going through their papers. There were endless questions, and then the group were turned away. One large man started to argue and Jack thought there would be a fight. But another member of the group took the man's arm and led him off. It clearly didn't do to argue.

"Come," said the long-suffering man at the table and Jack and Jane presented their papers, and the invitation bearing the coat of arms. The man looked it over indifferently and then handed it back. He said nothing, and for a moment Jack thought that they were not being let through either, but then Jane was leading him by the wrist through the high wooden gate.

They found themselves in a smaller courtyard with a second gate and another snaking queue. Another bored guard inspected their papers and made them sign a pledge that they would abide by the city's regulations.

"And if you breach the contract..." said the guard, but didn't finish the sentence. He just nodded towards another three gibbets hanging from the inner wall.

Jack and Jane surrendered their various weapons in exchange for a receipt, emptied their packs for inspection and allowed a wild-eyed man to poke and prod them to check for signs of disease. He squinted at Jack's prosthetic leg, but they assured him it was lost to injury rather than sickness. Finally, they were allowed through the second gate, across another bridge and through a third gate—where a nervous woman in uniform stood waiting.

"Ms Crowther, Mr Bedford. I'm Constable Ahaiwe. I'm afraid your meeting has been unavoidably delayed."

"You're kidding me," said Jane, making Ahaiwe flinch.

"What my colleague means," said Jack, amiably, "is that we've had quite a journey and that's rather a disappointment. Can you give us any idea how long we'll have to wait?"

Ahaiwe managed to smile. "I'm afraid certain matters need going into and they have to take precedence."

"Of course. By 'certain matters,' you mean...?"

The constable was taken aback. "I'm not at liberty to go into it."

"No, of course not," said Jack. "Well, it can't be helped. I suppose we should find some accommodation."

"That's already been seen to," said Ahaiwe. "You might be here some days. We are, of course, sorry for any inconvenience."

"Oh, you're fucking *sorry*, are you?" muttered Jane, quite distinctly.

"Now, now," Jack told her. "You only came in the first place so you could look round the library. And now we'll have time to do that." He turned to Ahaiwe. "I assume that can be arranged. Given the inconvenience."

"It's really not my role to—" she began, then caught Jane's expression. "I'll see what I can do."

"As long as it's no trouble," said Jack.

Ahaiwe was actually shaking. "Of course not," she said. "Now, if you'll follow me, we can find you a rick."

*   *   *

"Ricks" TURNED OUT to be rickshaws, pulled by strong, gangly teenagers Jack assumed must be students. He and Jane shared a single rick, clinging to their luggage as they made their bumpy way. It didn't do much for Jane's mood.

Jack, who'd never been to Oxford before, sat back in his seat contentedly, drinking it all in. The ancient spires and buildings, the students in their gowns. Bookshops and market-stalls and pubs, all from another era.

There were also the gun installations and masked patrols with assault rifles. He could see it in the faces of the people, too: a pinched, over-earnestness you never got at St Mark's. People living in fear of the rules, of the gibbet—and whatever else was happening. Whatever Jack had been called here to discuss.

They ducked through an archway and found themselves in the courtyard of one of the colleges. Jack had a sudden flashback to his time at Harrow, and a life and identity he'd long put behind him. What if someone here recognised him from that time? Well, he'd deal with that as and when.

They pulled up at one end of the quadrangle, where a line of small children wearing suits waited to carry their bags.

"I can—" Jack started to protest, but the children looked so aggrieved that he let them get on with it. As they followed the children inside, he saw Jane brush her hand against her hip, reaching for the gun that wasn't there.

"Want me to go first?" he asked—and she pushed past him.

It was warm and homely inside the college, but so much quieter than St Mark's. Children—in waistcoats and tails—were not allowed to chat or run. There was something rather sad about them as they passed. The children with the luggage led Jack and Jane through a warren of corridors, eventually stopping at a door like all the others.

"This is you," said the boy lugging Jack's bags, showing them into a simple, square room with adjacent single beds. There was a folded pink slip of paper on each pillow. "No food in your dorm at any time," he continued, "and no alcohol in college buildings. You share the loo with the rest of the corridor, but married quarters have a sink and running water."

"We're not—" Jane began.

"—used to such luxury," said Jack. He tried to give the boys a coin each as a tip, but again they looked affronted.

"Why do we have to be married?" said Jane, after the children had gone.

"Don't want to risk losing a top room like this," he said.

"Fine," she said, starting to unpack. "Just don't get any ideas."

"You should be so lucky."

"I could do better than you."

"Yeah, bit of make-up, a frock, do something with your hair, you'd almost pass."

She ignored him.

"Are you okay?" he said.

"No," said Jane. "I don't like being kept waiting. And I don't like not knowing what's going on. That woman at the gate."

"Constable Ahaiwe."

"She knows more than she let on. She was clearly terrified— of what?"

"You looked in a mirror recently?"

"Ha, ha—but it's not us. We're clearly not important, or there wouldn't be this delay."

"Oh, there's another explanation for that. Isn't it obvious?"

Jane sighed. "I don't want to have to hurt you."

Jack grinned. "Well, it's a classic power play, isn't it? Call us here urgently, then make us wait. Put us in our place."

"It's almost as if they don't know you're the rightful King of England," said Jane. Then understanding dawned. "Or they do, and they don't like it. You suspected, didn't you? What you said about them not sending an escort."

Jack nodded. "I think we're being tested—or played."

She sighed. "Politics. I should have listened when you told me not to come."

"I'd be dead if you'd hadn't. And hey, I got you into the library, didn't I?"

"You think? Now Constable Thing knows that's what I want, they can use it against us. Keep us in our place."

Jack looked stung. "I'm counting on psychology. I put it on their honour."

"And there's a lot of that around. Fuck, we've come all this way. I abandoned Lee! And now, if they don't let us in…"

"Then we find someone who works there who can look the stuff up for you. We need to do that anyway."

"Why?"

"So when you're back home, you can send letters back and forth. What, weren't you thinking long term? Besides, Lee is happy being babysat by Caroline. He's got her round his finger."

"You make it all sound simple."

"I do, don't I? But you're right: this is important. The medical books they have here can save a lot of lives."

"Or give us tips so we don't do so much harm. Then there's their botanical garden. We could be making new medicines!" She shook her head. "It can't be that easy, can it?"

"Probably not." There was an awkward silence, and Jack picked up the pink piece of paper on his bed. It was a free ticket for the Ashmolean Museum. He showed it to Jane. "Fancy this, then?" he asked her. "It's a bit late today, but they might just let us in. It's your sort of thing."

"Yes, I'd like to see it. But it's pretty obvious, isn't it?"

"What is?"

"Another power-play. We go where they tell us, we do what they want. More putting us in our place."

"Sure, but what can we do about it?"

"Not much until we know what they're all so scared of. But meanwhile, we don't go where they tell us."

"Okay. Then what?"

"The pub."

DOWN A NARROW alley they found a centuries-old pub with low ceilings. Regulars argued points of philosophy and discussed the books they'd just read. Feeling out of place, Jack and Jane moved to a wooden table outside in the gloom. A sign to one side of them proclaimed that they were sitting where Bill Clinton had famously not inhaled. Jack needed the reference explained to him, and then Jane teased him about heads of state who could never escape their own history, no matter how embarrassing or awkward. He let her take the piss: it had been a long time since he'd heard her laughing.

"But you do want to be King," she said at length.

"I *am* the King."

"You know what I mean."

He took a deep breath. "All right. I think we need a leader. Someone to unify all the different factions—the Rangers, the Cleaners, the Steamies, whoever."

"Make us one happy family."

"They fight," said Jack, "because they all want to be in charge. If there was someone else in charge, but who only had nominal power..."

"A constitutional monarchy," said Jane. "With what, the Rangers and Steamies as kind of political parties?"

"We'd need to work out the system," said Jack. "But yeah, that's my idea."

"And why should it be you? It could be anyone."

"Yeah," said Jack. "But you don't want someone who's grasping for power. You want someone who'll serve."

Jane watched him for a moment. "That's why you made us queue, and were so charming to the constable. Make them think you're a team player, a public servant."

"I *am* a team player."

"A good man in a crisis. A steady pair of hands. And not out for yourself. You don't tell them you want to be King. You let them come to their own conclusion that they want you on the throne."

"If it's what the country wants."

She smiled. "You've read that book on Napoleon that props up the shelf in the loo."

"It gave me some ideas. Think it could work?"

"I can think of a hundred reasons why it won't. But we're out of beer. Same again?"

She went to get the pints in, leaving Jack alone in the dark. He needed her to approve. That's why he'd risked sharing his ambitions with her now, when he'd not told anyone else. Jane was well respected. With her on his side, the rest of St Mark's would support him.

But as he waited for her to return from the bar, he picked over what she'd said—about heads of states and their pasts catching up with them. Was she right? Surely things were different since The Cull; it was more difficult to unearth people's secrets. His whole plan, his whole future, depended on that fact. Because while a select few knew Jack was the King of England, he alone knew the truth: that there'd been a mix-up. He was a nobody called Ben Wyman, and the real Jack Bedford was dead.

Where had Jane got to? Jack—he even thought of himself as Jack now—stood up to look in through the window, but couldn't see her at the bar. No, there she was, with a group of four young men. The men were thick-set and muscular, and none of them were smiling. Great.

He hurried in, slouching a bit and pretending to be more drunk than he was. "Darling," he said. "We're going to be awfully late. Constable Ahaiwe will be waiting." By the men's reactions, they recognised the name.

"Right," said Jane, staring one of the men down—though he was a full head taller than she was. Jack took Jane's hand.

"Nice to meet you, gents," he said, dragging Jane with him. "Another time, perhaps." They went out into the alley. "Chatting you up?" he whispered as he marched her on.

"Not exactly," said Jane. "Wanted to buy me a drink. I said no, nicely, and they started to insist. I know what you're going to say."

"I'm not going to say anything!"

"Well, I'll say what you're thinking. Why me? There were other women around. Young and pretty ones who don't have faces like thunder."

"You're pretty on the inside."

They were almost out of the alley and on to the main street when a figure stepped in front of them, blocking the way.

"Sorry, 'scuse us, mate," said Jack, but the man didn't move. Jack glanced back down the alley, where the other four men were approaching.

"No cause for alarm," said the man who had spoken in the pub, sounding posher than Jack expected. He held his arms out in front of him, showing his empty hands as he held them up in surrender. "I apologise if I scared you. We forget how it is outside Oxford. You folks must be wary of strangers."

"Who are you?" said Jane. "What do you want?"

"Messengers," said the man, approaching slowly. "Got a message for you."

"Go on, then."

"Well," said the man, lowering his voice. "It's a rather sensitive matter. About what's been happening. We don't want the whole world to hear."

Jane turned to Jack—she looked just as surprised as him. But what could they do? There was no way they'd push past the big man behind them, and they were curious. Jane nodded to Jack to remain where he was while she made her way back down the alley to meet the spokesman.

Who punched her hard in the face.

Jane collapsed backward, blood spouting from her nose and lip. Jack hurried forward to help her but the man behind him grabbed his shoulders and propelled him into the wall. Jack hit the bricks with the side of his head and his attacker clamped a hand round his throat, scraping Jack's face against the wall while he strangled him. Stunned and stupid, Jack tried to get purchase on the man's powerful hand. He tried to kick out, he tried to do anything, but knew that it was hopeless.

"Why?" he managed to say.

The men weren't listening. They looked down at Jane, prostrate on the floor. She held a small pistol up at them.

"Naughty," the well-spoken man told her. "That's a capital offence."

"Worth the risk, it turns out," said Jane, getting to her feet. She nodded towards the man still throttling Jack. "Let him go."

The hand eased from round Jack's aching throat. He leant against the wall, gasping for air.

"You get out of the way," Jane told the man who had throttled Jack. "We're leaving."

"I mean it," said the man. "The patrols catch you with that, you're done for. They'll do your boyfriend, too, for being an accomplice."

"Who are you?" Jane asked him. "Why pick on us?"

The man glanced involuntarily back at his friends. "Tourists. Don't know your way around town. Easy pickings."

Jack's throat was so raw he could barely get the words out. "He's... lying."

The spokesman only smiled.

"Someone sent you to kill us," said Jane. He didn't answer, so she raised the gun, pointing it right in his face.

"Nothing quite so permanent as that," said the man. "Call it a friendly warning."

"From who? About what?"

"Oh," he said, "I can't tell you that. You really would have to shoot me." He saw her finger tighten round the trigger and he smiled again. "I think you could do it, too. But I'll remind you you're in Oxford and there are strict rules about who can and can't carry guns. Actually killing someone? The gibbet, if you're lucky."

"He's right," said Jack, woozily. "We don't want the aggro."

"No," said Jane, her gun still on the man. "We never do, but it comes all the same." She glowered at the man. "Right now *I'm* the messenger. Friendly warning for whoever sent you our way. You don't fuck with us."

Still with his hands raised, the man bowed politely, then backed away down the alley with his men. The man who had throttled Jack was already gone.

Jack went over to Jane. Blood poured from her nose, but it didn't look broken. From the look she gave him, he was in a similar state. "You brought a gun into the city," he croaked, frowning.

"You're welcome."

"But if they find it..."

"They're not going to," she said, and started to slip it back into the holster in her sleeve.

"Um," said a voice behind them. "Actually..."

They turned. At the end of the alley stood Constable Ahaiwe, and two masked patrolmen with assault rifles.

CHAPTER THREE

"I'D BETTER TAKE the pistol," said Ahaiwe. Her hand trembled as she held it out, as if she thought Jane might shoot her.

"Five men just attacked us," said Jane. "If I hadn't had this on me, we'd be dead."

"It's true," said Jack. "I mean, look at the state of us. We weren't all bleeding when you spoke to us earlier."

"I see," said Ahaiwe. "Where are these five men now?"

"You just missed them," Jane told Ahaiwe. "Conveniently enough."

"You must have seen them," said Jack. "Five great big blokes. They were right here."

"Did you see anything?" Ahaiwe asked her patrol.

They shook their heads. "No, ma'am," one man grunted.

"They were *your* thugs," said Jane, slowly.

"I don't know anything about it," snapped Ahaiwe, though she wouldn't meet Jack and Jane's eyes. "But if they're not here now, you can give me the gun. Please. I don't want to use force."

There didn't seem to be any point arguing, not with the patrolmen and their assault rifles, so Jane handed over her pistol. Ahaiwe took it gingerly, as if it might bite her, and stowed it away in the pocket of her uniform.

"Good," she said to the patrolmen. "Take them to the castle."

The patrolmen gestured for Jack and Jane to move. Jack glanced back down the alley, but there was no hope of reaching the door to the pub at the end. He shrugged at Jane and led her the other way, out of the alley and on to the main street.

It was still early evening, a good hour before curfew, and there were plenty of people about. Academics discussed their studies, young couples held hands, a group of teenage boys shared a joke. It looked idyllic; to Jack, it seemed false. This was a police state, conspiring against him and Jane.

People turned to watch as they were led down the street by Ahaiwe and the two patrolmen. Jack held his chin up and walked with purpose. This would be part of the legend, he told himself. They'd remember his dignity and poise at this moment when, sometime in the future, he had become King. Yeah, he could hold on to that thought. He even grinned at Jane and she gave him a rueful if bloody smile in return.

"Um," said Ahaiwe behind them. "Could the prisoners both stop?"

Jack and Jane did as they were told. What now? They waited, but nothing more was said. Jack started to turn round but something poked him hard in the back—the end of a rifle. He stayed resolutely still. A crowd gathered round to watch, keeping their distance. This had to be something out of the ordinary.

"Yes," said Ahaiwe after a moment, speaking to the patrolmen. "I'm sorry but the, er, operational directives are clear. When a concealed weapon is located, the officer must be sure that there are no further concealments."

Beside Jack, Jane sighed. "You mean you want to search— oof!" She, too, had been jabbed in the back.

"Um," said Ahaiwe. "You must both remove your clothes."

"What, here?" said Jane.

"It's kind of a public place," said Jack. "Lots of public. All staring. And it's cold."

The gun ground into his back. "Son," sneered the patrol

man, "you were given an instruction. You get your bits out or we'll do it for you."

THEY STOOD COMPLETELY naked in the street, watched by what felt like the whole city of Oxford. Ahaiwe took her time gingerly examining their clothes, as if at any moment a garment would explode. Jack tried to keep his composure, but it was fucking freezing and he couldn't help shivering— and shrivelling. People pointed and jeered. He was acutely conscious of his prosthetic leg. This wasn't helping the legend.

His head throbbed from being bashed against the wall earlier. He was also bothered by Jane. Her nose had stopped bleeding, which was good, but she just stood there, staring straight ahead, blotting out the world. The same dead-eyed look she'd had all those years ago when Lee—little Lee's father—had died. It had taken her a couple of years to fully come out of it, basically when her son was of an age to demand conversation.

"Um, okay," said Ahaiwe after what might have been an hour. "I'll take these." She'd found a blunt bit of pencil, a paperclip and the key to Jack's flat at St Mark's.

"Very dangerous weapons, those," said Jack.

Ahaiwe ignored him, quickly turning away. "Take them to the castle."

"Wait," said Jack. "Can't we get dressed first?" Again, a gun jabbed him in the back—so hard he stumbled forward. Naked it was...

Jane nonetheless quickly scooped up her clothes in a bundle. Jack did the same, though one shoe had rolled away towards the crowd, and when he made to collect it he got another jab in the back. They marched through the streets, awkwardly pulling on clothes as they went. When Jane stopped to put on her boots, a patrol man shoved her forwards. They went on, barefoot but otherwise dressed.

They marched west, away from the pubs and colleges to a wide open space with the remains of white markings on the tarmac. It had once been a car park, but the cars had long since been taken away. They crossed the empty space, heading into pitch darkness. Oh, shit, thought Jack.

He considered making a break for it, but the car park offered no protection from the guns. Besides, he didn't fancy being shot in the back.

They came to the edge of the car park and a shape loomed from the darkness. There wasn't enough light to see, but the military police ushered Jane forward and she stumbled up a narrow path. Once he was on it, Jack could just make out the gravel pathway winding up the side of the steep hill. The stones were agony on his feet. Not being able to see didn't help—the ascent was treacherous. They must have climbed the equivalent of four of five storeys, still nearly blind, when they heard the creak of a door.

"I can't see where I'm meant to—" said Jane, and her voice cut off abruptly.

"Hey!" said Jack, starting to turn. As a result, when the patrolmen shoved him forward, he fell arse over tit through the thick curtains masking the door, landing in an undignified heap in the blazing light.

Spots danced before his eyes as Jane helped him up. "You're an idiot," she told him.

"I know. Ow—I can't see a thing."

"Electric light," she said. "Electric light!"

They were in a sumptuous hallway, with plush red carpet under their aching feet. A slightly chipped statue of a lion grappling with a unicorn took pride of place. The patrolmen with machine guns had not followed them inside.

"Where are we?" said Jack.

"A court house, I guess," said Jane. She turned at the sound of footsteps.

An elderly, thin man with an immaculate uniform and an immaculate moustache gave a little bow. "Your Majesty, ma'am: if you'd care to come this way?"

The alternative was to rush back outside to the dark and the patrolmen, so Jack and Jane followed him. He led them down a corridor and up a staircase. Lush paintings of English scenes—all of them post-Cull—adorned the walls.

"I should say: I am General Singhar and this is Oxford New Castle, the largest brick building constructed anywhere in the country since The Cull. We're all jolly proud."

"Right," said Jack. "Very cosy. And it's where you sentence us to death?"

The man found the thought amusing. "Not quite, sir. It's the government building."

"If the Council knows we're here," said Jack, "they could put in a word for us. Get us off the charges."

General Singhar rubbed at one of the gleaming buttons on his uniform. "I'm afraid the Council no longer exists."

"What?" said Jane. "Since when?"

"Since just over a month ago," said the general. "It's rather been superseded. We now have a provisional national government, made up from all the regions—or at least those willing to take part. This is where they meet."

Jack stared at the man. "Nobody asked us to take part. I mean, St Mark's. The whole district of Kent." A horrible thought struck him: perhaps some communities in Kent *were* a part of this, but had kept the fact from him.

"Well, ah, no," said General Singhar. "The initial member communities felt, rather strongly I'm afraid, that a break should be made from the former system of governance. Some were very keen that the new government should not be based in London, let alone at Westminster."

"And there's some who don't want Jack being part of it," said Jane. "They need to see us brought down. That's what just happened out there."

The general looked uncomfortable. They had reached a pair of double doors, guarded by a man and a woman in robes that didn't quite hide their body armour. The general kept his voice low so the guards wouldn't overhear.

"I'm an old-fashioned soldier," he said to Jack and Jane. "Politics isn't really my thing. But a long time ago I made a vow to serve the monarch of this country. Frankly, I don't see how the end of the world should make one damned bit of difference to that." He stood up a little straighter. "So, as much as it's practicable and for the little it might be worth, I am, humbly, Your Majesty's servant."

Jack overcame his astonishment and extended his hand. General Singhar shook it gratefully.

"So what now?" said Jane.

"Now," said the general, "you're called before the government. I hope it all goes... well, the best it can, in the circumstances."

"Hang on," said Jane, indicating the doors. "You mean the government's in there?"

"They've been waiting some time for you. I'm afraid they can be impatient."

"But," said Jane, "we can't go in like this. I've got blood encrusted down my chin and His Majesty has a black eye. We're not even wearing shoes."

The general nodded. "Battered, but unbowed," he said. "Give 'em hell."

He gestured to the guards, who opened the double doors onto a chamber crowded with people.

Jack stood up straight, sucked in his stomach and put out his elbow. Jane took his arm and they strode boldly forward to address the new English government.

CHAPTER FOUR

AAMNA MOSS DIED in agony. A copy of the one-page medical report listed the efforts not to save her life but to make her death less appalling. Jack scanned quickly over the unsettling details. Jane would be able to explain the technical words to him later, but Aamna had died bald and burned and withered, literally melting away as a result of what she'd been exposed to.

And yet, weak and sick as she had been, Aamna had dictated several pages of what she'd seen at Heysham. A V-shaped tear right the way down the shore-side wall of the power station, and billowing smoke that glowed amber. A last page, written by one Professor Owens, offered some analysis of what those things might mean.

"A nuclear explosion," said Jack, putting the pages down on his lap to hide the fact that his hands were shaking. "Or a... core melt?"—glancing back down at the notes—"which caused an explosion." He looked around the room. "So, what can be done?"

He and Jane were sat on two not very comfortable chairs

in the centre of the chamber. Around them sat the sixty-four members of government, in two rows of benches arranged in a horseshoe. Clerks and a stenographer stood off to one side, so it was just Jane and Jack in the ring. But Jack's question seemed to impress the members of government. Yes, the thing was to look for solutions.

"It might help," said Jane, "to know what you've done already."

One of the members got to his feet. He was a Ranger, one of fourteen in the government. It was odd to see Rangers with their hoods down and not carrying bows. This man was of Asian descent, and had a flap of hair slicked flat across his bald spot. He spoke with cool authority.

"When we had Aamna's report," he said, "the Rangers began an evacuation of Lancaster and the region. It was already too late. The poison is in the air. We're seeing the effects now over more than a hundred miles."

"Christ," said Jane. "It's a national emergency."

"So," the Ranger went on, "we sent a delegation to Oxford to consult the books. And it seemed appropriate to summon the Council while we were here. The Council identified Professor Owens as a project lead."

"He's a nuclear physicist, is he?" said Jack. There was a murmur of discontent from the members around him. "Sorry, go on."

"Before The Cull, Owens was an astronomer. But there was no one else. He had a grounding in physics and read up what he could—and identified the problem. When The Cull hit, the technicians at Heysham did what they were supposed to. They instituted the shut down and SCRAM procedures."

"You mean they ran away?" said Jack.

The Ranger glowered at him. "Does His Majesty understand the mechanics of a nuclear reactor?"

"Um," said Jack. "Not exactly."

"It's to do with neutrons," said Jane. "You fire a neutron at an atom of the right kind of element. The neutron is absorbed but splits the atom apart. The result is that you produce a bit of energy, and—if it's the right kind of element—two more neutrons. They fly off and hit two more atoms of the stuff, splitting them to release more energy and four more neutrons. You quickly get a chain reaction: neutrons whizzing off everywhere, releasing more energy. If you've enough of the element in the first place, the reaction is self-sustaining. So lots and lots of energy for very little effort. Right?"

The Ranger smiled. "Very basically," he said. "And, very basically, you can slow the reaction by inserting rods of material that absorbs the neutrons. In an emergency situation, you insert all the control rods, absorb all the neutrons and so stop the reaction. Then you leave the building. That's what they did at Heysham at the time of The Cull."

"But it didn't work," said Jack. "What went wrong?"

"Shut down and SCRAM deals with the problem in the short-term," said the Ranger. "But a nuclear power station can't just be switched off, it must be properly decommissioned."

"And what with everything else going on, that didn't happen," said Jack.

"We assume the technicians died in The Cull or in everything that happened thereafter. The Blood Hunters were active in that area, until the Rangers dealt with them."

"And all that time, the power station is sitting there, like a ticking bomb. So, back to my first question: what can be done? We send the experts up there..."

"That's been done," said the Ranger. "The library supplied us with the best information available on the decommissioning process. From the Blood Hunters, we have a limited stock of protective suits. So Professor Owens led a team of delegates from all the different regions."

"Which helped knit you all together," said Jack. "This new government forged in the time of England's greatest need."

The Ranger didn't smile. "Owens was successful. Heysham is in the process of being decommissioned, the pile disposed at sea."

"But there's still hundreds, maybe thousands of people, who'll get sick or die from contamination already in the air," said Jane.

"That's one problem," said the Ranger. "Of more concern is that Heysham was just one site. There are nine more nuclear reactors, all around the country. They all need urgent attention."

"So," said Jack, "you leave a group at Heysham, and send Owens and his team to each one of the others in turn. But I guess then it's political; where do you send him first?"

"Owens didn't survive his time in Heysham," said the Ranger. "Only two of the delegates did. We've lost the knowledge of those who died. We've lost the suits they were wearing—though the protection they gave was clearly limited anyway. The books they had with them are contaminated, and cannot be moved from the site. So we've a pressing, widespread problem, requiring expertise we don't have. As you put it yourself, what can be done?"

Jack didn't know. He turned to Jane. She stared coolly at the Ranger. "You're asking for volunteers."

The Ranger simply nodded.

"But who in their right mind would do that?" asked Jack.

"You should think better of your subjects, Your Majesty," said the Ranger—which got a mumble of approval from the other members round the chamber. "We already have volunteers for most locations. They know their chances, but they know what's at stake if someone doesn't come forward."

"Right," said Jack, awed by the thought of such sacrifice. "It sounds like you've got it all wrapped up. So where do we come in?"

The Ranger hesitated. The members around him sat forward, eager for this moment. Jack felt the hairs on the back of his neck standing up.

"Your Majesty," said the Ranger, "there are two nuclear reactors at Dungeness, in Kent. If either explodes, no one will be able to use the Channel Tunnel. Even by boat, it's the shortest crossing to France. It would effectively cut off this country from Europe."

Someone muttered from the back bench that that might not be such a bad thing. There was a roar of laughter, a welcome release of tension. Then all eyes returned to Jack.

"Well," he said. "A nuclear meltdown isn't exactly us controlling the border. We should send people down there as a priority."

The members agreed with his sentiment, a little too keenly.

"Dungeness is fifty miles from St Mark's," said the Ranger.

"Right," said Jack.

"He means," said Jane, "that it's our responsibility."

After a moment, Jack understood: what the government wanted, and how perfectly they'd gone about it. His heart hammered in his chest.

"You want me to volunteer to walk into two nuclear power stations that might be about to explode any moment and somehow make them safe?" He got up from his seat to address them all. "You want me to give up my life because of some noble sentiment about the good of the country?" He was practically shouting by now. "You want me to die, to kill myself, for the benefit of your new government?"

He let the words ring in the air above the horrified members. Then Jack grinned. "Well, of course, I accept."

"YOU'RE A LUNATIC," Jane told him later. They'd been found a room in the castle where they could freshen up. They shared a bowl of warm water and the luxury of clean towels. The room had no window and no furniture but two chairs. Apart from the plush carpet, it might have been a prison cell.

"I know," said Jack, mildly. "But they didn't leave me a choice."

"You could have said no."

"How would that have looked?"

"It doesn't matter how it fucking looks!"

"And what if I don't go? Think about it. You said about that president whose past caught up with him."

"This isn't like smoking a spliff."

"But it is. If I don't go, I'll never live it down. 'Oh, he wants to be King and it's all about serving the people, but the moment you ask him to do anything...'"

"That's ridiculous."

"If I don't go, I'm a coward, a hypocrite. That's how they can play it." A thought struck him. "I think that's what they wanted. They hoped I'd turn them down. That would make sense of what happened before. They knocked us about, humiliated us in public, then put this in front of us. They thought I'd tell them where to get off."

Jane studied him, as if seeing him for the first time. "Do you want to be King this much?"

"The country's in trouble. There's still too much fighting between different groups and no vision for the future. And anyone else I can think of would be a whole lot worse."

"You could make a difference," she told him. "You might even do some good. But are you ready to die for it?"

"If I have to."

"Well, then. Good luck to you." She went over to him and kissed him on the cheek. "It is kind of noble. And maybe you're right: a crisis to unite the country. So I'll tell your story. Make sure the children grow up knowing your name. King Jack. The fucking lunatic."

ONCE THEY WERE washed and had shoes on—Jack was brought a new pair—they were taken to a drinks reception in the chamber with the members of government. The mood was meant to be sombre, but many of the members clearly saw something to celebrate. They had won. But Jack wouldn't let them crush him so easily. He mingled, shook hands, swapped pleasantries, and looked them all in the eye.

It had been a long time since Jack had drunk wine, and he made a point of not letting them refill his glass so he could keep track of how much he was drinking. Jane, he noticed, was doing the same, covering her glass with her hand when the waiters came around. While Jack moved from person to person, she got stuck in the orbit of the Ranger who'd addressed them before. Jack went over to rescue her.

"You'll have everything we can do to support you," the Ranger assured him. His name was Dr Ranjit, and before The Cull he'd worked in a bank. "I think you've met General Singhar, who has offered to go with you. He'll take a couple of soldiers to make sure there are no problems en route."

"And that Jack doesn't run off?" suggested Jane.

"I'm not going to run off," Jack told her.

"In addition," said Dr Ranjit, pretending not to have heard them, "we can offer two technicians. They're library staff who assisted Professor Owens in his research, and among the most qualified people at hand to advise on what must be done."

"Great," said Jack. "For a minute, I thought I was going to have be the one to press all the switches."

Dr Ranjit nodded. "You will be. Our technicians have vital knowledge. We can't afford to let them go into the reactor buildings. As you make your way to Dungeness, they'll brief you on the procedures. They'll have notes that you can read on the way. We'll need those back, as well."

"Okay," said Jack, feeling suddenly very sober.

"You think he can learn it all in that time?" said Jane.

"We have every faith that he'll do his utmost," said Ranjit. "And, of course, you'll be there to assist him."

Jane just about held her cool. "Jack spoke for himself. I'll be going home."

"Ah," said Ranjit. "My mistake."

"Yes," said Jane.

"A shame, though," said Ranjit. "You clearly understand the physics involved. The neutron chain reaction. His Majesty might have found that of use."

Jane actually laughed. "You had the extent of my knowledge before. Your technicians will be more than enough."

"And I understand you're a doctor," said Ranjit. "Again... Well, never mind."

Jane almost said something and then thought better of it. She turned to Jack.

"I don't want Jane with me," he said. "She's needed at St Mark's. And she's got her son."

"That's perfectly reasonable," said Dr Ranjit. "Although there is a complication. If she isn't part of this operation, which is so urgent that it takes priority over any other concerns..."

"What concerns?" said Jack—but he already knew.

"There's the matter of a serious breach of city rules. You brought a gun into Oxford. You brandished that gun at our citizens. When searched, you were found to have other items." He turned to Jack. "Items *you* admitted, in front of myriad witnesses, were 'very dangerous weapons.'"

"A paperclip and pencil," said Jack. "Come *on*."

"The rules are very clear. As are the consequences."

"Now, wait," Jack began. But Jane put her hand on his arm. She didn't need defending.

"I just want to know why," she said. "Him, I get. He's a threat to you. To the new government you've got. But I'm not anyone. Why are you so keen to kill me?"

Ranjit's eyes were cold as he smiled at her. "It isn't personal. But you are a doctor and you understand physics better than he does. The operation stands a better chance of success if you're there. And we need success. As does St Mark's and your son."

Jane nodded. "All right," she said. "I can see you've stitched us up. I'll go, I'll do this. But there's something I want in return."

Dearest Lee,

You're a good boy, I love you and I'm proud of you and wish I could be with you now. But there's a bad problem and if I don't help fix it a lot of people will be very hurt. That includes you, and I'd do anything to save you from danger.

I'm going to try and fix the problem, which means going somewhere dangerous, but it's the right thing to do. Sometimes it's not easy to do the right thing, but you have to be brave.

I've done a deal with them. If I go, they'll send you this letter and they'll share the books that tell us how to make sick people well again. It's the best I can manage. That's all I've ever tried to do.

I hope one day you can understand, and forgive me. I wish I had more space to say more. I love you so much. Be a good boy for Caroline. You've always been a good boy.

Mummy ✗✗✗

PART TWO

CHAPTER FIVE

TYRES THRUMMED ON tarmac as they hurtled down the motorway. Jack glanced round to see Jane grinning just as much as the rest of them. It was a glorious morning, the sun on their faces and knuckles as they gripped the handlebars. Ancient cars sat rusting all along the wide expanse of the M40, but they easily cut round them.

There were nine riders: Jack and Jane on mountain bikes; General Singhar on a Raleigh racer, looking like an old print Jack remembered of Don Quixote; Kit and Nina, the two teenage boffins who hadn't yet realised they were in love; a Ranger called Barnden who didn't say much; a Steamie called Jaye who never stopped talking; and two of Ahaiwe's patrol, Nathaniel and Alice. Huge and muscular, Nathaniel wore thick glasses held tight to his head by a strap of elastic. Alice had a hook instead of a right hand. It didn't seem to affect her cycling, but seeing it made his left leg twinge.

As they rode, Kit and Nina called out lessons to Jack and Jane on nuclear reactors. Jack tried to concentrate as they explained "decay heat," "coolant loss," and "core melt incidents," but feared it wasn't going in. It didn't help that he had to cycle as well, but the children weren't the best teachers anyway—to them this was all painfully basic stuff and they couldn't hide their impatience. The more Jack failed to grasp the concepts, the more it showed Dr Ranjit had been right: he depended on Jane showing him what had to be done.

"Fuck's sake," said Jaye, riding past as Jack got it wrong again. "Decay heat is the heat you get from radioactive decay! The radiation—"

Everyone joined in with the answer: "—whether alpha, beta or gamma radiation, is converted into a thermal movement of atoms."

"Oh, yeah," said Jack. "Okay, next one."

For all the horror that might await them, they were eager to get on. It wasn't just the mission; they also knew they would be targets for bandits. So, ignoring their aching muscles and the sheen of sweat, they kept going. Sometimes there were hills to ride down at break-neck speed, Jane calling for caution in case there was an accident, and everyone else ignoring her. They made good progress and just before noon—about five hours after they set off from Oxford—they passed an abandoned village that looked no different from others they'd seen along the way. Nina's hand-drawn map identified it as Fulmer, the last landmark before their turn-off to the M25.

"I think we should stop before we enter London," announced Singhar, climbing wearily from his bike. The others pulled up beside him, watching as the old soldier withdrew a blanket from his backpack.

"Lunch," he told them, spreading the blanket out beside the road, setting out a picnic.

All eyes turned to Jack. Not that he was in charge; it was more a courtesy the others paid to a condemned man. "Yeah, okay," he said. "Before we do London. And my bum is killing me."

Nathaniel and Alice volunteered to keep watch by walking further up the road. The others settled on Singhar's blanket and ate bread and ham and cheese. Jack and Jane reluctantly continued with their lessons in physics.

"Fuel cladding," said Nina.

"Um," said Jack. "It protects the fuel from coming apart—corroding—and spreading through all the system. But it isn't meant to interfere with the reactions, so it's made of stuff that won't absorb neutrons. Which means it doesn't count as shielding. Right?"

Nina nodded curtly. "Core catching."

"That's to do with a big meltdown," said Jack. "But remind me what."

They persevered. But as they reached the end of the pages of handwritten notes the two young boffins had brought with them, they were distracted by Singhar telling Jaye a rambling story about his days in the Army. Jack exchanged glances with Barnden, all braced for some tiresome anecdote aimed at building team spirit. But it soon went a different way.

"It seemed to us," explained Singhar, "that Trenchard being such a shit, we should repay him in kind. So one evening we came up with a marvellously convoluted plan to lace his evening meal with laxatives."

"No!" said Kit and Nina together.

"I remember once, when I was with my crew—" Jaye began, but Singhar didn't let her take over.

"It took a whole team to put the plan into effect," he said. "Someone to get the potion, someone else to make sure Trenchard's food was served up early and set on one side. I was part of the distraction in the kitchen so no one would see the plate being dosed. And then, very pleased with ourselves, we went into dinner, all eyes on Trenchard as he guzzled it down."

He paused, enjoying their rapt attention. "Oh, we'd been promised by our supplier that this stuff would work strong and quick. By God, he was right. Except Trenchard sat there happily stuffing his face, no cause for concern. Well, there didn't seem to be much we could do, so, thinking dark thoughts about our supplier, we got on with eating our own grub. And that's where the trouble began. You see, due to a small miscommunication in the pipeline, the laxatives hadn't been added to the plate set aside for Trenchard. They got stirred into the pot for the rest of us."

After a moment of shock, the others started to laugh. Singhar sighed. "In a matter of moments the whole mess... Well, 'mess' was the operative word. We all came down with the most explosive diarrhoea—every one of us *but* Trenchard."

The laughter mounted, contagious—the more they tried to stop, the harder they laughed.

"No way!" said Jaye. "Like I was saying, there was this time..."

"Now, really," Singhar persisted. "It's no laughing matter. It's really most unkind. You see, we had only a limited number of toilets. God, it was awful, crap every which way. I've never escaped that smell."

"What happened to Trenchard?" asked Jaye.

"Oh," said Singhar, eyes twinkling. "It all looked rather suspect, being as how he was the only one to escape. Command hauled him in front of a tribunal and then booted him out of the Army. So, a happy ending."

"And you got off scot-free," said Jane.

"Ma'am," said Singhar with his eyes lowered. "The guilt has been an awful burden all these years." But his smile faltered and he looked quickly up the road. Alice was coming down to join them.

"If you've finished eating, we should be on the move," she said.

"Is something wrong?" asked Jack.

"We've got a job to do," she told him, but she kept glancing round. The north side of the road was flanked with slabs of concrete, a curtain to stop the trees spilling out on to the road. South, the road looked down on a plain of untended trees and brambles. Jack saw no immediate cause for concern.

"We've hardly had an hour," protested Singhar as the others got to their feet. "It won't help anyone to arrive at the reactor exhausted. We're likely to need our wits when we get there. Isn't that right, ma'am?"

He addressed the question to Jane, who hadn't expected it. "Yeah, um, we don't want to over-do it on the first day."

"Yeah, right," said Jaye. "Of course she's going to say that. She and her boyfriend hardly want to rush anyway."

"What?" said Jane.

"Sure," Jaye went on. "The longer you put it off, the longer you live. And the more chance you've got to escape."

"I am not—"

"But you would—"

"How dare you fucking—"

"No one is escaping," said Barnden—the first time he'd spoken since they set off. He didn't smile. "I'll kill you first. Any one of you."

They stood in silence for a moment. "And I'll kill you," said Jaye to Barnden. "I mean, if you try and run yourself. Just to be fair, you know."

Barnden nodded. No one looked set to say anything, so Jack thought he'd better step in.

"Well, there we are, then. We get moving. The more ground we cover today, the less we have tomorrow." They gathered up their things and were soon back on their bikes.

It LOOKED AS if Nina had got it wrong: there was no sign of a turning to the M25. They pedalled on, feeling all the more exhausted for having stopped. Jack gave up trying to get his bike into a lower gear and opted for brute stubbornness, swearing under his breath at every step he planted down. Sweat dripped from his nose and chin. His breathing was ragged and his lungs ached.

The rest of the gang seemed just as knackered. Nathaniel and Alice led them, Alice calling out when she wanted Nathaniel to lean over and change her gears—something she couldn't manage with the hook on the end of her arm. Flashes of light kept catching on Nathaniel's glasses as he continually looked right and left, watching out for danger. Yet there was nothing to see: the wide road walled off to their left, and on the right looking down on the surrounding land. There were trees and foliage where bandits might be hiding, but surely they would have to step out into the open to try anything—and then they'd be lower than the road, so Jack and his gang would have the advantage. Wouldn't they?

No one else seemed troubled. Heads lowered, gritting their teeth, they concentrated on the ride.

All except Singhar, at the back of the group, clearly exhausted but trying not to show it. He rode his racer straight-backed, head up, a benign smile on his shining face.

He saw Jack looking and rolled his eyes. Then he fell over sideways. Singhar and his bike hit the road with a horrible crunch.

The others stopped to see what had happened. Singhar wasn't moving, tangled up in his bike.

"Fuck," said Jack, dumping his own bike and hurrying back to the old man. There was a pulse, and Singhar was breathing. "Hey," said Jack. "Can you hear me?"

"Is he okay?" called Jaye. And there was another sound that made Jack look up. He saw Alice and Nathaniel running toward Kit and Nina.

"What—" said Jaye, and the side of her face exploded. Jack threw himself at the ground, pulling the pistol from the holster at his hip. Alice and Nathaniel bundled Kit and Nina into a gap between two rusted cars.

There were more bullets, though Jack couldn't tell how close they were landing. He struggled to look round without lifting his head. A bullet smacked the tarmac about a metre from Jane as she crawled on her elbows towards the cars sheltering the others—and was soon lost from sight.

Jack was on his own. There was no way he'd reach the cars. He cast around desperately for cover. It would help, he thought, to know the location of their attacker—or attackers. A bullet spanged off the side of a car door, leaving a small pock-mark. From the angle of the dent, they were somewhere out in the plain on the right. A raised position to shoot at them on the road. Possibly up a tree.

There was a car blocking his view—but it might be giving him cover and keeping him alive. He didn't dare move, but then if the sniper had a good, raised position to shoot at them, he or she couldn't move either. Stalemate.

Jack heard a sound behind him.

He turned slowly to look back the way they'd come. There was no one on the motorway behind them—or off the road, for that matter—but a few metres away from him Singhar's body twitched.

Fuck, thought Jack. There was no way he could get to the old man without leaving his tentative cover.

"General," he whispered. "General!"

Singhar seemed to hear. Slowly, he turned his head to look up at Jack. Bits of gravel protruded from the blood on his face. Another bullet hit the road a couple of lanes to one side of them. Jack pointed in the direction he thought the sniper must be, and Singhar slowly nodded.

"Others?" he mouthed.

Jack pointed again, towards the cars sheltering their friends. Again Singhar nodded, then he started to move. The bike scraped against the road loudly as Singhar tried to free himself. Jack mouthed, "No!" but Singhar wasn't looking. He had to lift the bike to free the leg trapped under it. Then he let the bike fall with an almighty crash.

Jack watched horror struck. But Singhar was on his hands and knees, arse too high in the air as he crawled towards Jack. Any moment a bullet would strike him. Any moment—

But no, Singhar reached Jack and collapsed down beside him, panting. Blood poured from a gash in his cheek.

"That was stupid," whispered Jack. "They could easily have shot you."

"Already did," said Singhar.

"Shit," said Jack. "Where?"

Singhar shook his head. "All that matters is the mission. So, what are we going to do?"

"Right," said Jack. "Well, they can't get any closer without us having the advantage. So we're stuck like this. Unless the others..."

"The others can't help us. They're hemmed in."

Jack nodded. "Right. Then it's you and me."

"I'm not sure I'll get very far," said Singhar. And then, more firmly: "I can give you covering fire." Painfully, he shifted round and took the pistol from his hip. "What are you going to do?"

Jack considered. "We need to get to whoever is shooting. I'll use the cover we've got to reach the verge. When I signal, you try and draw their fire for as long as you can. I'll get down the side of the road and into cover. Then make my way towards them. If I can at least distract them, the others have a chance to come help."

Singhar nodded. "Good plan."

"You'll be all right?"

"Don't worry about me, Your Majesty. Good luck."

Jack ran, keeping low, towards the car providing him cover. He reached it without a bullet coming his way, and grinned back at Singhar, who gave him a thumbs up, then raised his gun, ready to go to work.

Jack edged towards the far side of the car, not sure at what point the sniper would see him. He felt sick with fear. Fucking hell, this was ridiculous. He edged forward, almost out into the open. Beyond the tarmac at the edge of the road was a strip of grass and a rust-speckled crash barrier that he could easily leap. Then there was a steep drop down to sprawling brambles. He'd be in the open for a matter of seconds. If he wasn't shot and didn't break his neck, he would be okay.

Jack readied himself to make the leap. Three, two... He turned back to Singhar to check he was ready.

Singhar had followed Jack round the back of the car—he couldn't offer covering fire. Yet his gun was raised, and he bore an expression that only meant one thing.

"But—" began Jack.

Singhar shot him.

CHAPTER SIX

JACK HURLED HIMSELF backwards, trying to twist his body—but there was no way he could dodge a bullet. It punched him, hard and burning hot, just above the right breast. God, it hurt. He'd been shot before, but it didn't lessen the shock.

Something slashed against his calves. He was already falling before he realised he'd hit the crash barrier at the edge of the road. Shit. Fuck! And there was Singhar, readying another shot...

Then Jack lost sight of him. For a moment he arced gracefully through the air, escaping his assassin. He'd got away!

He hit the steep incline with his head and shoulder and tumbled over and over down, trying to use his legs and arms to catch hold of anything to slow himself down. He did—his arm caught on a branch and his whole body seemed to explode, flaring from the hole in his chest.

Next he knew, he was tumbling again. He couldn't breathe, the blood from his gunshot wound spattered in his face and eyes. Then he crashed through brambles that caught and cut at him, and he slid the rest of the way down the hill, head first, on his back. Stunned and in agony from the wound, he lay in an undignified heap at the bottom of the slope, looking back the way he had fallen.

Singhar stood up on the motorway, behind the crash barrier, gun pointing down at him. Jack felt a sudden fury. This wasn't how he'd planned to go out. He wanted to shout something, he wanted last words. He managed a strangled squeak.

Then Singhar let go of the gun, letting it slide down the slope to where Jack lay.

Jack thought about reaching for it, but the slightest movement meant blazing pain across his chest. So he lay there, watching as Singhar raised his hands.

Barnden stepped up behind Singhar and pressed a gun into the back of his neck.

"Jack?" called Barnden. "You dead?"

Yes, thought Jack, as everything faded to darkness.

ALICE HEAVED HERSELF up the side of the concrete wall on the other side of the road from the sniper. A van provided cover; she hoped she hadn't been seen. She hauled herself through the dense thicket of branches at the top of the wall, then started running, following the line of the road back the way they'd come—away from the shooter.

She should have brought Kit and Nina, she thought. They would have been safer here in the foliage. But it was too late now. She'd just have to be quick.

Alice kept running, and at last found the old farmhouse she'd spied as they passed it. A strip of road led down and under the motorway—or it had done once. She used her hook-hand to push through the foliage blocking the old track and found herself in stale-smelling darkness. Light peeped from somewhere in the distance—the other side of a tunnel under the motorway. She couldn't see anything else and her instincts screamed at her that it wasn't safe, but she hurried on.

Her boots echoed loudly in the confined space. She splashed through foul-smelling muck, then fell over something right in her path, ploughing headlong into the concrete floor. Her hook hit the ground with a loud, metallic crack and shockwaves flailed up her arm.

But no one shot her. Alice got quickly to her feet. She still couldn't see much in the dark. Whatever she'd fallen over—she wasn't going to investigate—had badly scraped her shins and knees. She hobbled on towards the light.

Again, the foliage had grown up round the mouth of the tunnel and she had little choice but to force her way through. The splitting, snapping branches deafened her, the daylight was blinding, and as she plunged through, a branch thwacked her head. She lay in the muck on the concrete outside the tunnel—and still no one shot her.

Alice got to her feet and dared a quick look round. Back along the ridge of the road, she could just make out the overhanging stick Nathaniel had positioned to show the way to the sniper. It pointed away across the overgrown field to a line of trees. And yes, she saw something glint high up in one of the branches. What were the odds that whoever had shot at them would be on their own?

Carefully, Alice headed straight ahead, then made a wide arc around the edge of the field, watching and listening all the way. A snort made her drop to the ground.

She edged forward—and found two horses tied to a tree. A crude tripwire had also been set in a ring around the horses to catch anyone approaching. Alice traced the wire to a couple of grenades, which she quickly freed from the apparatus. Might come in handy.

She went on more cautiously, and now she saw the man in the tree. He sat about ten metres up, a rifle nestled in the nook of a branch ahead of him. She noted the mask and hood: not a Ranger, but perhaps trained in their methods.

Then a footstep crunched behind her. Alice whirled round and caught the other man in the face. She punched again and broke the fucker's nose. The man had a gun and fired, but the shot wasn't even close. Alice struck again, right in the throat, with the outer curve of her hook. Then she ducked round the man and grabbed him, using him as a shield, the point of her hook now pressed against his throat.

"You drop your weapon," Alice commanded the sniper. "You drop it to the ground, or I slice open this fucker."

The fucker she was throttling said something a little like, "glurk."

"I haven't got all day," said Alice.

The man in the tree left it another moment. Then he let the rifle fall. "Please," he said, his hands raised. "Don't hurt her."

"You got any other weapons on you?" Alice asked him. He produced a pistol and a penknife, and let them fall. "You sure you've got nothing else?"

"Nothing," said the man. "We surrender."

"You're not bandits," said Alice. "Crack shot like you is ex-military. And you've got good kit. Who sent you?"

The man didn't answer, so Alice pressed the hook against the woman's throat.

"Ask Singhar," said the man quickly. "You've captured him anyway—your friends did, I just saw."

"He hired you to shoot him? Come on." The man hesitated. "I'm not fucking about," Alice told him.

"If I tell you everything, will you let us go?"

Alice smiled. "So you know everything, do you?" She dragged the hook across the woman's throat, releasing a great spurt of blood. The man in the tree cried out in horror. The woman gagged and fought, and Alice simply stepped back, letting her flail about. She tried to reach for a pistol in her belt, but Alice took it from her—and shot the man in the tree. The bullet hit him in the leg, and sent him toppling off his branch.

The woman on the ground was gasping and spluttering as blood pumped from the gash in her throat. Alice stepped around her, making her way to the screaming man by the tree, trying to drag himself to his rifle. She got to him first and kicked his wounded leg. He howled and swore at her, and shouted to the dying woman behind them. It turned out her name was Daphne.

"Daphne's dead," Alice told him. "But we're on a mission to save the bloody country and I could do without this shit. So you get on with telling me everything, then I'll let you join her."

"THIS IS WHY they insisted I come along with you," said Jane, as she pulled the bandage tight.

Jack winced. His right arm had been lashed to his chest in

thick layers and something had been clamped round his neck, restricting his movement. Not that he wanted to move.

They were sat on the road, just the two of them but for the horses Alice had taken from the snipers. Kit, Nina, Barnden and Nathaniel had gone down the slope to bury Jaye. Alice was with them, guarding Singhar, making him watch.

"He wanted me to run," said Jack.

"He wanted you disgraced," said Jane. "Shot in the back for cowardice. Leaving your friend to complete your assignment. That's why they only supplied us with one protective suit— they knew there'd only be one of us."

"Well," said Jack. "Now you can go home. You should go home."

"Yeah," said Jane. "Well."

"But Lee."

"I explained about Lee. But Barnden has his orders. If you or I try to get away, he is going to shoot us." She smiled. "Singhar told him you would do a bunk. That's why he came looking for you before, and caught Singhar in the act."

"Jane," said Jack. "While they're all down there. You'd get away." She didn't say anything, finishing with the bandages. "Jane."

"I know," she said. "And I want to. But what if there's more trouble on the road?"

"Did Singhar say there would be?"

"He hasn't said anything. That's why they didn't just shoot him."

"They think he'll repent?"

"Or at least try to explain."

"It doesn't matter," said Jack. "He's played us since we met him. All that stuff about how loyal he was. Appealing to my vanity. And I completely believed him."

"You thought you had a friend. Well, that's why I have to stay."

"No. I mean it, please."

She didn't say anything. But after a moment she got to her feet and walked towards the concrete wall on the north side of the road. She put her foot on the crash barrier, ready to haul herself up. Then she turned on her heel and hurried back to Jack, checking again on his bandages.

Kit and Nina clambered over the barrier on the far side of the road, soon followed by everyone else. Kit and Barnden had both been crying. Singhar looked about a thousand years old.

"Still here?" said Nathaniel.

"No, we're in France eating cheese," Jack said. He let Jane help him to his feet. "So, all done?"

"Not quite," sniffed Barnden. "There's still him." He indicated Singhar.

"What do we do with him?" asked Kit.

"Isn't that obvious?" said Nina, bitterly. "We can't let him go."

The words hung in the air. Singhar looked down at his feet, as if embarrassed.

"Fuck it," said Alice, raising her gun.

"No," said Jack.

"Fuck off," said Alice. "The girl's right: we're not letting him go."

"No," said Jack. "But I'm the one who'll do it."

Alice glanced around the others. "Why you?"

"Because," scoffed Nathaniel, "he thinks he's bloody King." Jack noticed Kit and Nina—even Barnden—looked uncomfortable at him taking the piss.

"I'm a dead man," Jack told them. "That's all I am now. But whatever happens to me, you lot go back to Oxford, where there will be people who helped set this up. If I do this, then it's between me and them. You keep out of it, carry on with your lives."

Barnden shrugged. "You don't know if any of the rest of us are in on it."

"No," said Jack. "I don't. So this is the deal. We do the job, whatever it takes. Then you lot get to go home. No more complications."

The others didn't argue. Jack had to take his pistol in his left hand and couldn't quite hold it steady. Singhar smoothed his moustache and smiled pleasantly at Jack, like a kindly uncle. Oh, the little shit was still playing head games.

"It's not about me," Jack told him. "It's not Jaye or any of the rest of them. But we're in a national crisis and you threatened our mission to put that right. You betrayed your country."

A flinch; that one struck home. Jack squeezed the trigger and a bullet punched a hole through Singhar's face. The old man staggered back. Jack fired again and ended it.

No one said anything. Jack handed the gun back to Alice and made his way to the horses. He chose the smaller horse—it would be easier to get on to—and Jane hurried over to help, but he got into the saddle himself. He winced as he shifted his weight in the saddle; it felt like his insides might explode.

Eyes wet with tears, head throbbing from the pain, he looked down on the others. Jack knew he looked ridiculous, with his neck in a brace and his body all bandaged up, his trousers torn and covered in muck, his acne and greasy hair. And yet the looks on their faces—a mixture of surprise and awe at the way he'd just taken charge. For this fleeting moment, he'd got them.

"Let's go," he said. They collected their bikes and followed him, leaving the corpse on the road.

CHAPTER SEVEN

JACK KNELT BY the roadside, chucking up his guts. The stench from the steaming pool of sick turned his insides and he vomited again. At last, there was nothing left to come and he lay back on the cold tarmac, catching his breath.

It was a cold night and a half-moon made everything eerily silver. Jack's wound and throat ached, his whole head was on fire. And yet, for all the shivery awfulness, he felt a blessed relief to be off the horse at last.

"We should check the damage," said Jane, and Jack didn't resist as she and Kit began to unpick his bandages. The others were off to one side of the road, setting up camp and sorting out a meal. They moved slowly, wearily, after the day's long ride.

Barnden cradled the rifle they'd taken from the sniper, which he assured them had a better range than his own gun. He kept watch while the others worked in silence, weary and apprehensive of more trouble to come. They'd chosen a patch of road that had good views all around—though they'd felt the same about the road where Jaye had died.

"Shit," said Jane as the bandages revealed the mess of Jack's chest. He couldn't see what she was looking at.

"No," said Kit, leaning in for a closer look, a nerdy fascination on his face. "A lot of this is sweat and muck from the journey, but look—the wound is pretty clean." He smiled down at Jack. "You've been lucky, Your Highness."

"Urf," said Jack, and with more effort added: "Don't feel very lucky."

"We need to put on new dressings," said Jane. "It's probably going to hurt."

"It already hurts."

"Hey," said Kit. "We don't have many dressings left in the bag."

"We can't risk leaving him like this," said Jane, and to prove the point she tore off the dressing in one sudden movement. Jack screamed and kicked out, then fell back, hitting his head on the road.

"Sorry," said Jane. "Better to get it over with. I'd give you an aspirin, but I don't think you'd keep it down."

Jack was in no state to respond. Now the ordeal was over, the evening air whispered round the hole in his chest, cool and soft and soothing. He was so desperately tired.

"He's not going to make it," he heard Kit whisper to Jane.

"Of course he will," snapped Jane. "I'm not letting him go."

But Jane's words—and Jane—were fading.

He FELL THROUGH lucid battles and explosions, warped echoes of those he'd fought, populated by those he had lost. As he dodged the gunfire, he had to apologise for having forgotten everyone's names...

When Jack woke, he found himself wrapped in sweat-sodden blankets by a campfire, Nathaniel keeping watch as the other slept. Beside Jack, Jane stirred and wearily sat up. She took his temperature, frowned and got him to drink water. It burned his throat and the hacking cough sent needles of pain through his chest. His piteous weeping woke the others, who muttered about the noise as they turned away and tried to get back to sleep.

Jane wedged her bags against Jack so that he could sit up, which seemed to help with the coughing. Then she draped her own blanket on top of his, and snuggled up beside him. He tried, miserably, to express his gratitude, but she hushed him, cooing gently in his ear that it would okay, that he would soon be through this.

As he drifted back to his nightmares, he didn't know whether she meant that he'd recover or that he'd die.

He felt pretty much dead the next morning, and the others looked little better. It seemed he'd kept them awake through the night. When he tried to apologise, Alice told him to fuck off.

"Does that make you feel any better?" he asked her

"Yeah," she said, not backing down. Jane hurried to Jack's side, ready to defend him. Alice raised her hook in accusation. But Jack grinned.

"Then that's good," he said. "Anyone else want to say it?"

The others weren't sure, until Nathaniel good-naturedly said, "Go fuck yourself, Your Majesty."

"Yeah, fuck off," agreed Barnden.

Kit whispered it. Nina laughed at him and took great delight in proclaiming, "Fuck off, King Jack."

Finally there was Jane. "You're a fucking nutcase," she told him.

They settled down to breakfast over the fire. Jack managed some sausage and egg without throwing it up, though it felt like knives inside him and then he had to stumble away to the hedge at the side of the road when his bowels turned to water. His friends—that's what they were now—grinned ruefully or offered a thumbs-up. He told them to fuck off.

While the others packed up the camp, Jane stripped Jack naked and scrubbed away the shit and crusted blood. He lay there, cold but unembarrassed in front of everyone else. In fact, as Jane worked him over, he managed a bit of an erection.

"Sorry," he said when she noticed. She only rolled her eyes.

By the time Jane had got Jack dressed again, the others had started to argue. They were all determined to get moving, to lose no more time. But Kit insisted there was no way Jack could get back on the horse and that he should have a day to rest. Jane backed up Kit.

"I mean, look at the state of him," she said.

"I'm okay, really," said Jack, as the others appraised him. The argument went round and round until Barnden stormed off and Jack thought they might have lost him. Then he was back, hauling an old two-wheeled trailer he'd liberated from an abandoned car. With ropes, they managed to harness it to the horse, which Nathaniel offered to ride. Jack proved too long to lie in the trailer, so they used their packs to prop him up in a seated position, which would have to do.

Finally the gang set off, the trailer bumping and bucking over every imperfection in the road. It made Jack want to be sick again. He closed his eyes, trying to shut out the dizziness. It didn't seem possible that he would ever be able to sleep. And yet soon enough he did.

THEY MADE STEADY progress south round the M25. Along the way they met people: fellow travellers or enterprising locals offering items for sale. Some were welcoming, most were wary, especially of Barnden, as Rangers had a bad reputation south of London—more than anything because they were so rarely seen there. Kit and Nina tested Jane on the physics of nuclear reactors from their handwritten notes, Jack half listening as he dozed. In his more lucid moments, he found he knew most of the answers. The words didn't mean anything, but he could recite them back.

One time he woke to an argument between Jane and Alice about the gibbet cages hanging from the walls of Oxford.

"You've got to have discipline," said Alice, as if it was obvious. "We've seen enough of what people are like without the rule of law."

"I agree we need rules and laws," said Jane, just holding on to her temper. "But displaying the rotting corpses of those who step out of line?"

"How else do you make people take notice? You can't go up to some thieving, murdering wretch and say, 'Please, love, can you not?'"

"So the gibbets aren't about punishment. They're about scaring everyone else."

"Yeah. Why not?"

"So no one else breaks the rules."

"Yeah!"

"Yet somehow, despite this deterrent, you've still got a steady supply of bodies to put on display."

"Well," said Alice. "We get a lot of people visiting the city who don't know how to behave. Look, it's not like we haven't had this discussion ourselves. The Council, then the new government, they went over and over all the different angles."

"Yeah, well," said Jane. "Forgive me if I don't exactly take that as an endorsement."

Alice shrugged. "You think His Majesty would do anything else if he was in charge?"

Jack remained very still, his eyes closed—but the two women didn't seem interested in what his opinion might be.

"Jack doesn't want to be a dictator."

"But where would he stand on the rule of law? Look, we've all lived through a pretty shitty time. We've seen things— we've *done* things—we can't get out of our heads. The whole country is still acting batshit crazy. If we're gonna survive, we need clear boundaries about what is acceptable behaviour. And more than that, we need to know that *everyone* has to follow the same rules, and what happens if they don't. It's the only way."

Jane didn't say anything for a time. Then, in a small voice, she said, "Jack won't agree with you."

"Well," said Alice. "We can ask him when he wakes up."

Jack maintained the pretence of being asleep and the gang carried on in uneasy silence, just the sound of the bikes and the horse and the trailer. Then Kit and Nina started asking Jane about physics and Jack slept. When he next opened his eyes, night had fallen and they were off the M25 and on narrower, less tended, potentially more dangerous roads, and Alice was too busy watching for assassins to ask his views on capital punishment.

When they finally set up camp, Jack felt better for a day of relative rest and made a point of cooking a meal to thank the rest of the gang. It wasn't much—a stew much like the one from the previous evening—but they appreciated the gesture. Alice passed round a flask of whisky so they could toast the health of their chef.

"A good day," Jack told Jane later, as they took turns on watch.

"For you, maybe," she said. "Some of us did a lot of cycling."

"No one died," he said, and she sighed.

"No. But tomorrow..." Tomorrow, all being well, they would reach Dungeness. They sat in silence, watching the flickering campfire.

"The worst thing," said Jane at length, "is being so close. I mean, we're practically in sight of St Mark's. We could have popped in."

"We still can. If you want to."

She shivered at the thought. "I couldn't see Lee again, then go on with what we have to do."

He took her hand. "It's got to be done. Whatever it takes, we do it."

"I know."

"But if there's a way where you don't have to go inside..."

She smiled at him. "Let's have another drink." She twisted round to reach for the flask of whisky. That sudden movement meant the bullet sang over her shoulder rather than right through her head. It hit the horse instead, who tottered over with a pitiful groan.

The others sprang awake. Jane was already pointing a gun into the darkness, letting off a couple of shots. But with the fire behind them, they could see little out there.

"Fuck!" said Jack. "Now what?"

Barnden suddenly shoved Kit, sending him reeling—and out of the path of another bullet. Jane cracked off a shot in the direction it had come from. Nathaniel pushed her out of the way, crouching forward in her place and clipping something to the front of his glasses. A night-vision attachment.

"Alice," he said softly. "Two of them. Half past seven and about fifty yards."

Alice expertly bowled one of the grenades she'd confiscated from the snipers the day before, then had to dive to the ground as a volley of bullets came her way. A moment later, a deafening explosion lit up the night, spattering them with clumps of mud. There was a scream, too, but Nathaniel and Alice were already rushing out into the dark. Barnden looked tempted to follow, then opted to check on the horse.

For a moment, the others crouched in silence, straining to see what had become of their friends. The wind carried the voice of a man—not Nathaniel—begging for mercy, and then screaming. The screaming stopped. After a moment, a single gunshot rang out—horribly close. They turned to find Barnden standing over the horse, his pistol smoking.

Nathaniel and Alice marched out of the darkness, Alice wiping her bloody hook on her sleeve. They made for their blankets, returning straight to bed.

"There might be more of them out there," Jack protested.

Nathaniel shook his head. "The boy told us everything. Thought they'd scare us off, then help themselves to what we left behind." He snorted with annoyance. "Just a pair of kids."

Alice, wrapped in her blankets, reached for the flask of whisky, lying where Jane had dropped it.

NATHANIEL AND ALICE tucked into their breakfasts the next morning, but no one else had much of an appetite. Jack felt hollow and sickly, yet Jane had to admit her amazement at how much he'd improved.

"Another day and I'd have let you back on the horse."

"We don't have another day," he shrugged—then realised what he'd said.

Without the horse, he and Nathaniel had to walk. The others rode slowly and haltingly, while Alice and Barnden disappeared off to scout the road ahead.

"There's a town," they reported a little after noon. "Lydd. Last town before Dungeness. Only way in is over a bridge across the old railway. They've got barbed wire and machine guns in place. Not exactly encouraging."

"We could go round," said Jack, from where he sat exhausted on the roadside, prosthetic on the ground next to him, massaging his aching stump with his one free hand.

"There's signs saying man-traps," said Alice. "But that might be a trick."

"Okay," said Jack—and found them all watching him expectantly. He tried not to show his surprise. "The sensible thing is to send one or two of us up to the town, see how they get on."

"You volunteering?" said Barnden.

"Sure." Jack reached down for his leg. "You going to come, too? Make sure I don't run away?"

"Don't think there's much chance of that," said Nathaniel. "You can only just about walk."

"I'll manage."

"Suppose they don't like the look of you," said Alice.

"Hey," said Jack. "I'm quite respectable."

"Suppose there's trouble?" said Alice. "Like he said: you can't run, or fight."

"Then I'll use my powers of persuasion."

No one seemed convinced. Instead, Nathaniel and Alice offered to go in his stead.

"You'd better dump some of your weapons first," said Jane. "Don't want to give these people the wrong idea."

Alice didn't like it, but she and Nathaniel unloaded most of their arsenal into Barnden's care. Nathaniel gave his night vision attachment to Jane, who was clearly astonished and touched. Alice removed a yellow brick of plastic from her pack.

"Unfolds into the protective suit for the reactor," she said, offering it to Jack.

"He can't carry any more," said Jane.

"Fine," said Alice, offering it to Jane—who instinctively stepped back as Alice let it go. The pack thudded to the ground. "What are you playing at?" the patrolwoman snapped. Nathaniel grabbed her arm and dragged her away.

"Sorry," said Jane to no one in particular, staring down at the package at her feet.

Jack took her arm. "Bit soon," he said. "Bit real." She nodded.

"I'll take it," said Nina, stepping in. "It makes sense anyway, to have it with all the notes." She beamed at Jane, who smiled back, eyes wet with tears.

"Right," said Nathaniel. "Then we'll be off."

"Be careful," said Jack. "No chances, no fucking about."

"'Course not," said Nathaniel. "I like a quiet life. We'll be back in an hour."

"Or we won't," said Alice. "Joke."

She and Nathaniel considered using bikes but opted to walk, looking casual. It was almost comical, watching them head away down the road as if taking a stroll.

"Right," said Jack. "An hour. I might have a nap."

FIVE HOURS LATER, there was no sign of Alice or Nathaniel. Barnden and Kit dared to head down the road to within sight of the town, on the off-chance they might spot some clue. There were people on the machine gun at the gate, and the sound of activity from inside the town: voices and movement, the usual bustle of a community.

"Do we even know they're in there?" said Kit, after he and Barnden had returned to the others. "I mean, they could have just wandered off."

"They wouldn't abandon the mission," said Barnden.

"Their mission was to get us to Dungeness," said Jane. "We're pretty much within sight of it. Maybe they thought it was enough. I wouldn't blame them for not sticking around."

"No," said Jack. "I don't think they'd leave us. They must be in the town."

"So something has gone wrong," said Jane.

"Maybe," said Jack. "Or there's a complication and they don't think it's safe to come and find us just now."

"So what do we do?" said Barnden. "We can't hang around. If they're interrogated or tortured, they'll tell them we're all out here."

Jack considered. They didn't have the resources to mount a rescue—and they didn't know one was warranted—but they couldn't wait around. The answer was obvious, wasn't it? The problem, he saw looking round his remaining friends, was that no one wanted to be the arsehole who said it.

"All right," he said. "We move on."

Jane was appalled. "You really want to abandon them?"

"What I want doesn't matter," he told her, as calmly as he could. "It's about what we are capable of. We cut around the town. We can't take the bikes through the field, so we'll stash them and continue on foot."

"And the man-traps?" said Jane. "You said we couldn't risk them. That's why Alice and Nathaniel went into the town!"

"We go now while it's still light, and we watch our step. Look, I don't like this either. But Alice and Nathaniel are big enough to look after themselves. They'll catch us up."

No one believed him, but they nodded their assent. That only disgusted Jane all the more. "Those two saved our lives—twice in as many days."

"I know," said Jack. "But we put the mission first."

CHAPTER EIGHT

Barnden went first through the field, treading lightly and carefully but moving quickly. The others followed in single file, trying to tread in his footsteps. It meant concentrating on each next step rather than looking where they were heading or watching for movement from the town. They kept low, hunched over, which made Jack's gunshot wound throb.

"There aren't any mantraps," he said after maybe half an hour, sweat dripping from his brow.

Ahead of him, Barnden slowed to a halt. Kit didn't notice and bumped into Nina, and she pushed him away. Barnden moved swiftly, grabbing Kit's arm before he fell back—then pointed at the ground.

Jack couldn't see it at first and had to crouch down for a better look. But yes, protruding from the soil he saw a rusted fragment of metal, a pattern of teeth in a curve. He made out the circular shape of the buried trap.

"Home-made," concluded Barnden.

"Um," said Nina. "What do we do if we stand on one?"

Kit, adrenaline pumping after his near-escape, tried to make light of it. "Say goodbye to your leg," he said. "Ker-splatch."

Barnden shook his head. "This thing snares you, so the townspeople take you prisoner. If you stand on one, we get you out."

"But I wouldn't advise it," said Jane. "Those teeth will do enough damage. Then there's the chance of infection."

"Nasty way to go," nodded Barnden. "So, watch out for your feet."

"But what about the others?" said Nina. "If Nathaniel and Alice follow us this way..."

Barnden looked to Jack.

"They'll leave the town by road," Jack said. "No need to come this way."

"But they might try to find us," said Nina.

"They saw the signs," said Jack. "And they'll know to be careful. We can't discuss it now. Look—it's getting dark. We need to be out of here while we can still see."

They went on, playing close attention to exactly where Barnden trod.

A PALLID MOON shone down as they at last stumbled on to what Nina's hand-drawn map said was Dungeness Road. It felt foolhardy to be out in the open—surely someone in the town behind them would see them on the road. Yet the only hope of cover was in the fields on either side of them, which meant man-traps and who knew what else.

The road wound through marshlands, an ancient sign proclaiming what had once been a 'National Nature Reserve'— from a far away age when nature required guarding from man. Wild animals barked and cried in the darkness, and Barnden took the bow from his shoulder, ready to shoot anything that dared to approach. Something large watched them as they passed, eyes shining in the night, but didn't come any closer.

Suddenly Barnden halted, looking back up the road they had come. Jack followed his gaze but couldn't see anything.

"What is it?" he whispered.

"Off the road," said Barnden. They scrambled down a shallow bank of mud. There was no way—or time—to check for man-traps; they just slithered down into the muck. Barnden told them to huddle together and keep completely still. Jack lay between Kit and Jane. The mud stank wetly, and didn't help his sudden urge to pee.

Then, on the wind, he heard it: a rumble like distant thunder, off towards the town. He didn't relish the thought of being caught out in a storm.The sound became more distinct: something on the road, something wheeled and moving at speed. He dared to raise his head and look, but could see nothing coming. Barnden smacked him lightly on the back of the head to make him duck back down. He waited, face down in the mud, as the noise got ever nearer. There were footsteps—a whole group of people, racing down the road. And the heavy wheels of whatever vehicle they ran with.

The vehicle and the footsteps passed by their hiding place and carried on down the road. Jack and the others lay in the mud for an agonising time, listening to it recede. Then Barnden crept forward and dared to take a look. He gestured, silently, for Jack to follow him.

In the feeble moonlight, Jack just made out a group of people hurrying away down the road. They surrounded a structure twice their size, apparently pulling it along as they ran. It took Jack a moment to recognise the shape, it had been so long since he'd seen one. A horse box, like you'd attach behind a car.

"Bit late for making deliveries," he whispered. "And why such a rush?" Barnden didn't say anything, only stared after the horse box as it disappeared into the night. Jane, Kit and Nina joined them on the road.

"They might have been friendly," said Kit.

"Better to be wary," Jack told him. "For one thing, they outnumbered us."

"Do you think they're heading to the reactor?" said Jane.

"Maybe, but we don't know what else is down here," said Jack.

"Then you don't think Nathaniel and Alice were inside that thing?"

Jack shrugged. "I can't see why they would be." But as they continued down the road, he was haunted by the thought that they might have missed a chance to rescue their friends.

They trudged down the road through the marshlands, the night chill piercing them to their bones. Jack's gunshot wound ached horribly and he wanted to sleep, but he kept on, trying to stay alert to the sound of more people on the road, or the return of the horse box.

They came to a junction. To their left, enclosed in the remains of a barbed wire fence, stood the terminus of a railway—without a station or name boards. On the right was a road junction, the lane closest to them painted blood red. *PRIVATE PROPERTY* declared the fierce capital letters straddling the road.

"This is it," said Nina. "The approach road. It's just over a mile down there."

"Great," said Jane. "Then we're here."

"Hang on," said Jack. "It's very exposed. If that horse box comes back, they'll see us straight away. Let's at least wait till morning, when we can see what we're facing."

They left the turning and followed the Dungeness Road until they heard the crash of the sea somewhere up ahead. Barnden found a secluded spot off the road where he felt they could set up camp. He wouldn't let them build a fire.

"Death by frostbite," said Jane. "Fucking hell."

"Make the most of it," Jack chided her. "Our last night under the stars."

They cuddled up under their blankets, the five surviving members of the expedition, holding each other close solely for the warmth. With the sea, and the panorama of the Milky Way glittering above them, Jack felt small and insignificant and not worth being afraid.

THE SEA AIR made their blankets clammy and cold, so they had no choice to get up in the morning and face whatever the day had in store. Barnden checked the road for signs of activity, then allowed them a small fire on which to cook breakfast.

They ate their paltry slops and were tested one last time on their physics. Jack and Jane recited the answers together, in the same bored monotone—making Kit and Nina laugh.

"Word perfect," concluded Nina as she reached the end of the last handwritten page.

"I'm still not sure what we actually do when we get in there," said Jack.

"They'll have information in there," said Jane with confidence. "We just read the manual."

"Because it's going to be that easy."

"'Course it is," said Jane. "What can possibly go wrong?"

After breakfast, as the others packed up and hid the traces of their camp, Jane helped Jack wash and unbind his arm from the bandages. He had pins and needles as he flexed his fingers, and couldn't hold his razor still; Jane had to shave him, too. She helped him into his one clean shirt without too much jagging pain. She scraped sweet-smelling oil over the top of her head, then washed it away with the last of the bucket of sea water Barnden brought them. Then she changed her bloody, dirty top for a clean black jumper with a hole in one elbow.

"Okay?" she asked Jack.

"Bit nervous. Like we're going on a date."

She grinned. "Won't be as bad as that." She turned to Barnden, Kit and Nina. "We're ready to go."

THE ACCESS ROAD cut through a wilderness of rock and scrub and shallow pools of water. An icy breeze came at them from the sea. It started to drizzle, the cold pinching at their faces and hands where they were exposed.

About half a mile down the road stood a burnt-out building. It might once have been an office or hotel. Two men with rifles emerged from the doorway, but didn't raise their guns.

"What do we do?" whispered Jane.

"Keep going," said Barnden. "Like we're meant to be here."

He nodded to the men and one of them nodded back.

A little later the road curved round to the right and then they could see the nuclear power station, a huge complex of windowless grey buildings inland from the sea and surrounded by some kind of wall. Pale smoke rose from various chimneys and they could feel the thrum of energy from the complex. Beyond, row after row of enormous pylons stood rusting and coming apart. Jack's mouth felt horribly dry.

Closer, and they saw that the wall around the reactor

buildings was some kind of high fence, covered in all kinds of junk: blankets and scarves, flapping in the wind; signs with crudely painted slogans about peace and destiny and the end being nigh. People milled around the fence at regular intervals—but there was no one beyond it.

There was movement, too, in what looked like a sprawling rubbish tip to the left of the main complex, centred around a low, grey building. The building was only low, Jack realised as they got closer, compared to the rest of the site; it was probably three or four storeys high. People scoured the rubbish tip for items of value, bobbing in and out of sight. Children scurried about, playing games and shouting. It wasn't a tip, but a shanty town.

"There could be two hundred people down there," said Jane. "What if they don't like the look of us?"

"Too late," said Barnden. "They've seen us."

A delegation of people was on the road ahead, coming up to meet them. Barnden glanced at Jack.

"No problem," said Jack. "Like you said: we act like we're meant to be here." They carried on, Barnden going first, shielding Kit and Nina.

The approaching men and women—there were seven of them, outnumbering Jack's band—looked half-starved and a little crazy. No, Jack realised, they were overjoyed.

"Hello, there!" cried one woman in a bedraggled cardigan. "I'm Laura Hoffman, one of the committee here." Her accent was cut glass, every syllable perfect. "Call me Laura, please. We don't stand on ceremony here."

"Hello," said Jack, stepping forward. He then wasn't sure what exactly to do, so unthinkingly extended his injured arm in greeting. Laura shook his hand warmly, making him cry out.

"Oh, dear darling," said Laura, embracing him—he got a whiff of charcoal and cats. "You must have suffered on the road."

"It's not much," he said, embarrassed to have shown her such weakness.

"We've doctors and medicines," she told him. "You'll have all you need."

"Like what?" said Jane, and one of the men in Laura's group began to list their facilities. Jane was visibly impressed; they even had what they referred to as a surgery.

Laura led him and the others down the road towards the commune.

"The reactor," said Jack. "It looks like it's still working."

"Oh, don't be deceived," said Laura. "There are no lights on, as you can see. But the noise and smoke, it's brewing up in there. Ready to explode, any moment now. Just like in the north."

"Right," said Jack. "Well, that's why we're here."

Laura took his hand. "Are you ready to die?"

"If that's how it's got to be."

She squeezed his hand tight. "It has. But we shall all be cleansed."

Jack tried not to show his surprise. "Yes, that's what we all hope for. Um. What does it involve? I mean, exactly."

"You're afraid. A lot of us are, there's no good denying it. But it's going to be all right. There won't be any pain. And you don't need to do anything but wait with the rest of us. We have games for the children—yours might be too old for that. But you can help us with the fence. We're putting up symbols to represent those who've gone before us. To make them part of the end."

"Right, yes, of course."

Her eyes twinkled kindly. "I can see you're not a believer. That's okay. We've all sorts here. There are those who think the radiation will cure all ailments or even heal the world. And there are those who know it's the end of days and it's better to go in the explosion, not drag it out over months or years. We've lost so much already and the world is so cruel that we should be thankful."

"Um," said Jack. "Has no one tried to get in there?" Laura looked stung. "I mean," said Jack, "people who aren't so enlightened. Do you have to guard against it?"

"Some have tried," said Laura, sniffily. "We discourage it."

"But it's not forbidden."

"Of course it's forbidden," laughed Laura. "That's why we discourage it."

"Sure," said Jack, reasonably. "It's just I want to understand how it works. What's happening here is so important."

Laura nodded. "We're vigilant at the fence. But we've not had to shoot anyone in a good while. That's because of the discouragement. The ones who were shot we put on display."

She indicated the grey building around which the shanty town clustered. Now they were closer, Jack could see the skeletal remains tethered to the roof. At least a dozen up there, one of them small, possibly a child. Crows wheeled round the bodies, idly pecking at the flesh. Some of the bodies looked fresh.

"I thought you said you hadn't had to do it in a while," said Jack.

"Oh," said Laura lightly. "That's not people who rushed the fence. We work with the local communities. You must have come through one of the towns earlier today."

Jack nodded, his mouth dry. Nathaniel and Alice had gone through the town.

"And they welcomed you in, offered you something to eat?" asked Laura, with a smile.

"They were very hospitable," nodded Jack.

"And they asked why you were heading this way?"

Jack didn't answer, staring up at the gruesome spectacle hanging from the side of the building. The poor unfortunates being picked apart by crows up there had given the wrong answer to that question, daring to suggest that they wanted to stop a nuclear explosion killing everyone for miles. Now he knew, he could see them clearly. The sunlight glinted on a pair of thick spectacles held on with elastic, and on a hook instead of a hand.

CHAPTER NINE

DESPITE THE IMMINENT nuclear holocaust, Laura's community were keen to keep up with the paperwork. Jack and his friends sat at a line of tables inside the low, grey building, working their way through pages and pages of forms. They were all numb with shock from the brutal loss of their friends. Nina had to choke back tears, for they were all desperately aware that any slip up they made in front of Laura and her cult would see them meet the same fate as Nathaniel and Alice.

Jack couldn't help going over what he might have done differently. If they'd stopped the horse box as it passed them on the road, he thought. If Nathaniel and Alice and been inside it, and if they'd still been alive...

He was also worried about the others sat with him now. Yet he himself didn't feel afraid. There was little hope he'd survive very long anyway: he'd die trying to get into the nuclear reactor, or because he managed to. But his fearlessness was mostly down to the fact that it hadn't sunk in. Filling in paperwork while sat in what was basically a village hall felt almost homely and normal, not the prelude to horrible death.

Around them, children chased each other back and forth in a complex game of ever-changing rules. The children were aged, Jack guessed, between about three and twelve, all noisy, healthy kids without a care in the world—presumably not knowing of its imminent end. When one small child slipped and crashed to the ground, another, older child scooped her up for a hug then set her on her feet, and the game continued.

Jane had been watching, too. Jack saw her face and guessed she was thinking of her son. Catching Jack's eye, she quickly turned back to her papers. "They actually want to know what I got in my GCSEs," she said.

"Make it up," said Jack.

"Best to be honest," said Barnden. "They might test us on our answers. That's why the forms are so long—it's harder to remember everything we put."

"We're going to die," sniffed Nina. Jane took her hand.

"Not if we're smart," she said. "And you're the smartest one of us all."

"Bad news for Jack," said Kit, and despite everything—or because of it—they laughed.

They continued writing. Jack felt a pang as, under 'parents,' he wrote out the names, birth and death dates of Emma and Scott Bedford, mother and father of the real Jack. He'd seen the names on so many documents that 'proved' his claim to the throne that he knew the details off by heart—but this was the first time he'd had to spell out the lie himself.

"Hey," said Jane.

"I'm fine," he said, but she looked over what he had written.

"It's not right to ask stuff like this," she said. Barnden coughed, but it was too late—Laura, coming over with a tray of steaming cups, had clearly heard her.

"The idea," said Laura, forcing a smile, "is to leave behind a full testament. Who we are, that we do this of our own volition."

"Of course," said Jane. "I only meant it dredges up some difficult memories."

Laura handed out the cups, which contained the foul "coffee" made from roasted acorns that older people insisted on drinking. "Good to get these things out in the open. Deal with it now, before the end." She stood patiently waiting for them to drink. Barnden sniffed his coffee suspiciously, but Jack took a sip. It was utterly disgusting.

"Lovely," he told Laura. "Just stronger than I'm used to."

Kit came to his rescue. "Can I ask a question? How will the answers we give here survive? Paper is sort of flammable."

Laura nodded. "We've secure storage under this building—a shelter, in case of emergencies."

Jack and his friends resisted the urge to swap glances. "Um," said Jack. "I imagine that has to be closely guarded, just like the fence."

Laura laughed. "Oh, if anyone has a sudden change of mind, they're welcome to enter the shelter. There's room inside for a large part of our community if that's what people want. But I doubt many, if anyone, will change their minds. We all know what conditions will be like after the explosion. We've enough reports from the north."

"I don't understand," said Jane. "I mean, you shoot anyone who tries to get to the reactor..."

"That's completely different," said Laura, patiently. "We explain this to the children: what's happening now is about how we face the end with dignity, as rational beings. But we don't interfere to hasten the end."

Jack chose his words carefully. "They say in the north that it's possible to fix things so there isn't an explosion. Do you get that being said here? You know, by people out to make trouble."

Laura shook her head sadly. "We had to deal with some very disagreeable sorts, and others who meant well but could have done a lot of harm among the community. They couldn't understand that the evidence is clear. The people who tried to fix things in the north were all killed by the reactor, weren't they? The reactor still poisoned the area for hundreds of miles. They didn't save anyone, just prolonged the agony. Imagine: the situation as bad as it is, and you make it worse."

"Of course," said Jack. "Awful."

"So we wait it out," said Laura. "Like decent, civilised people. After all, we're British, aren't we?"

The others made affirmative noises. Barnden looked like he might laugh, or punch something.

"You don't think people will go crazy waiting it out?" said Jane. "I mean," she added quickly, "that's what we heard can happen in the north."

Laura sighed. "Yes, we've heard that, too. But we run a timetable of scheduled activities and entertainment to keep people busy, and open counselling workshops where we can all share our concerns. You're invited to join us for the session tonight."

"We'd love to," said Jack.

"Good boy," said Laura. "And you look like you've almost finished your form."

He had, signing his name at the bottom of the last page and sitting smugly back in his seat. Nina—who'd studiously completed her form while the others had been talking—sat back, too. A thought occurred to Jack and he took her form and put it on top of his, as if helpfully collecting them up. Then he just happened to notice the details on the first page of her papers.

"You're from Oxford," he said, as if it were news to him.

"Uh," said Nina, "yeah."

"Funny," said Jack. "We spend all this time on the road together, and we don't really know the first thing about each other."

Jane got what he was doing. "Barden's a Ranger, he must be from Nottingham."

"Macclesfield," said Barnden.

"Oh," said Jane. "Well, we can get to know each other while we're here."

Laura didn't seem very interested, so Jack laid it on a bit thicker. "You see," he told her, "we met on the road, but we're not really together." He hoped that when he and Jane made their break for the reactor, that distinction might save his friends.

Laura only shrugged. "Well," she said. "We're all together now. One big family of friends. So long as everyone behaves."

JACK AND BARNDEN strolled toward the barbed wire fence that encircled the huge, square buildings of the nuclear reactor.

The ground trembled with whatever infernal forces were being generated within. Men and women with shotguns regarded them coolly as they approached. Barnden had his arms slightly out to the sides of his Ranger's cloak, showing he carried no weapons and presented no threat. Jack copied him, though he felt awkward—like the more he tried to convince these people he meant no mischief, the more they would suspect it.

"Afternoon," he said to the men and women with shotguns. "Just arrived here. I'm Jack, this is Barnden—he doesn't say much but he's all right, really. Our other friends are with Laura, looking for a space in the—the shanty town? You know what I mean. But that doesn't need all of us. Frankly, we were getting in the way. So they sent us out for some air."

"No sudden moves," was all he got in response, from a woman in a battered old trenchcoat, worn over a glamorous ballgown. She had make-up and jewellery, too—things Jack had barely seen for years. One man behind her wore a black suit and tie, for all they were threadbare and spattered with mud. The guards were in their best clothes, proud to be first in the coming holocaust.

"Can't be too careful," agreed Jack. "You're all doing a great job." He gave them a thumbs up. They clearly thought he was a twat, but a harmless one.

The chain link fence stood some ten feet high, but close up it was difficult to look through it to the tall grass and buildings; scraps of coloured fabric had been threaded through the links, together with long lines of coloured wool and bits of old plastic packaging, any old rubbish with a splash of colour. Faded photographs in plastic coverings smiled cheerily at him. He saw drawings, too—crude stick people by children and portraits that captured a likeness. As he and Barden got closer, they could read messages on some of the litter: names and dates of loved ones, simple notes of remembrance and prayers that they'd be reunited.

These tokens and memories so crowded the fence that it took Jack a moment to spot the strands of barbed and razor wire also threaded at regular intervals. The rows were a hand's span apart—a gap he couldn't have wriggled through—and the barbs looked rusted and nasty.

The men and women with shotguns were still watching, so Jack, trying to look casual, pointed to one of the portraits.

"Hey," he said to Barnden. "I think I knew this girl."

The Ranger leaned forward to examine the picture. Jack moved his finger out of the way, and tapped the protruding tip of a piece of barbed wire. Barnden nodded—yes, of course he'd seen it—then stepped away from the fence.

"Could be anyone," he said, carrying on round the perimeter, as if the fence itself held no particular interest. Jack hurried after him.

The fence and its guards entirely encircled the reactor buildings. Barricades had been added in front of the site's old gates and along the slender strip of beach on the south side of the complex. Jack's heart sank as they idled their way round. There was no obvious way in. The wind blew the acrid smoke into their faces, making Barnden sneeze.

They left the beach and made their way back towards the low building. Just for this short distance, they would be out of earshot of anyone else. "Well?" asked Jack.

"Easy," said Barnden. "Plant a grenade by one of the fence posts and it'll knock the thing down or make you a hole you can duck through. Best to do it up by where you pointed out that picture. Fence post with the blue jersey tied to it has the least distance to the buildings inside."

"Right," said Jack, his insides turning over at the prospect of this actually happening. "How do we plant a grenade without that lot seeing us, or shooting us when it goes off? And I'll need to put on my protective suit before I head through the fence. Which might just make them suspicious. And I can't go quickly or I'll tear the suit on that wire. So all together, fuck."

Barnden shrugged. "You see the guns they've got stored away, where we were signing the forms?"

"Um," said Jack. "No."

"Narrow, oblong crates, stacked up by the wall."

"I was busy getting our story straight with Laura, so she wouldn't have us strung up."

"They've got enough people wandering round with shotguns. Those crates must be their back-up. Some kind of heavy artillery. Which I'll use on the ones stood in front of the fence."

"You mean just shoot them?"

"Before they shoot you."

Jack ran his fingers through his matted, greasy hair. "Fucking hell," he said.

"We've a job to do," said Barnden.

Jack had faced death before. He'd run headlong into heavy fire. He'd felt then the same mix of terror and complete certainty he felt now. Fuck it, he could do this.

"Okay," he said. "When?"

Barnden smiled. "Tonight—we can't lose any more time."

"Right," said Jack. "But look. Jane and Kit and Nina..."

"We send them away. Not immediately—that'll draw attention. But the moment we're ready to move, Jane will get the kids out of here."

Jack nodded. Jane wouldn't be able to argue with that. It would make things easier when it was time to say goodbye.

"Okay," he said. "A plan."

But Barnden didn't smile. He looked back towards the long building where they'd filled out the forms. Jack could just make out a figure framed in the doorway, arms raised and waving.

Barnden began running. Jack trailed after him, though with his gunshot wound he could barely keep up.

"What is it?" he called. "What's happened?" But Barnden didn't answer, racing towards the figure—who Jack could now see was Jane. She had a horrified look on her face.

CHAPTER TEN

"THEY WENT THROUGH our bags," said Jane, trying to keep her voice steady. They were back at the tables where they'd filled out the paperwork, and Laura had brought them more of the horrible coffee. The children were still playing. Stacked up against the far wall, Jack could see the crates Barnden had mentioned, containing the heavy artillery. He had to resist the urge to run over and grab something, to shoot the whole place down right there and then. Instead, he concentrated on Jane.

"They do it with everyone," she continued, "to see if we've anything dangerous, or if there's something that might benefit the community as a whole."

"People hoard medicines," said Laura, reasonably. "Then there's the problem of guns. We don't mind people keeping them—we just need to know who has what."

She might have been discussing the washing-up rota, thought Jack, and not a couple of teenagers now facing death. Nina's bag had contained the protective suit and all the hand-written notes. They couldn't exactly deny their intention to get into the reactor, but Kit had said it was his idea. He'd obviously hoped to take Nina's place in custody, but now they both faced execution. It offered little comfort that they denied that Jack, Jane or Barnden had known about their plans—and the forms they'd filled out backed up the story that they'd merely met on the road. That seemed good enough for Laura.

"So what happens?" asked Jack. "I mean, what's the procedure?"

"Obviously there's a trial," said Laura. "That's going on at the minute—a formality really, as they don't deny the charge. Then there's the paperwork, which won't take long. No, the main thing is letting word get around the community so no one has to miss out."

"We all gather to watch," said Jack, his mouth dry.

"Those who can be spared from their duties," said Laura. "It's an occasion for us all to come together. It builds unity."

"They're children," said Jane.

Laura sighed. "Perhaps in the old days. And we have to consider the other children here." She smiled at those chasing about at the far end of the hall. "If we spare the rod now, what sort of example are we offering?" Then she shivered, turning to Jane with such sadness in her eyes. "It's not easy, we don't like it, but it has to be done."

Jane looked ready to respond, but thought better of it—getting herself in trouble, too, wouldn't help.

"If that's all settled," said Barnden, irritably, "did you find us somewhere to sleep?"

Laura seemed shocked by his lack of concern for the teens.

"You'll have to forgive Barnden," Jack explained. "He's from the north." He didn't know what Barnden was planning, it just seemed wise to go along with it.

"I told you those kids were up to no good," said Barnden. "Now they've been caught and they'll get what they deserve. But that's nothing to do with us, is it? So: did you find us somewhere?"

"No," said Jane—also trying to play along. "I mean, we'd just started looking when they opened the bags."

"Fuck's sake," muttered Barnden. "How hard can it be?"

"I'm not your servant," said Jane.

"You had *one fucking job*," he snapped, shocking the children at the far end of the hall. "You said you were going to sort it. I'd have done it myself if I'd known you wouldn't bother."

Before Jane could shout back at him, Laura raised her hands. "Now, please," she said gently. "You've all had a long journey, and now this nasty surprise. But there's no need for any unpleasantness. I can see you're tired, Ranger Barnden. It won't take me a moment to find you somewhere to sleep."

Barnden actually smiled at her—a big, cheesy grin, completely unlike him. "That would be very kind. I don't want to be any trouble."

"Of course not," she preened, rising to her feet. "Now, you make it up with these two, and by the time you've finished your coffee I'm sure I'll have found something."

"You're an angel," he told her, and she blushed and hurried away.

"All right, Casanova," said Jack when she'd gone. "What's the plan?"

Barnden glanced about, then reached deep into his cloak and produced something dark and round. He placed the grenade in Jack's hands. Jack quickly moved it to the pocket of his coat.

"She said everyone who can be spared gets to enjoy the fun," said Barnden. "That might mean fewer people manning the fence."

"Right," said Jack.

"We can't let them string up Kit and Nina," said Jane.

"I've got an idea about that," said Barnden. "When they think I've gone for a kip, I create a distraction. Then I rescue the kids."

"On your own?"

Barnden held Jane's gaze. "Think you could do it?"

She stared back at him for a moment, then shook her head. "But I could help—give covering fire, or something."

"Yeah," said Barnden. "But not for me. You need to get Jack through the fence. We think the crates by the wall over there—"

"They're full of assault rifles," said Jane. "I read the labels when Laura led us past on the way to the shanty town."

Barnden nodded. "When I start my distraction, you each grab a gun and you charge the fence. One of you has to get through."

"But—" began Jack.

"No arguments," said Jane. "He's right, I'm coming with you."

"Fine," he said. "But if we both get up there, I'm the one who goes inside."

She smiled. "We can discuss that when we get there."

"Do you know what they did with Nina's notes and the protective suit?"

"I couldn't really ask," she said.

"No," said Jack. "But we'll have to find them."

Barnden shook his head. "We need to be quick about this, take them by surprise."

Jack wanted to argue, but Jane took his wrist. "That suit wouldn't save you anyway. You've heard the reactor, you've walked through the smoke. We've probably had a lethal dose as it is."

Jack, Jane and Barnden regarded one another across the table. Jane was right: there was nothing more to be said—and just as well, because Laura made her way back to join them.

"Ranger Barnden," she said. "We've found you a lovely spot with a hammock. I'm rather envious, to be honest."

Barnden got to his feet. "Thank you, Laura," he said, making her beam. He winked at Jane before he left, but didn't say goodbye.

As the crowd gathered outside the long building, Jack made a point of not looking up at Nathaniel and Alice, the friends he'd failed to save. He wouldn't be able to hide his revulsion, which wouldn't help him or Jane.

Yet, as they congregated with the rest of the community waiting for the show, a woman in a stripy jumper caught his eye and nodded, sharing his horror at what was being done but not daring to say it out loud. Jack gaped at her then quickly turned away, so no one else would spot the moment of connection.

So, not everyone delighted in the killing of two teens. In fact, Jack could spot them, the individuals in the crowd whose smiles didn't convince.

He could have made a speech, tried to rally them—and perhaps others would have joined the cause, made a stand. There was the tantalising prospect of being torn down by this crowd, which seemed a bit more heroic than a slow death by radiation. This was exactly the kind of thing that made him want to be King: giving people a cause, something more than brute strength and the baying of the mob.

Jane clasped his arm and he thought he must have been showing his anger. No, she'd seen something and it took a moment to follow her line of sight. A ladder had been set against the side of the building, and there was a team busy with two long ropes. Each rope had a hangman's noose at the end. The idea seemed to be that Kit and Nina would both be alive as they were pulled up to the roof, kicking and flailing for the crowd's delectation.

That wasn't what had given Jane the start. Next to the men with the ropes was a brightly coloured stand, at which people in tall hats cooked bubbling blobs of meat. A queue had formed to receive these tasty treats, the food served right where Kit and Nina were about to die.

The cooking meat made Jack's stomach turn over. Jane led him away, back towards the door into the building, dodging children feasting on toffee apples on sticks. He felt hot and giddy, tears streaming down his face. Around them, adults and children guzzled food and chattered, caught up in the excitement.

And didn't immediately notice the fire.

The first Jack knew of it was a woman screaming. Then there were more shouts and people running off to the shanty town. Jane held Jack tight by the arm so they wouldn't be separated. And then they saw the flames, licking round the side of the building, reaching up right to the roof to taste the first of the bodies hanging there.

"The town's on fire!" someone shouted.

"Save the children!" shouted another. Jane led Jack to the door of the building, against the stampede.

They walked into sudden darkness. A blanket of smoke crept its way across the ceiling, blocking the sky lights. Jane and Jack hurried to the far wall, and could feel the incredible heat of the blazing tents and sheds on the other side. Amid the roar of the flames were desperate, pitiful cries, people calling out instructions and names. Jane didn't hesitate, tearing the lid off the first of the crates and seizing two rifles. She checked they were loaded, handed both to Jack and took two more for herself.

Without a word, they marched out the building and made their way up the low rise to the fence. There were fewer men and women with shotguns guarding it—some had clearly been allowed to enjoy the execution party. The rest seemed torn about what to do about the blaze. Some came forward as Jack and Jane approached. Others raised their shotguns.

"Laura sent us," Jack called ahead—his throat sore, his voice gravelly from the smoke he had inhaled. "We can cover the fence with these, so more of you can help with putting out the fire."

Some of them dropped their shotguns and ran. The man in the suit Jack had seen before turned to one of the women pointing a shotgun at Jack. Jack could see her wavering, eyes on the blaze down the hill. Fuck, thought Jack, they might just pull this off without having to shoot anyone.

"Stop!" yelled a voice from far behind them. "Don't let them near the fence!"

The woman in front of Jack fired at him and he let her have it with the rifles. The recoil almost knocked him backward, juddering through his arms and shoulders and jaw—and the weapons tore the woman apart. He sprayed more bullets into the man in the suit and the others at the fence. They didn't stand a chance.

"Fuck!" said Jane, beside him in the silence that followed the shooting. "Fucking fuck."

"You're not the one who did it," he said, hurrying forward to the fence.

"Yeah, but what about the rest?"

Jack looked behind them. The whole building was ablaze, and the shanty town beyond it, the flames blinding to look at, black smoke filling the sky. No one could get close to the flames, let alone combat them, which left nothing for them to do but follow Laura, brandishing shotguns, as they made their way up the hill.

Jack dropped his rifles in the bloody earth and reached into his pocket for Barnden's grenade. There was the fence post with the blue jersey, but with the grenade in his hand, Jack realised he didn't know how to set it off, at least not without being caught in the blast.

"Fuck's sake," said Jane, handing him one of her guns and taking the grenade. He covered her as she worked at the base of the fence. He fired over the heads of the crowd, but they kept on towards him, brandishing shotguns and knives. The mob included children.

"Move," said Jane, and she led him along the side of the fence for about fifty yards, then turned back in dread. Nothing exploded behind them. *It hadn't fucking worked.*

A bullet spanged off the fence. Jack fired back at the crowd, now easily within range and two people danced backward and fell. Others dropped to the ground beside them—he couldn't tell if they'd been wounded or not. But the rest of the mob kept on coming.

Jane raised her other rifle, firing down the line of the fence, back the way they'd come. "Get down!" she yelled at him over the noise—just as the ground whipped away under his feet.

Jack hit the ground hard and tumbled head over heel, losing grip of the rifle. Stunned and sore, he scrambled back to his feet and retrieved the weapon. Jane, crouched down as she'd fired, was already running. Jack caught her up, and they gazed in dismay at the carnage.

The grenade had obliterated the fence post and all the rubbish entwined in the fence for about five metres either side, but the fence itself remained intact. There was no way through. Jack stood before it, gun trained on the mob now gathered around them. Men, women and children, baying for his blood.

"Sorry," said Jane. "Thought I'd dug it in properly."

"It's going on your permanent record," he told her. "Might affect your chances of promotion." They both trained their guns on the crowd.

"Thought it was a stupid idea coming here," said Jane. "I mean, what else can go wrong?"

He was formulating an answer when someone shouted from the crowd.

"Your Majesty!"

Jack and Jane stared in horror as Nina stumbled forward through the mob and into the open. Her nose had been broken, there was bruising round her eye, and Laura jabbed a pistol into her throat.

"She says you're the King," said Laura, as if it were a joke. Some of the crowd around her even laughed. Jack didn't say anything. He couldn't think of any way to save Nina without killing an awful lot of people, and he could see that Nina knew it. She stared back at him, tears cutting lines down the blood and muck on her face.

"Does it make any difference what I am?" Jack asked Laura.

"It might have done. We're reasonable people."

"Apart from stringing up children," said Jane.

Laura smiled, showing bloody teeth. "We had a system. Regular sacrifice to keep everyone else in line." Her smile faded. "The Ranger's dead. This one told us what you're planning to do. I'm afraid we can't allow it."

"What about Kit?" said Jane.

Laura shrugged. "A lot of people are missing in the fire. Who knows how many you murdered? If you're the King, surely you agree that there must be justice. Drop your guns, surrender to us. Or I shoot the girl."

The fire raged behind the crowd, but a cool sea breeze whispered around Jack. He felt perfectly calm and sure.

"Shoot her," he said. Some of the crowd gasped, but Laura stood her ground.

"Don't doubt that I will," she said.

"I know you'll kill her," said Jack. "Whether we surrender or not. You need to, to keep your hold on power. But I can't let you prevent us doing the job we came to do. We can stop the reactor exploding and we can save everyone here. And we're willing to die to do that. All of us. Even Nina."

Nina was weeping, shaking her head, but that didn't matter. Neither did Laura, finger twitching on the trigger of the gun pressed into Nina's neck. What mattered was the crowd, the confusion on their faces—and, in some of them, the slowly dawning hope.

"It's true," Jack told them. "I'm the rightful King of

England—and my life is yours. You can kill me yourselves, or you can let me die by going into the reactor to save you."

For a moment he had them: he could see their need to believe.

"Fuck you," said Laura, and Nina's head exploded. Then so too did the crowd. A dozen pairs of hands reached for Laura, grabbing her, pulling her backwards, tearing her clothes and flesh. She tried to scream, but more hands smothered her mouth.

The crowd wasn't united. People pushed and shoved and threw punches. Guns went off. But Jack could see the light in the eyes of those his words had affected.

"We need to get through the fence!" he yelled, and the mob descended on him. Jane tried to drag him out of the way as people surged forward, but they were caught in the throng and knocked back into the barbed wire. Barbs pricked through his clothes and skin, but the crowd kept pushing. He lost grip of Jane's hand. He couldn't breathe.

Then, somewhere something snapped and he was falling backward as the fence gave way.

There was no jubilation as the crowd unpicked themselves from the fence and long grass to get back to their feet. Many people looked horrified by what they'd done. They backed away, not daring to stand in such close proximity to the thundering reactor, as if a few paces would make any difference. A little distance off, Laura knelt in the mud by Nina's body. A man stood over her, a knife glinting in his hand.

"What you want done with her?" the man asked Jack.

Laura looked up imploringly. Jack hated her for all that she had done. If he'd had a weapon in her hand, if there hadn't been a crowd watching him, he might not have hesitated. But there she was, on her knees with everyone looking on.

"Let her go," he said. The man looked astonished, then appalled. "We defeated her," Jack told him. "There's nothing more she can do. Nothing worse than I'm about to face anyway."

The man didn't like it but wouldn't argue with Jack. He poked Laura with his toe.

"Go on," he said. "Get." She didn't need any encouragement, and scrambled away into the night.

"That really such a great idea?" whispered Jane.

"Am I not merciful?" he said, but his smile faltered. For all that people were slinking away, there were still plenty watching Jack and Jane, eager to see the King head into the reactor and save the world as promised.

Through the tall grass, he could see a door in the wall of the reactor building. There was nothing between him and the door; he just had to start walking.

"Well, then," he said.

"Well, then," said Jane.

"You don't have to come with me."

"No," she said.

"You should go home to your son."

"Yeah."

"I might just about manage without you."

She sighed. "Not a chance."

"Well, then," he said.

She took his hand in hers and they went together.

Dear Lee,

This note is for when you turn 16. I hope the world is better than when I knew it, that there's some kind of peace.

But I also know that it's the quiet times that can do the worst damage, because it's when people deal with what they've been through and lost. I looked after lots of kids at St Mark's and I saw how the quiet could eat them up. So you need to hear this:

What happened to me isn't your fault. I chose to do what I'm doing so you'd be happy and safe. That isn't me giving you permission, it's an order: be happy and safe. Don't feel bad for what happened or because you forget me.

I love you.

Mum xx

PART THREE

CHAPTER ELEVEN

THE DOOR WOULDN'T open. Jack almost wanted to laugh. He and Jane tried again, smacking and battering the cold metal surface to no avail.

"Makes sense though," he said at length. "They wouldn't just let you wander into a nuclear reactor."

"What are we going to do?" said Jane. Behind them, beyond the broken down fence, a crowd continued to watch them.

"We could go round the building," said Jack. "See if there's another way in. You know, a main reception with big displays about how completely safe this place is."

"Maybe," said Jane, then ran back the way they'd come. People jeered, disappointed that she'd given up so soon, but Jane clearly had no intention of abandoning the mission. She searched the mud around the fallen fence and retrieved one of the assault rifles.

"Right," she said, hurrying back. "Improvised skeleton key."

Jack got quickly out of the way as she unleashed a deafening torrent against the metal surface. The door buckled under the onslaught. Jane stopped firing and replaced the clip on her gun while Jack inspected the damage. The door steamed and hissed, so he didn't dare touch it. But the shooting had exposed a square shape just under the metal on the right hand side. He was looking at the mechanism for a swipe card.

Jack pulled off his jacket and wrapped it round one hand. Suitably protected, he bashed at the square mechanism until it popped out and fell to the ground. He grasped the torn metal of the door and pulled—and, with effort, it creaked open.

They stared in amazement at the corridor within, bright with electric strip lights.

"The power's on!" said Jack.

"Well duh, it's a power station," said Jane.

"It's working!"

"That's not a good thing. Means they didn't shut it all down."

"But we might be able to, I don't know, just push the right buttons," he said. "We just have to track down the control room." So saying, he stepped into the corridor. "In and out quickly, minimum of exposure."

"We want to decommission it, not just shut it down."

"Okay, but maybe it means there's been no damage to the cooling system yet, and we can take our time. I'm trying to keep positive."

The corridor smelled stale and damp. Water dripped from the ceiling and pooled on the smooth concrete floor, and mould dappled the walls. The strip lights buzzed as if they would explode at any moment. Jack's footsteps echoed eerily as he made his way forward.

"What are you afraid of?" said Jane, making him jump. "It's not like there'll be anyone here."

"Yeah, all right. It's just weird."

"Well, no shit. Come on. Talk me through the reactor core controls we expect to find here."

"Um, yeah. Coarse shut-down controls are boron control rods, with fine control from stainless steel rods."

"Which means?"

"Basically, we insert any rods that haven't been already. Then we look for what safety manuals or procedures they've got for us to follow."

They continued to test themselves as they made their way through the building. The vestiges of decoration were prehistoric—from perhaps as far back as the 1970s. But over-written on this were signs of life from the time of The Cull. Notes on a notice board advised on handwashing and reporting symptoms, invited staff to join a pub quiz league with a cash prize of £100, and said there'd be a collection for Muneet's baby. Jack and Jane moved on.

At the far end of the building, they found a cutaway diagram of the site, detailing escape routes in case of a fire. It was a very old diagram, from when the complex had been built. The spacious car park contained just three pictured vehicles, all from the 1960s, including an open-topped sports car. The sun was shining and behind the complex of buildings families played on the beach. Nuclear power, it seemed to suggest, was more than just safe—it was fun.

"Okay, we're here," said Jane. "Administration block. We carry on this way to reach Dungeness A." That was the first of the two reactors on the site, with—remembering from Nina's notes—four turbo-generators housed in the turbine hall.

"We could split up, do one each," he suggested.

"Might take longer," said Jane. "We figure out the first one together, then the second one is just doing the same."

"Dungeness B is different," said Jack, piously. "The reactors there are 545 rather than 225 megawatts, and have advanced gas-cooled systems."

"Bet the off-switches look the same."

"Fine." Jack traced his finger over the diagram working out the route to the main station control room. "We want to avoid the big machines if we can—there's a higher risk of contamination. So we head for the services unit and then up this staircase to the viewing balcony. Should be simple enough."

They left the administration block and stepped out into darkness, just able to discern a path through the overgrowth to the huge reactor block. A vast cylinder towered overhead, the concrete weathered and cracked from years of neglect. The path took them to a wooden door with a window, but the view inside was obscured by drapes. Jane tried the handle and the door opened easily. They ducked under the curtain of black felt.

"I guess that's to keep the radiation from escaping," said Jack. "We must be in a hot part of the site."

"Oh, good," said Jane.

There wasn't the same stale smell as in the accommodation block. Jack tried the light switch and the lights blinked on. There were more details to be gleaned about the staff who'd worked in the place before The Cull—a politely furious note about putting money in the tin for the coffee pods. All the windows they passed had been covered in black felt.

They made their way towards the services unit, continuing to test each other on physics. Suddenly Jane stopped, grabbing Jack's arm and dragging him through a side door. They hid in an abandoned office, the computers buried under dust and cobwebs. Jane flattened herself against the wall. Jack followed her lead, and they remained perfectly motionless.

Nothing happened.

"Now who's jumpy?" said Jack. Jane flinched at the loudness of his voice, watching through the crack in the door—but watching what? Gingerly, he edged round the door to look.

The corridor stretched off ahead of them, ending in double doors inset with windows, reflecting the lights he'd turned on back at him.

Then he saw something move. A shape, far down the end of the corridor, slowly coming towards them. He ducked back into the office, then dared to peep again. Definitely something approaching, a blobby, roughly human shape.

Jack watched in wonder as the figure came slowly nearer. The double doors creaked open, revealing a person in a faded yellow radiation suit. He or she—there was no way to tell in the suit—looked left and right, as if lost.

"Anyone there?" the suited stranger called, a man's voice. "Hello?" He had an accent—German, maybe.

Jack didn't dare to answer. What the fuck was going on? Beside him, Jane raised her rifle.

The man took a few steps forward, and called out again. "Hello? Someone there?"

"What is it?" called a woman's voice from behind the man.

She, too, had an accent. In the darkness up the corridor, Jack saw another blobby shape, a figure in a protective suit.

"Lights are on down here," said the man.

"Ack," said the woman. "Then turn them off."

The man reached out a gloved hand to the wall, and the lights went out. Again he twisted round, left and right, scanning the now dim corridor. Then he shrugged and lumbered back through the double doors after his friend.

"What," said Jane after a moment, "the actual fuck?"

"Just what I was thinking," said Jack. "The felt on the window: it's to hide the lights when they're on, so no one knows those two are here. This could be good: they've got the right kit, so they must know what they're doing."

"We don't know anything of the sort. How did they get in here? They can't have come through the community—they'd have been strung up."

"There must be another route in. Do you think it's just the two of them? Or are there more people here?"

"Fuck," said Jane. "What do we do?"

Jack considered. "We can't just walk away. We find out who they are and what's they're up to, and whether there's anyone else." He smiled. "They might be friendly, and on top of things here. This might turn out okay."

"Oh, yes," said Jane. "And we'll all get to have cake and a sing-song."

THEY CHECKED EACH doorway as they made their way down the murky corridor—but there was no sign of the man and woman in protective suits. According to the cutaway diagram they'd seen before, they would soon reach the turbine hall, where they were likely to be exposed to a huge dose of radiation. Jack felt tired and itchy already.

Jane skidded to a halt, pointing ahead to a line of light, blinding in the darkness. They crept closer: the light emerged from the gap under a door. They could hear rumbling through the wall, like some kind of machinery. There was no sign or marking on the door to tell them what lay beyond. Jane raised her gun—she would cover Jack as he went inside. There was no handle, he just had to push the door inwards. Gingerly, he did so.

A cloud of smoke erupted from the doorway. Jack fell back, clamping his hands over his mouth and nose so he'd not breathe in the toxic fumes. The door swung shut again, cutting off the steam. Jane grinned at him.

"Know what this is?" she whispered. Jack shook his head. "Shower rooms. Decontamination."

"So?"

"So, they're knocking off work for the day. Which means they'll be off guard. We can handle two of them. And then we can ask them what they think they're playing at."

"If there's only two of them in there," said Jack. But he pushed the door anyway and stepped through the wall of steam.

He found himself in a square-tiled room, dazzling white in the glare of electric lighting. The air was hot and moist. Steam curled thickly from a doorway in the far wall, through which he could hear running water.

Jane followed him, gun on the doorway. With Jane covering him, Jack made his way over for a better look. His clothes stuck to him as he moved, soggy in the heat. Now, under the sound of running water, he could just hear the man and woman, calling out to one another as they washed. A tiled wall cut off his view of the washing facilities—he couldn't tell if the man and woman were alone.

Beside the doorway stood a plastic bin with a lid. A handwritten sign pointed down to the bin with the words *Kern Strahlenschutz Anzug*, and a pretty good sketch of a radiation suit. A box on the wall bore a green cross symbol, and beneath it—reachable from the floor—was a red emergency button. There was nothing else.

Jack mouthed "Okay?" at Jane and she nodded. He took a step towards the shower room and the merry chatter of the two Germans. Then he stopped, glancing back round the room. Jane met him with a look of puzzlement, and he held up a finger: they couldn't make a sound. She nodded her understanding, so he moved to the plastic bin and removed the lid.

The visor of a radiation suit stared sightlessly up at him. Carefully, quietly, Jack extracted the suit from the bin. It was surprisingly heavy, especially the visor and the mask that fitted beneath it. He tried to hand the suit to Jane, but she still held her rifle. So, to her surprise, Jack started to pull on the suit.

It was warm and damp, with a strong whiff of its previous occupant. The face mask fitted tightly round Jack's eyes and nose and mouth, the thick plastic making him gag. Jane had to help him with the zip that reached up the side of the suit and then over, across the top the visor. His breathing echoed around him, he felt hot and trapped and dizzy. But there was also a heart-racing excitement. They had a protective suit! There might yet be a chance of surviving.

He nodded his head towards the door out of the room, but Jane shook her head and handed him the gun. Jack couldn't argue without making noise, so could only watch as she clambered into the second protective suit, pulling on the mask with more skill than he had shown. The mask obscured her features, and reflected his own anonymous visor back at him.

He pointed back to the door they'd come in by. Jane nodded, took the machine gun from his hands and they lumbered stiffly back out into the corridor.

"Go on, then," said Jane, her voice muffled by the suit. "Why didn't we question those two in the shower?"

"There can't just be two of them here," said Jack. "The lights are working, they've got showers. This is a big operation."

"We'd know for sure if we asked them."

"Did you see the alarm button on the wall? What if there was one in the shower room, too? They'd have called for help before we got to them."

"You don't know that. And they might still call for help when they miss the suits."

"They don't come back that way. There were no towels, no clothes to change into. You must go out a different way."

"They'll notice eventually."

"Then we'll have to be quick. But wearing this, we can have a good look round and no one will challenge us."

"And we might just get away."

"There's a chance, isn't there? Come on."

They wanted to see the main reactor, and there were two options. They could head through the turbine room and round, a long and circuitous route where they would potentially meet lots more people working on the site, or they could duck outside and cut across to that part of the building.

The cold night air pinched at their suits. It was difficult to see much more than straight ahead in the suits; Jack had to twist his whole body left and right to get his bearings. A path led across a strip of roadway to the Reactor B building, another huge fat cylinder on top of a cube-shaped block. The windows above them looked dark, but they could feel the thrum of huge machinery inside.

A series of concrete blocks and low walls in the road had, Jack assumed, been put there to prevent vehicles getting too close to the reactor buildings. He'd seen similar defences outside the Parliament building in London.

They crossed the road, heading for a pair of doors. Suddenly, the doors burst open in a blaze of light. Jack shielded his eyes. People emerged from the glare, at least ten of them in protective suits. Light glinted on their visors, and on the assault rifles in their gloved hands.

"Play it cool," said Jane under her breath and continued to lumber onwards.

Jack kept by her side. The armed personnel spreading out in a line to block their path. Jack and Jane had no option to stop as well, just a few metres in front of what looked very much like a firing squad.

"Excuse us, please," said Jane, mildly.

There was no response—the armed personnel might not have understood. Or they understood too well. They were raising their guns...

Jack grabbed Jane's arm and dragged her away down the road as the shooting began.

CHAPTER TWELVE

JACK THREW HIMSELF round the side of a concrete wall and landed on top of Jane. She swore at him and hit and kicked him as bullets flew over their heads. He rolled off, badly jarring his shoulder and the wound in his chest. Jane was on her feet, edging round the concrete wall to return fire with her own rifle. The concrete echoed the sound, deafening Jack. Without a gun of his own, he couldn't help Jane, he could only keep out of the way. Back against the concrete, knees bent so his legs were against his chest to present the smallest possible target, he cast around for anything he could use, or any way to escape.

They were trapped between two large chunks of concrete that barely gave adequate cover. Between them and the next bit of a wall was a gap of at least five metres where they would be exposed to the firing squad. There was nothing else, just some stones at the side of the road. Well, Jack could throw those at the armed personnel, it was better than nothing. But as he grabbed the stones another thought struck him.

Jane stopped shooting. A tense silence hung in the air, just the hiss of steam from the gun.

"Did you get them all?" whispered Jack. "Pretty helpful if you did."

"I can't see," said Jane. "There's a wall in my way." She glanced back behind them, quickly assessing their chances of escape. "Fuck."

A Germanic voice cut through the silence. "If you are still alive, if you lay down your weapons and step out into the open, we will let you live."

"What do you reckon?" whispered Jack to Jane.

"We don't have any choice. If they capture us, they have to tell us what they're up to. And they might not be quite as homicidal as everyone else we've met in the past few days."

"I suppose—" began Jack, but his words were cut off by a hail of gunfire, blasting chips of concrete from the wall just above his head.

"I say again," called the Germanic voice. "Lay down your weapons and step out into the open."

"I don't trust him," said Jane. "He's enjoying this. Fuck."

"Get ready to run," Jack told her. She didn't question him, but nodded.

"Five," called the soldier. "Four. Three..."

Jack threw the stones in his hand up over the wall in the direction of the armed personnel. He heard a yelp and hurried bootsteps on tarmac, by which point he and Jane were already racing for the next wall, diving down behind it as the armed personnel realised he hadn't thrown grenades. Bullets battered the wall beside Jack, and a chip scored across his visor like a blade.

"Go," said Jane, covering the way they'd come with her assault rifle. He didn't argue, he didn't look—he half-ran, half-crawled to the next section of wall, keeping his head low. Bullets spanged off the road and concrete ahead of him, blocking his path. Then, behind him, Jane was on her feet and firing, a huge volley of bullets clattering on stone. Senses dulled by the noise, Jack threw himself round the next chunk of wall, tucking himself up tightly to leave space for Jane. He realised that he was crouched on a metal hatch, the surface pitted with ridges. A hefty padlock secured the hatch.

"Jane!" he shouted—but she couldn't hear him over the

noise of the gun. He dared to duck back round the side of the wall, where Jane knelt in the open, spattering bullets at the gap in the concrete ahead of them.

"Jane!" called Jack again. She didn't turn, but she must have heard him because she got to her feet and quickly made her way back towards him, gun still trained on the gap in the wall.

"Here," he said, pointing to the padlock. She swept bullets across the metal surface and the padlock flipped up and broke apart. Jack hurriedly wrenched open the hatch, revealing a ladder down into darkness. He started down the steps.

He found himself in a narrow passageway, the walls on either side lined with pipes and ducting. Lights on the floor revealed a passageway gently curving in each direction—it seemed to make a circuit round the main reactor building. There were the familiar warnings of radiation and reminders to wear a protective suit, with the number to call in case of emergency.

Jane slid down the ladder to join him. He couldn't see her face through the mask and visor, but her breathing was ragged and she stood hunched and exhausted. Jack could feel the heat of the gun in her hand.

"Okay?" he asked her.

"Not really," she said.

They raced down the passageway, bashing their shoulders against the thicker pipes. Jack found a grille in the wall that they might have been able to get through if they'd not had an army right behind them. They went on, and he had the awful thought that soon enough they'd be back where they'd started. Then he found the door.

It was a huge, heavy door with a tiny window in one side; it appeared to be a good hand-span thick. Levers and a wheel had to be released before it would open. A series of pictures beside the window explained the process, and Jack and Jane worked together to get it done—not easy in their gloves. The door sighed as if pressurised, opening into another passageway—this one in total darkness.

They hesitated before plunging into the gloom, but somewhere off—behind or ahead of them, it came to the same thing—they heard clanging footsteps on the ladder. Jane went first as she had the gun, and Jack used his shoulder to heave the door shut behind them. Hefty locks *clunked* into place as it sealed. The tiny window created a feeble spotlight that reached less than a metre into the room, illuminating a small patch of floor.

Something bashed into Jack's arm. He recoiled—but it was Jane, reaching out to grab him by the wrist. Gingerly, they made their way forward through the total darkness. The floor was smooth concrete under their feet.

They crept onwards for what seemed an age. Then Jack could see something—a patch of brightness ahead. It was another spotlight created by a window in a door, though the light beyond seemed far brighter than that in the passageway they'd just come from. Still clutching Jack's wrist, Jane knelt to peer through the small, square window. Jack glanced back the way they'd come but couldn't see anything in the dark. Surely the armed personnel couldn't be that far behind them.

Then Jane was on her feet again. Without enough light to read the instructions, they fumbled over the levers and wheel, trying to remember the process. The last lever wouldn't shift, no matter how much they forced it—and then there was a noise behind them, the door opening and admitting booted feet.

"Fuck," he heard Jane say.

"Try again," he said. "From the start."

They raced through the levers and the wheel—and this time the tumblers turned and with another sigh the door heaved open towards them, letting in dazzling light. A shout went up from some way behind them and they heard running footsteps, but by then they were already hauling on the door to close it again.

Jack and Jane found themselves looking up at huge, rumbling machines. It was hot, too, Jack's skin already clammy with sweat. They hurried along the side of one huge machine, searching for a door.

"What do you think?" he asked Jane.

"Gas circulator," she said, pointing up to a gantry overhead supporting a vast mechanism, stretching across the room. "Leads to the reactor. After you."

He led the way, scrambling up the ladder to the gantry.

Behind them, Jack could hear the door shushing open and armed personnel spilling out into the room. Jane still had hold of her assault rifle, but he couldn't imagine her using it inside the reactor building itself. Perhaps she wouldn't need to—just the threat of her firing it would mean everyone else would have to back off.

They reached the gantry, ducked round the side of the huge gas circulator apparatus to keep out of sight. The gantry didn't offer them any escape route: it stopped abruptly, looking out over a huge open space from which they could see the enormous, cylindrical structure of the reactor itself. Jack let out a gasp of surprise. Around the reactor, at myriad control desks and stations, there were twenty or thirty people working, all in yellow radiation suits. Jack almost wanted to laugh. What could they possibly do against an organisation like this?

"They've got it under control," said Jane in astonishment, leaning back to stare up to the top of the reactor core. Beyond it, many levels above them, a long window looked in on a control room, computer banks staffed by men and women wearing lab coats instead of protective suits. "Look at them," said Jane. "They're running the place! Like there was never a problem."

"Who are they?" said Jack. "How long have they been here?"

"And how did they get past Laura?"

"It doesn't make sense," agreed Jack. Then he fell silent. Below them on the main floor, the squad were searching for them. One—it seemed to be the leader—hurried over to a supervisor. There was a hushed conversation, the supervisor leaning in to listen. Then he stood back, yielding authority to the people with the guns. In pairs, the squad spread throughout the room, interrogating the workers. The leader and supervisor watched the floor for anyone who tried to run.

Jane quickly placed her gun in a gap between two of the machines beside them. She hovered by one of the machines, making a show of checking the reading given on a screen. Jack examined the display on the next machine, some distance apart from her.

"They'll look up eventually," whispered Jane.

"I'll go first," he said. "Back down the ladder. Then round the reactor to the stairs. I'll wait for you there, then we go up together. To the control room."

"Without the gun?" said Jane.

"With it, we won't get across the floor. Without it, we at least stand a chance."

"If you say so." He assumed, somewhere underneath her visor and mask, she was rolling her eyes.

Jack made his way back to the ladder, stopping to check another of the readings as he went, taking his time and showing anyone who might happen to glance up towards the gantry that he was in no rush. His feet clanged horribly loud on each rung as he made his way back down to the main floor but no one came to investigate. Not too hurried, not too casual, he walked over to the main working space around the reactor core, just one of the many anonymous people in protective suits getting on with their jobs.

So far, he thought, so good. The vast reactor core thrummed with deafening power. The whole floor trembled with energy. Jack could almost feel the radiation pressing close against his suit.

The leader of the squad Jack had seen earlier still stood with the supervisor. Closer, Jack could see the supervisor had blue stripes on his or her protective suit; otherwise, the only difference between Jack and the other people around him was that some of them carried assault rifles.

He didn't make directly for the doors at the far end of the huge room, but headed to a computer bank as if to check the readings and confer with the two operators there. The men or women working the controls reacted in surprise—at least as far as he could tell. One backed away from him, and in their visor Jack saw reflections of a couple of the armed staff suddenly taking an interest. He couldn't walk away without drawing more attention, so he walked on until he was stood with the two nervous operators.

Jack couldn't think of anything to say or do that might not give him away. His silence only seemed to make them more nervous.

"It's Alexa," said one, her accent Germanic just like everyone else. As she spoke, she tapped her chest then indicated her colleague. "That's Boas. I can vouch for him. Hasn't been out of my sight."

Jack nodded curtly and kept moving. No one intercepted him as he crossed the floor. He stopped at another bank of controls. On one display screen, a needle hovered in the safe zone of whatever it was reading. Jack kept his body posed as if inspecting the data, but behind the visor of his protective suit he turned his head to look back the way he'd come. A number of blank-faced visors stared back at him.

Jack caught his breath, remaining rigidly where he stood, trying to work out his next move. He couldn't tell if any of them were actually watching him, or just happened to be facing that way. The doors were near enough that he could make a run for it and they might not catch up with him. But that would cause problems for Jane. He couldn't see her, either—she should have been following him across the floor. But then he couldn't be sure which one of the identical suits was her anyway.

There didn't seem to be much option but to carry on, so he backed away from the readings and then, as if an afterthought, made his way to the doors. He pressed again the door with his hand—and it didn't budge. He felt rising panic, then spotted the green button to one side and stabbed it with his gloved finger. The door yielded and he went through.

He stood at the bottom of a stairwell. Signs warned him that he was still in a high exposure zone and not to remove his suit. He didn't want to linger at the bottom of the stairs, as that might look suspicious if anyone saw him. Jack made his way up the stairs, waiting at the first turn, where he could keep an eye on the door. If anyone appeared—at the door, or from further upstairs—he would be mid-stride, heading somewhere with purpose.

Jane didn't come. Through the wall, he could feel the thrum of the reactor, but apart from that all was agonising silence. His heart hammered and the mask over his face made it difficult to breathe. Sweat pooled around his toes. Where the fuck was Jane? Something must have gone wrong.

Then there was a click from the door below him. A suited

figure entered the stairwell—a suited figure holding a pistol. Jack froze—as yet unseen. The figure with the gun closed the door carefully, then looked all round. He felt a sudden relief, recognising Jane's body language.

"Hey," he called to her, and she almost shot him. Jack held out his hands reassuringly and made his way down the steps to join her. She didn't say anything but held the gun at him. He realised he'd made a terrible mistake and raised his hands, surrendering.

"Gotcha," she said.

"Funny," he told her. They headed back up the stairs. It was slow going in their heavy suits. At each level, a door led off to some department or area—the signs explaining that the viewing balcony and main station control room were still some way above them. Jack, short of breath as he climbed, still had questions. "Where'd you get the gun?"

"Easy," said Jane. "The ones with the rifles also have these in holsters. I figured the holster is on top of their protective suits, as well as whatever they're wearing underneath. So if I slipped it from the holster, they wouldn't feel a thing."

"Risky," said Jack.

"No one spared me a glance. Not like Mr Nonchalant Stroll Around The Room."

"I was trying not to be noticed."

"So we all saw." She stopped. "Shit."

Jack looked back the way they'd come, but couldn't see or hear anything. Jane was staring at something on the wall, reflected dead in the centre of her visor; a camera. Jack hadn't seen a working camera since he was a child. He'd certainly never seen one twitch.

The movement made him jump. "Fuck," he said. The camera turned to regard him. A small red light winked on and off.

Jane grabbed his arm and they raced up the stairs. They passed another level and another door, and Jack wished the signs leading still further upwards gave some indication of how far they had to go. Then, below them, they heard charging footsteps as armed personnel poured into the stairwell.

"Stop!" shouted a man from at least two levels below them—still horribly near. "Stop or we fire!"

"They can't risk it," Jack told Jane. "We're too close to the reactor."

They hurried on, bounding up two stairs at a time, though Jack's thighs were already burning and his stump jarred with each impact. Suddenly, gunfire echoed in the enclosed space of the stairwell. Something ricocheted off the bannister just by Jack's side. He and Jane kept running as more bullets clattered around them.

"Fuck!" said Jane, falling forward to smack hard into the stairs. Her pistol rebounded off the concrete and out of her hand, but Jack caught it before it arced away down the stairwell. He quickly handed it back to Jane, then grabbed her under the armpits to help haul her to her feet. She cursed him under her breath and her whole body was shaking. When she tried to put weight on her left leg, it buckled and she fell backwards, threatening to send them both tumbling down the stairs. Jack held onto the bannister tight until she could right herself.

"Fuck," she said again, looking down. Blood seeped from a neat, round hole in her calf.

"It's not so bad," said Jack. "Come on."

She clutched her arm round his shoulder and they struggled up the next flight of stairs—each step agonising to Jane, and agonisingly slow.

"Go on without me," she told him.

"Not a chance."

But she shoved him onwards up the stairs. "I mean it. I'm dead anyway. Hole in my suit; I must be taking a full dose."

He wanted to argue, but she sat on the stair, resolutely turning away from him to aim the gun towards the soldiers fast catching them up. Jack, furious with her, hurried up the stairs. This hadn't been the plan!

The gun shots continued. A man screamed and there was a pause before the shooting resumed. Jack dragged himself up the next flight of stairs and reached the next landing.

More armed guards stood waiting there, assault rifles trained at his head. Behind them, through thick glass, he saw the main control room—a row of ancient-looking computer banks, staffed by intelligent young people in lab coats, all staring back at him in alarm. At one desk, a tall, thin woman in a black suit jacket stood poised by a silver bulb on a stick. When Jack caught her eye, she smiled thinly at him—and then turned to someone else, another, shorter woman, sat in a chair to one side.

It was Laura.

The thin woman turned back to face Jack and silently pressed a button by the silver bulb on a stick.

"Your Majesty," a Germanic voice said from a box in the wall of the stairwell. "You seem to have killed us all."

CHAPTER THIRTEEN

THEY STRIPPED JACK naked, sheared off his body hair and forced foul gunk down his throat that made him spasm and vomit and shit. The mess was cleared with jets of icy water, the pressure so high it propelled Jack, all knees and elbows, across the hard, tiled floor and wedged him against the wall. He might have blacked out in the numbing onslaught, and then they were on him again, clipping his toe and finger nails, swabbing the insides of his ears and nose and arsehole, before turning the hoses back on.

Eventually, a fey man with a Geiger counter decreed that Jack has passed whatever line constituted danger, or that they could do no more. Jack was coarsely towelled dry, then manhandled into loose cotton pyjamas a few sizes too big. His prosthetic leg wasn't returned to him. His head pounded, he was covered in bruises where they'd held him down and his insides felt scraped out. But the fey man checked him over and, not hiding his surprise, concluded that Jack would live.

"Jane," he asked them. "What about Jane?" The fey man wouldn't say. Jack felt the loss deep in the pit of his stomach.

He would have sobbed were he not utterly exhausted.

They put him in a square room with an ancient bald man who had to be carried in. No, he realised with a start—that was his reflection. Apart from the mirror, there was no furniture, no window, just a strip light on the wall that made everything over-bright and unreal. They lay Jack on the thin carpet on the concrete floor, and before they'd left the room he'd succumbed to sleep. There were fitful, indistinct nightmares, his body dissolving as dead friends looked judgementally on.

When he woke, his first thought was of Jane. But no, sat cross-legged by the wall was the thin woman he'd seen in the control room. Her piercing black eyes watched him with amusement as Jack struggled to sit up.

"Jane," he said.

The woman's mouth twitched in what might have been sympathy.

"We're doing what we can," she said.

"I want to see her."

"We will have to see."

He got himself into a sitting position, propped against the hard, cold wall. "You're Germans."

She smiled. "You think we're an invasion."

"I don't know what to think. You seem to know what you're doing."

"I am Doctor Sara Brandt, formerly of the Max Planck Institute for Kernphysik—for nuclear physics—in Heidelberg. Since The Cull, I have been part of the cabal of scientists under Chairman Weber."

The name didn't mean anything to Jack—and Brandt was clearly disappointed. "We have a simple ambition," she went on. "To lead the world through enlightenment and science. Look at this institution. We rendered it safe, we had useful electrical power and restored some semblance of the civilised world. Speaking of which..." She clapped her hands, the sound sharp and echoing in the unfurnished room.

After a moment, the door opened and a woman walked in with a tray. Jack instinctively edged away from the sight of Laura. She looked different in a lab coat, her hair tied back in a neat plait. But there was the same steely look in her eyes.

"Join us, please," said Brandt, the tone making it an order. Laura didn't seem keen, but did as she was instructed, placing the tray down and sitting beside Brandt by the far wall. The tray contained two china cups and saucers, a plate of homemade, elegant little biscuits and a cafetière. Jack's stomach turned over and he thought he might be sick, and he had a sudden, vivid impression of his mother smiling.

"You see?" said Brandt, leaning forward to push down the plunger on the cafetière. "Civilisation. When was the last time you experienced real coffee?"

Jack didn't answer. He watched Brandt pour the coffee and took the cup she offered him. His hand trembled, and dark, strong-smelling coffee slopped over the side of the cup, scolding him. He put the cup down quickly, and his smarting hand to his mouth. The coffee tasted extraordinary. Brandt was clearly delighted by the wonder on his face.

"Civilisation," said Jack bitterly. "That's what you call what's happening outside? Her stringing up children who step out of line?"

Laura snorted—and spoke in her native German accent. "We had a system of control. Deaths were kept to a minimum."

"You lied to all those people!" Jack snapped back at her. "You made them complicit in what you were doing, butchering innocent people. My friends!"

Laura only nodded. "The operation demanded it."

Brandt was more conciliatory. "We had to keep people out of the reactor buildings—for their own good."

"You could have told them the truth," said Jack.

Brandt sighed. "The irony is, for all we wish to advance enlightened thinking, people remain irrational and afraid. They would have interfered with our work, and we could then not have made them safe."

He didn't like it one bit, but Jack needed to know one thing. "Is it safe?"

Brandt took a deep breath. "It was, at least in the short term. We engaged a number of protocols and brought the systems under control. But the A reactor had ceased to generate power before The Cull, and is long overdue for defuelling. We do not have the resources to effectively decommission the site.

Our colleagues have had to attend reactors in other parts of the world—those in Russia have taken priority. We hoped to maintain safety levels here until more of our team could be deployed. But now that won't be possible, thanks to you."

"Me?" said Jack. "What have I done?"

Laura snarled at him. "The community outside! Oh, they're cowering now, waiting for you to do what you promised and put everything right. But how long do you think they will last before they need to see what's happening? Come the morning, they'll be here."

"And they've got guns," said Jack.

"So have we," said Brandt sadly. "But a gun battle around the facilities of a nuclear reactor would not be a good outcome for anyone."

"You could evacuate now, before they arrive."

"How far would we get? And what would happen to the reactor without us to maintain it? If the people streaming in here decide to vent their frustration and fear, who knows what damage they could do? And if they manage to contain themselves, it remains a ticking clock. It is quite the dilemma, but I must say I prefer they destroy it quickly. Better to die in a sudden explosion than wait for slow and lingering death. So we will stay, and if need be we will be the ones to ignite the final end."

Jack could hardly take it in. "I'm sorry," he said.

"You've killed us all," spat Laura. "You've killed the children out there! Your country!"

She was right. Jack felt sick inside, thinking of what he said to Singhar before he took his life. He was only thankful that Jane couldn't hear any of this, that she might never know how massively he'd screwed it up. He knew what she would say: that it was all his fault for trying to game the situation, to use it to his advantage, as a ploy to help him take power.

And a thought struck him. He started to smile. Laura glared at him with hatred, but Brandt watched him curiously.

"It's probably a stupid question," he told her.

"It is a saying among scientists," she said. "There are no stupid questions."

"Well," he said. "The thing is, why does there need to be a fight at all?"

"Because," said Laura wearily, "the people outside will only stay outside for so long."

"Exactly," said Jack. "They want to know what's happening. They want to know if there's a possibility that things can be okay. So, why don't we go tell them?"

Laura opened her mouth to protest—but the words stuck in her throat. He could see it in her eyes, the sparking of hope.

"We are scientists, foreigners," said Brandt. "We tricked them. They will not listen to us."

Jack didn't answer, because he could see she was getting it, too. Brandt started to smile.

"But," she said, "they will listen to their King."

THE SKY AND sea were blood red as Jack stepped out that freezing morning in an ill-fitting suit. He didn't think anyone would recognise the frail, bald figure but, of course, the people waiting out in the cold only expected him or Jane. They were clearly shocked by his appearance, but also delighted to see him alive. He walked with confidence—still getting accustomed to his new prosthetic—and smiled a reassuring smile. They couldn't help but applaud.

Jack made his way to the broken-down fence. The crowd gathered round him: men, women and children all gawping at him in desperate wonder. A hush descended over them, a perfectly still moment but for the lapping of the sea to Jack's right and the soft rumble of the power station behind him. He let them wait, building the moment, the legend that would follow this.

"My friends," he called out to them. "I have a few things to tell you and that you need to hear. But the first and most important thing is that I did as I promised you: the reactor is safe."

The words hung in the air. Then someone cheered, and others joined him, and soon there were shouts and more applause. People held on to each other and wept. One old woman shook with hysterical laughter. Jack remained poised and calm, and soon enough they hushed again to listen to what else he had to say.

"It is safe for the time being, but we—you and I—have a great deal of work to do to make it safe for ever more. I need your help. I need volunteers. It will not be easy. There might be some danger. But you'll have protective suits and training. We'll work side by and side. And together we'll put things right. We'll make the reactors here safe. Then we'll move on and make the other reactors safe, up and down the land. We— you and I, together. We will save the country."

"You've sold us out," said Jane, weakly. "The whole fucking lot of us."

She sat propped up by pillows in her bed, bald and emaciated, her leg encased in plaster. A trace-work of old scars shone silver on her scalp, and her skin was dry as paper. Jack had to disguise his horror at the sight of her, but Jane's eyes burnt just as fiercely as ever, piercing into him as he sat at the end of the bed.

"We don't have any choice," he told her. "If we don't work with these people, the reactor goes *foom*. This way, we exploit their skill and experience and we make things right. All the reactors in Britain, not just the ones here."

"And a grateful nation is then only too happy to see you on the throne."

Jack grinned. "If they insist, it would be rude not to take it."

It was the wrong way to play it. Jane tried to turn away from him in disgust, and that caused her wrenching pain. She swore, then tried to pretend that it hadn't hurt. Tears glistened in her eyes.

"And the government in Oxford?" she said. "How do think they'll react?"

That surprised him. "They'll welcome the help. It's a national crisis."

"Which just so happened to take place on their watch. They failed us, didn't they? Just as you come swanning in to the rescue... how very convenient."

"It isn't like that! I'm not going to use this."

Jane held his gaze for a long time. "Yes, you are," she told him. "And so are these friends of yours, the Germans."

"They're scientists, they're not political."

"The ones who say they're not political, they're the ones with the biggest agendas. Ask yourself: why all the secrecy? Why not tell people in the first place that they were trying to help?"

"I... I guess it was easier."

"You saw what they did to Nathaniel and Alice—and Nina. God, Barnden, too. And who knows what happened to Kit. Has he been found?"

Jack felt utterly ashamed—he hadn't thought to ask. "Not yet," he told her.

"And all the others hanging from that roof," she went on, missing his look of guilt. "They had a whole town waiting to trick people, sending them to that kind of death. A whole system— that's power and politics right there! Jack! Can't you—?"

But she started to cough, her whole body convulsing. Jack saw bright droplets of blood on her chin and hand, where she tried to cover her mouth. He reached over her for the button that would call the nurse.

"I'm not dying," Jane told him, battering him feebly away. "Just been sick so much, I tore the lining of my stomach. You don't get rid of me so easily. Which is worse luck for you."

He stared at her dumbfounded. "What? Why? We're friends."

She choked back a laugh. "Then take some friendly advice. These people are vicious, ruthless fucks. They'll knife you, first chance they get. And in the meantime, while you're being their boy, dancing on their string, they'll be knifing everyone else."

Rain began to patter against the windows. The sky was a thunderous grey. "What do I do?" said Jack.

Jane regarded him for a moment, then sank back into the embrace of the pillows. "Not my problem," she told him. "Soon as they let me out of bed, I'm going home to my son."

"Jane," said Jack. "Please."

"I won't be a part of this," she told him. "I've had enough. So you do what you like. It's your choice." She closed her eyes, shutting him out. "And you'll have to deal with the fall out."

THE END

ABOUT THE AUTHOR

Simon Guerrier has written countless *Doctor Who* books, comics, audio plays and documentaries—including *The Scientific Secrets of Doctor Who* (BBC Books, 2015). He also produces documentaries for Radio 3, has written award-winning short films, and created the original science-fiction series *Graceless*, broadcast on Radio 4 Extra.

CHILDREN OF
THE CULL

CAVAN SCOTT

Original cover art by Sam Gretton

CHAPTER ONE
CURE

I USED TO dream. Every night, without fail.

The specifics would fade almost as soon as I opened my eyes, the details lost to daylight; but the colours would remain, a lingering afterimage of my nocturnal adventures.

I liked that. Part of my life that I knew was there, but just out of reach. A comforting echo. A mystery.

Not anymore. I assume I still dream. Everyone dreams, don't they, even if they can't remember it? I haven't remembered; not once, since the Cull. No more colours. No more echoes.

Just an empty void from the moment I slipped away to the alarm rudely jolting me back to consciousness the next morning.

The sleep of the dead, that's what Mum used to call it.

THE DAY STARTED like any other. I threw my hand out, trying to find the snooze button on the alarm, anything to cut off that electronic squawk. I lay in the darkness and sighed. Why prolong the inevitable? She would be waiting for me, out in the corridor, like every morning.

Pulling back the sheets, I swung my legs over the side of the bed, reaching for the light switch. The room came into view with the buzz of ancient bulbs, the nylon carpet cold beneath my feet. I sat there for a minute, staring at the pile of clothes I dropped on the floor the night before. She'd notice the creases, passing judgement if not comment.

And what do you care? came a voice from the past, my mother standing in our old kitchenette, hands on impressive hips.

She hated whingers.

If you have time to complain about something you have time to do something about it, my girl.

Yeah, yeah, Mum, very good. Now get out of my head. There are enough voices in there as it is.

Stretching, I pushed myself up from the bed and padded over to the shower. The alarm kicked back in as soon as I'd closed the door behind me.

"GOOD MORNING, DR TOMAS."

I jumped as soon as I opened the door. Stupid. As if I didn't know she'd be there—but standing right in front of the door? What a freak.

I leant on the doorframe, willing my heart to stop hammering so hard in my chest. "Olive, what the hell are you trying to do to me?"

My assistant removed her ever-present clipboard from beneath her arm to check something off the top sheet.

"Sorry doctor, but we have a busy day ahead. You told me to—"

"I know what I told you." Sighing, I shut the door behind me, slipping the ID-card from around my neck into the pocket of my medical scrubs so it didn't swing back and forth as I walked.

You're not going out in that! my mother twittered in the back of my mind. *Why can you dress like a lady for once in your life?*

Why can't you stay dead?

Would mother approve of Olive, in her smart navy dress?

Of course she bloody would. She'd probably wish that Olive was her daughter, rather than me.

I watched her sashaying ahead, hearing Mum's verdict of Olive's little black dress. *Now* that's *an outfit, sweetheart—tasteful. Cut just below the knee, with a high neckline; close-fitting but not slutty, just tight enough to accentuate the curves God gave you. Why can't you dress like that anymore?*

Yeah, Mum would have loved Olive.

I started down the corridor after her, trying not to be annoyed by the sound of my assistant's heels clicking along the floor. Who wore heels these days?

"So, what have we got on today?"

"There's the morning briefing, naturally..."

"Naturally."

"Followed by your ten o'clock with Dr Atkins."

A little bit of me died inside.

"Do we have to do that today?"

"You put him off yesterday. And the day before."

"Then he won't mind if we bump him to tomorrow. If I don't check the resistance reports today, they'll never get done. Oh, and I want to schedule a series of allergy tests for Samuel. If we're going to take him out—"

The wail of a klaxon cut me off, and my heart sank. Not again. Not now.

Breaking into a run, I snatched the walkie-talkie from my belt, opening a channel.

"Control, this is Tomas. Come in."

There was a burst of static and an American accent replied. Des Moore, chief of security and almost as much as a pain in the arse as Olive. "*It's another attack, ma'am.*"

"I gathered. How many this time?"

"*The cameras have picked up three. No, wait—there's four. They jumped the fence to N-4.*"

"At four? I thought you'd secured that?"

"*So did I! A team is on its way to intercept. They won't get far.*"

"That's what you said on Monday."

"*And we stopped them on Monday. Ma'am, I need to oversee this.*"

"Yes, yes. Oversee. And then make sure it doesn't happen again."

I killed the channel. Arguing with Moore wouldn't do any good. The bastard would just dig his heels in. He knew his job, no matter what I thought of him. My first priority had to be the children. Always the children.

I flicked the toggle on the side of the handset, switching channels.

"Allison?"

"Jasmine? Can you believe this?"

The neurologist sounded as frustrated as me, and with good reason.

"Don't even go there. How are they?"

"How do you think? We don't need another day like Monday." Her Dundee accent was somehow more pronounced over the radio.

"Tell that to Chief Moore. Don't worry. They're targeting Neighbourhood Four. Obviously after supplies. It should be over soon enough."

"Until next time. This is the third attack in a week. Sooner or later they're going to get lucky."

I turned the corridor, decided to take the stairs rather than the lifts. The last thing I wanted was a power outage trapping me in a metal box with Olive.

"I'm on my way," I replied, starting down the stairwell. "Monitor the subjects' reactions to the alarm. We might as well make use of all this."

"Every cloud has a silver lining. Will do. See you in a minute."

The handset fell quiet and I clipped it back onto my belt, reaching the ground floor. As Olive clattered after me, I yanked open the door to the main corridor and made for the exit.

"Dr Tomas," Olive called after me. "If the alarm sounds..."

I sighed, stopping in my tracks. I hated when Olive was right.

"All personnel should use the tunnels, yes, yes."

I turned on my heels and stalked back to the stairs, Olive standing beside the door, clipboard clutched to her chest. For once, would it hurt her to open a door for me? Isn't that what assistants were for?

Still huffing, I stomped down to the basement, pressing my ID card against the card reader. The scanner beeped twice, its lights flashing red.

Bloody hell.

I looked up at the camera above the door, waiting for one of Moore's numpties to check their screens at the hub. What's the betting it was Lam, playing games in the middle of an emergency?

"This is ridiculous," I moaned.

"The base *is* in shutdown."

The lights flashed green, and with an angry buzz the lock clicked open.

"One more word from you," I said, yanking open the door to step out into the tunnel, "and I'll shut you down, permanently."

Olive smiled as if I was joking. I didn't hold the door open for her.

"I get why they lock the doors," I continued, more to myself than to the girl tottering after me. "But why include me in the deadlock? What's the point of being the project leader if you can't even open a door by yourself?"

For once, Olive read my mood and kept her smart-alec remarks to herself. I knew she was still thinking them, though, which managed to annoy me even more.

Out feet echoed down the low-ceilinged corridor as we walked in the direction of Neighbourhood Two, a route I knew on auto-pilot, even down here.

"Dr Tomas?" Olive asked quietly.

I couldn't repress the sigh. "Yes?"

"Have you taken your medication this morning?"

Damn.

Every day the same question, and always the same answer. You'd think I would remember.

I fished around in my scrubs pocket and brought out the small brown bottle. A shake revealed that there were only a few capsules left, maybe three or four. I'd have to get Chemistry to make up another batch.

I unscrewed the lid and shook one of the small blue-and-red capsules onto my palm. Coming to a junction in the tunnel, I popped the pill into my mouth and swallowed it dry.

I shoved the bottle back into my pocket as we took the corridor to the right. "Happy now?"

"Just doing my job, doctor," came the smug reply.

It was going to be a long day.

CHAPTER TWO
KILL

IDIOTS.

They didn't have a clue.

Their first mistake was going over the fence. They'd thrown blankets over the barbed wire so they could scramble across without slicing their bellies open, but why waste the energy? Better to cut the wire at the bottom, easing it aside. That's what I would have done. You didn't need a massive gap, just enough to crawl through. It wasn't as if any of them seemed to have much meat on their bones.

Either way, the cameras would have picked them up long before they reached the top. I watched them drop to the ground on the other side, making enough noise to wake several legions of the dead, and wondered how long it would be before the alarm was raised.

The howl of a klaxon provided the answer precisely twenty seconds later. They hadn't even made it to the first wing.

I could have scripted what happened next. The idiots—I

counted four of them—dived for cover, making for the corner of the building, where they stopped, waiting for the guards to arrive.

Mistake number two.

What did they expect would happen? Even if they survived a firefight, mowing down whatever security forces the base was about to throw at them, what then? Did they really think that would be it? The base would surrender, brought to their knees by the superior force of four scrawny twats?

I almost didn't want to look, but couldn't help myself. It was like picking a scab. Entertainment was hard to come by, so you took what you could, even if that meant lying on the roof of an abandoned supermarket, peering at a botched infiltration through a cracked scope.

The idiots stayed where they were, guns raised, having literally backed themselves into a corner as the guards arrived. Six guards, clad in full body armour—or as full as you could get, these days—spilling out of the adjoining building. They raced across to a barricade of skips and storage crates.

There was a shout, one of the guards yelling for the idiots to give themselves up. No reply. That, at least, was promising. The last thing anyone needed in this scenario was bullshit bravado. In the real world, no one came back with a witty retort when facing the wrong end of a gun.

You'll never take us alive, copper.

No shit.

Then, something happened that actually surprised me. One of the idiots drew back his hand and threw a small canister. It was belching yellow smoke before it bounced in front of the barricade.

One of the guards let off a shot, but the idiots were already on the offensive, throwing themselves around the corner to pepper the rag-tag blockade with bullets.

Another shout followed—no, a cry this time; strangled, sharp—and a body was thrown back in the yellow cloud.

First blood.

The shooting continued, but the guards had no chance of hitting the targets. They couldn't see in front of their face, and certainly couldn't risk breaking cover.

Now came the bravado. The idiots surged forwards, guns raised as if they were in an old gangster movie, firing indiscriminately.

That's it, boys. Show me what you've got. MP7s, maybe a 7A; better than I expected. The skip doesn't stand a chance.

Maybe I owed the idiots an apology. Maybe they weren't as incompetent as I'd first thought.

Then again...

Without warning, a bloom of red mist obscured the side of idiot number one's head, and he went down, hard. Idiot two turned in the direction of the shot, a bullet to the shoulder spinning him into a graceless pirouette, the second tap to the back of his head sealing the deal. Idiots three and four at least had the sense to double back, realising too late that they'd rushed into an ambush.

They didn't get far.

A second team of guards had been waiting for the idiots to break ranks. The raiders had been so intent on the barricade that they hadn't seen them till they were shooting. Now, with the smoke clearing, the first set of guards dropped idiots three and four in a heartbeat.

The impromptu battlefield fell quiet, save for the alarm that warned any other would-be attackers to keep their distance.

When it was obvious that none of the idiots were getting up any time soon, four of the guards darted out from behind the blockade, compact rifles up and ready. L22 carbines. Effective enough, but not great over distance. Worth noting.

Splitting into pairs, the first checked the bodies on the ground, while the second made sure no one else was lying in wait. Of course there wasn't. The attack had been bungled from the start; the guard who'd been shot was unlucky in the extreme.

I lowered my scope as the siren finally died, a strange hush settling on the surrounding fields. I looked around, taking in more of the landscape. It had been years since I'd been here, long before the Cull. The complex had just opened, the pride of the MoD, the biggest base of its type on home soil. There had been much back-slapping and congratulations among the top brass, but I had found its location as funny then as I do now.

A classified installation built slap bang next to an out-of-town retail park. Well, I guess civil servants needed somewhere to mooch around during lunchtime, even if it was just Asda. Oh, and Matalan. All those cheap polyester shirts and garish ties had to come from somewhere.

Stow it, soldier. No need for lip.

Sir, no sir, etc.

I suppose the point was that the original occupants of MoD Abbey Wood weren't soldiers, not the majority anyway. They were pencil-pushers, bean-counters. Put a gun in their hands and they'd have been just as effective as the idiots who'd just tried to storm the place.

The dead idiots.

A smile tugged at my lips, pulling at scar tissue that I barely noticed any more.

These idiots are no more. They have ceased to be. They've expired and gone to meet their maker. These are late idiots.

It's funny what you miss, even after all this time. I always liked a bit of Python. Can't remember who introduced me to Graham, John, Terry and the rest; everything before the Cull sort of blurs into one. Could have been my Dad, or old Tony next door, maybe even someone from a school.

It certainly wasn't Jasmine. She couldn't stand John Cleese. Made her skin crawl, she said. Something creepy about him.

Stowing the scope in my pack, I eased back from the edge of the roof, scuttling on my hands and knees like a spider.

Well, maybe not scuttling. Not that fast anymore. Not if I don't have to.

I made my way back to the air-conditioning unit before standing, although I stayed in a crouch. Not that anyone would be looking this way. They had problems of their own to deal with.

As I crept over to the ladder, I wondered what they did with the bodies. Fresh meat in the staff canteen tonight?

It should have been easier going down the ladder than it was coming up. My body shouldn't ache this much. I told myself that it was because I'd stayed in one position for too long. Yeah, that had to be it. There was a nip in the air, winter's last hurrah. I looked up. Clouds were gathering, dark and full, first drops of rain already falling, icy cold. I needed to get to cover.

I jumped down the final three rungs, the impact jolting my body.

And there came the rain, heavier now. It always rained whenever I came to Bristol. Bloody city. Anyone would think it wasn't pleased to see me.

I pulled up the collar of my jacket and set off at a run along the back of the old superstore. There was no danger of being spotted now. An unkempt ridge of bushes separated me from the base, blocking my view of the guards dragging the corpses away.

I knew what I should do. Stick to the plan; see it through. But the ache in my back said otherwise. Would it hurt if I headed back to the empty house I'd made a temporary home last night? It was dry, and still in possession of most of its windows. I could make a brew, get some warmth back in my bones. Come back tomorrow. It wasn't as if the idiots were going anywhere.

What's wrong with you, man? Orders is orders.

Sir, yes sir, et—

Something hit me in the head as soon as I turned the corner. I fell back, stunned, barely felt the back of my head connecting with the floor.

I groaned, rolling onto my side, my hand going to my throbbing forehead, brushing already bruised skin.

Someone grabbed my shoulder, hauling me up as if I were a sack of spuds. I allowed myself to be pulled to my feet, a voice yelling at me to get up.

I stumbled, my assailant supporting my dead weight from the scruff of my jacket.

What was it with these idiots and their mistakes?

I threw my body into him, taking him by surprise. My head met his nose, and I felt a satisfying pop.

Now we were falling, gravity taking hold. He hit the deck, my full weight upon him, my shoulder planted firmly into his stomach for added effect. And then I was back on my feet, booting him in the side.

That sudden movement was my undoing. The world spun and I pitched forward, throwing out a hand to break my fall. The barrel of a rifle smacked me in the side of my head. I crashed to the ground and moaned, and this time it wasn't a ploy. I had no surprise moves left. I was having enough trouble not throwing up my guts.

A boot thudded into my shoulder, kicking me onto my back. My moan turned into a racking cough, but I didn't try to get up. There was no point. The man who'd attacked me stood silhouetted against the clouds, rain coming down in sheets over us.

I spat rainwater and blood out of my mouth as I realised it wasn't a man at all. She was big, well over six foot, and as solid as she was long, her tightly-cropped hair plastered against her scalp. There was no way of telling if it was light or dark in the rain. Only one thing was obvious—her nose hadn't been that squashed a moment ago.

Lying there, the rain in my eyes, I didn't know what was more intimidating—her furious glower, or the rifle she aimed right at my face.

I smiled, hoping that the rain would at least wash some of the blood from my teeth.

"Hello, gorgeous!"

Yeah, I know, I know—no one bothers with one-liners in real life. So sue me.

Since when have I played by the rules?

Do you think this is funny?

Sir, fuck off, sir.

CHAPTER THREE
CURE

I COULD HAVE kissed Allison when the alarms finally stopped.

"Thank God for that."

The phone on the neurologist's desk rang almost immediately. She pushed it in my direction.

"That'll be for you?"

"Gee, thanks."

I picked up the receiver, glaring at Allison. She laughed, pointing two fingers at me and miming a shot. Putting me out of my misery. It shouldn't have been funny seeing what had just happened outside.

"This is Tomas."

"*Ma'am, I'm pleased to report that the crisis has passed,*" Moore responded brusquely on the other end of the line.

"For now. How long to the next one?"

"*I am doubling patrols, and the tech team are fitting new cameras on weak spots along the perimeter.*"

"Last week you told me that there *were* no weak spots."

"*Dr Tomas, my resources are limited. It's not like I can advertise for more staff.*"

I sighed, rubbing the bridge of my nose. "I know."

"*If you would allow me to make a recce of the surrounding area, we could discover where these low-lives are coming from, how many there are.*"

"No."

"*Ma'am, three attacks in a week...*"

"We've been attacked before."

"*But never in such quick succession. This has to be the work of a gang. The guns recovered today match those on Monday.*"

"Are you telling me we have an army at our gates?

"*We many never know, unless we go and look.*"

"I'm not going to repeat myself, chief. No one goes off base. There's no need. You've proved that you can handle anything they throw at us."

"*Three or four at a time, but if they attack en masse...*"

We were going around in circles. A change of subject was required. "Was anyone hurt?"

"*Eckstein, but not badly, thank God. He's in the infirmary.*"

"Could have been worse. And the raiders?"

"*No longer a threat. I'll have a full report with you in an hour.*"

"You do that," I said, putting down the phone.

"Do you get the feeling he's enjoying himself just a little too much?" Allison asked, leaning back in her chair.

Tension was working its way up my neck, a headache beginning to form. I looked out at the rain lashing against the window.

"Little boys playing soldiers."

"Was he complaining about resources again?"

"What do you think?"

"Have you thought about requesting"—she snorted at her own melodrama—"reinforcements?"

"And make Moore's role any bigger than it is?"

Another laugh. I sighed, marshalling my thoughts. The truth of the matter was that the Cabal would be over us in a flash if I so much as suggested that the project was in jeopardy. It was hard enough keeping them at arm's length at the best of times.

No, better to keep quiet and see where the next few weeks led. Moore was probably right. The attacks we'd suffered in the past had been opportunistic. A former MoD base was always going to be a hot target, especially in a relatively remote location. Places like this suggested weapons and supplies, even after Operation Motherland and the Americans had cleaned most of them out. And it was obvious that the base was occupied, in a sea of empty fields and derelict housing. No wonder interested parties got cocky from time to time, chancing their arms.

This felt different. Our defences were being tested, by someone who didn't care if their men came back dead or alive.

But we were safe, I was sure of that. Whatever Moore claimed, the Cabal had provided more than enough. Weapons, supplies, even a lorry-load of books and DVDs.

"All work and no play leads to exhaustion and poor results, Dr Tomas. Remember, you are running a scientific community, not a work camp."

Our benevolent masters.

Enough. I pushed the chair back and rose to my feet, Allison mirroring the action, surprised by my sudden movement.

"Are we leaving?"

"I want to check in on Ruth," I replied, turning to leave the small office, "make sure the attack hasn't unsettled her."

Olive stepped forward from where she had been hovering by the door, my constant shadow, as silent as a ghost until required. Some days I even forgot she was there.

"Dr Tomas, the morning briefing..."

I ignored her, opening the door and emerging into the windowless corridor.

THE CHILDREN'S DORMS were on the top floor of Neighbourhood Three, one storey up from the heads of department. We took the stairs, Allison regaling me with the argument she'd had with Bets last night. I made all the right noises and nodded in what I hoped were all the right places, barely taking in any of the details. I had no problem with relationships among staff members; it was inevitable, living in such proximity. But

I didn't need a blow-by-blow account of their domestic bliss or otherwise. There was a reason my personal quarters were in the east wing of Neighbourhood Two, while the rest of the staff had taken over the west wing. Allison said that all the empty corridors would give her the creeps, knowing that she was alone in a wing at night, but I didn't mind. I was only there to sleep. Why would I need anyone near?

It suddenly occurred to me that I had no idea where Olive was barracked. She had to be with the rest in the west wing, but I'd never asked. Better that way. I wasn't here to make friends.

What a shame Allison didn't seem to realise that. I just hoped she wasn't about to get into how she and Bets had made up.

"Have you seen Ruth this morning?" I asked as we approached the Dorm corridor, bringing Allison's attention back to our patient.

Allison nodded breezily. "I checked in as soon as the alarm sounded. She was fine. She's *always* fine, you know that."

"I don't know," I replied as we approached the door marked with Ruth's name. "There's been something about her recently."

"Like what?"

"If I knew that, I wouldn't be worried. Something in her manner."

Allison opened the door to the suite and stepped into the small antechamber that preceded Ruth's actual quarters. Like all of the children's dorms, the rooms had been converted from old offices, each with an observation area identical to the one we were standing in. Allison lowered her voice, even though Ruth wouldn't be able to hear a thing. The place was completely soundproof.

"Her test scores are consistent, her responses exceeding expectations. There's nothing wrong with her."

I stared through the one-way mirror that separated us from the 12-year old girl we were discussing. Allison was right—on paper, nothing had changed, but...

It was a hunch, nothing more.

Ruth sat in her stark quarters, cross-legged on the floor, staring up at a television screen set into the wall. A games controller twisted in her hands as she threw the racing car around the circuit on the screen, the soundtrack playing through her headset. Crowds lined the side of the racetrack, waving their pixelated arms above hoardings for long-forgotten soft drinks. It was a world Ruth had never known, one that even I struggled to remember, and yet what could be more normal than a girl sitting in her bedroom playing computer games?

"Let her know we're here," I instructed, and Allison went to the adjoining door, pressing a button on the intercom, and a doorbell chimed. Ruth barely looked away from her screen.

Allison laughed. "I doubt she can even hear us over those things."

She tried again, and this time the girl answered, calling over the intercom.

"*Yes.*"

"Ruth, it's Dr Tomas and Dr Harwood."

"*Come in.*"

I nodded at Allison, who entered, holding the door open for me to follow. As always, Ruth's room was immaculate, a place for everything and everything in its place. My mother would have been proud.

Ruth was wearing her usual light blue pyjamas, one of the few splashes of colour in the largely white space.

Allison closed the door behind us, shutting Olive in the observation area. I walked over to Ruth's small functional desk, pulling out the chair to sit down. The papers on the desk were perfectly ordered in neat piles, the pens lined up in order of colour and size.

"Good morning, Dr Tomas," Ruth offered, still engrossed in the game.

"Good morning, Ruth. How are you today?"

"I'm fine," she replied. "How are you?"

The conversation was hardly what you'd call spontaneous; we said the same thing, day after day, never deviating from the script.

"Very well, thank you. Are you enjoying your game?" I said, glancing at the screen. Ruth's car slewed round a tight corner.

"It's my favourite," came the reply.

You wouldn't know by looking at her. She was concentrating,

but there was no sign she was enjoying the activity. Her face was a passive mask, and she played in total silence at all times. There were seven other subjects, similar in age to Ruth, in similar rooms, and we had allowed them the headsets to communicate when they played their video games. The results hadn't been what you'd expect from children their age. No shouting or yelling, no grunts of frustration as they misjudged their cars' speed and crashed into the barriers. Just an indifferent, one-tone commentary of the race, politely praising each other on their gameplay.

"Can you pause it, please?" I asked, remembering the tantrum that would have followed whenever my mum had asked me to turn off the Commodore 64 when I was Ruth's age. *Just five minutes longer, please!*

Not Ruth. She complied without question, hitting a button and placing the controller down in front of her, the headset obediently removed. Without a flicker of emotion, she shifted on the floor to face me, every movement controlled and calculated.

"Thank you."

"You're welcome."

Even as she looked at me, I could hear what Olive had said about Ruth the previous day.

Such a shame, really. She could be quite pretty, if it wasn't for... well, you know...

For the fact she was a subject in ongoing medical research, restricted most of the time to these four walls. I had told Olive what I thought of her comments, that in this day and age, after everything that had happened, surely it didn't matter if someone was pretty or not. Why were we still using looks as a yardstick, what difference did it make?

Olive had pouted those full, painted lips of hers and returned to her clipboard.

It was true, Ruth was a striking child. Her features were symmetrical and smooth, her eyes a brilliant, almost breathtaking shade of blue. She was a little underweight for her age and height, her cheekbones pronounced without being gaunt, but held herself in perfect posture at all times, her back ramrod straight. Her pallor was, understandably, that of someone who spent too much time inside, although she regularly took part in Dr Heslin's PE sessions out on the hard courts behind Neighbourhood Two. I couldn't say she enjoyed them, as none of the children seemed to enjoy anything. They didn't complain or moan—quite the opposite—but attacked every task, from studies to pastimes, as jobs that needed to be completed as quickly and efficiently as possible.

"She's a machine," Olive had decreed on another self-opinionated occasion. "A nice enough kid, but... unsettling, you know?" When I'd ignored her, my assistant had simply seen it as carte blanche to continue. "It would help if she had some hair. Even eyebrows would be an improvement. You could at least give the poor child a scarf to wear."

I'd offered Ruth a headscarf the next day.

"There is no need, doctor," Ruth had replied flatly. "I am quite warm, thank you."

Olive had just rolled her eyes.

I leant forward, Ruth's chair squeaking beneath my weight. "Did you hear the alarm this morning, Ruth?"

The girl nodded. "Of course. Was there a problem on the perimeter?"

"Just a drill," I lied.

"There was shooting," Ruth replied, a statement of fact, nothing more.

I nodded. "There was."

"Part of the drill?"

"Yes."

I searched her pale face for a response. Could she tell that I was lying? Any indication that she was aware that she was being deceived?

"How did it make you feel?"

"Curious."

"You weren't scared?"

"No."

"Why not?"

"Because we are safe here."

"You and the other children?"

Ruth paused, and there it was again; the same twitch in her eye that I had noticed yesterday. Was it a reaction to the mention of her fellow subjects? I wanted to turn to Allison, to ask if she'd seen it, but forced myself to focus on the girl.

"Were any of them scared?" Ruth asked, her tone as even and considered as ever. "The other children, I mean."

"I don't know yet. I haven't asked them. I came to see you first."

She nodded, accepting this at face value and the moment was gone. What was she feeling? Pride that I'd favoured her? Frustration that I couldn't answer her question?

Something must have been going on behind those azure eyes.

"Doctor, may I return to my game?" Ruth asked.

"Yes," I conceded, "but not for long. Your breakfast will be arriving soon."

"Of course," Ruth replied, slipping the headset over her ears again. She picked up the controller and hit the start button, the car on the screen accelerating away.

I watched her play, Olive's words coming back unbidden: *a machine*.

I turned to Allison, who shrugged and mouthed a silent *See?* Business as usual.

I was about to say goodbye, when the door crashed open. It was Ed Dunning, one of the medical staff, his face almost as pale as Ruth's.

I jumped up. "Nurse Dunning?"

"Doctor, you need to come." Ed flashed a look at Ruth, who was lost to the game again. "Right now."

His expression told me not to ask any more questions until we were out of the room. I hurried after him, Allison shutting the door behind me, so we could speak freely.

"Ed, whatever's happened?"

The nurse's eyes were wide and full of tears. "It's Samuel. He's... he's dead."

CHAPTER FOUR

KILL

I LAUGHED OUT loud when I realised where I was being taken. Two goons had appeared to pull me to my feet and march me across the abandoned car park, long-established weeds reaching for the sun between gaps in the crumbling tarmac. The woman with the broken nose stalked behind us, my confiscated backpack slung across a muscular shoulder.

Crossing to what was left of the stores on the other side of the shopping precinct, I was marched around the back of the warehouse-sized buildings and in through a back entrance. Our footsteps echoed along once-busy corridors as we moved from unit to unit to our final destination.

They were taking me to Matalan!

"What's so funny?" Broken-Nose asked.

"I was just thinking I could do with some bargains. New shoes, for a start. The leather on these boots is as cracked as you."

That's it, soldier. Keep needling away at the enemy. Make them angry. Make them sloppy.

We stepped into the huge stockroom. The racks had been rearranged to form shelters, tarpaulin stretched between metal struts. I doubted the residents of the hastily-assembled shanty town had found many spoils when they set up home—the store would have been looted long ago—but as camps went, you could do a lot worse. The walls were sturdy and, if the rain hammering against the iron roof was any indication, the place was reasonably watertight, save for the odd isolated leak. Sure, the building was cold, but here and there braziers had been lit, providing welcome heat, although my chest could have done without the smoke that hung like a cloud in the stuffy air.

"Keep going," Broken-Nose commanded as I slowed to check for available exits. The service doors were open, revealing even more tents in what would have been the shop floor.

This is where they'd come from, those idiot raiders; part of a community, a tribe.

I was shoved through a doorway at the end of the warehouse. A gloomy flight of stairs awaited me, which I duly climbed, ignoring the weariness of my joints. My head still throbbed, but I seemed to have avoided serious concussion. None of the tell-tale signs were there: I knew exactly what was going on, and was no more sluggish than before I'd received a rifle-butt to my forehead. The slightly brighter light as we stepped into the staff canteen didn't worry me at all. Good.

Of course, I wasn't about to let my captors know any of this. I stumbled forward as we crossed the open space, as if I was in danger of losing my balance, or my breakfast.

Make them think they've won. Lull them into a false sense of security. Then, when they least expect it, you're ready to strike.

"I need to sit down," I croaked, lurching to my right. One of the goons reached out to steady me. I could have taken him right then, but I wanted to see where I was being taken, who or what would greet me when I got there.

We pushed through double doors into a long corridor. Pin boards dotted the walls, some still smattered with remnants of the building's past life. Health and safety notices. After work clubs. A picture of a missing dog.

REWARD

Male, 2-year-old, Jack Russell Terrier
Answers to T.J.
Last seen on Filton Ave July 19th

I wondered if T.J. had ever been found.

"In here," Broken-Nose said, the goon on the left grabbing my arm and guiding me roughly towards an open door. I teetered through to find the room empty save for a high-backed swivel chair in the middle of the floor, and an office desk pushed beneath the window.

Broken-Nose shoved me towards the chair. "You wanted to sit? Sit."

"Thank you," I slurred, dropping harder than I needed into the seat. The hydraulic support shifted slightly beneath my weight, but it was comfortable enough, not that I had any intention of relaxing.

I let myself slump forward, resting my genuinely throbbing head in my hands. I heard Broken-Nose drop my backpack onto the desk and open the zip. Soon she was rifling through the contents; the billy can full of what little rations I had left, a flask and my scope. I wondered if she would uncover the Colt stashed in a hidden compartment at the bottom of the bag. The Walther P99 I usually kept in my shoulder holster had already been confiscated along with my knife, the gun tucked into Broken-Nose's belt. Through my fingers, I saw her weighing the seemingly empty pack in her hands. Then she was reaching back in, searching the lining until she discovered the concealed pocket and pulled out the Colt with a snort of satisfaction.

She was good.

Footsteps were approaching the room now. Brisk, confident. How many? I let my head drop, listening carefully.

At least three. They slowed slightly as they reached the office, but walked straight in.

"So, who do we have here?" The voice was female, the tones of a woman who was used to being obeyed. Northern Irish.

I couldn't tell how old without looking. Not young, but not ancient either.

"He was on the roof, across the way," Broken-Nose reported.

"Did he do that?"

No spoken reply.

"Have Brassey look at it. So, he can handle himself, then."

"Not enough, by the look of things." A new voice. West Country, but not Bristolian. Devonshire, possibly Barnstable way. Nasal. Sneering.

"He put up a fight, I'll grant him that." How generous. "Two guns and a Bowie knife, recently sharpened." I heard the slide on my P99. "Both guns are well-maintained. He knows what he's doing."

Still I didn't look up. I could see their boots ahead of me. Scuffed leather, but sturdy. Cargo pants and military surplus, no jeans. The smaller pair of boots (brown) belonged to the Irish woman, the larger Doc Martens (black) to the Devon lad. Broken-Nose's boots (also black) had clattered as we'd walked across the concrete floor of the store room below. Hobnailed, then, probably with steel toecaps. Good job she hadn't returned the favour after I'd hoofed her in the side. Those things might have caved in a couple of my ribs, given the size of her.

Irish strolled forwards, Barnstable crossing to stand beside my chair. Jesus, he stank. I mean, people generally smelled these days, especially on the road, but seriously? How did the others put up with it?

Concentrate soldier. Don't get side-tracked. Focus.

Sir, yes, sir, etc.

Irish stopped in front of me. I didn't react, relaxing my shoulders, guessing what would happen next.

And I was right.

Fingers gripped my hair, jerking my head up to face her. I didn't have to pretend to cry out, my bruised forehead saw to that. I let my breathing remain ragged, forcing my eyes wide as I stared up at the newcomer.

She was a good ten years younger than me, maybe more. It was hard to tell. People looked older now. Late thirties, early forties at a push.

Short ginger hair, cropped close, like Broken-Nose. Made sense. Less chance of lice.

She had green eyes. No, that wasn't right. One green, one brown. I used to know what that was called. Hetero-something. Like Bowie. There was a scar on her chin, not deep, but noticeable, and her nose and eyebrows were pierced with simple studs.

She looked slight when compared to Broken-Nose, but so would Sly Stallone. It was clear from the way she held herself that she'd be handy in a fight.

"Where'd you come from?"

I coughed once before answering. "Around."

Barnstable yanked my hair, not satisfied with the answer.

"I travel. Here and there."

"Pretty well-armed for a tourist."

"Can you blame me?"

She smiled. It wasn't entirely pleasant.

"So why the roof? What were you doing up there?"

There was no point lying.

"I wanted to see the base."

"Why?"

"Why do you think? It's MoD. There'll be... stuff in there."

She regarded me coldly.

"What kind of 'stuff'?"

"Medical supplies, equipment. There's lights on, so there must be power."

"Clever boy. You planning a raid?"

"I was, until someone got there first."

Her eyes narrowed.

"What did you see?"

"That they're well defended. Guards. Guns. The works. Which means..." I left the sentence hanging.

She couldn't resist filling the silence. Good. "Yes?"

"There's something worth protecting."

Broken-Nose stepped up behind the woman. "How did you know about it?"

"What?"

"It's a good question," Irish said. "How did you know a base was even here?"

I shrugged. "Followed the signs, from the motorway."

"Is that right?"

"MoD base. Simple as that."

She glanced to my right, and Barnstable yanked at my hair, stretching out my neck, cold steel at my throat.

"Try again," he hissed in my ear, his breath perfectly matching the rest of his general bouquet.

"O-okay, okay," I stammered, raising a hand to signal capitulation. "I'll tell you."

The pressure of the blade relaxed, only for a moment, but long enough for my other hand to grip Barnstable's knife arm. I pulled it down, away from me, planting my feet firmly against the floor. Shoving back, I rammed the chair into the scrawny git, smashing my elbow into his face for good measure.

Twisting his knife arm, I sprang out of the chair, feeling hair rip from my scalp. Something cracked and he dropped the knife with a yelp, his arm hopelessly over-extended.

I heard the others' guns as I pivoted around to pin him to the floor, knowing full well that I was hopelessly outnumbered.

In fact, I was dead where I stood.

So I answered the question properly.

"MoD Abbey Wood. Opened 1996. Headquarters of the DE&S. Seven thousand staff across four buildings with an annual budget of roughly thirteen billion. There were plans to build a fifth building, but the Cull put pay to that. Would you like me to continue?"

All the time I didn't look up, staring at the back of Barnstable's head. He was wearing a faded blue baseball cap, his lanky brown hair riddled with dandruff.

I had to wait, to see what the boss-woman would do.

She took her time.

"Put them away."

There was a moment's hesitation before the guns were holstered. I didn't react until she spoke again.

"I would prefer if you didn't break Fenton's arm."

"That you?" I asked the man still beneath my knee.

His only reply was a curse. I released his arm and stood back. Fenton scrambled to his feet, massaging his shoulder, looking for the world that he wanted to punch me in the face.

"That's enough," his boss commanded, and Fenton retreated, like the good dog he was.

I stared at him, my expression neutral.

"DE&S?"

I turned back to the woman, who was standing as relaxed as ever, her eyebrows raised expectantly.

"Defence Equipment and Support," I explained. "Procurement for all the major services, from paper clips to aircraft carriers."

"And you know all this how?"

"I've been inside, only a couple of times, but enough to know my way around."

"Military?"

"The staff? Not largely. I'd say an eighty-twenty split, civilian to military."

"I meant you."

"Once upon a time."

She peered at me, weighing me up. I let her look.

"Niamh Brennan," she eventually said. "Fenton you've already met."

"And what about you?" I asked Broken-Nose.

"Beck," came the reply. It was strangely anti-climatic for such an impressive specimen.

"They were your men? The ones the guards took down."

"They were."

"Shame. I thought you might know what you were doing."

Brennan found my audacity funny. From the depth of her scowl, Beck did not.

"I mean, I get it; testing their defences. Very wise—but a frontal attack? A waste of good men. A waste of bad men, for that matter. How many have you got here?"

"Just men, or do you want to know about the women too?" asked Beck pointedly.

"Either. I'm all for equal opportunities when it comes to incompetence."

Brennan gave another laugh. "You've got balls, I'll say that for you."

"You want into that place?"

"I thought that was obvious. As you said, they must have something worth protecting."

"But you don't know what?"

"Do you?"

I shook my head. "Don't care, but I can get you in. For a price."

She nodded. "So, you're a gun for hire."

"I prefer 'consultant.'"

"And what's your price?"

That was simple. "Drugs."

Brennan raised her eyebrows. "You don't look like a junkie."

It wasn't up for discussion. "You asked me what I wanted, and that's my answer. Take it or leave it."

"Says the man who I could have shot at a moment's notice."

I shrugged. "If you do, you'll never get in. Your choice."

Brennan smiled again, this time showing teeth that instantly aged her. I doubted they had a dentist in the camp.

"Forty-two."

Her answer confused me. I didn't like being confused.

"Sorry?"

"You asked how many of us there are. Forty-two. Until this morning it was forty-six." She looked around herself. "Living here, in the place... we've had it worse. But living *there*, with fences and a moat?"

"A palace fit for a queen."

"Get us inside, and I might just make you my king."

I grinned. "How can I refuse... Your Majesty?"

CHAPTER FIVE
CURE

THE DOOR TO Samuel's room was open, the observation area full with medical staff, Dr Atkins, Dr Heslin, a smattering of nurses. They stepped back as I entered, clearing a path to Samuel's quarters.

"Show me," I told Ed, letting the nurse take the lead. I followed him into the room, Allison and Olive leading the rest of the staff in behind me.

I took one look at what greeted us and ordered everyone out.

"Dr Tomas—" Olive began, but I herded them from the room like cattle.

"Everybody out! If you're not Dr Harwood or Nurse Dunning, leave immediately."

Olive tried to argue—of course she did—but she was the only one. The rest of the staff obediently filed from the room, George Atkins glancing over his shoulder to take one last horrified look.

"Clear the observation area, too," I barked, shutting them out. "We don't need an audience."

And then there were three—four if you included the body.

I took a breath and turned to face the boy sprawled on the floor.

Allison was standing with her hands over her mouth, staring down at Samuel. "Jesus Christ, Jasmine."

Beside us, Ed Dunning flinched, his Catholic upbringing clearly offended—but a little blasphemy was the least of our concerns.

I reached into my pocket. This time I wasn't going for my meds. I pulled out a small silver voice recorder and, checking the available space on the SD card, hit record.

"Time stamp: oh-seven-forty-three. Dr Jasmine Tomas, Dr Allison Harwood and Nurse Ed Denning present."

Allison stood aside as I walked over to Samuel's body. There was every chance that she wanted to pass comment on the need for making a recording straight away, but protocol was all that held us together at times like this.

I crouched beside the corpse, still recording. "The subject has been found lying beside his bed, in a state of advanced rigor mortis. His eyes..." A glance at the boy's face caused my detached facade to slip for a moment. I coughed, clearing my throat, all too aware of the quiver in my voice as I proceeded. "His eyes are open, staring up at the ceiling. There is... evidence of subconjunctival haemorrhage."

Behind me Allison reached the end of her tether. "*Evidence?* His eyes are bright red, Jas. Look at them."

I rose, my cheeks burning. "Allison, please."

"Sorry, am I interrupting your report? Worried you might miss something. Okay, let me fill you in." She grabbed my hand, pulling it towards her face. "Samuel's—that *the subject*, by the way—is dead. Did you get that? An eleven-year-old boy in our care, dead at our feet."

"Perhaps I should go," Ed muttered, turning towards the door.

"Oh, no, you don't," Allison called after him. "Someone else needs to be here. That's regulation, isn't it, Jasmine? Three people present at a report. That's the way we do things? Moore will be proud."

I shut the voice recorder off. "What is wrong with you?"

"What is wrong with *me*? I'm not the one pretending to be Mister-Bloody-Spock."

"I'm being a doctor," I snapped back, louder and with more force than I intended, but it did the trick. Allison clamped her mouth shut, crossing her arms in frustration. She glanced away from me, her eyes wet, biting her bottom lip.

We stood in silence, Ed shuffling uncomfortably.

"I know," Allison finally admitted, wiping a solitary tear from her cheek. "I'm sorry. It's just the shock. I... I was with him last night. He... laughed. Or at least, he tried to. To please me." A sad smile broke across her face. "It was such a ridiculous noise, so false, but I could tell he was doing it for me, to make me feel better about... well, how *I* was feeling. It was the most empathy I've received from any of these kids. And now..."

She looked down at Samuel and the tears welled again. "Go on," she said. "Please."

I knew that I should reach out, to touch her arm, even pull her into a hug, but also knew she wouldn't thank me. I restarted the recorder.

"The subject's features show signs of risus sardonicus, the lips drawn back into a rictus grimace."

"Tetanus," Ed cut in.

This time I didn't bother to stop the recorder. "I'm sorry?"

"I've seen it before, in cases of tetanus." He looked embarrassed, realising that he was telling me things I already knew. He was only trying to help.

"It would explain his back," Allison pointed out, quietly. She coughed, raising her voice for the benefit of the recorder. "Samuel's body has pulled into a bridge position, his spine arching."

"Opisthotonus," I agreed. "Caused by severe, and usually erratic, muscular contractions." I could see where they were going—both phenomena were classic symptoms of tetanus—but I had my doubts. Still, it was better to cover all bases. "Had Samuel cut or scratched himself recently?"

Ed shrugged. "Not that I know of."

I turned to Allison. "And you said he seemed in good spirits last night?"

"As far as he ever did; as any of them do."

"No signs of a fever? Stiffness of the jaw?"

"He didn't complain of anything."

I turned back to the body. "If it was tetanus, you'd expect a four-day incubation period at least, and we'd have seen the signs. And that's with a normal patient. With Samuel? It's impossible. And to accelerate so quickly..."

I touched the boy's throat, feeling the bunched muscles beneath the skin. They were like rock.

"Death appears to have been caused by asphyxia, the muscles in his neck effectively crushing the trachea. Time of death is difficult to place, although I would estimate that it has been no more than two or three hours."

Behind me, Allison nodded. "Rigor mortis would have set in immediately."

I pointed at a pool of vomit beside the bed. "And there's this..."

Samuel had been sick during his convulsions, rolling into the mess as he'd thrashed about. There were traces on the side of his face—but the vomit on the floor hadn't completely dried, glinting in the light from the ceiling lamps.

"But if it isn't tetanus?" Ed asked.

Before I could answer, the door was thrown open, Des Moore bursting in without invite.

"Good God."

So much for keeping everyone out.

The security chief rubbed the back of his thick neck. "I came as soon as I heard. Do we know what happened?"

"That's what we're trying to determine. Shut the door, will you?" If Moore was here, I might as well use him. The man had been originally assigned by the Cabal themselves. Soon after he'd arrived in Bristol, we'd got drunk together, one of the last times I allowed my guard to drop. He told me how he'd been a teenager at the time of the Cull, how he'd moved from city to city as the world fell apart, joined various militia. It had been a hard life.

There was something in his eyes when he spoke of the past, a loss I recognised... Before I knew what I was doing, I'd leant forward and kissed him. We never told anyone about that night. Over the years, mutual embarrassment had given way to passive-aggressive sniping on both sides, but I knew I could rely on him when push came to shove—like now.

"Chief, I need you to find out exactly what Samuel was fed over the last week."

"I can do that," Ed offered, but I cut him dead.

"No, it's better that Chief Moore handles this. Get to the kitchens, quarantine any ingredients used in Samuel's meals, and check the trash, too. They may have been thrown away."

"What may have been thrown away?" Allison asked, touching my arm. "You're not suggesting that Samuel was poisoned?"

I ignored her. "Ed, Allison—check if any of the other subjects are exhibiting symptoms. Tightness of the jaw. Difficulty breathing. I'll perform the autopsy on Samuel myself." I looked down at the pool of vomit beside the body. "We'll need a sample of that too, to see what he ingested."

Allison was running her hands through her hair, not wanting to believe what she was hearing.

"Did you get all that?" I asked, switching off the voice recorder. "Allison?"

She nodded, not looking sure at all. "Yes, got it. Sorry." She dithered for a moment, before ushering Ed out of the room. "You heard the lady. Let's go."

Moore also turned to leave, but I stopped him. "Des, we need to check the storerooms too, specifically any poisons we use for pest control."

His scowled, the dark skin between his brows forming deep furrows. "You mean like rat poison?"

"I mean *exactly* like rat poison." I looked down at Samuel's body. "Especially anything containing strychnine."

FIVE HOURS LATER and the prospect of a dreamless night of sleep had never seemed so appealing.

I sat in my office, staring across the complex. The storm had passed, although the clouds were threatening a repeat performance any minute.

The base was eerily quiet—not that it was ever what you'd call bustling. A complex built for thousands, now home to about sixty. It must have been impressive when it was first opened, with its winding pathways and immaculate gardens, like a university campus. Most of the green spaces were overgrown now, although some were maintained by staff keen to stave off boredom when they weren't on duty. There were vegetable plots, of course, and a surprisingly healthy orchard near Neighbourhood Three; but some of the gardens were actually quite stunning. Allison and Bets maintained one of the plots, growing roses of all things. It turned out that Allison had quite the green fingers. She'd even asked me if I wanted to join them.

I'd killed every plant I'd ever owned, including a potted cactus. Who kills cactuses, of all things? They're like cockroaches.

Not that it made much sense to me, anyway. Growing flowers in the midst of all this. I looked up to the horizon, seeing the derelict houses across what was once a busy ring road. Shops, schools, even a sports centre... there would have been people everywhere.

Sometimes I imagined them all. Children hanging around the car park when they should be heading home. Trains thundering past on their way to London, cars navigating seemingly endless roundabouts, shouts from the football fields beside the sports-centre, a plane flying overhead...

It made me smile and ache at the same time. I would have hated it. Weekends traipsing around out-of-town shopping centres. No, thanks. But it still hurt.

Most of the buildings in the base were empty now, although we maintained some of the amenities. From what I've read, Abbey Wood had four restaurants when it first opened—the largest now acted as our staff canteen here in Neighbourhood Three. There were hairdressers, a gym, tennis courts and a five-a-side football pitch, which I could see from my office window. We even had our own Sunday league; technicians vs medical vs security and so on. I'd never made it to a match, but had spent many a long hour watching the teams practise.

The puddle-strewn pitches were empty now; not because of the weather, more the threat of being shot during the second half.

Raids stop play.

"Dr Tomas, should we call a general meeting?"

I jumped, looking up to see Olive at the door, clipboard in hand. I hadn't heard her come in.

"How long have you been there?"

She gave me what she obviously thought was a kind smile. Poor Dr Tomas, lost in thought, cracking under pressure. Losing control.

And all the time Olive stood in her perfect little dress, with her perfect hair and perfect make-up. Where did she even *find* lipstick anyway?

"It's just that people are starting to talk..."

"I bet they are."

Olive took a tentative step forward. "There's talk of poisoning. Rumours are already spreading." She glanced at her clipboard. "We should clear the rest of the day, hold a town hall, in the atrium maybe."

The look on my face told her what I thought of that suggestion.

"We need to something," she insisted. "The last thing we want is people putting two and two together and making five. You know how quickly gossip spreads around this place. Only last week, Nurse Tyler told me—"

"Yes, yes," I said, raising a hand to stop her mid-flow. "You're right, we have to do something."

Olive beamed. "Excellent. Shall we say five o'clock, then?"

"Let's say nothing, yet." She went to argue, so I shut her down quickly. "I want to have all the facts at my disposal before we do anything. Some people..."—I let that hang in the air for a moment—"are going to gossip come what may."

There was a knock at the door and I felt a rush of gratitude for whoever it was.

The door opened and Des Moore entered. I felt my heart sink a little bit, but seized the moment all the same.

"Chief, please, come in." This was going to be tough, but anything was better than hearing my assistant drone on. "Thank you, Olive, that will be all for now."

She left with a face like several thunderstorms rolled into one. Chief Moore shut the door behind him.

I let out a sigh, and rubbed my temples. My long-awaited headache was gaining ground.

"Are you all right, doctor?" Moore asked as he strode over to my desk. I nodded, motioning for him to sit.

"It's been quite a day, one way or another."

"And it's not over yet."

Ain't that the truth. Well, there was no preventing the inevitable.

"Any luck with the discs?" I asked.

The subjects' rooms were all fitted with closed-circuit TV, the feeds automatically burned to recordable DVDs. A dreadful invasion of privacy, but necessary to the project.

"I'm afraid not."

"They're still missing?"

"Not just Samuel's; the entire floor."

"Every disc? But that's—"

"Impossible, yes. I just don't understand it. They would have been swapped for the new batch at 7am, but the cases are empty."

"The computer back up? All footage is stored on the servers for twenty-four hours. It must be there."

"Wiped."

"What?"

"It could only have been done by one of the technicians."

"Have you asked them?"

"I spoke to Lam Chen—he was the one who showed me the files, or rather the lack of them."

"And you can trust him?"

"I've had no reason not to."

"Up to now."

I leant back in my chair, letting my head fall back to gaze up at the ceiling tiles.

The last thing Samuel had ever seen.

For the first time in years I could kill for a drink—which in present company might not be wise.

"Do we know when he was poisoned?" Moore asked bluntly. There was no question of it now.

I leant forward on the desk. "Around 5am, as far as I can tell. As suspected, there are traces of strychnine in both his stomach and the vomit we found on the floor."

Moore balled his fists on the arm of the chair. "I just wish we knew it was from the stores."

"It has to be, you said that it looked like there was rat poison missing—"

"As far as I can tell, but it turns out that our caretaker is somewhat lax when it comes to stock-taking—"

"We have no way of knowing for sure?"

Moore glowered as he shook his head. Like Olive, the chief prided himself on running a tight ship. Today we were discovering corners being cut across the base, left, right and centre.

"How much had he been given?"

I glanced down at the freshly written report on my desk. I could just imagine the ripples this would cause when it arrived in Germany.

"More than enough. A lethal dose for an average adult is as little as 100 milligrams. I found traces of twice that amount. The effects would have been near enough instantaneous, certainly no later than ten minutes."

"So it couldn't have been in his evening meal?"

"Not in the concentration required. It must have been swallowed in the earlier hours."

"But there was no sign of a struggle?"

"As if he'd been force-fed the poison? Not that I could find. No skin under the fingernails. No lesions or bruising."

"So someone went into his quarters at around half-four in the morning, gave him the poison, without excessive force, and then left him to die?"

"Or watched it happen."

It was a thought I'd avoided vocalising until now.

"But why Samuel?"

"I don't know."

"And why now?"

"Same answer." Another thought occurred to me, this one more encouraging. "Could we... fingerprint the door handles, see who's been in and out of the room?"

"Who hasn't, over the last six hours?" Moore pointed out. "You. Me. Half the medical team."

"What about the card readers? At that time of the morning, you'd have to use ID to get near the children."

Des Moore's stared at me, and looked dismayed. He sprung from his chair. "I'll check the logs. That could be just what we're looking for."

He started for the door without permission to leave, keen to follow up any line of enquiry after so many dead ends.

"One more thing, chief," I said.

He stopped, turning back to me. "I'm sorry, I should have asked—"

I waved the apology away, dreading the words that were about to come out of my mouth. "Confine all the staff to their quarters."

His eyes went wide. "Are you sure?"

I held his gaze. "What alternative do we have? Could someone have broken into the base to poison Samuel?"

"In theory, yes, but—"

I raised my eyebrows, and he finally relented.

"It's unlikely."

"Then we're probably looking at an insider. Until we've at least narrowed down the suspects, I can't take any risks. You, me, two guards you can trust. That's all. Everyone else is confined to barracks as of this moment."

"But, the subjects..."

"I'll looked after them myself. I can cope with eight children—" I stopped myself. Seven, now.

"The staff aren't going to like it."

I gave him a look that made it clear the conversation was at an end. "They're not supposed to."

CHAPTER SIX
KILL

"Here," said Beck, thrusting a chipped mug at me.

"What is it?" I asked, eying her with suspicion.

"What does it smell like?"

Tentatively I raised the mug to my nose and took a sniff. My eyes widened, the bruise on my forehead twinging.

"You're kidding me? *Coffee?*"

"Or as near as dammit," said Beck, taking a sip from her own blue-and-white-checked mug.

"Where did you get it? Actually, no. I don't care. Thank you."

I took a sip, the hot liquid burning my lips. The bitter taste washed over my tongue. It had been a long time since I tasted coffee. I could barely remember if this was good or bad—but it was welcome.

To be honest, while my introduction to Brennan's gang had been less than welcoming, things had rapidly improved. They'd given me a room among the old offices to change—

even providing some reasonably clean clothes and, miracle of miracles, showed me where they had installed a makeshift shower in the corner of the storeroom downstairs. It was cold, of course, using rainwater they'd collected in giant butts on the roof, but alongside a bar of gritty chemical-smelling soap, I wasn't complaining. It was also far from private, what little remained of my dignity protected by loose plastic sheeting draped around some old clothes horses, but, again, I barely gave a fuck. So, I was washing under the gaze of curious gang members nearby. What did it matter? I was clean, *properly* clean for the first time in months.

Who would have thought I'd care?

Certainly not me.

"How's the nose?" I asked Beck, taking another swig of the coffee.

She shrugged, although it had to hurt. It had been set—to a fashion—beneath a long plaster, but the bruises around her eyes were obvious.

I almost felt sorry.

"How's the head?" she responded.

"Still as thick as ever."

She almost smiled.

"So, how long have you been with Brennan?"

"Long enough."

"Quite some time, then."

"Does it matter?"

Small talk wasn't her thing. I got that. Even appreciated it. But she'd been the one to offer the java-infused olive branch.

"Thanks for the coffee," I said, finishing the cup.

"No problem."

Why was she even here? I looked at my watch, looking past the cracked face. It still worked, that was all that mattered. Besides, it had been a present from Jasmine. It was the nearest thing I had to a treasure.

"Brennan's on her way," Beck said, assuming I was getting twitchy. "She had things to attend do."

"She's the boss," I said, putting the mug on top of the papers I'd carefully laid out on the table beside us. "I'm not going anywhere."

"What about you?" Beck asked, surprising me with the question.

"What about me?"

She took another sip. "How long have you been a merc?"

I was tempted to say 'long enough.'

"Since a little after the Cull. A lifetime."

"And before?"

I grinned, mocking a yank accent. *"That's classified, ma'am."*

This time she did actually smile, showing a row of yellowed teeth. "Special forces?"

"Something like that. Who trained you?"

"I was brought up on the streets. Can't remember much about life before."

"Don't know what you're missing, eh?"

"I wouldn't say that."

There were footsteps from the hall outside. Brennan was on her way. Beck's posture changed. She'd started to relax for bit, there. Now it was back to business. She drained the last dregs from the mug and placed it on the side of the table, standing up straight, her arms behind her back.

Chat time was over.

Brennan walked in, Fenton beside her, strutted along like a '90s Brit-Rocker. I wasn't looking forward to having him by my side. Beck I could trust, at least to handle herself in case we got in trouble. *When* we got in trouble. Fenton, well, one glance told you that he was full of it. A legend in his own mind. Shame his body didn't match up. As scrawny as a smackhead, with a pock-marked, ratty face. And the stink. Why didn't Brennan insist that *he* take a shower? Perhaps they didn't notice anymore. Live with shit long enough and you no longer smell it.

"Did you enjoy the coffee?" Brennan asked, coming to a stop in front of me.

"From her own stash," Fenton pointed out, wanting me to be impressed.

I ignored him, replying directly to Brennan instead. "Best brew I've had for years. Thanks. For everything."

"The least we could do," the woman said, stepping forward

to look at the papers on the desk, "seeing that you're going to get us into... what did you say it was called?"

"Abbey Wood."

"Sounds like a retirement home," said Fenton, sneering.

I brought the largest sheet of paper to the top of the pile. "I don't know about that, but if you're looking to build a nest, you could ask for a lot worse."

I'd drawn a rough map of the complex, half from memory and half from my observations that morning.

"As I said, the base is made up of four main Neighbourhoods—"

Brennan interrupted immediately. "Neighbourhoods?"

I had to give him that one.

"Sorry—MoD speak. Four main buildings, each with four or more wings. Back in the day, each building corresponded to a different service." I pointed out each building as I ran through the list. "Navy, Army, Air Force and so on. Each had accommodation, offices, cafés..." I shot a look at Fenton. "Shower blocks. The whole kit and caboodle. Moat on one side, fencing on the other."

"Which they've added to since," cut in Beck.

I nodded. "From what I saw yesterday, the entire campus has been surrounded by a secondary perimeter fence, topped with razor-wire." I tapped on the former entrance to the base. "The road in here has been barricaded, new gates constructed, and subsequently clad with metal plates."

"Iron sheeting," Brennan confirmed.

"Have you tried to take them?"

"We have a van parked round the side of the store," Fenton revealed. "We were going to drive through the gates, you know, like a battering ram."

"But?"

"But we haven't enough fuel," Brennan admitted.

"We have a few canisters of gas for the generator," added Fenton, "but not enough to get her started."

"So, scratch that," I concluded.

"That won't be a problem though, will it?" Beck asked. "You said you can get us in."

"Not a problem at all," I assured her. "So far you've attacked the potential weak points, yes?" I put my finger on the location of today's failed attempt. "Here—"

"And here and here," Brennan said, pointing.

I nodded, feigning appreciation. "All good spots, but you're missing a trick. It's not your fault, of course. You weren't to know."

"To know what?" Beck asked, frustration creeping into her voice.

"About the tunnels."

Brennan's eyes lit up. "Under the buildings."

I gave her a conspiratorial grin. "This is an MoD base. Tunnels, bunkers. You name it, it's under there. There are storerooms full of enough dried rations to survive a nuclear war. Weapons, vehicles. Probably even fuel."

I pointed out of the window, towards the tall white roofs in the distance. "What you can see is only the tip of the iceberg."

Brennan was looking hungrily at my maps now. "That's how we get in? The tunnels?"

I picked up a pencil. "The tunnels were built to allow movement between Neighbourhoods in case of emergency— but they also offered escape."

I pulled the paper towards me and drew a cross on a blank space above the moat. "This is old farmland, not worth much back then, although the farmer received a healthy subsidy from the Ministry of Defence."

"Because of the tunnels?" Beck asked.

"There was a hidden entrance on his land," I confirmed. "I don't think it was ever used, but it's there. And if it could let people out..."

"...it can also let people in," Brennan said.

"I'm not saying it'll be easy. They'll be deadlocks and security systems."

"But you can get past them."

"It shouldn't be a problem if we work together. How many guns do you have?"

Beck looked to her boss, cautious. Brennan nodded.

"About forty rifles. More handguns; most of us are armed."

I whistled, actually impressed. "Why haven't you just stormed the place?"

"I didn't say we had the ammo to match," Beck admitted.

"Ah, okay." That wasn't so good. "Have any explosives?"

Fenton snorted. "You think those gates would still be standing if we did?"

I tapped the end of the pencil against my teeth and flashed Fenton my brightest smile.

"Then I better take you shopping!"

THE EVENING WAS drawing in as I led my new allies back across the car park towards the old Woolworths.

"What's this about?" Fenton whined.

"You'll see," I said, bringing them to a door on the side of the building, a door that Beck had marched me past without so much as a second glance that morning.

Keep them on their toes, soldier. Knowledge is power.

I stopped at the door and tried it. It wouldn't budge.

"Locked," Beck concluded.

"Stuck," I corrected her, putting my shoulder to it. The door burst open, and I fished a flashlight out my jacket pocket.

They followed me into the building, past an old reception and into a corridor. I paused to listen, just to make sure.

There was nothing, bar the scampering of tiny paws along ancient lino.

"This way," I said, counting office doors as we continued. One, two, three—and here we were. Another door, this one opening easily enough. I flashed the torch inside, revealing a narrow closet.

"A cleaner's cupboard?" Beck commented.

I glanced back at the tall woman. "It's amazing what you can hide in cleaning cupboards."

Passing my torch to Brennan, I crouched down beside a set of shelves, grabbing the battered holdall I'd stashed at daybreak.

"I didn't want to lug this up to the room," I explained, carefully lifting it onto the floor.

"Or mention it when we found you?" Beck pointed out.

"Neither of us were that chatty this morning. We hadn't even gone for a coffee yet."

I opened the zip. Brennan aimed the light into the bag.

"Damn."

That was the reaction I wanted.

Fenton was more obvious. "Explosives!" he grunted, like a kid who'd just found a box of sherbet Dib-Dabs. There was no way I was letting him near this lot.

"Just a little C-4 I've picked up on my travels. Not a lot, but enough for what we'll need. Oh, and then there's these."

I reached towards the back of the shelf and pulled aside the broken-up cardboard box I'd use to cover the last of my cache. Carefully, I pulled out the box of six remote grenades.

"Now, who wants to mount an invasion?"

CHAPTER SEVEN
CURE

"Jasmine? Jasmine, wait up."

I sighed and stopped as running footsteps approached from behind.

"Dr Tomas," Olive warned quietly beside me. "We still have five more subjects to—"

I silenced her with a look and turned to greet Allison.

"What do you think you're doing?" she asked.

I tried to play the innocent. "I'm just checking in on Ops, and then will see to the children. Everything—"

Allison didn't let me finish. "Did you really order Moore to lock us up?"

"That's... not exactly what's happening."

"Isn't it? The medical staff has just been marched back to their quarters by armed guards. People are scared here. It's like some kind of coup. What's next—firing squads?"

I raised hands, trying to calm her down. "You're being hysterical—"

Allison jabbed a finger at me, stepping far too close.

"Don't give me that. I've just been threatened, Jas. Physically threatened."

I took a step back, if only to avoid having an eye poked out by an angry fingernail. "Threatened? By who?"

"I didn't stop to ask his name; one of your stormtroopers."

"Hysterical and melodramatic," muttered Olive, but if Allison had heard her, she didn't rise to it. Good job; she was furious enough as it was.

"Tell me what happened?" I asked, keeping my voice level.

"I was checking on David, making sure he was secure, and he just barged in."

"He?"

"One of Moore's lot, telling me that I had to go back to my quarters. I told him I was busy, and he tried to grab my arm. Jasmine, he had a gun."

There was little I could say to make her understand. "Allison, what with the attacks and—"

But there was no stopping her. "This wasn't in the observation area, Jas. We were in David's room, right in front of him."

I cocked my head, intrigued. "How did he react?"

The question derailed Allison for a moment.

"What?"

"David," I prompted. "How did he cope with the situation?"

Allison shook her head, running a frustrated hand through her hair. "The same as normal... I don't know. He just took it in his stride."

I nodded, making a mental note. David was one of the younger subjects, only eight years old. His IQ tests were off the scale, even compared with the others, but he kept himself to himself, barely uttering a word.

"But it shouldn't have happened, Jasmine. You get that, don't you?"

I rubbed the bridge of my nose. "Of course I get it, but Allison, Samuel was *murdered*."

"I know. But—"

No. Now it was time for me to talk. "Someone killed him. It wasn't an accident. It wasn't a mistake. It was planned, premeditated. Someone *wanted* him dead."

Allison just stood there, stunned by the force of my words. When she spoke again, her voice was small, deflated.

"Someone in the base."

"That's what I have to assume, until we find evidence to the contrary. Allison, I don't want to do any of this, but I'm having to make it up as I go along. None of this is in the instruction manual."

The corners of her mouth tucked up. Not much, but it was a start. "There's a manual? You kept that quiet."

I returned the gesture. "I'm sorry that people are scared. And I'm sorry if Moore's team are getting carried away; I'll have a word. But trust me, no one is getting locked in, unless they want to themselves."

"And what about the guards? Once we're all safely tucked up, will they be confined to quarters?"

She had me there. "Not all them. We need to make sure everyone—"

"—stays where you want them."

"Yes."

Allison crossed her arms. "I see."

"I'm sorry," I added, somewhat redundantly.

"It's fine," Allison replied, giving a weak approximation of a smile. "You have to do what you think best."

"I do," I insisted. "For the children. For all of us."

"I better get on, then," she said, turning. "But you will have a word with Moore?"

I promised I would.

"You know what he's like."

Better than most.

I watched Allison walk away, still hugging herself.

This was madness, all of it. Talking of which...

"How long since I took my meds?" I asked Olive.

Down the corridor, Allison stopped, looking over her shoulder. "What was that?"

I waved her away. "Nothing. Don't worry."

She nodded, still looking hurt, and carried on.

The nearest thing I had to a friend on this base.

Olive was checking her clipboard. Of course she was. "Not since this morning," she replied, answering my earlier question. "You're overdue."

I nodded, pulling the bottle out of my pocket. Damn. I'd forgotten to ask for more, what with everything that was going on. Still, I had enough to last until tomorrow, at least.

The last thing I needed was an episode. Someone had to keep their head around here. I unscrewed the lid and popped a capsule into my mouth, swallowing.

"Come on, then," I said, walking on towards the security hub.

"Dr Tomas, should I return to my quarters?" Olive asked, sounding terrified at the thought of me being alone for a second.

"I'm sure you won't mind. You've probably got some spreadsheets to play with, or whatever it is you do in your spare time."

She laughed. "Spare time? Doctor, looking after you is a full-time job, twenty-four-seven."

"Sorry to be such a handful."

"No need, I enjoy my work."

How the hell could she remain so cheerful? It wasn't normal. Perhaps Olive was the exception to the rule. Perhaps her quarters *should* be locked. And bolted.

And then set on fire.

I smiled to myself as I reached the hub door and swiped my ID card over the reader. The door clicked and I walked into Moore's domain, happy to see that he was off playing Hitler somewhere else. The operation room was on the other side of the open plan office, which Moore's team used as a rec room, chairs and coffee tables dotted around.

I slipped inside Ops, glancing up at the wall of monitors, rotating through camera feeds from around the complex. Only the top eight screens—the feeds from the children's dorms— were static. That was odd.

Someone had attached a scrap of masking tape beneath each screen, scrawled with the children's names:

Ruth. David. Matthew. Samuel. Michele. Katy. Adam. Dawn.

It was a strangely personal touch.

I watched the screens for a moment. Some of the subjects were reading, some were playing on their games consoles.

Ruth was sitting at her desk, building a model from LEGO. All so normal, save for the near identical clothes and lack of hair. Children without a care in the world. Did they even realise how important they were?

How could they?

My eyes lingered on the picture of Samuel's empty room, the lights still shining but no one home.

You must think we're made of money, my mum echoed in my head. *Turn your lights off when you go out. It was like the Blackpool illuminations in this house this morning!*

"Dr Tomas?"

Olive's gentle prompt snapped me back to the present. I looked around in shock, suddenly aware of my surroundings again.

"Sorry. Miles away. Now, where are we?" I pulled out the operator's chair and sat down in front of a PC on the desk. A wiggle of the mouse and its screen sprung to life, a box appearing and requesting a password. I typed my own, which could access any computer on the base.

Incorrect Password.
Please try again.

I blinked at the message. Maybe I'd typed it wrong.
I tried again, the chunky keyboard clattering.

Incorrect Password.
Please try again.

"This can't be right." One more failed attempt and I'd need a network administrator. I frowned at my hands, as if it was their fault.

"Perhaps you're using an old one," Olive suggested, making me want to throw the keyboard at her stupid smug face. Of *course* I wasn't. I knew my password. I'd only changed it last week.

I tried again. One last chance.

Incorrect Password.
Please contact the administrator.

I slammed my fists down on the desk, and then jumped as a voice spoke behind me.

"Excuse me, but what *the hell* do you think you're doing?"

CHAPTER EIGHT
KILL

Now everyone had torches, although I'd told them to kill the lights as soon as we crept out into the field.

"I could break my neck," complained Fenton.

Only if there was a God...

"We don't want to advertise our presence," I suggested, pushing through waist-high grass. "There's no way of knowing who's watching—so keep your voices down for that matter. Sound travels after dark."

The night air was cold, but thankfully dry at last, although the mud beneath our boots squelched with every step. In the distance a fox screamed. I'd always hated that noise. When I was a kid I'd stayed entire summers with my Gran, staying in the attic of her cottage. You wouldn't believe the horrors I'd imagined when one of those bastards started up in the middle of the night.

"It's okay, pet. Just a vixen." Show no weakness, soldier. You've nothing to fear.

"Yes, Gran." Sir, yes, sir. *Nothing to fear but fear itself.*
And the bullets, and the mines, and the gas, and—
I had the feeling there would be more screams before the night was out.

We kept moving on, everyone heeding my words and shutting the fuck up. Even Fenton. Brennan was on my heels, leading the rest of her pack; Beck keeping some distance between her and Fenton, and behind him, the two goons who had grabbed me that morning. The man-mountain to the left was called Garret, and his hulk of a partner Curtis. Neither were what you'd call chatty, but they weren't here for conversation. Garret had a fireman's axe strapped between his monstrous shoulders, while Curtis was lugging a portable battering ram on his back. The thing must have weighed twenty kilos. Say this for Brennan, the armoury she'd salvaged and jury-rigged was impressive, and her people weren't the idiots I'd written off this morning. Inexperienced, yes, but they would come good, given the right orders.

I almost believed we had half a chance of surviving the night, if everyone—I'm looking at you, Fenton—if everyone did what they were told.

BECK, GARRET AND CURTIS were packing automatic rifles, Fenton a pump-action shotgun and Brennan a handgun, with another at her waist.

I was happy to stick to my handguns, the P99 in my hand and the Colt in a belt holster along with the Bowie knife. The remote grenades were hanging from a strap slung across my chest, a quarter of the plastic explosives stowed safely in my pack.

Just another day, ready to cause merry hell.

I was counting my paces, leading the group to what I had found the day before. I slowed, raising my gun hand so the others did likewise.

"Is it here?" Brennan asked.

I stepped onto the concrete rim of the grate.

"What do you think?"

It was round, about six feet in diameter, the metal bars old and rusted, although, as I'd found out yesterday, they were still strong enough.

Slipping my Walther back into its holster, I crouched down as Brennan and the others formed a semi-circle around me. I shone the light into the shaft, my beam of light picking out a floor covered in bird-shit and clods of mud some twenty feet beneath us.

Fenton lit his torch, mirroring my action. "That's a long way down," he sneered, before hawking loudly and spitting a ball of phlegm through the grate. It dropped, illuminated by his beam before landing wetly on the floor below.

"It's not far," insisted Beck. "No more than six metres at most."

Brennan reached forward and grabbed hold of the grate with a gloved hand, testing its resistance. "So, how do we get down?"

Getting to my feet, I stepped three quarters of the way around the grating and flashed my torch down again, tracing the bars.

Brennan dropped down onto her haunches, running her hands along the metal. "They've been cut!"

I nodded. "If Beck had searched my bag yesterday, she would have found a hacksaw."

Brennan looked up into the light. "You did this?"

"Last night, just before the sun went down," I confirmed.

"You were lucky no one saw."

To say the least. In daylight there had been a direct line of sight to the top floor of Neighbourhood Four. It was a calculated risk.

Brennan slipped her fingers through the grating, grabbing hold and pulling sharply. There was movement, but not enough. I shone the beam around the semi-circle I'd managed to cut. The torchlight found solid metal.

"You didn't finish the job?" said Fenton.

"The blade snapped," I retorted, annoyed. "It was old."

He looked me up and down. "You're telling me."

It would be so easy to dash his brains out on the concrete.

I flashed the torch in the direction that we had walked. "There used to be a hardware store, about half a mile that-a-way."

"Yeah, we found it," Beck confirmed. "Cleared out."

"I thought I might find a saw lying about," I admitted. "But no such luck. The ceiling's come down."

Brennan tested the grille. "There's some give in this. If we could bend it up..."

Fenton boggled. "You're joking!"

"It should be wide enough to climb through."

"And then what?" Fenton asked. "Drop to the bottom?"

Yeah. Hopefully, you'd land on your head.

Beck grabbed Fenton's arm to shine his light down the concrete walls of the shaft.

"There's a ladder."

"Why do you think I cut here?" I said.

Beck crouched down, Brennan stepping aside to let the larger woman examine the grate. Putting down her gun, Beck grabbed the bars with both hands and heaved, grunting slightly with the effort, and then let go, nodding.

"Yeah, that'll come. Garret, you and Curtis, with me."

The two meatheads fell in, crouching either side of Beck.

I stepped around them, shining my light onto the spot where the blade had snapped.

"On three," the woman commanded. "One... two... three."

They began to pull, the metal squealing in protest. They made little progress at first.

"Hang on," Fenton said, passing his torch to Brennan so he could produce a crowbar from his pack.

Perhaps he wasn't such a waste of space. I guessed there had to be a reason Brennan kept him around. It certainly wasn't because of his charm.

Fenton dropped to his knees beside Garret. "That's it," he said, shoving the crowbar into the ever-growing gap. "Almost there."

He was right. The metal was beginning to buckle.

"I'm in,' said Fenton, pushing down on the lever. "That's it. That's it."

Then he slipped, the crowbar springing into the air. It landed on top of the crate, upended and then tumbled down the shaft to clatter on the floor below.

The sound rang out across the night.

We all froze.

Nothing. Not even another bloody fox.

Brennan breathed out. "It's okay. No one could have heard that, not this far away."

I wondered who she was trying to convince.

"It bloody hurt," whined Fenton, taking off a glove to rub his aching palm.

Someone get the boy a tissue.

"We can do this," Beck said, and they redoubled their efforts. The grille was giving way now, opening as if on a hinge. In theory, we could probably wriggle through already, but it would be a bit tight. Curtis shifted position, pushing from underneath now, Beck pulling from above. The cords of her neck were bunching, looking ready to break, before she slipped and fell back with a cry.

It didn't matter. The twisted metal stood proud, pointing up towards the clouds that smothered the stars above.

"That'll do," panted Beck, taking my hand. She hauled herself back to her feet and retrieved her rifle. "We should be able to get through now."

Fenton shone his torch over the roughly hacked hole. "You sure?"

"Who wants to go first?" I asked, knowing full well what the answer would be.

"You can lead the way," Brennan said simply.

"No problem," I said, passing my pack to Beck. "Pass this down to me when I'm through. I don't want it catching on the sides."

Slipping my torch into my pocket, I sat myself on edge of the shaft and swung my legs down, searching for the rungs of the ladder.

CHAPTER NINE
CURE

I TURNED IN the chair to find Lam Chen standing in the door, a coffee mug in his podgy hand. Lam headed up the technical department, and could usually be found up to his elbows in fibre optic cables or squinting at a screen.

Now, his eyes went wide behind thick-rimmed glasses. "Dr Tomas, sorry, I... I didn't realise it was you."

"Something's wrong with your terminal," I said, brushing past the moment. We had bigger problems.

"I know," the technician said, pushing past Olive. He slapped his mug down on the desk, black tea slopping over the rim to leave another mark on an already stained table top.

Lam ran his hand through his wispy black hair as he stared at the monitor. I pushed my chair back to let him get closer to the keyboard. He grabbed the mouse, placing the cursor back into the dialogue box and tried to enter his own password.

Access denied.

"I just don't understand it," he admitted, tapping a long nail on the desktop. "It's been like this since I checked the files with Chief Moore."

"Can't you bypass it?"

"None of the passwords are working."

"None of them? But you're the administrator. Don't you have a... I don't know... override?"

"My account *is* the override," he replied irritably.

"Could it be a virus?"

"I wish I knew."

Lam fetched a second chair from the other side of the control room, removing a battered guitar. The place was a mess, Lam's little kingdom, with piles of comics scattered around the workstation and a games console and headset pushed to the edge of the desk. How did Moore cope with it?

Leaning the instrument against the wall, Lam sat down, wheeling himself back towards the keyboard. He began furiously tapping the keys, his fingers a blur. I had a feeling that he'd tried all of the combinations before, but couldn't help repeating the process, just in case one of them suddenly worked.

"The definition of insanity is doing the same thing over and over again, but expecting the results to change," Olive commented from the door. "Benjamin Franklin."

"Einstein," I snapped, Lam looking up from the screen.

"What?"

"Don't worry about it," I said, glaring at my assistant.

Lam shot a look at the door. He'd obviously having been so engrossed in his work that he hadn't heard Olive's snide remark. Probably for the best.

"What's the solution?" I asked, pulling him back to the problem at hand.

He took another sip from his mug of tea. "At the moment, I honestly don't know. Chief Moore told me to go back to my quarters, but..."

A thought struck him and he tried entering a different password with his left hand, only to be greeted by the same error message.

"But, what?" I prompted. I wasn't surprised the technician

had chosen to ignore Moore's instructions. Lam had always been a law unto himself.

He sat back in his chair, sipping more tea, staring at the computer screen as if he could will it to unlock.

"I can't leave it like this," he admitted. "It's bad enough that someone got in here and wiped the files—"

"Not to mention taking the discs," I reminded him, looking up at the bank of DVD recorders beside the games console.

"But to lock us out?"

"You think the two things are linked?"

"You don't?" came the reply. "If I didn't know better I'd say the lockdown happened *because* we were looking for the missing files."

"Like a... what? A booby trap?"

Lam pushed his glasses up his nose. "They didn't want us rooting around."

I leant forward, resting my arms on my legs. "Who didn't?"

"I don't know. Whoever offed the frea—"

Lam stopped himself, trying to cover his gaff by taking the biggest gulp of tea yet.

"The what?"

"The kid. Steven."

"Samuel," I corrected.

"Yeah, him." Lam put his mug back on the table, concentrating too hard on the computer screen.

I sat back on my chair. "What were you going to call him?"

Lam played with the mouse, moving the cursor pointlessly around the screen.

"Nothing."

"I beg your pardon?"

"I didn't mean anything. It's just a nickname."

"Freak."

"Everyone calls them that."

I crossed my arms, raising my eyebrows. I knew full well how certain members of technical and security support viewed the subjects, but to hear it from Lam? He'd never talked like this before.

"Do they?"

"Yes—well, no. Not everyone. Just a few..."

"Who?" I wasn't about to let him off the hook, no matter how much the guy squirmed.

"Look," he said, turning to me and raising a hand as if to stave off a blow. "What you guys are doing, it's nothing to do with me."

"Nothing to do with you?"

"I get it, I've heard the speeches—it's for the good of humanity."

This was too much. "Speeches?" I parroted. "They're speeches now?"

Lam flailed. "Your... you know, your updates—talks. I get what you're trying to do."

My hackles were up now. "But you don't approve?"

Lam looked like he wanted to run from the room. What had I stumbled upon here? "Do we have to get into this now?"

I leant forward again. "Lam, one of our subjects has been killed, brutally murdered. This is *exactly* the time to get into this."

Lam's mouth opened and shut like a fish. He pointed at the screen showing Samuel's empty room. "You don't think *I* had anything to do with that?"

"I don't know, Lam. Let's think about it." I started ticking off points on my fingers. "The computers records have been wiped, the DVDs have gone missing."

Lam clasped his head between his palms in disbelief. "This can't be happening."

"No one can get into the system."

He looked up in dismay. "Not even me."

"So you say. How do I know you're using the right password?"

"This is nuts."

"Says the man who calls our patients—what was it? Freaks?"

Lam stood, pacing back and forth. Behind him, Olive took a step forward as if worried he was about to lunge at me.

"It's just a name, okay, just a name."

"You should know better," Olive snapped.

"I didn't mean anything by it. People call them plenty of things. It doesn't mean anything."

"Then why don't *we* try a few names?" Olive pitched in

again, with more venom than I had ever heard. "What about 'geek'? 'Nerd'? *'Chink'?*"

I stood up, sending my chair spinning away. "That's enough," I said, shocked at her behaviour. No matter what Lam had said, there was no need for that kind of talk, not in my base. She sank back to the door, eyes down, her cheeks flushed.

I turned back to Lam.

"I'm sorry—" I began, but the technician interrupted me.

"No, I am," he said, rubbing his chin with a shaking hand. "I shouldn't have said that. Look, I may not be entirely... comfortable with what we're doing here, but he didn't deserve that. I like the kids, and what happened to Sam..."—he glanced up at the empty monitor again—"it was horrible. I'm just... I just trying to figure out what happened, that's all."

Or trying to cover your back.

The thought came from nowhere. At first I thought Olive had said it, but my assistant remained tight-lipped, glowering at the technician's back.

"Okay," I said, trying to calm the situation. "Okay. Can you compile a report?"

Lam looked puzzled. "A report?"

"Everything that's happened, step by step. It might help... make sense of this."

While keeping you nice and busy, fat boy.

I frowned. What was wrong with me? Was it time for more meds already? My mouth was dry, my throat raw. I licked my lips. It was just the pressure of the day, everything that had happened. I knew that Olive had shifted her gaze to me now, assessing my condition, my risk. I concentrated on Lam.

Hold it together, girl, my mother said in my ear. *You can do this. I know you can.*

An electronic buzz made all of us jump, the walkie-talkie at my hip crackling.

"Dr Tomas?"

I blew out in shock, snatching the handset from its belt-clip. "Yes, chief?"

"Where are you?"

"In the hub."

"The hub?"

"I'll explain later. Is everything all right."

"*Stay there*," Moore ordered. "*I'm on my way.*"

I exchanged a worried look with Olive. "To the hub."

"*I need to check the cameras.*"

"Why?"

"*I'm not sure. I think I saw something. Outside.*"

CHAPTER TEN
KILL

THE SILENCE IN the tunnel was stifling as we waited for Fenton to descend. He got to the bottom rung and jumped the remaining metre to the floor, his boots splashing in the shallow puddles at the bottom of the shaft.

I shone my torch in the direction of the base, picking out crumbling concrete walls.

"Is this place safe?" asked Beck.

"It was built to last," I said, even as the light found cracks in the ceiling, roots hanging down.

The passage was about two metres from side to side, just about wide enough to drive a jeep down without removing too much of the paintwork. The floor seemed smooth enough, save for a scattering of debris from the damaged roof, which thankfully didn't look too substantial.

"Aren't there any lights?" Fenton moaned.

"Not this far out. There's security doors that way," I said, waving ahead. "Things get more civilised when we're past them."

Brennan shone her own light into the gloom. "And how easy will that be?"

"Well, they open from the other side..."

"Of course they do," groaned Fenton.

"Then it's a good job you're here to help Curtis with the battering ram, isn't it?" pointed out Brennan.

Fenton sneered and spat on the floor, while behind him, Curtis looked like he'd bitten into a shit sandwich.

Evidently deciding that the conversation was at an end, Brennan took the lead, marching into the darkness. "Let's go."

I fell in beside her, the lights of the other's torches bobbing behind us.

"Are there cameras?" she asked.

"I doubt it, not this side of the security doors."

"'Doubt it'? I thought you knew this place?"

"I performed a security review nearly two decades ago. A lot's happened between now and then."

"So, this is what you do now? Travel the country, offering your services?"

"I get around."

"I bet you do. But why?"

"I told you."

"Because you need drugs."

"That's right."

"To numb what exactly?"

This was getting uncomfortable. It was time to deflect the spotlight.

"What about you? Why do all this?"

"All what?"

"Playing general."

"I'm not playing."

"Sorry. I didn't mean it like that. But how—"

"How did I end up with this lot?"

"She got lucky," Fenton piped up, behind us.

"Or I was very bad in a previous life," Brennan shot back.

Fenton laughed with something that almost resembled camaraderie.

"There's nothing much to tell. I was a kid when the world went to crap. Joined a gang to survive life on the streets, and soon learnt to use my fists to survive."

"Until you'd beaten everyone else into submission?"

"For a man who doesn't like talking about himself, you sure ask a lot of questions."

That shut me up. I laughed it off. I liked this woman. She was quick and smart, and told it like it was. It made what I was trying to do easier.

Get your contact on side, soldier. Feign interest, ask questions. Get them talking about themselves. Never fails.

Except when it does.

We marched on, our boots scraping on the concrete, until the doors appeared in the torchlight.

I felt my mouth go dry.

I must have slowed up, Brennan immediately picking up on my subconscious hesitation.

"What's wrong?"

"They've redecorated," I replied, raising my hand to stop the group.

"What do you mean?" Beck asked, coming to a halt.

"There used to be double doors here."

We all looked ahead. A solid metal plate barred our way.

"They upgraded their security," Brennan said.

Fenton wasn't so subtle. "I knew it! I fucking *knew* it!"

"Knew what?" Beck snapped.

"This is what happens when you trust jokers like him."

I didn't respond to the insult. I didn't have to.

"Stow it, Fenton," Brennan ordered. "You're not helping."

"And he is? Standing there gawping at the fucking door? What are we going to do? Use this?" He slapped the battering ram on Curtis's back, drawing a glare from the giant.

"It would have taken down the old doors, no problem," I admitted. "This... well, I guess we'll have to improvise."

Fenton wasn't giving up the argument. "Improvise? What are you going to do, knock on the door and hope one of the little piggies let you in?"

"Enough," Brennan bellowed, her voice echoing down the corridor.

"Quiet," I hissed, raising a hand. "We need to keep our voices down."

Fenton scoffed. "Worried they're going to hear us?"

"Not yet," I replied, turning and marching towards the bloody door. "But they will in a minute."

Brennan took after me, rushing to catch up. "What are you thinking?"

I reached the door and rapped lightly on the metal.

Little pig, little pig, let me come in.

It was solid, too solid. Resting my hand on the cool metal, I looked up, running a beam of light around the edges.

"It must slide down," I muttered, mostly to myself. "There isn't room for it to swing open, not if they want to drive vehicles through, so it has to come down from the ceiling, on hydraulics."

"So, what? We blast our way through?"

"And bring the roof down on our heads?" Fenton spluttered.

I crouched down and slapped my palm on the concrete floor. "It wouldn't work anyway. These things are built to withstand most explosions..."

"But..."

I swung the pack from my shoulder, unzipping the main compartment. "What time is it?"

Beck shone her light over her wristwatch. "Six forty-nine."

"We haven't got long." I started unpacking what was left of my plastic explosives.

"I thought you said explosives wouldn't work?" Fenton pointed out. I briefly fought the urge to stuff the C-4 down his stupid whining throat.

"Not against the door," I replied. "Now shut the fuck up and let me get to work."

CHAPTER ELEVEN
CURE

MOORE GROWLED AT Lam as he stalked into the Ops rooms. "What are you doing here?"

I raised a hand. "He was trying to access the computers. The system's in lockdown."

"It's what?"

"We're shut out," Lam told him. "None of the passwords work."

"What about the cameras?" the chief said, barging the technician out of the way to get to the security controls.

"They're on a different system. Everything else seems up and running."

"But for how long?" Moore asked, pulling Lam's chair towards him and sitting down. He jabbed at the CCTV control console, cycling through the feeds, the grainy images switching from one camera to another on the screens.

"What are you doing?"

Moore peered up at the central screen. "I've established patrols around the perimeter."

"Patrols? Chief, I said two guards, max—everyone else is supposed to be confined to quarters." Couldn't anyone follow a simple order today?

The chief glared at me. "And you'd rather we were left unprotected?"

How many times would I have this argument today? "Until we find out—"

"The medical staff are contained, as are technical support"— the security chief scowled at Lam—"at least, most of them are. I've only got a few men out, a handful; the ones I can trust."

"Can we trust *anyone*?" Olive asked by the door. I raised a single finger to silence her. Not a fight worth having.

"So, what are we looking at?" I asked.

Moore manipulated a joystick, the image on the screen zooming in to focus on a section of fencing illuminated by floodlight.

"The east perimeter. Team Three called it in."

"Called in what exactly?"

"Movement, beyond the fences. In the bushes."

The picture continued to zoom in. There was nothing there, save for blurry, pixelated images of overgrown shrubs.

"Isn't that where we were attacked this morning?" Lam asked.

Moore nodded, sitting back in the seat. "Yes. I wouldn't have expected them to come back for more, not so soon."

"Could it have been an animal?" I asked. "A dog, or something?"

"My men know the difference between a dog and a human being."

Still the screen showed nothing.

"Well, if there was anyone there, they've gone now," Olive added unhelpfully.

Moore snatched the walkie-talkie from his belt and opened a channel. "Control to Team Three. Come in."

"Team Three responding, chief."

"I'm in Ops. There's nothing on the camera." He flicked along a line of buttons, scrolling through corresponding feeds. "On any of them."

On screen, we saw three guards cautiously approaching the

wire mesh, torches mounted on their rifles. Circles of lights swept across the no-man's land between the two fences.

"Are you sure that's a good idea?" I asked.

"They know what they're doing," Moore insisted, before bringing the walkie-talkie back to his mouth again. "Well?"

"*There's nothing, sir,*" came the distorted reply, the lead guard raising his own handset on screen. "*It might have been kids, mucking about?*"

"Remind me of the last time we saw kids?" Moore's eyes flicked up to the top row of screen. "Outside the perimeter, I mean."

"*There was definitely something there, chief, but it's gone now.*"

The three men stood their ground, swinging their gun-lights along the perimeter.

My stomach was in knots. This was like those old movies we used to watch before horror became an everyday occurrence, the hero creeping into an empty house, the soundtrack dropping away to nothing; no music, no dialogue, just the poor hapless bastard inching forward. You were yelling at the screen, knowing what was coming. *Get the hell out of there! What are you doing? Haven't you seen these films before?* And then the monster would strike.

My nails stabbed into the palms of my hands.

Moore had seen enough. "Okay, pull back. There's nothing there. Continue your patrol."

"*Roger that, Control. Three out.*"

I relaxed, placing my stinging palms on my hips.

"I'm not sure how much more of today I can take."

Moore swung around to me. "It was better to make sure. If there had been something out—"

A rumble reverberated through the building.

Above me, the lights flickered, a siren sounding in the corridor outside. "What the hell?"

"Was that an explosion?" Olive yelped.

On screen, Team Three whirled around to face the direction of the blast, their backs to the fence. There were flashes of light in the darkness, and the guards hit the ground hard.

"Jesus!" Moore's walkie-talkie was back to his lips. "Team Three, come in! Team Three!"

They weren't moving, shadows appearing in the bushes beyond the perimeter, men and women, guns in hand.

"Definitely not dogs," Lam stammered, as the would-be invaders started climbing the fence.

Calls were coming in from all over the complex.

"Control, explosion at the main gates. Guards down."

"Chief, intruders scaling the north perimeter."

"Fire near Neighbourhood Three." The sound of breaking glass came through the tinny speaker. *"God, they're throwing petrol bombs."*

On the screens, all hell was breaking loose. One of the front gates hanging askew. Liquid fire rippling out from smashed bottles, bushes and shrubs already ablaze. One of Team Three was trying to crawl away, dragging a ruined leg. Behind him a girl had made it over the first line of defence. She raised her gun and dispatched the guard with a single shot. His body jerked and lay still.

Moore yelled into his handset. "All teams, stand your ground." He was up out of the seat, charging towards the door.

"Where are you going?" I called after him.

He stopped at the doorway. "I need to get out there."

"But what about Control? Surely you need to co-ordinate—"

"You're here, aren't you?" he replied, before disappearing out of the room.

I sank down into the seat he had surrendered, staring up at the screens, not really knowing what to do next

Flames spread.

The murderers at the east perimeter scaled the interior fence.

Get the hell out of there! What are you doing? Haven't you seen these films before?

They were coming from all angles at once. So many. So fast.

"The chief was right," I said, as Lam audibly whimpered by my side. "They were testing our defences, preparing for a full onslaught."

"Why don't you call him up and congratulate him?" Olive suggested, but before I could yell at her to get out, Moore's voice crackled over an open channel.

"All guards to positions. Code nine, I repeat, this is a code nine."

"There he is," shouted Olive, pointing at a screen to the right. Moore burst out of a door, gun in hand, running towards the east perimeter.

I pulled the walkie-talkie from my belt. "Chief, what the hell do you think you're doing? I need you back here."

He ignored me, running off-camera on one screen to appear on the next, ducking behind a barricade. He never made it. One minute he was running, the next he was spinning on the spot as something hit his shoulder, dropping him to the ground.

"Moore!"

A boy dashed into shot, a teenager, wearing a leather jacket and jeans. He ran behind the barricade, pointed down at the floor and fired once, twice.

"Oh, God," burbled Lam. "Oh, God; oh, God."

I switched channels, addressing anyone who could hear. "All guards, this is Doctor Tomas. Fall back. Secure the Neighbourhoods."

The first raiders made it safely over the gate.

A guard's voice cut through the channel. "*Ma'am, are you sur—*"

"That's an order. Fall back. Now!"

"Have you lost your mind?" Olive squawked, gaping at the screens. "You need to take the fight to them."

"No, we have to secure the children."

The raiders were on every screen, swarming over the fences, through the gates. There were even inflatable dinghies crossing the moat, paddles strafing through the water.

I stood up, making a decision. "Lam, you're in charge."

The technician's eyes stretched wider than ever, and he shook his head frantically. "No. I can't."

I slammed my walkie-talkie down in front of him. "Use this. Just make sure everyone gets inside, and seal the buildings. We can use the tunnels."

I ran for the door.

"Where are you going?" Olive called after me.

I was out of the room before I answered, "To get the kids."

CHAPTER TWELVE
KILL

"Right on cue," I said as a distant siren sounded. "I have to say, Brennan; your guys are punctual, if nothing else."

"'If nothing else'?" Fenton said. "I'd like to hear you say that to them up close."

"Wouldn't be a fair fight," I said, reaching out to Garret. "The poor sods wouldn't know what hit them."

Garret almost cracked a smile as he handed over his axe. I weighed the weapon in my hands, noticing the notches and stains on the blade. It had seen a lot of action, and hadn't been cleaned as often as it should. I didn't want to ask too many questions.

I bent down, running my fingers across the concrete in front of the door, finding a hairline crack. That would have to do. I put my torch down on the floor, so its beam shone across the imperfection, and rose to my feet.

"You'd better stand back."

Raising the axe above my head, I brought the blade down onto the crack. The impact shot up my arms, the metal *clank*ing dully against the floor. I crouched, running my hand over where I had struck. The concrete had chipped; not excessively, but I knew it would work.

Brennan and the rest watched as I set to work, slamming the axe into the floor, grunting with the exertion.

Once.

Twice.

Each strike like a thunderclap in the tunnel.

Four.

Five.

Chips flew from the widening crack like shrapnel, bouncing against my legs.

Seven.

Eight.

I began to lose count.

Fifteen?

Sixteen?

I had no idea any more. My arms felt like lead, my elbows stiff.

I stopped on what felt like the hundredth blow, breathing hard, sweat running down my nose.

"Do you need any help?" It was Beck, hovering behind me.

"It's fine," I huffed, punctuating my words with further blows. On the final strike, the blade slipped and I dropped the axe, dancing out of the way before it could take a chunk out of my leg.

"You sure about about?" Fenton asked.

Trying to control my breathing, I knelt down, exploring the shallow crevice I had opened. It wasn't great, but would have to do.

I stood, handing the axe back to Garret, who ran a thumb against the blunted blade.

"Don't worry," I panted, running the back of my hand across my mouth. "It'll still cleave heads, or whatever you have planned."

Rubbing my shoulder, I walked over to the backpack I had leant up against the tunnel wall and carefully lifted out a rectangular block wrapped in tight, green plastic. As the others watched, I peeled the wrapping away to reveal a milky-white block that looked for all the world like modelling clay.

I wouldn't advise anyone to throw pots with this stuff.

Kneeling, I pushed as much of the explosive as I could into the crack. When I was a kid, the war novels I read always insisted that C-4 smelled of almonds. That was crap. If anything, the stuff reeked of tar or pitch, but I wasn't about to stick it under my nose.

Without looking up, I raised an expectant hand. Beck stepped forward, handing me the reel of detonator cord and blasting cap I had given to her for safe keeping.

I zipped my backpack shut and passed it to the tall woman. "Take this, will you?"

"Your wish is my command, *sir*."

I smiled, pressing the blast cap into the explosive. "Careful. I could grow to like that."

"In your dreams," came the gruff reply.

"Just shut up and let him work," Brennan said, peering over from what she presumably hoped was a safe distance. She was an intelligent and resourceful woman, but obviously didn't have much experience with half-a-kilo of C-4. By the sound of the muffled thunder high above our heads, the rest of my stash was being put to good use.

I connected the detonator cord to the cap and retreated along the corridor, unreeling the spindle. I went slowly, carefully; the last thing I wanted to do was slip and end up on my backside. We walked all the way back to the shaft and beyond, the cord trailing between us and the blast door, the sounds of gunfire drifted down the shaft as we passed beneath the grille. I wondered who was winning.

I stopped when the cable ran out.

"Is this far enough?" Brennan said, looking over her shoulder; we were rapidly running out of passageway, a set of heavy double doors blocking our way.

"It'll have to do," I said, fishing in my jacket pocket for the detonator itself. "That's got to be around sixty feet. I'd rather have more, but you play with what you're dealt."

"Sixty feet?" repeated Fenton. "What's that in English?" Jesus. He must have been younger than he looked.

"Nearly twenty metres," Beck translated, holding her torch up for me so I could attach the detonator. It occurred to me that I had left my own flashlight by the doors. I could wave goodbye to that, then, unless Fenton wanted to go back and fetch it. No-one would blame me if I pressed the detonator at just the wrong moment, would they?

Stay focused, soldier. You've a job to do.

Sir, yes, sir, etc.

I slipped the empty reel into my pocket. "Okay, is everyone ready?"

"No," muttered Fenton.

"Do it!" ordered Brennan.

"Cover your ears," I said. Not waiting to see if anyone followed my advice, I pressed down on the detonator.

The explosion was amplified in the confined space, painfully so. Light flared white in the darkness as a wall of sound and air rushed towards us, bringing with it dust and the acrid tang of atomised concrete. I held my breath, listening for the near-inevitable roar of the tunnel collapsing in on itself, but there was nothing, save for the patter of loose debris dropping to the floor.

"Can I have your torch?" I asked Fenton, holding out my hand.

"Fuck you."

"Here, have mine," Brennan said, handing over her flashlight.

Tentatively at first, we walked back towards the door, speeding up as it became clear that the ceiling wasn't about to drop on our head yet. I covered my mouth, trying not to choke on the dust that hung heavily in the air.

The torchlight cut through the smoke, revealing the blackened, but resolutely solid blast door.

"Nothing," Fenton groaned. "Not even a scratch."

"I told you—I wasn't trying to blow up the door." I lowered the torch, revealed the hole that had appeared beneath the barrier.

It wasn't as deep as I'd hoped, but it would do for now.

Fenton stared at the newly-excavated but worryingly shallow pit, the penny finally dropping. "You expect us to crawl through there?"

"Under the door, yeah. I'm not saying it won't be tight, especially for the bulkier members of the group." I shot an apologetic look to Curtis, to find him already swinging the battering ram from off his back.

"Don't worry, Fenton," said Beck, also removing her pack. "A scrawny streak of piss like you will have no trouble."

I smiled, turning to Brennan. "Ladies first?"

"Age before beauty, I think," the Irish woman responded.

I'VE MADE MORE dignified entrances. The explosion had cleared just enough space beneath the door, although it was tighter than Garret and Curtis would have wanted. I lay on my back and wriggled beneath the thick metal. My jacket repeatedly caught on jagged shards of broken concrete, and for a horrible moment I imagined the door dropping inexplicably halfway through, slicing me clean in two.

Keep your head, soldier. You've been in tighter spots than this.

Sir, yes, sir. Very funny, sir.

Less concrete had been disintegrated on the other side, but there was enough room to manoeuvre, pulling myself up into pitch darkness.

I reached inside my now-torn jacket to recover Brennan's torch.

"What do you see?" she called through the gap as I tentatively crossed over to the wall and flicked the lightswitch I'd discovered. The fluorescent strips above my head blazed into humming life, chasing the shadows away with a sterile white glow. The walls on this side of the blast door were covered in smooth plaster, dusty cobwebs draping the white paint. The tunnel hadn't been used for years.

I wondered if the same could be said about the CCTV high on the wall, pointing in the other direction.

The fact that it hadn't swivelled around to face me was encouraging. Hopefully whoever was sitting in the control booth was too busy with the mayhem on the surface to care about what was happening down here, but there was no point taking chance. I pulled my P99 from its holster and dispatched the camera with two shots that somehow seemed as loud as the explosion.

"What the hell was that?" Brennan yelled.

"Don't worry," I called back. "It's all clear. Garret, can I have the axe?"

I used the handle to knock lumps of loose concrete clear on my side of the hole to make it easier for the others.

"Okay," I said, leaning the axe against the door. "Start passing things through."

Bags and weapons were slipped beneath the door, which I piled to the side, before the rest of the party began to push themselves through. Brennan was first, as lithe as she was steely. Then came Fenton, and I had to resist the urge to accidentally kick his perpetually whining head as it appeared beneath the door.

As predicted, crawling through the hole proved more difficult for Beck, and almost impossible for Garret and Curtis. The latter looked as though he was stuck as he attempted to squirm through, and I finally heard our resident goliath stringing more than two words together, although most only had four letters. All looked lost, until he twisted abruptly, dislocating his shoulder with a *crack*.

"Oh, Christ. That's disgusting," gagged Fenton, but Curtis didn't even grunt, pulling his now-displaced arm through the gap. Garret reached down to help his partner up and Curtis nodded, giving permission for what was about to happen. With a sickening crunch, Garret pushed Curtis's shoulder back into place. Everyone winced, but it was clear this was a trick they had performed before. All the time, Curtis barely uttered a sound, although the colour drained from his face, only returning as he rolled his aching shoulder in its socket.

"What now?" asked Brennan, as we recovered our various loads.

"Now you follow me," I said jogging ahead to a T-junction. I paused, mentally placing the buildings I'd seen earlier.

Left. It had to be.

"This way."

"Are you sure?" Fenton asked, sounding even less confident in my abilities than usual.

I didn't answer. Now we were inside, I wasn't sure about *any* of this anymore.

CHAPTER THIRTEEN
CURE

"*Doctor Tomas, come in.*"

"Don't answer it," said Olive, running beside me, still clutching that bloody clipboard.

"Don't be stupid, I have to."

I thumbed the button on the handset. "Go on, Lam."

"*Neighbourhoods Three and Four are secure, but we've lost contact with Team Two.*"

"Where?"

"*Neighbourhood One,*" came the squeak of the reply. Lam was in One.

"Do you have a weapon?"

"Only his breath," muttered Olive.

"Shut up!"

"*What was that?*"

"I said, do you have a weapon?"

"*What do you think?*"

"Lock yourself in. What do the cameras show?"

"*Only that they're everywhere. The front gate is down, and they're all over the perimeter.*"

"And the children?"

Lam drew a breath and expelled it loudly. "*All tucked up safe and sound, although a couple are looking... agitated.*"

I turned a corner at speed, almost going over on my ankle. "Who?"

He paused, and I pictured him reading the labels on the screen. "*Er, Davie and Michele.*"

"Davie?"

"David. Whatever."

Still, that was interesting. David was another of the more taciturn subjects in the experiment.

"Always working, doctor," commented Olive. "You just can't help yourself."

"I'm almost with them," I told Lam, ignoring her. "I'm going to get the children down into Bunker Three. Team One are meeting me at the dorms."

On the other end of the channel, Lam gave a cry of alarm.

"What was that?"

"*I heard something,*" he whispered, holding the mic close to his mouth, the sound distorted. "*Someone's outside.*"

"Shut the door. Barricade yourself in, with anything you can. I need you there. Do you understand?"

There was no response.

"Lam?"

The walkie-talkie crackled. "*Yes, I'm here. I was just shutting the door. Going to see if I can pull the bookcase in front of—*"

"Excellent," I said, cutting him off. "Tomas out."

We continued down the corridor, Olive matching me step by step. "I thought he'd never shut up. It would serve him right if he gets a bullet in the brain!"

"How can you say that?"

"You've seen the way he looks at us, looks at you. He's probably watching us now, on those little screens, hunched over, jerk—"

"Olive!" I said, stopping in shock. "What is wrong with you?"

She stared back at me with wide eyes, her cheeks flushed,

breathing hard. "You know he is, dirty little pervert. Fuck him."

Oh, God, she'd cracked. I *knew* she would. So prim, so proper, so many neuroses squirming beneath the perfect facade.

"That's enough, Olive. You need to go back to your quarters, right now."

She took a step closer. Too close. "We can't. We need to save the children. They're all that's important. They're the future."

I stepped back, putting space between us. "That's what I'm going to do, but I can't look after both them and you. Do you understand?"

If she did, she showed no outward sign. She was hugging her clipboard to herself, the papers crumpling against her chest. Sweat was beading on her forehead, running down her throat as she tapped her foot in agitation. "No, I can help you. That's what we do. You and me, together."

She was getting hysterical. I considered slapping her across her face—it was either that or landing a punch to her jaw.

Unless...

"You want to help?"

She nodded eagerly. "The children, yes. We need to help the children."

"Go to my office, get all the files. I'll need them in the bunker. Can you do that?"

She stared at me as if I was mad. "Of *course* I can. You couldn't find a *thing* without me." She frowned. "But what about you? Will you be okay?"

"I'll be fine, I promise. Now, go. And hurry."

"Yes," she said, spinning on her heel and tottering off, pausing only to remove her stilettos. "I'll be right back. You can rely on me."

And she was off, racing around the corner as if all our lives depended on it.

Poor bitch.

I wondered if I'd see her again, and stopped myself asking if it would be such a bad thing if I didn't.

I had to hurry. The sirens were still wailing, the shots still sounding outside. The children must be terrified.

I sprinted towards the Dorms, turning the corner to crash headfirst into someone racing the other way. They screamed, pushing away from me, before realising who I was.

"Jas," Allison cried out, flinging her arms around me. "Oh, thank God. I thought you were... I don't know *what* I thought you were. But you're okay."

I pulled out of the embrace. "I'm fine. Things aren't good. Moore's dead."

"Dead? Are you sure?"

"And I've no idea how many guards are left. We need to get the children down to Bunker Three. Once they're safe, I'll send word to the Cabal."

Allison nodded, gathering herself. "Right, okay. Bets is checking on the wards. I know you said everyone had to stay in their quarters, but—"

"Things have moved on, I know."

"Where are the others?"

"Still back in N-2, I think. The doors have sealed."

I couldn't remember if Lam had said Neighbourhood Two was secure. They'd have to look after themselves.

Allison led me back the way she'd come. "The children are confused, to say the least. It's not exactly surprising, they haven't a hope of understanding all this."

Her tone annoyed me. "They're not stupid, Allison."

"No, but they're not exactly normal, either."

I stopped short, Allison taking a few steps before she realised I wasn't following.

"What's that supposed to mean?"

"What's what—?"

"*Not exactly normal.*"

"Really? You want to do this now?"

"It's bad enough that I have to listen to this crap from Lam, but from you?"

Allison grabbed my arm, pulling me on. "I didn't mean it like that, you know I didn't. It's just been a hell of a day, that's all. What did Lam say?"

She wasn't getting off that easily. "If you've got something to say, Allison, now would be a good time."

She blew out in exasperation, raising both her hands to the

heavens. "There's nothing, honestly. I'm just worried about them, that's all. Jesus."

"You don't approve of what we're doing? All this time and you've never thought to mention it before?"

"Seriously, Jas—not now. Trust me, we can debate ethics until we're blue in the face once we're locked up in that bunker."

And then what? She'd tell me what she really thought? I fell silent as we dashed towards the dorms. I couldn't believe this, not of Allison. I thought she understood what we were doing. I thought she was on my side. All the time we had been working together, all those dark moments when I felt so alone, so wretched, she had been there for me, my right hand, my rock.

And now this? How long had she had doubts? How long had she been lying to my face?

We turned and entered the dorm block to find three guards waiting for us in full riot gear, rifles in hand.

"Doctor Tomas," the first said.

I frowned at him. "Eckstein?"

He raised a hand. "Before you say anything, I know—I should be resting, but—"

I nodded. How could any of us rest at a time like this? "Your side?"

"Holding together," he said as my eyes dropped to where he'd taken a bullet just this morning. The man was as pale as a sheet, his accented voice thicker than usual. "Just. Ma'am, Chief Moore is—"

"I know." I looked at the other two men, reading the names on their uniforms: Wright and Stones. "Any more of you in the building?"

"Decker, Southern and Krause. They're patrolling the ground floor."

"Is that all?"

"Why do you think I'm up and about? But the doors are secure. No one's getting in."

"Not yet," said Allison, behind me.

"That's not helpful, Allison," I spat, walking Eckstein to the first dorm before she could offer an apology.

"Have you ever been in here, er...?" I realised I didn't know the German's first name.

"Stefan," he supplied, trying to hide the fact that he'd had to lean on the door post as we entered the observation room. "Only once, on a tour of the building."

He looked through the observation glass, seeing a girl sitting on her bed, knees tight against her chest, rocking gently back and forth.

"This is Dawn. I have to warn you; this might be difficult. The children often struggle with emotional situations. They... shut themselves off."

"Like a defence mechanism?"

"Maybe. We don't understand yet, but they have trouble expressing how they're feeling and have a habit of taking things literally, so let me and Dr Harwood do the talking, okay? We'll gather them together and take them down into the bunker."

"Understood."

That was more like it. Someone who was used to obeying orders without question. Why couldn't more people be like Stefan Eckstein?

I called back into the corridor. "Allison, you take the left hand side, starting with Adam."

"Sure," she said, making for the first observation suite. Just like that. One word and she was gone. But what was going on inside that head? What was she thinking?

I couldn't worry about that now. I slipped my ID across the card reader, waiting for the light to flash green. Then it was time to fix a calming smile on my face and get to work. I pulled the door open and entered the room.

"Dawn, hi. It's Dr Tomas. We need to go on a little adventure."

CHAPTER FOURTEEN
KILL

Getting into the building itself was easy, especially when you had a Curtis and a big hammer. Curtis and Garret grabbed hold of the battering ram's handles and took out an internal door in three bone-shattering blows.

We were through the door and up the flight of stairs in seconds, guns in hand and ready to meet resistance.

None had come by the time we reached the ground floor. Sirens blared, lights flashed, but no guns fired. Hopefully that meant that the plan had worked, and the guards were occupied holding back the frontal assault, too busy to even notice we were here.

I opened the door and poked my head into an empty corridor. This was it, Neighbourhood One. If I remembered correctly, and I hoped to God that I did, the Ops centre would be here, the security hub for the entire base. Even if Brennan's gang had breached the perimeter defences, they had little hope of breaking into the buildings if they were locked down. Every door was steel-lined, every window bullet proof, but the hub could open everything from the inside with a flick of a switch.

"This way," I said, leading our little band along the corridor. The hub was near the main entrance, not far away—I hoped.

Reaching the end of the passage, we slowed, peering around the corner. No one there. Good. I beckoned the rest on, thankful that even Fenton seemed to be keeping his mouth shut for once. For all we knew we were alone in the building, but there was no point taking chances.

Another corner, another corridor. Nearly there. It was just around this bend and—

I slid to a halt, darting back around the corner I'd been about to take. Brennan stopped short, mouthing a silent *What?*

Guards, I mouthed back, raising two fingers.

Had they spotted me?

They couldn't have. There were no footsteps, no shouts.

I looked around the corner again, staying close to the wall. They were standing with their backs to me, beside what should be Ops. Two guards a-guarding—and they didn't stand a chance.

I stepped back, Brennan indicating for Garret to take position. Garret nodded, flattening his back against the wall, rifle up and primed. Then he swung himself around, and sprayed the corridor. There was a cry and Garret pulled back, at least one of the guards returning fire, the plaster on the corner of the wall beside Garret disintegrating.

"One went down," Garret hissed, the most I'd heard him say. "I know he did."

The bullets stopped, our assailant waiting for us to make a move. Garret swung around again, squeezing his trigger.

"He's in the doorway," he reported, ducking as the guard retaliated.

"The other?" I asked.

"Out of the game."

"Move in," Brennan ordered and Garret twisted into the corner, his gun barking. There was a cry and Garret disappeared from sight. Curtis was straight after him, gun raised, and after checking around the corner, Brennan indicated for us to follow.

The first guard was on the floor, a ragged hole in the side of his neck. The second was slouched on the floor, clutching a wound in his shoulder, blood pumping between his gloved fingers.

Fenton took one look at the stricken guard, and put him down.

"What did you do that for?" I snarled. "He could have told us how many men they have left."

Fenton shrugged. "There's one less now."

"Next time you wait for the order," Brennan berated him as I looked around. Yeah, this was the place, and that was the Ops centre. I crossed to the door, flattening myself against the wood. P99 in one hand, I wrapped my fingers around the door handle. It turned, but was locked.

There was a cry from inside. Short, but distinct, as if someone had clapped a hand over their own mouth to shut themselves up. Brennan motioned for Curtis to bring the battering ram over and the man mountain obliged, hefting the heavy cylinder by himself. This lock offered little in the way of resistance, shattering on first impact, but the door smacked into something. They'd barricaded themselves in. Curtis dropped the battering ram to the side, putting his not insubstantial shoulder to the door. There was a scrape of wood against the floor and the door opened a fraction, enough for Curtis to get his hand into the gap to press against the wall.

Big mistake. Something clanged hard on the back of his hand, and Curtis roared in pain. He yanked his hand back, as Beck raised her gun and fired calmly into the door itself, the wood splintering.

There was a whimper from inside and Beck took her foot to the door. It shifted more and she was in, her gun sweeping up.

I didn't wait for Brennan to give me permission to squeeze through the gap. On the other side of the door, a Chinese guy cowered beneath a desk. He was shaking where he sat, nostrils flaring, a fire-extinguisher grasped to him like a shield.

"Get out of there," I ordered, keeping him firmly within my sights as the others followed me in, Garrett shoving the bookcase barricade out of the way.

"D-don't shoot," the kid stammered, crawling out from his hiding place, still clinging to the fire-extinguisher like a safety blanket.

"Don't give us a reason to," Brennan told him, looking around the messy room. "What's your name?"

"Lam."

"Okay, Lam. How many people have you got here? And I'd put that down, by the way."

Reluctantly, Lam did as he was told, although his eyes flicked to Curtis, who was massaging his bruised hand.

"Fifty-eight," came the reply. "Well, there was, before..." He glanced at the screens, many of which showed dead and injured guards slumped on the floor.

"Fifty-eight?" Fenton echoed. "All this for fifty-eight people?"

"What do you do here?" Beck demanded.

Lam shrugged. "Research."

Beck's grip on her gun tightened. "What kind of research?"

"Medical research," Lam babbled. "Experiments. I don't know much about them. I'm only the technician."

All this time, I had been checking the cameras. The wall was a mass of screens, all showing feeds from around the complex, except for the top row, which were all blank. One of them had a scrap of masking tape beneath it, half pulled off. I reached up and yanked it away. It read *Katy*. Curious.

"Well?" said Brennan, joining me at the console.

"Your people are in the grounds," I reported, working the controls to cycle through the external cameras. "Although the buildings are still secure."

"Not now we're here," said Fenton, smirking.

I turned to Lam and pointed at the blank screens. "What should those show?"

"Nothing. We don't use them." The reply had come too quickly.

"Is that right?" I showed him the scrap of masking tape. "Who's Katy?"

He shrugged. "I don't know, man. I'm just here to push the buttons, not ask questions."

Brennan was flicking through the internal cameras.

"Wait there," I said, as she brought up images of what looked like hospital beds. "Are those... children?"

"What are these rooms?" Brennan barked, pointing at the screen.

"I told you," Lam whined. "We... well, the medical team... do research. I really don't understand what. Diseases and stuff."

That was worrying.

"What kind of diseases?" Beck asked. I was interested to know myself.

"I don't know. Viruses. DNA."

"And those kids?" I said.

He looked even more uncomfortable. "They're the test subjects."

Even Fenton was incredulous. "Test subjects? Like guinea pigs? Shit, what have you guys been doing here?"

Lam started to stammer a reply. "I-I—"

"You don't know," interrupted Brennan. "We get it, but you must know how to work all this. You're the technician. You press buttons."

"Y-yeah, I guess."

"Then show me how to unlock the doors."

"I can't!"

Beck hefted the gun in her hands.

"Some technician."

"No, you don't understand. There's something wrong with the computer. We can't get access to anything except the cameras."

How convenient.

"So you're useless?" Fenton sneered.

"Not yet," I cut in, tapping on the picture of the hospital. "Where is this?"

"Neighbour Three, in the east wing. That's where all the research takes place."

"And this is Neighbourhood One, right?" Brennan asked.

Lam nodded. "Support and security."

"And the rest of your people."

"Mostly in N-2, in their quarters."

Now Brennan returned her attention to me. "We can move from building to building through those tunnels?"

"That's the idea."

Brennan turned to Lam, looking at the lanyard around his neck. "Will that get us through the doors? I'd like to keep at least some of the locks intact."

Lam fingered his ID card with shaking hands. "Yeah. There's a box of them, in that cupboard," he said, pointing at a metal cabinet across the room.

"Now you're using your brains," said Brennan, crossing over to the cupboard. She opened the doors, checking the shelves, Fenton following. Lam saw his chance and ran for the door. Stupid kid. Curtis stepped in front of him and whipped the butt of the rifle across the technician's head. The kid's glasses arched across the room as he went down, slapping against the floor to stay still.

Brennan slammed the door of the cupboard. "There are no cards in here. I'm almost impressed." She walked over to Lam's prone body and roughly yanked the lanyard over his head. The kid's head cracked against the floor as she pulled it free. "I'll take this one. Garret, Curtis; check the guards for passes and then get down to the front doors. Let the others in and then search the building. Your hand okay?"

Curtis nodded, flexing his fingers. "I'll live."

"Off you go, then."

The two grunts left, leaving us with the unconscious technician.

"What about him?" asked Fenton.

Brennan picked up a plastic bag of spare lanyards from the floor. They must have tumbled from the bookcase. "Tie him up. We'll need someone to show us how everything works. Beck, you go to N-2. Same thing. Open the doors, but be careful—you'll have company, by the sounds of it."

"What do you want me to do with them?"

"Round them up, but don't stand for any nonsense. We can always give them a choice..."

Fenton looked up from where he was tying Lam's podgy wrists together. "To stay?"

"If they're scientists, they could be useful. Besides, I want to understand what they've been doing here. We need to know the place is safe."

This was my chance to join the conversation again. "We should check out that ward, in Neighbourhood Three. I'm no medic, but I might be able to see what they've been up to."

"You read my mind. I'll come with you. Fenton, you too."

Joy of joys.

"Is he secure?" Brennan asked.

Fenton stood up to admire his handiwork. The kid's wrists and ankles were bound together, the knots more impressive that I would have given old rat-face credit for. Just to lower my opinion of him again, Fenton gave Lam an unnecessary boot in the side. "He'll be fine until we get back."

"Let's do this, then."

We turned to leave, and the walkie-talkie on the desk beneath the screens crackled into life. The voice that followed caused by heart to not so much miss a beat as explode in my chest.

"*Control, this is Dr Tomas. Lam, come in.*"

CHAPTER FIFTEEN
CURE

"Lam? Lam, are you there?"

There was no answer. Did that mean that Neighbourhood One had fallen to the raiders, or that Lam had done a runner? Either was possible, but I couldn't worry about it now. All that was important was getting the kids down to the bunker.

They were huddled in the corridor between the dorms now, all wide eyes and clasped hands. I'd never had a maternal bone in my body, but my heart went out to them. How could we expect them to cope with all this? We'd had drills, of course, but they never seemed real. Of course they didn't, locked up in our base, playing games.

No one was playing now.

"Nothing?" asked Eckstein.

I shook my head. "He's not answering."

"Do you have a security monitor on this floor?"

Allison pointed down the corridor. "In the far lab, beyond the dorms. There's a side office."

"I'll check," Eckstein said, clutching his side as he limped away from us. "You get the last kid."

I bit my lip. Of all the labs, I didn't want anyone going in there. Something else I didn't have time to worry about. I turned back to the children, giving them what I hoped was an encouraging look.

"You stay here with Dr Harwood. I'll fetch Ruth."

"Yes, Dr Tomas," they chorused, as one. It was unsettling.

"We'll be okay, won't we?" Allison said to them, Dawn cuddling into her side. Of all the subjects, she had been the most scared, barely saying a word since I'd coaxed her out of her room.

I glanced through the window as I walked to Ruth's door. The girl was sitting on the edge of her bed, her back to me. I slid my card over the reader, paused, and knocked on the door.

"Come in," Ruth called out.

I opened the door and stepped inside, and Ruth looked up at me, her face a blank mask.

"This isn't a drill, is it, Dr Tomas?"

As direct as ever. "No, Ruth, it's not. I need you to come with me."

"I don't want to."

That surprised me. Ruth was the oldest, but also one of the most compliant of all the children.

"Trust me, none of us want this, but I need to make sure you're safe."

"I'm safe in my room."

Inside I was screaming, telling her to move.

"Not any more you're not, sweetheart. Please."

She frowned.

"You're never called me that before."

"Called you what?"

"Sweetheart."

I hadn't even realised I had. "We need to go, Ruth."

She nodded, stood and looked around her room, taking it all in, as if it might be the last time she stood there.

There was every possibility.

I held out my hand. "The rest are waiting."

"The other children?"

"Yes."

That made up their mind. "Then I must be brave, for them."

She took my hand and I led her out to the others. "Okay, we're all here."

Eckstein's voice echoed down the corridor. "Dr Tomas?"

Ruth's hand tightened around my own.

"It's fine," I told her. "I'll only be a minute."

"I don't want you to go."

I couldn't take her with me. There was no telling what Eckstein had discovered.

"Here, you stay with me," Allison said, holding out her own hand. "You heard Dr Tomas. She'll only be a moment. We'll all look after each other, won't we?"

More nervously than I would have expected, Ruth let go of my hand and took Allison's.

I mouthed a *thank you* and then went to find Eckstein. The guard was in the office Allison had suggested, sitting awkwardly on a chair in front of a monitor.

"How is it?" I asked.

"Not good." He flicked a switch and showed the atrium of Neighbourhood One. The doors were open and the raiders were swarming in.

I gasped. "There's so many of them."

"And that's not all."

Another switch and the picture of a tall woman marching towards the front doors of N-2, followed by a colossus carrying what looked like a battering ram on his back.

"They're everywhere," he said, cycling through the feeds.

"Here?"

"Not yet, but it's only a matter of time, see?"

Another image, the tunnels. A smaller woman came into shot now, striding confidently. Beside her was a less impressive man, rail-thin, and behind them...

It was like being hit by a sledgehammer. One minute, I was standing behind Eckstein and the next I was on the floor staring at the screen in disbelief.

"Dr Tomas?" Eckstein was out of his seat, offering his injured hand without thinking.

And all the time I couldn't take my eyes off the display.

That face, after all these years. He looked older, of course he did, probably older than his years, but there was no mistaking him. His hair had receded slightly, his frame wirier than I remembered, but his eyes... As he passed the camera, he looked up, straight into the lens. Even on the grainy screen, they were so strong. So sure.

Looking straight at me.

And then he was gone.

"Dr Tomas."

Eckstein's voice. More demanding, insistent, bringing me out of my fugue.

"Yes, yes."

"Are you all right?"

"I'm fine," I lied. "I'm sorry. I... It's all been a bit much. I'm fine."

Yes, because repeating it made it true.

He offered his hand again, but I refused, pushing myself up to sway on my feet.

It wasn't possible, not after all this time.

Eckstein was talking again, although I couldn't make out the words. I forced myself to concentrate.

"...know what we have to do."

What the hell was the man talking about?

"The endgame? Ma'am, can you hear me?"

"Yes, of course I can."

He'd found me. After all these years. When I had given up hope.

"So will you give me the authorisation?"

"Authorisation? For wha—" Then I realised what he had been saying. The endgame. A dead man's switch. The Cabal's orders were clear. When all lines of defence have failed, the base would be destroyed by explosives set into the foundations, ready to blow on the authorisation of the base commander, or whoever was left.

I shook my head. "No, not that. Not yet."

"We have to, doctor. It's standing orders."

"Not *my* orders; besides, we can't. The computer system is inoperative. There's no way of setting off the charges."

"There is, from the bunker. We get the children down there, access the secondary system and then blow these bastards to the skies."

He grabbed my shoulders now. "A signal will be sent to the Cabal."

We couldn't. *I* couldn't. Not with *him* on the base. Not after he'd found me.

"They'll send a rescue party," Eckstein continued, desperately trying to make me see. "Take us back to Germany. All your work, it'll be safe. The children will be—"

"No!"

I didn't mean to push him that hard, and certainly didn't expect for him to fall. It must have been his injury, the loss of blood. He'd been unsteady on his feet all the time.

The crack as Eckstein's head met the table would have turned my stomach if it wasn't already churning. He crashed to the floor, and moaned, rolling on his front. It was like it was happening to someone else. I watched a hand—my hand— go for the gun in Eckstein's belt. I pulled it out, grabbing the barrel to pummel the butt into the back of the German's head. I couldn't stop myself. It wasn't real. The crunch of his skull. The blood. The gun falling from my shaking hand as I staggered back.

Eckstein didn't move.

Why wasn't he moving?

Oh, God.

Oh, God. Oh, God. Oh, God.

My training kicked in. See if he's breathing. Check his pulse.

"Leave him."

I whirled around to find Olive standing in the door. Christ. Where had she come from? Had she seen what I'd done?

Her tidy ponytail had come loose, hair hanging down in front of manic eyes. Eyes I recognised; I see them every time I look in the mirror.

"Jasmine, he's dead. But no-one will know."

I retched, turning to vomit in the corner of the room, inches from Eckstein's corpse.

Olive was by my side, rubbing my back. "That's it. Let it all out. It's fine. He deserved it, you know. He probably killed Samuel. Him and Lam. Working together. You never trusted them."

Didn't I?

I wiped a thread of drool from my mouth. Jesus. My scrubs. They were splattered with blood. Eckstein's blood.

"Quick, this way. Before the others come."

Olive led me into the lab, pointing to a box of paper towels.

"Clean yourself up, as much as you can. Wash your hands."

It was like I was on autopilot, moving over to the sink, running the water.

"But the blood..."

"There's a white coat on the back of the door," she told me. "Put it on. It'll cover most of it up, until we can get you changed. There are clothes in the bunker. It's going to be all right."

"Olive, I..."

She was beside me again as I slumped over the sink. "He's here, isn't he? You saw him, on the screen."

I looked up, laughing at the ridiculousness of it all. "Did you see him too?"

"Of course I did. I'm your eyes and ears on this base. Always have been. You want to see him, don't you?"

"Yes. More than anything."

"Then sort yourself out. Head up, back straight. Get a coat and get a grip."

I laughed, covering my mouth. "Yes. Yes, you're right." I grabbed another paper towel, dabbing my eyes, wiping my lips. Turning on the cold water tap again, I stuck my mouth under the stream and took a gulp. The cold liquid set my teeth on edge, but I swilled it around my cheeks and spat it out into the sink. "What would I do without you, eh?"

Olive rolled her eyes. "I've been telling you that for years. Coat, now."

I rushed to the door, grabbing the lab coat and slipping my arms into the sleeves. It wasn't a bad fit, a little bit big, but it would do. At least most of the blood was covered up.

"Right, I'll get Allison to move the children and then go and look for him."

"Sound like a plan. But aren't you forgetting something?"

I peered at Olive, not understanding.

She let out an exasperated sigh. "The case. Don't forget the case."

CHAPTER SIXTEEN
KILL

IT HAD BEEN her; the voice I'd heard every night when I slept. I'd worried for a while that I would forget what she sounded like. I already struggled to remember what she looked like. But not now. She comes to me as soon as I heard her voice.

Smooth skin the colour of coffee; dark curly hair; wide, expressive eyes that seemed to reach all the way to her soul.

And then there was the laugh. Oh, God, that laugh. People would turn and stare when she got going—and smile. Talk about infectious. She could start a pandemic, eyes gleaming, head thrown back without a care in the world.

She exuded passion in every way possible. In her laugh, in her work, in our arguments—and where it mattered most, too. Life was for the living, as far as Jasmine was concerned, and woebetide anyone who stood in her way.

That's why, even after all this time, I knew that she had survived, even when the universe told me that it was impossible. Blood-Type AB+. Cursed. Doomed.

But I'd heard her voice, all those years ago, by complete and utter chance, over a machine in the SIS comms-room. Just four words.

"Are... are you there?"

And there it was, my reason for living. The knowledge—because that's what it was—the *certainty* that I would find her again, would hold her in my arms, would pick stupid rows and laugh at stupid jokes and just be the way the universe intended us. Together.

And yes, I know that's enough to make you reach for the sick bucket, the kind of crap that's spouted in a thousand and one rom-coms full of beautiful people with beautiful lives, but I don't care. That's how I felt, how I feel.

And I was right. I'd followed her here—or rather, followed rumour and hearsay, from one continent to another. The trail had brought me to Bristol, to this place. I'd told Brennan I wanted drugs: it's what she wanted to hear, made me less threatening. The junkie who could get them into the base, with a one-track mind, thinking of his next fix.

I guess I should have felt guilty. All those people who had died. The guards, the gang-members. But hell, they were fighting for what they wanted, for a place to belong in an increasingly batshit crazy world. For a purpose.

So was I.

For years, as I'd drifted off to sleep at the end of every day, my prayer had been the same. Who gave a shit that I didn't believe in God? It didn't mean He wouldn't hear.

Just let me hear her say my name again, one more time.

That's all I wanted—and it could happen today.

"Is this the way?" Brennan asked, striding ahead of me.

I looked up, surprised by the question. "What's that?"

"The place on the screen? Is it this way?"

What did she want me to say? "I guess so."

"You guess so? Did you hear that, Brennan? He guesses so! I thought he was supposed to be the fucking expert!"

Fenton had been bad enough before. Now, it was all I could do not to snap his raw-boned neck.

"There weren't any hospital wings when I was here before," I snapped back. "They've obviously had some work done."

"Yeah," Brennan muttered darkly. "For these 'experiments.'"

I picked up the pace, storming past Fenton. The sooner I got this over with...

"But from what I could see on the screen, it has to be on this floor. Old conference suites, the only place big enough to fit in all those beds."

There were swing doors coming up on the left. I was sure I'd been in there before, staring at boring PowerPoint presentations, counting the seconds until I could escape.

I marched up to the doors, swinging them open... and froze.

Keep moving, soldier. Whatever the world throws at you. Keep moving.

Sir, yes, sir, etc.

The conference rooms had been partitioned into curtained cubicles, each containing a bed. Most were empty, but a few contained bodies wired up to life support machines, all tubes and wires and electronic beeps.

They were all so *thin*. Emaciated. A memory surfaced, a documentary I'd watched about holocaust survivors, from the concentration camps, living skeletons. Jasmine had made me turn it off. It wasn't upsetting her. It was making her angry.

How could they do that to another human being?

But this was worse, much worse. As I walked the length of the room, I realised that all the patients were children.

Experiments.

The technician had said experiments.

Is this what he meant?

"Jesus!"

It was a woman's voice, to my right. She'd walked through a door between wards, checking notes. Young, perhaps early thirties, tall and slim, with dark skin and short curly hair. Now her folder was on the floor and she was running back the way she came.

"Stop her," Brennan yelled, and Fenton was off like a greyhound after the rabbit. He tore past me, quicker than I would have thought, and soon caught up with the woman, grabbing her shoulder. She screamed, trying to pull herself free, and they went down, slapping against the floor, Fenton on top of her.

"Hey," I shouted, running after him to yank him back.

"What's your problem?"

"There's no need to be so rough."

The girl scrambled across the carpeted floor, putting an occupied bed between us and her, painting herself into a corner. Stupid, but understandable. She was scared.

Looking at the kids in the beds, so was I.

I took a step closer and she flinched, her back against the curtain. "We don't want to hurt you."

Fenton thrust his gun in her direction.

"That's not necessary," I said. "She's a nurse or something."

"Doctor," she told me. "I'm a doctor."

"Sorry—Doctor...?"

"Ezogu, Betty Ezogu."

"Okay, Betty. This is what we're going to do. My friend here is going to lower his gun—"

"Like hell I am."

I looked at Fenton. "You don't need it."

"Yes, he does," said Brennan from behind me. She stalked forward, never taking her eyes from Betty. And she had a gun in her hand too, a Glock, pointing straight at the young doctor.

"Not you as well. Listen—"

"Shut up." Brennan talked across me. And to think I'd been starting to like her. "Doctor Ezegu."

"Ezogu."

"What are you doing here?"

Betty wetted her dry lips. "I was checking on the patients. With everything that's been going on—"

"No," Brennan interrupted. "I don't mean now. I mean in general." She took in the ward with a wave of her gun. "All this. We were told you were conducting experiments. What kind of experiments?"

Betty paused, considering her options. At the moment, with an idiot like Fenton pointing a gun at her, they were limited.

"It's... classified."

Brennan laughed. "I need authorisation, is that what you're saying? This is my authorisation, right here. Seventeen rounds of nine-millimetre Parabellum, pointing at your chest. Who are you working for?"

That I could answer, although I kept my mouth shut for now. I had followed Jasmine here by picking up fragments of communications, mainly from Germany, from an organisation that only seemed to be known as the Cabal. The rumours weren't great. They weren't good people, but if the ends perhaps didn't entirely justify the means, they made them easier to swallow. The Cabal carried out sometimes-dubious research, but their work was making things better for a lot of people. Cleaner water. Better drugs. Could have been worse, a lot worse.

That was glass-half-full stuff, of course, but sometimes you had to believe the world was getting better. It helped you wake up in the mornings.

But this? Nothing about this smelled right. I picked up a board hanging from the end of one of the beds, reading the notes.

"You haven't been healing these kids," I said, flicking over a page. "You've been killing them."

"What?" Brennan asked, walking over to snatch the notes from my hands.

I didn't need to see any more. I looked at the child in the bed, a girl of eight. A girl with malaria.

Before she'd been admitted, she had been fit and healthy. She'd had a future.

I walked to the next cubicle, checking the notes of the boy in the bed. He was nine years old, and had been given anthrax.

I dropped the folder onto the bed.

"Why?" Brennan was asking. It seemed inadequate, considering what we had discovered.

"I can't—" Betty began.

"You can, and you will," Brennan insisted, before a thought occurred to her. "Are we in danger here? Are these things contagious?"

Betty shook her head. "No, they're not. We're all fine."

"*They're* not fine," I said. "Are they?"

"Last chance," Brennan warned, taking another step forward, gun half-raised. "Why are you doing this?"

The fight went out of Betty's eyes. "We've been researching immunities, developing... subjects that are immune to diseases."

"To the Cull?" I asked.

She shook her head. "We're all immune to the Cull, aren't we? I mean, immune to *everything*, from the common cold to the deadliest of pathogens."

"And what about these?" I said, indicating the beds.

"Not all the subjects have been successful."

I felt sick. Jasmine, what had they made you *do*? This madness would have been anathema to her, against everything she believed.

I was going to find the bastards behind all this.

"What about that?" Fenton was asking, pointing to a sealed room beyond the last cubicle.

"Quarantine."

"Contagious diseases, too?" Brennan's lips curled into a grimace. "You people are sick."

"What kind of diseases?" Fenton asked, panic in his voice.

"Influenza. Cryptoccossis. Ebola."

Fenton circled around Betty towards the isolation room, his morbid curiosity getting the better of him. "What about this one?"

"That's Mason. He's got tuberculosis."

Finally, someone with a name.

"I don't even know what that is, but I don't like the sound of it." Fenton peered through the glass as if he was at a freak show.

"How many have you got like this?" Brennan demanded.

"Only six. The other subjects are in good health."

"And where are they?"

Betty hesitated, which would only make Brennan's trigger finger itchier.

"You might as well tell them," I told her. "They'll find out in the end."

"Tell *them?*" Brennan repeated, a hint of betrayal in her voice. I didn't get a chance to respond. There was a crunch of boots behind us.

"Drop your weapons!" came the shout. "Right now!"

I spun to see two guards standing in the doorway, weapons raised and ready to fire. I was still reaching for my own gun when Fenton yelled a battle cry from beside the quarantine room and unloaded his shotgun; the guard to the right was hit square in the chest and went down. His partner returned fire and Fenton's cry became an agonised scream, bullets punching through his chest and arms.

Brennan threw herself behind one of the curtains—as if the soft fabric would somehow shield her. That left me. Before Fenton had even hit the floor, I was crouching behind the bed, my P99 out of its holster and ready to fire. I aimed at the guard's visor. The impact knocked his head back and he stumbled, losing his footing. I fired twice more as he fell, aiming for the body armour's weak points. The guard grunted as he hit the floor, the helmet spinning from his head. I waited to see if he was going to get up, but he stayed down, groaning with pain. My arm extended, I crept from behind the bed, noting dark pools spreading out from beneath both guards. The man I'd shot was coughing up gore, a deep wound in his side belching out blood.

I put him out of his misery and trained my gun on his compatriot, but he was beyond mercy, eyes staring blankly from beneath the visor.

"Good work," said Brennan, emerging from her hiding place. I didn't answer. I hadn't done it for her, and I certainly didn't take pleasure from it. Them or us; that's what it always came down to.

A wet cough made me turn. Fenton was lying beside the quarantine room, which had taken a bullet to a window, cracks spider-webbing across the not-so-shatterproof glass.

"Get me out of here," Fenton burbled, writhing on the floor. He needn't have worried about sickness; it was clear he wouldn't last long.

A set of doors on the far wall were swinging shut, Betty having got away in the confusion. I ran over to Fenton, not looking at the jagged holes in his chest or the blood flowing freely from a hole in the side of his neck. I snatched his shotgun, reaching inside his vest for spare shells. He grabbed my arm with bloodied hands.

"You've got to help me."

I shook him off, not giving him another glance as I made for the door.

"Hey, where are you going?" Brennan called after me.

"To find that girl," I replied, not waiting for her permission as I pushed my way through the doors, "before she brings more guards. You check the rest of this floor."

A quick glance up and down the corridor revealed I was alone.

Of course, Betty could live a long and happy life for all I cared. There was only one person I wanted to find, and until then, I had a job to do.

I ran up the corridor, heading towards a stairwell. Behind me I could still hear Fenton whimpering until a single shot silenced him forever.

CHAPTER SEVENTEEN
CURE

Gun shots.

There were gun shots in the building.

But who was firing the guns?

I ran out of the lab, racing back to the children, who looked to me with more emotion in their eyes than I had ever seen.

Fear.

"Did you hear that?" Allison asked.

Wright didn't wait for me to answer. "We need to move."

He was right. Of course he was. Everything was slotting into place.

He was here, in the base. He'd come for me, and together we could do this. Together.

Like it was meant to be.

I flashed my best reassuring smile at the children and herded them forward.

"That's right. Let's get everyone down to the bunker."

Allison's eye fell on the briefcase.

"What's that?"

"Notes," I said, surprised at how easy the lies were coming.

"You can do this," Olive whispered in my ear. "Eyes and teeth. Eyes and teeth."

Wright looked past me, towards the lab. "What about Eckstein?"

"He's going to follow us down. We've lost contact with Lam. Stefan's co-ordinating the resistance, at least until we get the children to safety."

"Are we not safe here?" Ruth asked, the slightest of tremors in her throat.

Allison jumped to my rescue. "You're safe with us. That's our job, isn't it? Keeping you safe."

"What about the codes?" Wright asked as we shepherded the children along. "If the computer has locked us out..."

My mind whirled. God, he was right. Assuming we got down there, could we even get in?

Olive spoke up beside me. "The bunker works on an isolated system."

"That's right," I chipped in, relieved. "I have the overrides."

"To what?" Allison asked.

"The bunker's computer." The pressure must have been getting to her. She needed to keep up. "It'll be fine. It's completely separate to the main network."

"Allison's losing it," warned Olive beneath her breath. "She's a weak link, like Eckstein was. We should get rid of her."

I glared at Olive, but luckily Allison hadn't heard, her arm around Dawn, telling the girl about the games that we kept down in the bunker.

Were there any games? I couldn't remember—but it didn't matter. It had strong doors; that was all I cared about. I'd get the children into the bunker and then go and find him. Bring him in safe with us.

I realised I was beaming.

"That's it," I called to the front of the group, the two guards leading the way. "Around the corner. The stairs are on the right."

Wright raised a hand, telling us to stop. The kids obeyed immediately, shrinking closer together, as the sound of running feet filled the corridor. Wright ushered us towards the wall as he and David raised their guns, waiting.

Surely the raiders hadn't reached this far already? I felt Olive tugging at my sleeve, trying to get me to run the other way. Leave the kids. Forget them. You know what you must do; who you must find.

But the figure that came sprinting around the corner had no weapons. She skidded to a halt, raising her arms in surrender as she saw the guns pointing at her.

"Don't shoot. It's me."

"Bets?" Allison broke from Dawn's embrace and ran to her girlfriend. "What's wrong?"

Betty grabbed Allison's hands, kneading them beneath her fingers. "They're downstairs. In the ward. I thought they were going to kill me."

There was no need to ask who she was talking about. "How many?" Wright asked, his voice professionally calm.

"Three, but one of them was shot, I think."

A fist gripped my heart. "Which one?"

Betty looked confused at my question. "What do you mean?"

"Which one was shot? I saw them on the monitors, two men and a woman—"

"You never said!" Allison turned to me.

"She was trying not to worry you!" Olive protested, aggrieved. None of that mattered.

"Which of them was shot?" I repeated, more forcibly.

"One of the men," Bets replied, looking unsure. "The skinny one. I got out as soon as I could."

The pressure on my chest released. The skinny one. Thank God.

"And our men?" David was asking.

Betty shook her head. "There were two of them. I couldn't tell who, with all the visors and everything, but..."

She didn't have to say anymore.

"We're going to the bunker," I told Bets, urging everyone on.

"What about the patients in the ward?"

"We can't help them now."

Dawn looked up at me, her mouth open. "We're leaving them behind?"

"We'll come back for them later," I lied. "But only after you're all safe."

"No! You can't!"

It was Ruth. I'd never even heard her raise her voice before. She broke from the group, trying to run around the corner. "We've got to get them."

Wright reached out, grabbing the girl. She screamed, fighting against the guard as he pulled her close into him, more gently than I would have thought possible. She shrieked, arms flailing as he held her close.

"No, no," he said, firm and sympathetic at the same time. "That's enough of that. Calm down, eh? Calm down."

The other children drew back, unnerved by Ruth's outburst. We moved to them—Allison, Betty and me—throwing our arms around them like hens around their chicks.

Ruth stopped thrashing, hugging Wright close, sobs wracking her thin body. "That's it," he cooed. "That's it. We won't let anything happen to you, okay? We'll look after you."

Ruth nodded, sniffed and stepped out of Wright's arms, raising her arm and shooting the guard point-blank in the face.

Brain-matter splattered over the wall as his body fell back. Ruth turned, Wright's blood across her face and chest, and pointed the handgun she had taken from his belt straight at Stones, who was staring in disbelief down his own sights.

"Drop the gun," he said, a little shakily. "Drop. The. Gun."

I gaped at Ruth. This couldn't be happening. It just couldn't.

"Ruth," I said, raising my free hand. "Do what he says. Put the gun down and you won't be hurt. You're scared, we're all scared, but this isn't helping."

Ruth didn't take her eyes off Stones. She didn't look at me or say a word. Instead, she did something I had never seen before. She smiled.

Without warning, the children surged at us, crying out as one. Taken by surprise, we staggered back, Allison stumbling against the wall and cracking her head.

Stones turned, just for a moment, distracted by the sudden confusion, but it was enough. Ruth fired, the bullet tore through the guard's exposed neck. He went down, his rifle skittering along the floor, where it was retrieved, coolly and precisely, by Dawn.

Ruth turned her gun on me.

"Show us the cameras."

"What?" I couldn't make sense of any of this. What were they doing?

"In the lab. I need to know how you access the cameras."

When I didn't respond, Ruth calmly turned the gun and shot Betty in the chest.

Allison screamed as Betty crumpled against the wall and slid to the floor, leaving a smear of blood in her wake.

"Show me the cameras," Ruth repeated.

The children were all looking at me, but not for help. They were waiting for me to obey Ruth's command, their eyes cold, Dawn standing behind them, her rifle trained on Allison.

Perhaps I did dream, after all. That had to be it. This was just a dream, and I would wake up any minute for another day of routine tests. There wouldn't be killers surging through my base, sirens blaring and Allison crying, trying to hopelessly revive the woman she loved.

There wouldn't be him.

"Jasmine," Olive said in my ear. "You need to do what she says."

I nodded, clutching the handle of the case tighter than ever.

"Allison," I croaked, my throat dry. "Allison, we need to go."

"No," she whimpered. "I can't leave her. I can't leave her."

Never taking my eyes off Ruth, I edged closer to Allison, leaning down and taking hold of her arm with my free hand.

She wailed, trying to shake me off, but my grip stayed sure. If she didn't move, they would kill her; that much was clear.

Michele and Adam had recovered Stones' other weapons now. We were outnumbered.

Allison finally let me pull her away, nearly doubling over in grief. "That's it," I encouraged her. "We'll come back for Bets later. When this is all over."

"The cameras, Dr Tomas," Ruth reminded me.

"Yes," I said. "This way."

I turned, half expecting a bullet between my shoulder blades, and, wrapping my arm around Allison's waist, walked back towards the lab. Olive said nothing. She had her arms raised in surrender, but I could see that she was thinking, the ultimate control-freak coming up with a plan.

It had better be good.

"AT LEAST THAT'S shut her up," Olive sneered as we entered the small control room.

Allison had sobbed all the way to the lab, trying and failing to pull herself together. I couldn't imagine what she was going through, seeing the love of her life gunned down in front of her.

What sickened me was the voice I heard in my ear, telling me to shut her up, irritated by her heartbreak and grief.

Now Allison was standing open-mouthed, staring at Eckstein, lying in the sticky contents of his own head.

She didn't say a word. She didn't have to. She stepped away from me, the disgust on her face more damning than any rebuke.

Olive immediately jumped to my defence. "It wasn't her fault. You don't know what he wanted to do."

I should have shut her up, but didn't have the energy anymore. I just looked away, seeing Eckstein's gun where I had dropped it, the drying flesh clinging to its handle. Why hadn't I taken it with me? I could have had it in my hand now.

But what good would it have done?

Ruth marched through the crowd of children, serene and confident, gun in hand. She had no need to threaten us now, not with her army behind us.

An army. Is that really what I had bred?

"These are the controls?"

I stepped up beside her, wondering if I could take her out before her cohorts fired. I had the briefcase. Slam it across her face, knock her to the side. She was only a child after all, no matter how special her physiology. Once she's floundering, grab Eckstein's gun. The children were bright, but they'd never fired weapons before today. They would hesitate, maybe even miss, the recoil shocking them. Sadly, I had plenty of experience. I could give the distraction Allison and Olive needed.

"Dr Tomas?"

Ruth was looking up at me, expectant.

"Yes, sorry. It's simple enough." I leant down to the control box, clicking through the feeds. "Use this unit. The cameras are on a cycle."

She all but slapped my hand out of the way, taking over, scrolling through the feeds. The other Neighbourhoods, the medical staff being rounded up, a few missing faces in the crowd. Then we were back in this building: the ward, with the guards sprawled on the floor; a corridor, the woman I'd seen creeping around the corner—and then him! I fought the urge to smile. It was real. He *was* here, crouching down in a corridor, his back to the camera—before Ruth moved on, flicking through the channels. It was all I could do not to wrestle the controls back from her to see him again.

I had to keep my cool, to remain calm. I could almost hear Olive's advice. *Just go with it, give them what they want and then we can leave them all to rot. We can find him.*

She was right. She was always right, although I'd never let her hear me admit such a thing. She was insufferable enough as it was.

"Thank you," said Ruth, the gratitude as false as any emotion she'd ever portrayed. "Matthew and Adam will take you and Dr Harwood down to the bunker."

"What about you?"

Ruth looked at me as if I was an imbecile.

"We must defend our home."

Our home, like it belonged to them.

Things started clicking into place.

"Samuel," I said simply.

Ruth didn't respond.

"You know what happened to him, don't you? You know he died."

"You tried to keep it from us."

"I was trying to protect you. But there was no need, was there? No one crept into his room. No one slipped poison into his food."

"He did it himself," Ruth replied, blandly.

"But why?" Allison asked. Ruth didn't answer. Why waste the energy? We'd raised them to be pragmatists. But I wanted to hear it. I wanted a reason to abandon them.

"He sacrificed himself," I offered. "To spread confusion amongst us. Mistrust."

Ruth watched me.

"Creating a crisis that would end with us letting you out of your rooms, moving you to a safe location, so you could strike."

"But how could they plan it?" Allison asked. "We were always with them; every time they were together, we were there."

And then I remembered Ruth sitting, engrossed in her computer game, controller in hand, headset clamped over her ears.

"Not all the time. We gave them a network to talk to each other, to interact. To plot against us." I snorted in derision. We had thought we were being kind.

Why hadn't we seen it coming? We monitored all of the chat over the network, there were recordings...

On the computer system.

"Lam," Olive said. "He has a console in the hub. He was playing with them. He was in on it."

"His pass is like mine. It can get him everywhere. Opening any door."

"Who?" Allison again, asking stupid questions. I couldn't blame her, I guess. She was in shock.

"Lam," Ruth replied, obligingly. "He wasn't comfortable with what we were doing. I persuaded him to let me out one night, when he was on duty. I told him that I wanted to see where he worked. He would wipe the record of it, no-one would know. He was cross when I ran away."

"To N-4, to the stores. You took the poison, slipping it to Samuel during Dr Heslin's PE session."

Ruth nodded. "Please don't be too harsh on Lam. He didn't know what we were planning. Although he panicked when Samuel died. He was going to tell you everything, until I pointed out that we could pin Samuel's murder on him. All those times he wiped the records. My secret visit. It wouldn't look good."

"You blackmailed him!"

"I assured his silence."

All that stuff about *freaks*. Had it been a bluff, Lam trying to distance himself from the plot?

"It didn't matter in the end," Ruth continued. "The raids were unexpected. Events have escalated." Her gun was raised again, pointing at me. "Please, make your way to Bunker Three."

"To keep us safe?"

"We have much to thank you for. You have made us pure in body—"

"If not in mind."

"And yet there is much we need to understand if we are to build upon your work. You will assist us."

"And if we don't?"

"We will find someone who can."

"If you survive any of this, you little bitch," Olive added, as gunfire echoed through the corridors outside.

Ruth turned to the monitor and flicked through the channels. "The raiders are in the building. We will all go to the bunker."

The children ushered us back through the lab and I turned to see Ruth retrieve Eckstein's gun, not even flinching as her small fingers closed around the gore-encrusted grip.

Waste not, want not.

She followed us out, just as three raiders chased us around the corner, two men and the tallest woman I'd ever seen, with a buzz cut and plaster strapped her nose. They raised their guns, warning us to stop. The children stood firm, caught in the one of the most bizarre standoffs in history. A hand brushed against my back, Olive drawing my attention to the swing doors behind us.

There was no way we could reach them.

"Drop the weapons!" the woman shouted, her rifle never wavering, although the men behind her weren't looking too sure. I could imagine what was going through their heads. Armed guards was one thing; but children, even with machine guns?

The woman took a tentative step forward and Dawn fired. The sound was deafening. The woman cried out, squeezing her trigger in reflex. There was a scream, not a child's voice, a woman's; maybe Olive, maybe Allison. I didn't know. I was running, head down, towards the doors. I flung myself to the floor, a bullet slamming into the door next to me, but I carried on, crawling on my hands and knees with the case in my hands. Struggling to get the door open, I squeezed through the gap. The door slammed shut, but I was up and running. I hugged the case to me, expecting to feel the impact of a bullet in my back at any minute.

There were stairs ahead. I had the vague sense of someone following me, shouting my name, but I didn't stop.

I wouldn't stop until I found him.

CHAPTER EIGHTEEN
KILL

THE REST OF Brennan's gang were in now. I could hear them, muffled shouts somewhere nearby, the percussive rattle of gunfire.

She might already be dead. Wouldn't that be the final joke? All this way, after all this time and I find her bleeding out in the corridor?

I couldn't think like that.

I pounded the corridor, snatching another remote grenade from my chest strap. More gunshots, up above, on the third floor. The grenade was cool in my hand. I stopped, stooping to fix it to the metal pipes, the magnets doing their work. A flick of the switch as it was primed, another link in the chain, waiting for the signal.

I stood up to find someone standing in front of me. My gun was in my hand in a heartbeat, even before I realised I was staring at Brennan down the sights.

Her Glock stared back.

"What the hell are you doing?"

I didn't answer, already planning my next move. She was standing beside a stairwell, but had little cover. I had even less. If either of us fired, this close to each other, it would all be over.

I tried to reason with her.

Yeah, like that ever works, soldier.

"This place is wrong, Brennan. You know that."

"What?"

"You saw what they were doing to those kids. What else are we going to find?"

"So you want to blow it up?"

"It'll send a message. To whoever's behind all this."

She took a step closer. Dangerous. "We've already sent a message. We've taken the base."

I snorted in derision. "And you think that'll be the end of it? Where did all that medical equipment come from, Brennan? The guns, the body armour? None of that was here before the Cull. It's been brought in from outside. Settle here and you'll find yourself under siege when the *real* owners turn up."

"Where's the trigger?" She hadn't heard a word I was saying.

"We could still get out of this alive."

"'We'? Are you sure about that? Downstairs it was *them*. 'You might as well tell *them*.' Now I'm supposed to believe we're in this together?"

"I never said I wanted to stay here. That wasn't part of the deal."

"Neither were your grenades. Drop the gun."

"Brennan, listen—"

"Drop it."

It was no good. I couldn't guarantee that I'd be the quicker shot, not anymore.

"Okay, I'm putting it down."

Slowly, purposely, I lowered my gun to the floor and slid it over to her. She stopped it with her foot as I straightened, hands in the air.

She stalked towards me. "It's a shame. I liked you. Thought you might fit in."

"Like Fenton fitted in? How did that end up?"

"Come on, you met him."

I gave her my best lop-sided grin—the full Han Solo. "Sure, and I wanted to put a bullet in his head from the first moment, too."

She was in front of me now, the Glock inches away from me. She wasn't buying my charm offensive. Couldn't blame her.

"The trigger."

"In my jacket."

She hesitated, weighing up whether to get me to take it out or do it herself. She went for the former, and I did as I was told, bringing out an old battered mobile phone, which I dutifully offered her, looking her full in the eye all the time. She glanced down at the phone, and I struck.

Dropping the phone, I swept my hand into the wrist of her gun arm. She fired, doing permanent damage to my eardrum, but the bullet ended up in the plasterwork, not me. There was no time for finesse. I shoulder barged her, sending us both crashing to the floor. Scrabbling for her gun arm with my left hand, I found her throat with my right. She kicked and thrashed, but I was too heavy, pinning her arm down, crushing the breath from her. She gasped, her eyes wide, her struggles diminishing by the second.

I took no pleasure from this. I'd liked her, too.

Perhaps that's what made me sloppy.

The knife went into my thigh, almost to the hilt. I cried out, releasing my pressure on her neck, enough for her to pull the blade free and find another home between my ribs.

She heaved against me and I rolled onto my back, the knife still sticking out of my side. Brennan scrambled to her feet, bringing her gun down to bear.

My hand went to my pocket as I cursed myself for being a stupid old man, and a shot rang out.

Brennan's body toppled forward to land beside me.

My head swimming, I looked up to see Jasmine standing at the bottom of the stairs, a briefcase in one hand and my P99 in the other.

IT WAS ALL a bit of a blur after that. I remember Jasmine falling to her knees beside me, checking my injuries. I screamed at her not to remove the knife. It was plugging the wound. If she pulled it out, there was no telling what damage it would do.

And then I think I was sick.

Some reunion.

After that there were only snatches of memory. Jasmine getting me to my feet, yelling at me not to die. My arm was around her shoulders, and we were stumbling through sliding doors.

A lift. You weren't supposed to use lifts in emergencies.

This was an emergency. wasn't it?

Sirens.

Gunfire.

More doors.

Darkness.

When I awoke, I was on a bed. I tried to move, but thick leather straps cut into my arms and legs. There were restraints over my chest as well. What was happening?

I struggled, and a shadow fell over me, blocking out the harsh lights in the ceiling above.

A face coming into focus.

Her face.

Of sorts.

Her skin wasn't as smooth as I remembered, her cheeks more pronounced, eyes sunken. Her beautiful hair had been cropped short, turned prematurely grey.

I wasn't exactly an oil painting myself.

"Jasmine?"

"Shhh," she said, stroking the side of my face. "You need to rest."

I looked around, taking in the drip beside the bed, tubes snaking down from the plastic pouch to the shunt in my arm.

"You're going to be okay. The knife's out. It was a clean cut."

"You patched me up?"

She smiled. "Just like new."

"And you're really here? I'm not dead?"

A laugh now, but again, not like I remembered; nowhere near as hearty, like she hadn't used it for a long time. "You're not dead. You're safe. We're in the bunker. No one can get in here."

I tried to move again, testing the restraints. I burned where the knife had gone in, despite the painkillers. Jasmine placed a gentle hand on my chest. "Stay still. You'll open the stitches."

She increased the dose down the line, my head swimming as the drugs flooded my system.

"Can you let me out of these?"

She was stroking my hair now, long fingers against my scalp.

"Soon, darling. They're for your own safety. I didn't want to, but she was right."

"Who was?"

Jasmine walked away over to a metal work bench, her back to me. "Olive, my assistant."

I looked around the room. The walls were whitewashed breeze-blocks, a heavy metal door, slightly ajar across from my bed. There was little in the way of furniture. The workbench, and a lighting array. A chair sat to the side, my jacket thrown over the back and the remaining remote grenades on the seat.

There was no one else here.

Jasmine was examining a security monitor, like those in the hub, flicking through camera feeds.

"We were lucky Ruth didn't get down here first."

"Who's Ruth?"

If Jasmine heard the question, she didn't answer. "Most of the others are dead, but I can't find Ruth. It doesn't matter. They can't get in."

She carried on clicking, the picture shifting on the display. I couldn't quite make out what I was seeing; an endless cavalcade of rooms and corridors, some empty, some with bodies.

I wondered if anyone had found Brennan yet.

Jasmine leant over and flicked a switch on the monitor. The screen went dead.

"Yes, I know!" Jasmine spat, her tone suddenly harsh.

"Jas?"

She laughed, turning to me. "Allison used to call me that."

"You're scaring me, sweetheart. Let me out of these things."

"You always were a terrible patient." She returned to the table top, a briefcase open in front of her. I watched her produce a small bottle, drawing some of the clear liquid it contained into a syringe.

"What's that?"

She turned, and her eyes gleamed, but not like before. They were cold, shallow—and quite, quite mad.

"It's the cure," she said, grinning as she walked towards me. "And our future."

The cure. My mind went back to the girl in the ward, the doctor. No one had forced Jasmine to do this. My Jasmine. She'd done it herself.

I struggled against my bonds. "Jasmine, whatever that stuff is, I don't want it."

"You don't understand. We've been performing experiments here."

"I've seen your experiments."

"But you haven't seen the results; you don't know what this will do. No more disease. No more suffering. Do you understand? When we take this, we'll have nothing else to fear. Just the two of us, together. Like it was supposed to be."

Then she looked up, her lips drawing back, angry.

"You don't *have* to be here!" she barked.

I looked where she was glaring. There was no one there.

She stroked my hair again, the syringe in her other hand. "Don't listen to her. She's just scared. But there's no need to be. Not now."

"Don't listen to who? Jasmine, who are you talking to?"

She stared at me as though I was delirious. "Olive. You'll get used to her. She's always banging on about something, yadda, yadda, yadda, day or night." She gave a peal of laughter. There was nothing infectious about it now. It made my skin crawl. "I just can't seem to get shot of the stupid bitch."

There was a thud from outside the room, like someone banging against metal. Jasmine returned to the monitor, re-activating the screen. A young girl in pyjamas was slamming an open palm against a vault door. She was bald, her clothes covered in what could only be blood.

"And there she is. It's about time."

I struggled to remember the name Jasmine had mentioned. "Ruth?"

Jasmine was transfixed on the screen, lost in her thoughts. "Such a shame, but we don't need her anymore."

Her head snapped around, glaring into empty space again. "Well, *you* go out there, then." She turned her attention back to me. "Don't worry. Ruth can't get in. No one can. And once we've done this, we'll set the charges, bring the place down around her ears. The Cabal won't be pleased, but when they see you, see what I've achieved..."

She flinched. Shutting her eyes, her head cocked to the side, as if she was waiting for someone to stop talking... or to leave.

Finally, she sighed, her eyes opening again. "Thank God for that." She leant close, conspiratorially. "Don't worry, we'll get rid of her, too. I need her to help set the charges for now." She rolled her eyes. "Just my luck she's the only one who knows the demolition codes, but as soon as we're out of here, we need never see her again."

"Olive?"

She nodded, smiling.

I understood.

Jasmine flicked the syringe, clearing the bubbles in the liquid before slipping the needle into the shunt in my arm.

"Now, I'm not going to lie, this is going to hurt. That's why we strapped you down. It'll be worth it, though. Besides, you know me. I'd scream the place down if I got a paper cut. If I can get through this, anyone can, especially you."

"You've taken the cure?"

"I couldn't exactly test it on anyone else, could I? I wanted to tell Allison, but Olive wouldn't let me."

"You told Olive."

"She said that they'd take the glory. This had to be my discovery." A shadow crossed her face. "To make amends."

"For what? Jasmine, what do you need to make amends for?"

She came to me, this new twisted version of my beloved Jasmine.

"Gently now," she cooed, applying pressure to the syringe.

It felt as if someone was pouring lava into my veins. I had experienced pain, but never like this. I couldn't move, every muscle in my body knotting at once. I tried to scream, but my jaws were locked together so tight I thought my teeth were going to crack.

And all the time, Jasmine whispered in my ear, telling me that it was going to be all right, that I had found her. We would be safe.

She knew it was true. Olive had told her.

Eventually, the pain subsiding, releasing my muscles, letting my body relax. I choked, tasting blood in my mouth. My head was spinning, my brain feeling like it was expanding, pressing against my skull, wanting to break free.

I could hear Jasmine a million miles away, although the words didn't make sense. It didn't even sound like her voice anymore. Not the voice I remembered, not the woman I remembered. This wasn't right. It wasn't how it was supposed to be.

The leather strap sliced into my forearm as I struggled to slip my hand into my pocket. My fingers curled around the transmitter, flicking the safety-guard up with my thumbnail, feeling the button beneath.

My vision was starting to clear, Jasmine's face coming into focus. For a moment she looked the way she was, before the Cull, before it all, but then reality rushed back.

She was speaking to me, but I couldn't hear the words. I thought she said my name.

Don't you give up now, soldier!

Sir, no sir, etc.

I pressed down on the detonator.

ABOUT THE AUTHOR

UK number-one bestselling author Cavan Scott is currently trying to work on everything he loved when he was ten. He has written for *Star Wars*, *Doctor Who*, *Warhammer 40,000*, *Judge Dredd*, *Blake's 7*, *Highlander*, *Danger Mouse*, the *Beano* and *Vikings*. His new Sherlock Holmes novel, *The Patchwork Devil*, is out now from Titan Books, with a sequel in the works. He lives in Bristol with his wife, daughters and an inflatable Dalek called Desmond.

FLAMING ARROW

PAUL KANE

Original cover art by Sam Gretton

*For all the fans of the Hooded Man novels; I
can never thank you enough.*

"Look back over the past with its changing empires that rose and fell, and you can foresee the future too."

—*Meditations*, Marcus Aurelius

PROLOGUE

ONCE, A LONG time ago, this was a world. A living, breathing world.

Now it's just a shell, a shadow of what it once was. Not that Mouse could remember the time before; he was far too young. This was the only world he'd ever known, the one he'd grown up in. Alone, more or less, since he was very little. He had vague recollections of a family, parents maybe—or at the very least people who had looked after him... to begin with. But they weren't around for very long. He couldn't remember exactly why: one minute they were there, the next they were gone. Anything could have happened to them really; as much as it was a dead world, it was also a dangerous one.

It hadn't always been that way. Somehow, Mouse knew that. Perhaps the people who'd been around during the first few years of his life had told him so. There had been peace... of a kind. Some sort of order, at any rate. It was all he did know, as he hadn't come across anyone who could tell him more. Not that he'd ask. It wasn't wise—you only fell for that once. Trust was a hard thing to come by in this day and age, so it was best just to not get involved.

He'd been scavenging all this time, and had become incredibly good at it. Hunger was a pretty good motivator, even when you were very small—not that he was much bigger now—and fear kept you safe. Mostly. It was a combination that had worked well enough up to this point. It had also seen him travel a lot, moving on if a place had already been picked over—or he'd found all he could. Flitting from one burnt-out town to another, just as he was doing today. Sometimes you got lucky, like when he'd found that untouched basement with the tinned goods in. Tins were his best friends, they survived anything.

More often than not, there were days like this, when he found nothing. Mouse took one last look over his shoulder, at the scarred remains of the structures he'd been searching. The latest city he'd entered, which looked pretty much like all the others he'd ever come across. Except it wasn't like all the rest, he felt. And there was a sadness he couldn't explain as his eyes took in the rubble that filled the streets, the caved-in walls of buildings, bricks sticking out like broken teeth.

He shrugged, hitching up his backpack and leaving. It was time to head off somewhere else, somewhere that held more promise than this.

Time to hit the road again.

Mouse hadn't been walking for very long down that road when he came across a curious sight in the distance.

He was used to seeing blackened stretches of land; there was little else sometimes, between the towns and cities. What remained of that living, breathing world he had never seen. But the landscape here was slightly different. It was uneven, rising and falling around him. As Mouse drew closer, he saw that it was littered with short, squat columns, fixed into the ground. He crouched and peered at one of them, running a finger over the surface, then wiping off the ash that covered it. Beneath were rings, lots of them: larger on the outside, then progressively smaller the closer to the centre they came.

There were lots of the strange objects here, all of differing sizes and shapes.

"It used to be how you could tell the age," came a voice from behind him.

Mouse jumped, whipping out the piece of jagged metal he used as a weapon. How anyone had crept up on him was a mystery; Mouse was the quiet one, the sneaker—though someone was obviously much better. But the speaker wasn't as close as he'd sounded. He sat on one of the odd columns, his cloak hanging down over the sides. He was leaning on something long and twisted, two hands clutching it for support. His white hair and beard rippled in the breeze passing through this place, and his skin was as wrinkled as old leather. Mouse had never seen *anyone* as old as him, in fact. The man looked older than time itself.

Mouse was simultaneously terrified and intrigued, fixed to the spot. But standing here out in the open like this, gawping, was a good way to get yourself killed. Perhaps it was a trap, and any moment now he'd be attacked from other angles, his backpack snatched from him as he was kicked and stomped into the ground.

He made a concerted effort to move forward, placing one foot in front of the other. "You... You stay where you are," warned Mouse, looking about him all the while as he covered the distance between them, expecting at any moment to have to defend himself.

But the attack never came.

The man laughed softly. "You have nothing to fear from me, I assure you." His voice was rough, but kindly. His breathing was laboured, though, as if it was an effort for him to speak at all. "I am quite alone."

Still cautious, Mouse took another few steps. Out of habit, he looked the man over for anything that he might be able to steal. Wasn't the usual way he did things, he preferred not to get his hands dirty, but when the opportunity presented itself he would grab it with both hands. The man shifted his position, took one of his owns hands off the twisted thing in front of him, and held it up.

At first Mouse thought he was commanding him to halt,

then realised he was showing that he had nothing of worth about his person. Just his clothes, by the looks of things; no belts or pouches, certainly no food or drink. Mouse's eyes flicked sideways again to the oddly-shaped thing the man was still gripping with his other hand.

"You like this?" the old fellow asked, laughing softly again. "I bet you've never seen anything like it before, have you?"

In spite of himself, Mouse shook his head.

"Or like this..." Now the old man tapped the thing he was sitting upon. "Most forests were completely obliterated, but, well, this one is a little bit special." He sighed. "Only the stumps remain, however. All that's left of the trees."

Mouse frowned. "Trees?" He had no idea what the word meant, nor what a *stump* was. Or a *forest*, for that matter.

"Yes. There used to be trees here, so many of them. Huge, tall trees that reached into the sky." He craned his head back and without even realising it, Mouse did the same. When he looked down again the man was patting the thing he was leaning upon. "These grew from the sides, they were called *branches*. It's called a *staff*; it helps me to walk."

Trees, branches, staffs... It was like gibberish to Mouse's ears.

"So you see, I cannot give it to you—much as I'd like. And I have nothing else to offer a... *collector* such as yourself." That much Mouse had figured out already. "Oh, wait. Except, perhaps..."

Mouse held his breath, waiting for the man to continue.

"...a story."

A story? Mouse let out the breath again. He needed something to eat, or maybe even items to trade for food. What did he need with a story, with words? You couldn't— shouldn't—trade *them*. He shouldn't even be here talking to this old fool, had lingered too long in the one spot as it was.

"A story about the old days," the man clarified.

That made Mouse pause. The time before? Had this man lived through those times? He was old—*ancient*—that was for sure, but still... And how would Mouse know if he was telling the truth or not? Might be more nonsense like the thing with the trees, the branches. Yet there were the... what had he called them? Stumps? Mouse had never seen anything like those things before, with their rings for telling ages. He shook his head again.

"Are you sure? I would imagine someone like you would be very interested in those times. In what happened here in the past, back when this really was a forest." The old man grinned, revealing a mouth almost devoid of teeth. "It's a tale about good and evil and everything in-between. Heroes and villains, battles and wars."

Mouse edged just that little bit closer.

"In the beginning, there was a great plague," the storyteller told him. "It killed all but a handful of people with a certain kind of blood. And there was a man who survived, who was almost driven crazy by the death of his wife and child. He sought refuge out here in the wilderness, where he lived alone. Where he hunted with his bow and his arrows. Until he was needed, that was. Until he was called on to stand up for those who could not stand up for themselves. Who were being bullied by a lunatic who wanted to take over the world."

Without even realising what he was doing, Mouse had sat down opposite the storyteller on a nearby stump. He listened, head cocked, transfixed by what the old man was saying.

"He had help, of course, this man. This hooded man. There was a gruff farmer... Oh, a farmer is someone who used to grow food in the ground." He laughed at Mouse's reaction to that one; nothing could possibly grow in the earth that surrounded them now. "There was a priest, a holy man—you probably don't know what religion is, either, do you?" Mouse's silence was answer enough. "Anyway, that man believed in an almighty power called God, who created us all. Who created the world and watched over us, guiding events. The priest always thought that Hood had been sent to them by God... Then there was a giant of a man, Hood's trusted second-in-command. They were like brothers, those two. Fought side by side so many times. And there was a woman Hood met who taught him the true meaning of love." When the storyteller noticed Mouse frowning again, he explained: "That feeling of connecting with someone. Of trusting someone. Of wanting to look after them. No?"

Mouse shook his head yet again, this time much more emphatically. Maybe those people he could hardly remember had... had *loved* him. They'd tried to look after him, at any rate. But—whether it was through choice or not—they'd left him alone to fend for himself. Which is what he'd done; it was what he was still doing.

The storyteller shrugged, then carried on. "Ah yes, that's right. There was a young lad as well, about your age when he first encountered Hood." Now he really did have Mouse's attention. "Together they fought a number of foes, building up their own army in the process. A peace-keeping force like no other.

"Their enemies included a witch and a man who thought he was a dragon... Oh, that's a mythical creature, one with wings who could breathe fire." The storyteller realised he was going off subject and got on track again. "Not to mention other armies from different places, one a group who worshipped the opposite number of that priest's God."

Mouse pulled his legs up and folded his arms around his knees, his jagged metal weapon still in his fist, though he had loosened his grip slightly. The more the old man talked, the more Mouse wanted him to. There was something, not just about his tone of voice, but the story itself.

A story, the man continued, of what had once been this forest, of the city Mouse had just come from. Back when it had still been standing, back when it had contained something called a *castle*.

"So," said the storyteller, "should I go on?"

Mouse nodded, just as emphatically as he'd shaken his head before. Real or not, he was hooked.

"All right then. Well, this particular story takes place after the others, but is no less important. Indeed, it might just be the most important of all the stories concerning the legendary Hooded Man..."

CHAPTER ONE

THOUGH THERE WERE three of them, they moved as one.

They'd been trained to do so by the very best. To think alike, to act alike. To carry on the mission, even if one of their number was in trouble. The mission was all; that had been drummed into them time and again. There was no room for sentimentality, especially not on this occasion. No place for emotions. They'd had to become hard, cold.

Focussed on the task in hand.

The trio even looked the same, in their dark, skin-tight outfits and masks which left only their eyes visible: darting this way and that. Like clones. And like clones, they were expendable. Whatever happened tonight, whether they succeeded or failed, they would not be simply walking away from this place. How could they? It would prove impossible.

Gaining entry to the city hadn't been difficult... for them. Many had tried before, of course, and failed. Security was notoriously—and necessarily—tight here. Lessons had been learned from the past, obvious weak spots scrutinised and fixed. But if you wanted in badly enough, you could always,

always find a way. It was their job to find those kinds of ways and they were extremely good at it.

Guard shift changes had been monitored for some time now, patterns noted—even ones that changed. It was all a matter of routines, which these sorts of people loved. Then adapting to them, slipping in through the cracks. Even now they were approaching their target location, where yet more guards stood between them and their marks.

Taking these out wouldn't be difficult, but it would only leave them a limited window of opportunity before it was noticed. Time was of the essence. The first figure nodded to their comrades, indicating Phase Two of the operation had begun, and simultaneously they struck—raising their pistols, silencers ensuring that only the faintest of sounds could be heard. The guards by the main gate dropped sideways, hardly having any time to register what had happened. Moving forward, the trio took out the figures on the turrets as well, leaving the way clear for them to clamber up and over into the grounds.

The building loomed in front of them, large and imposing— to anyone else. Nottingham Castle. The three figures fanned out, dropping guards whenever and wherever they saw them, leaving a silent trail of bodies in their wake—only stopping to reload every now and again. All too soon they were at the building itself, disabling the alarm system. Breaking in through a downstairs window and slipping inside like burglars. But these men were here to steal something far more precious than paintings or jewellery, not that either had any value in the time after the Cull.

After dispatching a couple of internal guards, they made their way through corridors lit only by candles and up the stairs, not pausing once, determined to finish what they had started. Exhibitions and displays of local art had given way to bedrooms, after less thoughtful tenants had trashed them. The building had become functional again, but also strangely homely over recent years. If their intel was correct—and it was—they'd find the first of their targets on this level, the next in a bedroom above.

The trio split up, the first figures branching off to open two doors at once. The third was already moving up the stairs to do the same on the next level. The first of the men in black moved into the room, sharp eyes discerning outlines in the bed: on the left, a man. One of the Hooded Man's most trusted soldiers, known as Dale. To his credit, the Ranger woke as soon as he sensed a presence in the room, but it was already too late. The assassin's pistol was up and firing. Dale fell back onto the bed, where he sprawled out, unmoving. Then a couple of rounds were pumped into the waking female figure beside Dale. The assassin glided forward, checking pulses and nodding to himself.

In the other bedroom, the second assassin found another young couple, fast asleep. This was one of the major prizes they were after: Hood's adopted son, Mark, and his partner Sophie. Mark, too, sensed something was wrong at the last minute, looking up and over at the stranger in the open doorway. As the gun was raised, Hood's son was up and launching himself at the assassin. The man didn't even flinch; he just fired at the lad, catching him in shoulder and forehead. Mark dropped sideways onto the floor with a thump. His wife, Sophie, was now sitting up, still dazed and confused. She opened her mouth to scream, but a shot silenced her before she could get any sound out. Sophie dropped forward, doubling over, like a puppet with its strings cut.

Above them, on the next floor, the third intruder had located the next objective: the room where Hood and his own wife would be. He opened the door silently, stepping inside at the same time. On the near side of the bed, he made out a woman sprawled out, long hair splayed over the pillow. She murmured something and he thought she might wake at that point, but it was obvious she was just having a dream. The assassin raised his pistol, finger on the trigger.

He hesitated, his own senses tingling. Realising that even as he was watching the sleeping figure in the bed, about to take her life, he himself was being scrutinised. Someone was behind him, and it was only now—as his eyes adjusted—that he saw the other side of the bed was empty. Before he could react, he felt pressure around both his wrist and at his throat simultaneously. His first thought was: how could his attacker have gotten behind him? Had he been up already when they struck? The one thing they hadn't considered: Mother Nature and a full bladder nonchalantly tossing a spanner into the works?

It didn't matter, he needed to focus on the fact that his pistol was falling from his grasp; that he was blacking out because of the forearm jammed up against his windpipe, the arm crooked around his neck. The assassin jabbed backwards with his elbow, ramming it into his opponent's ribs hard enough to elicit a grunt. The pressure at his larynx eased slightly. Another jab removed it entirely.

The assassin shoved back with all his weight, sending the man crashing into the wall opposite. At the same time, the assassin spun and kicked, knocking his attacker backwards into the wall a second time. It would have been enough to fell most people, but the shadowy figure just shook himself and came at the third assassin once more.

The first blow to the face was blocked, but a second one—almost immediately after the initial one—thudded into the assassin's side. It was followed by a succession of jabs to the kidneys which hurt like all hell. Regardless of this, the assassin rose and brought the flat of his left hand up hard and into his opponent's chin. If it had been just a few centimetres lower, he might have broken the man's neck, but as it was it only served to whip his opponent's head briefly to the side.

Then the man brought a knee up hard into the assassin's stomach, doubling him over. He brought both fists down together onto the assassin's back as he withdrew his knee, and suddenly the assassin was on the ground. Before the killer could do anything else there was pressure on the back on his neck. Though he couldn't see, he reached back around and felt the foot there, but was at the wrong angle to dislodge it. This time his vision did swim and a moment later he was unconscious.

Underneath them both, the remaining assassins had met up again—puzzled that their comrade hadn't returned. They ascended to the next floor, to complete the mission if he had failed in his duties. The key members of Hood's elite must be put down tonight and nothing would stand in the way of that.

When they reached the next floor they saw no sign of their team-mate. Exchanging puzzled glances, they made their way cautiously down along the corridor towards the next target's room. The door was still closed, so the first assassin opened it. The bed was empty, no-one present at all.

He felt a tap on the shoulder, his fellow assassin drawing his attention to something. A figure down the corridor, head bowed, wearing a hood. Holding a bow and arrow. The first assassin couldn't help himself, he swallowed dryly—the gulping sound audible. The most sound he'd made all night.

Then came another sound as something whirred through the air toward them. Hood had raised his weapon and shot faster than either of them could ever hope to fire their pistols. They separated, one going left, the other right. The arrow passed between them, falling away behind.

The first assassin shot back, but Hood was no longer standing there. *Fuck!* he thought, fighting the urge to cry out loud, *where did he go?* Then he wished he hadn't asked, as Hood dropped from a ceiling beam to land on him, grappling him to the floor and knocking over a candle-stand in the process.

The other assassin trained his pistol on them, then felt something cold and hard pressing into the middle of his shoulder-blades: the unmistakable shape of a gun barrel. "I wouldn't, if I were you," said a female voice with such authority that he didn't dare argue with it. "Now drop your weapon!" Reluctantly, he did as he was told.

Looking over, the first assassin saw he was on his own now— saw the woman with long, black hair streaked with silver, dressed in a vest-top and pyjama bottoms, prodding what looked like an old-fashioned cowboy gun into his comrade's back. He would just have to do what nobody before him had ever done: take Hood down, and do it single-handed.

He angled his pistol behind him and fired a couple of shots, but couldn't tell whether either had winged the Hooded Man. Probably not, because the next thing he knew he was being struck across the back of the hand by the end of the man's bow. The pistol clattered to the ground and Hood kicked it away.

At the same time, flames rose behind them from the felled candle...

The assassin rolled away and rose into a crouch, facing his adversary, who was getting to his feet. The man wasn't overly muscular, but there was strength there—you could tell from the stance, the way he carried himself. He was also incredibly lithe, moved like some kind of animal: fluid and organic. The assassin tested him, shifting his body to the right, and Hood followed suit: a reflection in a mirror. The assassin reached into his boot and took out a knife, something Hood couldn't match. Then he lunged at Hood, blade downwards, slashing an arc first one way, which Hood dodged, then the other—catching him on the upper arm.

Hood growled; it had only served to make him madder.

But it had also distracted his wife, and her captive took full advantage of it. He spun as she cried out, knocking her pistol from her grasp with his elbow. The gun went off, deafening them both. The assassin shoved Mary backwards, pitching her to the ground, and scooped up his own pistol.

Now it was Hood's turn to be distracted, which cost him another slash with the knife-blade—this time across the thigh. In retaliation, he brought the bow up and smashed the assassin in the face with a grunt. By this time, it was too late—and the other assassin had fired several times at the prone figure in front of him.

"*Mum!*"

The cry came from two directions at once: from a small figure who had appeared at the other end of the hall—where Hood had started off—and from the Hooded Man himself. The child rushed forward, down the corridor; a little girl, no more than eight, with the same dark hair as the woman on the ground, dressed in pink pyjamas adorned with red roses. She launched herself at the killer, grappling his legs and bringing him to his knees.

Hood held out a hand for her to stop. "April! April, no! It's okay!"

The girl took no notice as she proceeded to bite into the assassin's calf. He let out a yelp. "Arrgh, get offa me!" the masked man wailed.

"April, sweetheart. It's okay." This was Hood again, rising and making his way over to the pair. "Look, Mum's all right."

He pointed and the little girl looked past the assassin, seeing the woman on the floor sitting up. There were splashes of colour on her vest-top, too light to be blood.

As the girl ran over and flung her arms around the woman, an alarm began to go off. The felled guards had obviously, finally, been discovered by someone and the flag had gone up. "About time," grumbled the Hooded Man. The first assassin was rising now, dropping the knife and grabbing a fire extinguisher to put out the flames. When he was done, he pulled off his mask to reveal a kindly face, framed by ginger hair and long sideburns. The other assassin, still clutching his leg with one hand, put down his gun and did the same: he had closely-cropped hair and a sour face, but was about the same age, in his early to mid-thirties.

"Bloody hell and bollocks!" he said, shouting above the alarm.

"Not in front of April," Hood admonished.

"Not in front of... She fucking..." He paused, then said more carefully: "She *bit* me."

A hand went up, one that was missing a finger, and the green hoodie was peeled back. The face was very different from the one who usually wore it. "She wasn't to know," Mark—the real Mark—informed him.

"It was all just a game, darlin'," said Mary behind them, rocking the crying girl on her shoulder, not caring that she was getting the purple paint from her vest all over the child.

"Just pretend," Mark added for emphasis.

"Tell that to my leg!" the man with the close-cropped hair protested.

"Oh, stop moaning, Chillcott," Mark snapped, showing him the wounds on his arm and leg. Even with the blade dulled, they'd done some damage. "Trevena got me a couple of times pretty good, and you don't see me complaining."

"As did you," said Trevena, rubbing his reddening nose. "And you were pretty damned close with that arrow."

"It was nowhere near you. Trust me, if I'd wanted to nail you, I could have... even with a rubber-tipped arrow."

Trevena ignored this, asking: "And what did you do with Jenkins, by the way?"

"Oh, he's okay. Sleeping it off in one of the cupboards, out of the way." Mark thumbed back down the hall. He switched his bow to the other hand, bending to clasp Mary on the shoulder and then stroke April's hair.

Mary looked up at him. "She'll be all right, just a little spooked. We should have told her, you know. Given her some warning."

"You know what Dad would say, don't you?" Mary nodded. "The real assassins won't give us any warning."

"No, but you all knew we were coming at some point over these past few days," argued Chillcott.

"At *some* point," said Mark. "Just like we know there's going to be a real sneak attack on us here, at *some* point."

"So what are you going to do, just wait up every night like you were tonight? Just in case?" Chillcott countered.

"If I have to," Mark told him, puffing out his chest. "It's what Dad... Robert would do. And with him not here, the buck stops with me."

"You do know that..." Mary began, then shook her head.

Mark frowned. "What?"

"Well, not only are you starting to look like him these days, you do know you're beginning to sound like him, too."

"I'll take that as a compliment," Mark said, with a smirk.

Mary smiled back. "That's how it was meant."

He patted the top of April's head. "And as for taking after people, you, young lady, are a chip off the old block. Both of them."

April—who had almost stopped crying—looked up and over at her brother, still hugely confused by what had happened, and now about what Mark meant.

"You'd better go check on the others," Mary reminded him, and Mark nodded, rising.

"Wait a minute, so who won?" Chillcott called after him as he began descending the stairs.

"Let's call it a draw," was Mark's reply.

HE TOOK THE stairs two at a time, hurrying to get down and see what the 'casualty' situation was. He'd managed to save his mother, but had any of the others survived? Doubtful, as his other two 'assassins' wouldn't have made it upstairs if they had.

That worried him. All of this worried him, in fact. Just another way in which he was similar to the man he'd come to call and think of as his father over the years. Who was he kidding? Mark was thinking about him like that not long after they'd met—when Robert Stokes had saved him from the Sheriff's men at that outdoor market. So long ago now; he'd only been thirteen. But he wouldn't go back to those times, wouldn't swap them for now. He'd been virtually alone back then, since the virus. After he met Robert and Mary, all that changed. He was given another family, and so were they.

There had been hard times, sure—things they'd had to tackle together. The Sheriff, De Falaise; The Tsars (both of them); the Welsh Dragon; the Widow up in Scotland. The Morningstars. But somehow, no matter how hard things had been, it had always brought them closer together in the end.

Mark remembered some of the times they'd had as a family and smiled again. That Winter Festival they'd held at the Castle. What a wonderful night that had been! He'd danced with Sophie until their feet hurt, laughed with her until their sides hurt.

It hadn't been too long after that they'd got engaged. It had been the business with that Native American, Shadow— who'd stolen into the castle, a little like his men had tonight, and kidnapped Mark—that had sealed the deal really. Sophie had been so worried about him, had realised she couldn't live without him then.

They'd married a few months after that, the Reverend Tate presiding over it just as he had done when Mary and Robert had got hitched. They hadn't wanted a big affair, just friends and family, with Mary heavily pregnant by this time. Dale had been his best man—strange, how close they'd become, when at the beginning they'd always been at each other's throats; mainly because Mark thought he was after Sophie, it had to be said. He'd been a bit of a ladies' man back in the day, had Dale. And who could blame them for falling at his feet with those good looks, not to mention he'd played lead guitar in a band back before the world went to shit. Then Dale had met

Sian—saved her from the Dragon—and fallen in love. The pair of them got married the year afterwards, back in Wales where they'd lived for a while until the Ranger presence there was well and truly established. Just like it was in most parts of the country now, not to mention Europe—thanks in no small part to their alliance with the current monarchy and its forces. And while they were still separate entities in their own rights, the Rangers and His Majesty's New Royal Infantry knew they could rely on each other when needed. They'd fought together on many occasions, not least when trying to quell the troubles in Russia and Germany.

Robert himself was currently travelling with a compliment of NRI himself, on a tour of some of the Ranger stations abroad. His second-in-command Jack 'The Hammer' was with him. As was Azhar, possibly the finest fighter they had in the ranks of the Rangers.

Mark understood that the trip was necessary, but the timing could definitely have been better. There was increasing unrest at home, rumblings from those who disagreed with the ban on firearms that had been imposed in the wake of what had happened with the Dragon and the Widow. The Rangers had simply reasoned that it was much easier to keep the peace when you knew you weren't going to get your head blown off, especially when they themselves still didn't carry guns. Robert had never approved of them, hated all they stood for— mostly all that was wrong about the previous world that had destroyed itself. It was bad enough that those who attacked from other shores had access to such weapons, without having to worry about stuff like that at home.

But it wasn't as if Robert and the Rangers just decided on their own. It had been in conjunction with the monarchy, and after a vote from the fledgling council system that had been set up—formed out of as many representatives from towns and cities as they could find. People who knew what Robert had sacrificed to defend them, who trusted him to carry on doing just that. It was no different from the system that had been in place before the A-B virus struck, anyway. Ordinary citizens couldn't take the law into their own hands then, weren't legally allowed to own firearms; they had to trust the police—

of which Robert was a former member himself—and military to protect them.

Of course, even back at the start there had been voices of dissent: those who argued that people needed a way of defending themselves, just in case. A small but vocal band that had grown in size over time, and now even had their own resistance movement. Their propaganda would have people believe that the council was a joke and the Rangers were lackeys of the new regime. That last one made Mark absolutely furious: the Rangers were *nobody's* playthings.

It was because of this misguided resistance effort—the so-called 'Defiants', who had stepped up their activities over the last year or so—that they all had to be prepared. Ranger spies had learned that they were planning on covertly striking at Robert's core leadership team to destabilise the Rangers. They weren't big enough to come at them head on, so it made sense that a small assassination unit would be sent to do this (a decision had been made to downplay all this, as Robert would have returned immediately).

They just didn't know how or when it would go down...

One of the reasons why exercises like this were so critical. The three Rangers involved had been trained to think as those people would, trained to be able to infiltrate a heavily guarded city and castle. And they'd managed to pull it off, maybe not getting to Mary or Robert—if he'd been here—but certainly taking out enough of Hood's most important people to cause the maximum amount of damage. The loss of Dale and Sian, of himself and Sophie... Mark closed his eyes, sucking in a breath and suppressing the tears that were threatening to break free. The thought of that last one—of losing her—was just too much.

He couldn't let his wife see him like that, see how worried all this made him—how scared for them all he was, for *her*. Mark was at the bottom of the stairs anyway, making his way along to his quarters. A Ranger called Abney had been standing in for Mark these past few nights, just as Mark had been standing in for Robert, providing added protection in case something did actually occur. Mark trusted Abney, both he and Sophie had known the guy and had been friends with him long enough for that. You'd have to, to let him 'share' a bed with you, in whatever capacity. But Mark had absolutely no worries on that score. Not only was Abney in a serious, long term relationship with somebody, that somebody also happened to be a guy.

So, it was quite a shock for Mark to round the corner and find not Abney, but a totally different Ranger there instead. A brown-haired guy wearing a tight-fitting T-shirt and tracksuit bottoms. Even through his top, the outline of his broad chest and six-pack could be discerned—and as for those arms... Not that Mark was any slouch in that department, he couldn't afford to be; it was just that being confronted by it for some reason made him feel strangely inadequate. The man was dotted in that same light purple paint, 'killed' by one of the assassins obviously, and was now sitting up on the bed crossed-legged. Booth, his name was, Mark recalled. One of a batch of new recruits the other month, who had only just finished his basic training if Mark remembered rightly. Something the bloke had relished, perhaps a little too much. Sophie was propped up at the head of the bed, pillows bracing her back; she too had been 'murdered,' judging from the purple paint that stained her white satin chemise—which had a plunging neckline Mark was altogether too aware that Booth was ogling.

It took a moment or two for them to register the fact Mark was even in the doorway, Sophie laughing—actually laughing—at something Booth had just said. Those freckles on her face, though less pronounced than when Mark had met her at fifteen, were infinitely more apparent when she smiled or had the giggles. But what was annoying him more? The fact that neither of them had taken this exercise seriously, or that Booth was making his wife laugh in a way he hadn't seemed to be able to do in a while?

When they saw his face, the laughing stopped. Booth went rigid, getting off the bed and saluting. "Sir!" he said, voice cracking slightly.

Ordinarily, Mark would have told him there was no need for all that: he wasn't in the bloody NRI. But right at that moment, Mark was glad of a chain of command, of his superiority over this man—even though he was at least five years younger than

Booth. Mark didn't salute back, however, and didn't give him permission to relax his own either. So there he stood, like a statue, or a robot awaiting further commands.

"Mark," said Sophie, rolling her eyes sideways and nodding, encouraging him to do just that and put the guy out of his misery.

"At ease, Ranger..." said Mark through gritted teeth. "Booth, isn't it?"

"Sir," replied Booth, sticking with the military theme.

"Where's Abney?" Mark asked, of either Booth or his wife, he didn't care who answered.

"Cried off sick tonight," Sophie told Mark, quickly. "Some sort of stomach bug. Tommy here kindly stepped in at the last moment."

Tommy now, is it? And I'll bet *he stepped in.*

"I see..." said Mark, drawing out the last word. "And what was so funny?"

Sophie and Booth exchanged a glance, as if struggling to cast their minds back all of a few minutes. "Oh," said Sophie, finally. "We were just tickled by the fact Tommy had fallen asleep by the time your guys burst in."

Booth looked extremely sheepish about that, it had to be said. "I pulled double shifts sir, sorry."

"Okay," said Mark. It was how he'd have ended up himself if he'd been here, but the fact remained that he hadn't been. It had been Tommy, asleep, in bed with *his* wife. "And you were both..." He couldn't bring himself to say *killed* about Sophie, even for an exercise. "You both got shot, I see."

"Yeah, 'fraid so," sighed Sophie, as if she'd just missed out on winning some sort of competition. Didn't she see the danger in all this, didn't she understand why they were doing it?

Mark couldn't help himself. "Jesus, if this had been for real—"

"But it wasn't," she said, sitting up even straighter in bed and folding her arms. "Was it? This was just some silly game."

"One that might save all our lives," Mark insisted.

"Won't happen next time, sir." This was Booth again. Next time? Mark wasn't about to let any of *this* happen again, either as an exercise or for real. He liked to think, with his reactions, tired or not—asleep or not—he would at least have been able to save Sophie.

Mark glared at him. "You're dismissed," he said. "Debriefing will be tomorrow morning, oh-nine-thirty." He wanted army talk? Mark could fucking do that.

Booth took one last look at Sophie, nodded, then left.

Sophie still had her arms folded, waiting for her husband to say something. When he didn't, she began instead. "You know, all of this was *your* idea, Mark."

He pouted. "Not just mine, we—"

"I just don't get what your problem is! I've played along, haven't I? Even though I think it's the stupidest thing in the world. How can you plan against a surprise attack? The whole point is you'll never see it coming."

"That's comforting," said Mark with an edge of sarcasm that wasn't lost on his wife.

"It wasn't meant to be. I think sometimes you forget how we first met," she said. That wasn't very likely: he remembered every moment of that day. Going on a ride-along to a village with the Rangers, spotting Sophie in that yellow dress. Feeling so sick and nervous talking to her. Then the Sheriff's men— grabbing and ripping her clothes. Mark offering himself up to go with them instead. Absently, he rubbed the stump of his missing finger, the one the Sheriff's torturer Tanek had taken from him... Maybe she had a tendency to forget as well? But he didn't bring that up—he hadn't done it to impress her. He'd done it because he felt something for her, even then, even having only known her for such a short space of time. "Look at the world we live in. These have always been dangerous times, there's no escaping that. And there's no 'planning' to prevent things from happening. You have to live for each moment."

"They're not as dangerous as they used to be,'" Mark replied.

Sophie snorted. "If you think that, then you're just kidding yourself."

Mark walked over to the bed, sat on the end of it. "Perhaps I am," he said sadly. "But it's only because I want to keep you safe."

She reached out and took his hand, noticing the cuts on his arm and thigh for the first time. "You're hurt."

He shook his head. "Just scratches. I've had worse." *A lot* worse. They both had. "Just some silly game, as you say."

"Maybe I should take a look?"

"I'll be fine, it was just..." But then Sophie was pulling at his top, pulling it up and kissing his stomach, then his chest. Mark let out a low moan; it had been a while since she'd done something like this. Something so spontaneous. What could have...

"Tommy," he said without thinking.

Sophie broke off from kissing him, pulling back. "What?"

Mark didn't know what to say now, hadn't meant for the thought to pop out of his mouth.

"What about him?" Sophie pushed, then when she didn't get an answer, said: "You think... What? *What* do you think?"

"I just saw the way he was looking at you, Soph. Especially dressed like that. He—"

Sophie pulled back abruptly, folding her arms once more.

"Not this again. I don't care how he was looking at me," she barked. "Doesn't mean I was looking at him the same way, does it? And this is what I always wear to bed, you know that. You said you wanted things to be as normal as possible during the exercise. You put him in here—where *you* should have been, I might add. For the last few nights, in fact."

"Actually, I put Abney in here."

"Yes, and we both know why. Don't you trust me?"

"Of course I do," he whispered. Why couldn't he just have relaxed, been in the moment, enjoyed the sensation of Sophie's lips on his skin? He had to go and spoil things again.

Sophie looked to the side, staring at the wall. "You've got a funny way of showing it, Mark." There was silence between them for a few moments, then Sophie turned to him and said: "This is just like what happened with Dale. You've got such a jealous side to you, Mark. It makes you—"

"Makes me what?"

"Sometimes..." Sophie drew in a breath, as if wondering whether she should say the next bit. "Well, sometimes it can be a bit ugly."

Mark felt those tears rising again, this time for a different reason. How could he tell her, that he only got that way because he knew how men looked at her—had *always* looked at her, even on the day they met? How he shouldn't worry, but couldn't believe his luck that she'd wanted to be with him in the first place. Was always terrified she'd wake up and realise her mistake, then want to leave him. The rational part of his mind was saying that if he kept up this kind of behaviour, he'd push her away anyway. But it wasn't logic that was in control when he had these feelings. He wanted to say all these things, yet in the end it was easier to just say: "I'm sorry."

"Hey, and how are you two lovebirds doing?" As if on cue at the mention of his name, Dale was at the door to check in on them. "Not interrupting anything, am I?"

Mark's expression told him he really wasn't.

"I see you got nabbed, Soph," said Dale, changing the subject, his hair flopping over his eyes so that he had to brush it back with one hand. Then he indicated the paint splodges on his own T-shirt. "Us too. Never would have happened a few moons ago. Must be getting too old for this shit, eh, Mark?" He laughed, but Mark didn't join in.

Probably because right at that moment, in spite of the fact he was only in his twenties, he felt ancient.

Old, useless—and very, very ugly.

CHAPTER TWO

He knew he was growing older, but still felt like he was in his prime.

He still felt young. Which was surprising, considering everything he'd gone through over the last decade or more. Having his new family helped, of course. And even when he'd been going through those sleepless nights, changing nappies and feeding April after she'd been born—a second chance for him, after the loss of Stevie to that damned virus—he'd never felt more alive. He had Mary, he had a brand new daughter to love and care for, and he'd seen his other son, Mark, settle down with Sophie.

Even the day-to-day running of the Rangers wasn't so much of a grind as it had been in the past. He'd always been fighting for a better existence, a world without dictators and madmen holding people to ransom or using them as slaves. They were far from finished yet, but Robert Stokes—Robin Hood, as many were now calling him—had made a decent enough dent in things. One day, he'd hand over the reins completely to Mark, knowing things would be in safe hands. That kid had always had an old head on his shoulders. But Robert wasn't done yet, there was too much work still ahead of them and it didn't do to become complacent. Whenever they'd relaxed in the past, that's when they'd had the rug pulled out from under them. He didn't intend to let that happen again.

Which was one of the reasons he'd agreed to this tour. Every now and again they'd do a sweep of their own country, which was in pretty good shape, all things considered. There were the usual naysayers, at the moment in the form of those massive pain-in-the-arse Defiants, but generally Robert was happy with the way things were ticking over at home. It was certainly a step up from what they'd all been used to, in the post-virus era. So, it was time to look further afield, to ensure that their outposts abroad were doing okay—after all, some of the most serious threats had come from there: France, Germany, Russia... all had taken a crack at Britain. Tried *to* crack Britain, more accurately, and they might have succeeded were it not for men like Robert and his band.

Of course, while he might feel young in himself, Robert was becoming increasingly aware of the toll the last several years had taken on his body. He'd been half-killed more times than he cared to remember, and become a little too reliant on the strange healing powers of his beloved Sherwood—the place he'd retreated to when his first family had passed away (even then, perhaps the forest had been working on healing his mind? Who knows... Robert had never questioned it, tried not to think about it too much if the truth be told). Sherwood was also responsible for those strange prophetic dreams he often had, particularly when he went and stayed there, as he did periodically to recharge his batteries. He knew that Mark also experienced them, though neither of them talked much about what they actually contained—they were always quite personal. Maybe they thought some of the magic would disappear if they discussed it?

In the last few, Robert had seen himself as the stag once more, only this time it had aged—the grey of the beast reflecting Robert's own salt and pepper hair now. Another reminder when he looked in the mirror that his body was growing older even if his spirit wasn't. In the dream, the forest had been ablaze, scattering the animals that lived there and decimating the trees. What it meant, he had no idea... But he would probably find out in the fullness of time, he suspected.

He always did.

Then there had been that thing in Spain, as they'd passed through after their tour of France was done with. The local Rangers had invited him to sit in on a display of combat techniques in one of the old rings that had once been used for bullfighting. One of their champions had then asked if he could have the privilege of sparring with the legendary Hooded Man himself: an eager and altogether too cocky individual called Vivas. Though the Commander there, Rojas, had refused on Robert's behalf—and both Jack and Ahzar had counselled against it (the ever silent Azhar had just shaken his head, and Jack's exact words were: "Don't be a dumbass, Robbie. Look at the size of him!")—Robert had accepted the challenge, like some kind of knight of yore or something.

Jack had reminded him of the sage warning as the NRI doctor who was with them—Cole, a heavily tattooed ex-field surgeon; even his bald head was covered in them—had treated his numerous cuts and bruises. "Yeah, but he went down, didn't he," Robert had said with a tight grin.

"Eventually," Jack conceded. "After using you as a human basketball for a while first." He then made Jack swear not to tell Mary; she'd finish the job and kill him if she ever found out. Jack had zipped his lips shut with a wink.

Robert had been tempted to cheat a little with his recovery, to utilise his 'secret weapon,' but he didn't like abusing it—especially as it had been his own pride that had caused the injuries. Mark and he had discovered a long time ago that by carrying a pouch containing items gathered from Sherwood—stones, twigs, grass, bark and leaves—the place's power would somehow be with them. It was like some kind of weird portable battery. Again, Robert couldn't explain it, and didn't question it: he was just grateful for it. In the end, he simply rested up until it was time to carry on with the next leg of the inspection.

Aside from Jack, Azhar and Cole, Robert was travelling with a mix of Rangers and NRI soldiers, the latter carrying weapons he didn't really approve of but had absolutely no say in. The current Monarch, King Jack Bedford (sometimes referred to as John II, in spite of the unhappy reputation of the last king to bear the name), the latest in the unfortunate bloodline of royals since the A-B virus, was quite stubborn when it came to that. Insistent that his men be fully equipped for any eventuality—particularly when in foreign territory. "Think of the kind of message that sends, when we're trying to keep guns off the streets," Robert had argued with him, but got nowhere. In a lot of ways Robert and King Jack saw eye to eye, enough so they could work together for the same goals, but there were still sticking points.

He also knew the soldiers Jack had sent were partly there to protect him, not that he needed it. Indeed, he railed against it when they'd huddle around him at times. Not only did he have his own men there, people he'd personally trained, but Robert was still more than capable of looking after himself—as he'd shown that huge Spaniard Vivas.

The locals were no less protective wherever he and his people went, though, laying on armed guards as they were ferried from one Ranger outpost to another. He remembered when they arrived in Rome, there had been that welcoming committee. They'd organised a brass band for the reception, the pomp and ceremony making Robert cringe inside. He'd smiled through gritted teeth as he'd shaken hands with the local official there, Baldinotti, a bespectacled individual who'd bent over backwards to make sure his visitors were given the VIP treatment.

Jack had nudged Robert as the band was playing, commenting: "Hail to the chief, baby." None of it had sat very well.

They'd been treated to a tour of the capital then, their guide bemoaning the state the city had been in for a long time—"Oh, the treasures we lost to mindless vandalism," he sighed—but it had been the same story everywhere, post-Cull. That had been the purpose of the peacekeeping force in the first place, to try and put some of this right. And, if nothing else, Robert felt proud of that fact. It would hopefully be a legacy beyond the whole 'Hooded Man' thing that had built up around him: the reason for the protection in the first place. He was the figurehead of all this. Shouldn't be taking pointless risks. But he was also Robert

Stokes, a man who didn't know how to do anything else. Who'd earned his reputation by doing precisely that.

At the same time, he was a husband and a father now—with all the responsibilities that entailed. He was keenly aware of the fact that, with one false move, April would grow up without her Daddy.

And Mary...

She hadn't really wanted him to come, he knew that. Knew his wife, and should do after all this time. But she also realised the responsibilities that came with his 'job.' It had taken them both a few years to come to terms with that, but they eventually had. "It'll only be for a month or so," he'd told her, dreading leaving her and April. "A whistle-stop tour."

"I know," she'd said, planting one of her tender kisses on his lips. Then: "You be careful."

"Hey, it's me," he'd said with a half smile.

"And that's *why* I worry," she'd said without any hint of humour.

"I'll be in touch whenever I can on the radio. And I'll be well looked after," he assured her, taking both of her hands in his.

He certainly had been, from place to place. A lot of effort had gone into co-ordinating this tour, which would now head further northwards towards Florence and Bologna. Robert had to admit he was dreading Venice, though. It was where he'd honeymooned with his first wife, Joanne, and would bring back memories. As with Paris when they'd passed through there, that place would—even now—forever be associated with romance and love. And, although Robert knew Jack would make some kind of jokey comment about them being there together, would probably even make to hold his hand or something, that the big guy would be feeling it, too.

Jack hadn't exactly been what you'd call lucky in love, even in the time Robert had known him. First he'd fallen for De Falaise's daughter, Adele, though he hadn't known who she was until it was too late. Then, on the mission to take down the Welsh Dragon, Jack had met Meghan, Sian's aunty.

He had been happy back then living over in Wales, and it was so nice to see, as everyone else was hooking up with people and Jack had always felt like he was missing out. But that hadn't ended well, either. Nothing sinister this time, she hadn't been murdered by a deranged lunatic, or died in a terrorist explosion. No, they'd simply realised—or at least she had—that things were not working out. Robert got the sense that Jack would have hung on in there for grim death, just to have someone by his side. But when a relationship goes sour, there's nothing you can do to fix it. Real life battles were one thing, but battles of the heart... they were something else. So, Jack had moved back to Nottingham Castle, they'd got drunk together and commiserated, going over all the shit that had gone wrong with women in both their lives, and Jack had started to get on with his own life again. Last Robert heard, Meghan was living with someone else, and by all accounts was happy. He didn't know whether Jack knew that—probably did—but wasn't going to be the one to tell him if he didn't. Someone would come along at some point and make an honest man of his best friend, Robert was certain of that. Jack had so much love to give the right person.

But all that was for another day. Today, right now, they were on the move. They were a small convoy: a couple of VTLM Lince personal carriers peopled by Italian troopers, about eight between them; an Iveco MMV general utility truck carrying Rangers and NRI in the back, including Azhar and Cole; then finally a black Lancia Thesis, official state car of Italy, which was chauffeuring Jack and Robert. The latter was in the middle, to ensure maximum protection. The modest size of the party was due mainly to the fact that they didn't want to draw attention to themselves. Regardless of how safe the route might be, there was still a chance they could come under attack from thieves or other organised criminals—which was why there were also just enough soldiers in tow to make those kinds of people think twice. The other reason was that fuel remained in such a short supply these days; more so than at any other time post-Cull. Which was why it was reserved for occasions like this.

Robert and Jack admired the scenery, as their driver Lagorio ferried them through the Italian countryside—made all the more pleasant as spring lazily made its way into summer. They were not far from Amelia, they were told, when chatter started coming across the airwaves. Even though Robert couldn't understand what was being said, he could tell from the voices that something was wrong. Leaning forward, he asked Lagorio what was going on.

"Is nothing. Some sort of communication problem, they say," the incredibly stubbled man told Robert.

"Communication problem?"

"They've lost touch with an outpost just east of here and are calling it in. Don't worry, Signor Stokes, it happens from time to time. Poor reception out here. They'll send someone to look when they get a chance."

Robert and Jack exchanged glances; they'd already been told how stretched Ranger forces were in more rural areas of Italy. "How far away are *we* from this outpost, Lagorio?" asked Jack.

The driver shrugged. "Not too far. An hour, maybe."

"Then we should check it out," said Robert.

Lagorio half turned in his seat. "Is not a major outpost. Is not on our list to visit. Our schedule—"

"Sod the bloody schedule," Robert answered back, drawing a frown from the Italian. "I'm altering it. We can afford an hour or so to see what the problem is."

Langorio looked back at the road, then turned again to face Robert.

"That's an order, by the way," he told Lagorio.

The driver nodded. "Si, signore." He let the other vehicles know they were making a slight detour, then turned the wheel. Soon they were heading off in the general direction of the outpost.

It took them a little over an hour and a half to reach the place, situated in the middle of a rolling green field, with hills behind and on either side. They passed through a forest to reach it—the only route along a narrow road. It made Robert feel almost at home. The outpost itself was a small converted fort—once called Fort Vittoria—with a high stone wall and a wooden gatepost: an odd mixture of Robert's twin homes, in fact, Sherwood and Nottingham. Even before they got to the gateway, they could tell something was amiss.

"No guards," said Robert.

"And the gate's wide open," Jack added. "*Busted* open, by the looks of things."

There were also bloodstains on the gateposts. This wasn't an ordinary communications problem; something very serious had happened here—and recently.

There was only room in the small courtyard for a couple of vehicles, in addition to the two battered jeeps already parked inside, so one Lince and the truck went on ahead. Robert made to open the door of the car they were in, but Lagorio urged him to stay inside. "I cannot... If something were to happen to you... *Please,* signore!"

Jack placed a hand on his friend's arm. "At least let them make sure the area's secure first, Robbie," he said.

Reluctantly, Robert nodded. Gone were the days when he could just storm in somewhere himself. Now there were rules and regulations to follow, some of them not even made by himself. And there was Mary and April to think of.

So they waited, and eventually Azhar came to the gate to beckon them inside. Encircled by armed Italian guards, Robert and Jack made their way inside the small outpost, only to be informed that no local Rangers could be found. Just more bloodsmears on the interior walls.

"What the hell happened here?" asked Robert of no-one in particular.

They were taken into the building that housed the main office area. The radio had been smashed to pieces, the chairs and desks around it overturned. "This isn't good," said Jack, always one for stating the obvious.

Suddenly, there was a noise from somewhere beyond the office—a rattling sound. A handful of Rangers and NRI led the way through into some kind of kitchen area. The noise was coming from a metallic storage cabinet at the back. Motioning for everyone to stand back, Azhar, one of those lethal-looking scimitars in his left hand, pulled on the door with his right. There was some resistance at first, but then it gave, and a body dressed in green fell out onto the floor with a thud, bags of what looked like sugar or salt falling out with it.

Cole rushed forward, turning the body over. One of the local Rangers, who looked like he'd been raked across the face and chest, blood still pumping from his wounds. Robert thought he was dead, until the man's body shook with a sharp breath.

"He's trying to say something," Jack stated.

Cole leaned in, then pulled his head away slowly, a hand subconsciously rubbing the top of his tattooed head.

"What is it?" asked Robert.

"I could only make out one word: *Monstri*."

Robert looked to some of the worried-looking Italian troops, although he feared he knew what it meant already. It was Lagorio who spoke.

"It means *monsters*," said the man, sounding like a child. "Signor Stokes, he is saying that monsters did this."

CHAPTER THREE

"*PULL!*"

The machine noisily flung the clay pigeon into the air, and he took aim. Tracing its trajectory with one eye closed, he pulled the trigger twice, letting off both barrels. The disc continued to soar, before dipping and beginning its descent.

The man—dressed in a tweed jacket, jodhpurs and boots, with a flat cap on his head—swore under his breath.

"Do you really think that's wise?" asked a voice from behind him. Virgil Sorin turned to see a woman in grey combats, black beret at an angle on her head, being escorted up the gentle slope by two of his armed men—themselves in dark blue jumpsuits, like something out of an old spy flick. "There is an embargo on and those things do make such an awful noise."

Virgil grinned, breaking the gun and resting it on his crooked arm, then waved his hand around. "Who's going to hear?"

"A passing Ranger patrol," she answered, stopping abruptly just metres away.

Virgil laughed out loud, shaking his head. "Passing? I think not. Too remote."

The woman inclined her head. "Besides which, it's not as if you're any good at it."

Virgil's smile became a grimace. He loaded up the barrels again and clicked the shotgun back into readiness. Then he pointed it in her direction. "Not likely to miss from this range, though, am I, my dear?"

She stood her ground, perhaps knowing he was all talk— Virgil had no intention of firing—but he thought he detected the slightest tremble of her ruby red lips. A tremor in her voice, perhaps even of pleasure (was she enjoying the thrill?) when she said: "Relax, Mr Sorin. We're all on the same side."

He laughed again, lowering his weapon.

"I do have to wonder, though," she continued.

"Yes?"

"What some of your followers—the 'Defiants' who are willing to give their lives for the 'cause'—might think if they saw you right now. Acting the part of the landed gentry of old?" Her turn to smirk, but it was a taut smile that held no humour.

It was a fair enough question, and as Virgil looked past her down the slope towards his country retreat—a virtual mansion that he'd spruced up and taken residence in—he couldn't help wondering too. Not that he gave a flying shit; it was his turn to get a bit of the good life. "The A-B Virus was a great leveller," he replied. "Rich, poor—it made us all the same. Broke down the barriers, if you like. At least to begin with. We're just trying to retain that equilibrium."

"Hardly an equilibrium," she pointed out. "The virus didn't make the strong and the weak the same, did it?"

"Well... no, that's true. But if you *were* weak and had brains and charm enough, you could use the strong for your own purposes."

"Is that what you are? Weak, but with brains?" Again that smirk was there. As much as he needed this woman—in more ways than one—it was incredibly tempting to just blow her head off right where she stood. But God, she was so sexy...

"You know exactly what I am," he answered, continuing the dance. "And you should also know what I'm capable of." He stared at the woman, waiting for her to blink. But it was he who cracked first. "Look, what is it that you want? I'm a busy man," he said impatiently.

"Clearly," she said with a snort, nodding towards the clay pigeon trap. "But to answer your question, I'm here to make sure things are progressing in a timely fashion. You have been known to drag your feet in the past."

"*Pull!*" shouted Virgil again, and the man controlling the trap sent another disc high into the air. Virgil aimed once more, firing off both barrels again. This time he at least winged the fake bird, sending it spinning off in another direction. When he turned back, beaming with satisfaction, he found the woman standing, hands on her hips. Her apparent annoyance just made him want her more.

Virgil handed his smoking gun to an aide waiting nearby, then joined his visitor. "Walk with me," he said to her, and when she didn't move, added: "Please. I'll try not to drag my feet." Now came the charm.

With a sigh, she fell in step beside him, pushing a strand of blonde hair that had come loose back over her ear. "I'm waiting," she said as they walked, trailed by more of Virgil's jumpsuit-wearing guards.

"I still don't see why this conversation couldn't have been conducted over the airwaves," Virgil moaned.

"But then you'd have been deprived of my scintillating company again, Mr Sorin," replied the woman beside him, her boots crunching on the gravel path—which led back to the house.

Was she flirting with him now? Or was his lust for her simply making him read too much into things?

"That and the fact our mutual friend doesn't trust such sensitive information to be broadcast, no matter what the frequency. You never know who might be listening in."

Doesn't trust me to get the job done, you mean, thought Virgil. *Has sent someone to gee me up, keep an eye on me. A good thing she had... charms of her own.* "All right. Well, things are definitely progressing in what you would call a 'timely fashion.'"

"So the Flaming Arrow is on target?"

"Set to be fired later on this very day," he reported.

She nodded firmly. "Good. That's very good. And the other small matter your movement were going to take care of?"

Virgil smiled. "Small? Hardly. But that's well in hand also. The person we selected is more than capable of the task. Hood's core command group is already in tatters, they just don't know it yet."

"Because I heard that they had got wind of your—our—plans and were taking steps to counter them." She looked across at him as they walked; he felt her eyes on him but this time didn't meet them.

"There's nothing they could do to counter *this*," he assured her.

"Because the timing needs to be—"

"I know, I know. I'm well aware of what's at stake here. But listen, it's all being taken care of." Virgil halted and faced her. "Now, I presume you will not be leaving for home just yet. Not after coming all this way?"

The woman didn't answer.

"Then I'd be delighted if you would be my guest for dinner tonight." Virgil knew full well she wouldn't be leaving, probably not until all this was over, in fact. So, why not get her to stick around so he could keep an eye on *her*? An extremely close eye. "I believe we're having roast pheasant tonight."

"Very well. As long as I don't have to wait for you to shoot them," the woman said.

Virgil studied her face, looking for any sign. Flirting, *definitely*. He understood women and this one *so* wanted him. Had a definite power and danger thing going on. He smiled again, then held out his hand for her to carry on walking. "After you. Ladies first," he said.

He checked out her arse as she strode in front of him.

It would be an interesting day today, Virgil thought to himself.

And, perhaps, an even more interesting evening.

"I GUESS I just don't understand women," he admitted.

Mary laughed softly. "We're honestly not that hard to figure out, son," she told Mark.

"Not to each other," he said, joining her at the kitchen table, having made them both a cup of coffee. The debriefing was over, and areas where security needed beefing up thoroughly identified. Though Mark hadn't really been as focused as he should have been, watching Booth and Sophie for any signs of... of what? That something more had been going on the previous night? Crazy and he knew it. His jealousy getting the better of him, as Sophie had said. But still...

No, Booth had just been standing—laying?—in for Abner when he was sick. There'd been nobody else available at such short notice, and even he had pulled a double shift before offering himself as a replacement—sense of duty, he'd explained. Nothing more, nothing less. So why was there this niggling feeling at the back of Mark's mind? He'd asked if he could have a chat with Mary, get her advice. Sometimes all you really needed to do was talk to your mum.

Mary took a sip of the steaming coffee. "You two just need some alone time, you need to reconnect with each other is all."

Mark looked unsure. "I think Sophie thinks we got together... got *married* too young," he confessed.

"Has she actually said that?"

"Not in so many words, but—"

"Mark," said Mary seriously, "Sophie thinks the absolute world of you. I know she does, I can see it in her eyes when she looks at you."

Mark wished that he could. He used to be able to see it, but now he wasn't so sure.

"It wasn't all plain sailing with me and your father, you know," Mary said, gazing down at the mug she was holding with both hands. "We've had our ups and downs, as you know. But if you're committed, you come through the other side stronger than ever. Trust me."

Mark rose, carrying his own drink to the window and gazing out—past the edge of the cliff-face and over the city he'd called home for such a long time now. "I just love her so much, you know?"

"And she knows that too," Mary said. "It's just that sometimes, especially when other stuff around us gets in the way, we can lose sight of what's important."

"We've been trying for a baby," Mark said, suddenly turning.

Mary almost spilt her coffee. "You've been... Wow," she spluttered. "You kept that pretty quiet."

He shrugged. "Didn't want to jinx things. Not that anything seems to be happening anyway."

"And... and this is what you both want?"

Mark's face was stern. "Of course! We've talked about it and everything. Starting a family and all." Or rather he'd talked and Sophie had listened, if he was being honest. There had been so much of it happening in the last few years, another generation being created that would take over from them someday. A repopulation of the planet, now that there was a certain amount of stability. Not that he'd put it in such dry terms; Mark just wanted to start a family, and figured Sophie would too.

"Because, well, a baby won't solve things if there are problems," Mary cautioned.

"You just said the only problem we have is not spending enough time together," Mark snapped.

"Mark, calm down."

"I *am* calm," he said, shaking his head. "I'm sorry, Mum. I just..." He shook his head again. "I just don't understand what's going on."

Mary took a deep breath and let it out again. "You're just going through a bit of a rough patch, that's all. Things will work out, you'll see."

Mark wished he could believe that. It didn't help to see Dale and Sian all loved up, it had to be said. The guy had certainly turned things around, was a one-woman man now and proud of the fact, while Sian seemed to love him more and more each day. It was quite the transformation from when he first arrived at the castle, but then he was—as he'd put it the previous night—older now. Not that early 30s was over the hill, but maybe it made him a little wiser too. Certainly more than Mark felt at the moment. Their fearless leader... *pah!*

As if reading his thoughts, Mary said: "You're also putting too much pressure on yourself right now. It won't be long before Robert gets back, and he can take over again—"

"So not only am I a crap husband, I'm not fit for command?" Mark slammed the coffee cup down on the side.

Mary scowled at him. "Don't forget who you're talking to, Mark," she said in a tone only mothers can muster; one she only rarely had to use with April, let alone her grown son. Mark went very quiet. "That's not what I meant and you know it. Your dad can take some of the workload, help get to the bottom of this threat we've learned about."

He hung his head, knowing she was right. Mark had admitted himself he could use his dad round about now. Jack too, and Azhar. But they were all off on their tour, enjoying the good life if Robert's calls home were anything to go by. And though he knew it shouldn't, that made him mad as well.

"Just don't let your imagination run away with you, Mark. That's all I'm saying. When it comes to the threat *or* Sophie." Mary got up, leaving most of her drink behind on the table. "It's not far off lunchtime; April will be finishing her class soon." There weren't many children at the castle—it wasn't the right kind of environment for kids, really—but Mary and Robert had initiated schooling for those who did live there, April included. Not that his little sister thought much to this idea.

"Mum... Mum, wait," said Mark, covering the distance between them and placing a hand on her arm. "I'm sorry. I really am."

Mary turned to face him, smiling. "You're a lovely young man, Mark. I'm lucky to have you as a son. And Sophie's lucky to have you as a husband. I think she knows that." Mary hugged him to her. "Just give it some time, okay?" Mark nodded into her shoulder, and she broke off the embrace.

He watched his mother leave. Give it some time... He'd never been the most patient of people. In a hurry to fight with the Rangers, not to be left out. In a hurry to love. In a hurry to marry? Perhaps they *had* rushed things a little, but they'd been together all these years. That had to count for something.

It would sort, he told himself. Mary was right; he just needed to calm down. Think about all this rationally. Clear his head.

And Mark knew just the way—just the place—to do that.

Nodding decisively, he left the kitchen and headed off in search of Dale.

CHAPTER FOUR

Classes sucked.

They were a complete waste of time. And the teachers were so patronising. All "What shall we learn about today, children?" and "Who can tell me what this is, class?" For fuck's sake! He'd learned all he needed to know by now, had taught *himself* most of it beyond basic reading and writing. Now it was all just holding him back. Getting on his nerves.

In the latest incident, he'd stood and swung a chair at Alistair Brooks, a hangover from another argument they'd had in the yard that dinner-hour. Alistair, a stocky lad who wrongly assumed he ruled the roost there, had called his father—his real father—a coward, who'd been put out of his misery like the yellow dog he was. Then Alistair and his friends, because there were always more than one bully in a pack, had started in on his mother for the first time.

"I heard she was some kind of a whore, back before you were even born," the boy had said to him, sniggering. "That your dad might not even *be* your dad."

Clive Jr had walked away from the fight then, like he'd tried to do so many times, and often failed—like he'd always been taught to do by Reverend Tate, his uncle in all but name. The *be the bigger man* thing, turning the other cheek. But when Alistair had continued in class that afternoon, whispering jibes from behind him all throughout French—one of the few lessons Clive Jr could actually tolerate—enough had been enough. Clive had risen, snatched his chair up and whacked the twat with it. Blood had exploded from the side of Alistair's head, splattering the desk and a couple of the other kids sitting nearby, who'd started screaming.

Clive, grinning all over his face, had been pulled from the class and his parents—well, the people who'd brought him up anyway, Karen and Darryl—had been sent for.

They'd all sat in the headmistress' office in silence, waiting for Mrs Berkley to arrive and pronounce judgement. When the po-faced woman—if you could even call her that, Clive had his doubts; and there definitely wasn't a *Mr* Berkley—arrived, she'd taken her seat opposite and shaken her head. "Here we are again, except it's a little more serious this time. Alistair needed stitches," Mrs Berkley informed them in her monotone voice. She wasn't even a real teacher, had been some kind of librarian or something back before the Virus, so the rumour went, and was making up for it now by throwing her weight around in the tiny school at New Hope.

"I'm sure Clive Jr feels really bad about that," Darryl offered. "Don't you?"

Clive shrugged.

"Whether he feels bad or not is irrelevant, I'm afraid I'm going to have to exclude him for a little while until all this blows over," said the headmistress. "And count yourself lucky that it wasn't reported to the Rangers."

He'd almost laughed out loud at that. Not only were they telling him he didn't have to come here for the foreseeable future, but they were threatening him with the 'police' over what amounted to a minor event at a school in the arse end of nowhere. Besides, the Reverend held more than a little sway with the Rangers.

"It's what Alistair's parents wanted to do, but I talked them out of it."

"Thank you," said Karen, casting her eyes in Clive's direction.

"And I assume the student will be suitably disciplined when you get him home?" Mrs Berkley tapped her finger on the table in front of her as she waited for an answer.

"The student"? I have a name, thought Clive.

"Oh... Oh, yes, he will," Darryl promised.

That punishment turned out to be a grounding for two weeks, and having his books taken off him. He didn't mind the former, but the latter was another thing altogether. He relied on them for information, to teach himself the important things. To give him a sense of what the world out there was like—or what it used to be like at any rate. History books, mostly, which spoke of emperors, kings and conquerors. He imagined himself like that one day, to have the unquestionable loyalty of those around him.

"We're taking them and that's that," Darryl had said, gathering up the books from Clive's room.

"No!" Clive spat back. "I won't let you!"

"You... *you* don't have any say in it, young man!" Clive got off his bed and stood in Darryl's way. They locked eyes and for a moment he thought his 'father' was actually going to back down. Then Darryl grabbed him by the arms and started to shift him sideways. Clive wasn't physically his match yet, but lashed out anyway—landing a kick on the shin-bone. Darryl yelped in pain, striking Clive across the cheek with the back of his hand before he could stop himself. "Y-You asked for that," he said to the boy, who glared up at him. "When I think what I went through to protect you when you were little..." He shook his head, then Darryl continued to collect the books, dumping them in a bag—not caring if he damaged them—took them and locked Clive's bedroom door behind him.

Clive wanted to cry, but wouldn't let himself. That was a sign of weakness, and true leaders didn't show weakness. Instead, he got up and started to trash his room, toppling over his wardrobe, picking up another chair—this time swinging it to crack the mirror on his wall—and upturning his bed. When he was finished, he stood in the middle of the room, breathing in and out quickly. Strangely, surveying the destruction he'd caused made him feel much better.

They must have heard the noise, but nobody came to see what was going on. Not then, at any rate.

A little while later, Clive heard the lock on his door being turned. A squat man walked—no, limped—in, looking left and right, then found the boy on the floor, knees pulled up, arms wrapped around them.

The older man tutted a few times. "It's all a bit of mess, isn't it." It wasn't a question, and it was unclear whether he was referring to the room or the situation. They were connected anyway, as were Clive and the Reverend Tate. "So, what have you got to say for yourself this time?"

The boy shrugged again, just like he had in the headmistress' office.

"We both know you can do better than that," said Tate, picking up the chair and sitting down on it, resting his hands on the stick. To look at him, you wouldn't think he'd been one of the Rangers' best fighters in the past. But then, Clive wouldn't like to get on the wrong side of him even now. He had a respect for this man, could sense the strength in him—which Tate said came from a higher power. So, Clive answered:

"I got angry. Darryl took my books away." He didn't mention the slap, as it had been in retaliation for his own kick, and Tate would know all about that.

"Your father, you mean?"

Clive dismissed this with a sniff. "He's not my father, and Karen's not my mother."

"They've looked after you since... All these years, Clive. They've loved you as if you were their own little boy." Tate gave him a warm smile. Clive couldn't remember ever seeing the man get mad at anything. Upset, maybe, uncomfortable, perhaps—but never actually mad, like he'd just been with his guardians. "They're good people."

"Like my real parents were? That didn't stop them from getting killed," Clive grumbled.

"Is that what you're scared of, that the same thing will happen again?" asked Tate.

Clive frowned, considering this for a moment or two. How *would* he feel if Karen and Darryl weren't around anymore? He'd miss being fed, having his washing done for him. But would he miss *them*? Nobody had ever asked him that before, and he was mildly troubled that the thought didn't scare him in the slightest, especially right now after the book thing. After Darryl's back-hander. Still, he nodded anyway.

"That's not going to happen," Tate said.

"You don't know that. Nobody knows what's going to happen."

Tate conceded this with a tip of the head. "Tell me about what happened at school," said the holy man, thinking he was changing the subject, but he really wasn't. That was connected, as well. Everything was.

"He got what was coming to him," said Clive.

"The Brooks boy? How so? What could he possibly have done to deserve being hit with a chair?" asked Tate, his voice patient and even.

Clive just looked at him. "He called my father a coward—*again*—and my mother a whore."

The Reverend's eye twitched. So, it wasn't just Clive who was stung by those remarks then. And little wonder—Tate had actually known his parents, Clive and Gwen. Loved them both, as you could see when he spoke of them—which he didn't often do, because it brought back such painful memories. The problem with that was Clive didn't really feel like he knew them at all: he could only recall vague memories of his mother, and his father had been killed before he was even born. "I see," said Tate eventually.

"Was he?" Clive asked.

"Hmm?"

"My father. Was he a coward?"

Tate blinked, as if he couldn't believe he was being asked such a question. "Clive Maitland founded this community, pulled all the original inhabitants together," said the Reverend.

"Yes, I *know* he did that," answered Clive; it was one of the few things he did know for certain. "But I asked if you thought he was a coward."

"He was one of the most courageous men I've ever had the good fortune to know. When the bad men came, the Sheriff's men, he refused to fight them."

"And that's what got him killed?"

Tate shook his head. "He refused to fight them, at first. But when they wanted to take your mother, he tried to stop them."

"That's when he got shot," said Clive. "And he didn't have any weapons to fight back with?"

Tate frowned, rubbed his chin. "Your father didn't believe in them, nor in violence to solve problems." He surveyed the damage in the room one more time.

"So," said Clive, his mind ticking over, "he wasn't prepared for the men when they came." Like Tate's line about the mess, it wasn't a question.

"No, it wasn't like that, he—"

"My father died because he didn't *want* to fight. Not until it was too late, and then he was shot and killed."

The Reverend held up a hand. "You're twisting things, that wasn't... His place is in Heaven now. He knows eternal life."

"Is what they said about my mother true?" asked Clive suddenly, veering the conversation off in another direction again.

"Of course not!" There was a note, just a note of anger in that reply.

"What happened after my dad died? Did those men take my mother? What happened to her?" asked Clive.

Tate hung his head, refusing to answer.

Clive got to his feet. "I have a right to know!"

Tate looked up at him, fixing the boy with a withering stare. "All you need to know is that your mother was strong. She *was* a fighter, her experiences made her that way. She fortified this place, prepared—as you call it—for the bad things to come. She still died; Gwen was still killed. But she saved your life in the process, Clive. That's the important thing."

Clive's eyes narrowed to slits. "You think she brought the badness on herself, don't you?"

Tate said nothing.

"If my father's in Heaven, then where is my mother?" Clive asked him.

"She's... She's with your father. The Lord forgives all trespasses." Tate was positively squirming in his seat now.

"What trespasses?" Clive demanded, storming over to the Reverend.

The man stood, and Clive saw then why he really shouldn't get on the wrong side of his 'uncle.' "That's *enough!*" Tate roared. Clive stopped in his tracks, shrinking back in fear.

When Tate saw this, his face returned to normal, and he held out his free hand to place it on Clive's shoulder. The boy pulled back even further.

"I think you should go now," Clive told him, attempting to keep his voice steady.

"Clive, I'm—"

"I said I think you should leave."

Tate nodded. "Perhaps you're right. I will call again soon." And with that, Tate left the room without saying another word.

Clive heard the lock being turned again, and backed up to the wall, slumping down it. It was only now that he cried.

Cried so hard he thought he might never stop.

HE DIDN'T EVEN realise he'd fallen asleep.

He'd shed so many tears, he dropped off. Hadn't even bothered to right his bed, had just fallen asleep right there on the carpet. He dreamed he was in Nottingham Castle— he'd visited occasionally with Tate. And he wasn't so much walking through its corridors as drifting through them; until he came to a heavy oak door, which thankfully opened on his approach. Clive found himself in a large room, much larger than the ones he'd seen there, and much higher. This was more like something that would have been around in the past, like something out of one of his history books. It was ornate, with pillars and carvings, exquisite paintings on the walls and maroon drapes that hung from arched windows. Diamond chandeliers descended gracefully from the ceiling, sparkling and twinkling.

The carpet in front of him matched the curtains, and stretched the length of the room, to a throne at the far end. Even at this distance, he could see it was made from gold, and probably priceless. Clive began drifting towards it, and the closer he came, the more he could make out the figures there. One seated, one standing just off to the left.

It was the standing figure who caught his attention first, and held it. Because the man was huge, but built with it. His skin was olive-coloured, and his sneer sent shivers down Clive's ethereal spine.

Wrenching his gaze away, Clive concentrated on the seated figure now. The one wearing a crown. He was a much smaller man wearing sunglasses, and when he smiled his teeth were yellow and crooked. Both men were dressed in military attire, though while the tall guy's clothes were functional—meant for combat—this one's were for show; more regal, Clive mused, complete with rows of medals.

Both also had wounds at their chests, where their hearts would be.

The smaller man beckoned Clive nearer with a white-gloved hand. When he spoke, it was with a French accent. "Ah, let me look at you! What a fine young man you have grown up to be, non?"

Clive didn't know what to say, so he shrugged.

"Do not keep doing that," the man ordered. "It is not the mark of a decisive person. And you *are* a decisive person, whether you realise it or not."

"Who... Who are you?" asked Clive, finding his voice at last.

"Do you not know?" The man looked up at his giant companion, then back towards Clive. "Has my legend not endured?"

"Legend?" Clive queried.

"I bet you have heard of that bastard Hood, though, have you not?"

Clive gave a slight nod of the head. Of course he had: the Hooded Man, Robert Stokes, was leader of the Rangers. He commanded the kind of respect and authority Clive aspired to one day.

"Typical. Do you not realise he stole it all from me? The power, the glory? It was all rightfully mine. Then *he* came along." The man made a fist and slammed it down on the arm of the golden throne, which shook. "Came along and butchered my people, slaughtered me. *Merde!*"

"You!" Clive blurted out suddenly. "You, you're—"

"De Falaise, at your service," said the man with a bow of his top half.

"The Sheriff," whispered Clive.

"I *was*," said the man, pouting. "Until *someone* stuck an arrow in my chest. Oh, forgive me, where are my manners? This is my right hand man and torturer extraordinaire, Tanek."

The giant said nothing by way of a greeting, just continued to sneer.

"He is much friendlier once you get to know him," said De Falaise with a chuckle. Then he leaned forward, pulling down the sunglasses a little and looking over the rims. "Now, to business."

Clive had no idea what was going on here. Why was he dreaming about the Sheriff? Unless it was because of all that talk about... He jabbed a finger at the man. "You killed my parents!"

De Falaise touched a hand to his bloodied chest. "Moi? Non."

"You did," Clive insisted.

"If you are talking about your namesake, then that was nothing but an unfortunate accident. One of my people being a little overzealous, I am afraid, and I can only apologise for that. As for your mother, I would not have hurt her for the world. I... I loved her. I cherished her. Tanek here will tell you that."

"You..." Clive couldn't believe what he was hearing.

"She lived with me at the castle. Did you not know? Ah, I see there are some gaps in your knowledge. Please allow me to fill them. Your mother was due to be my bride, you see. We would have had the classic fairy tale life together, non?"

"You... *you* and my mother?"

"Ask your friend, the holy man"—De Falaise's face screwed up—"if you must. He will confirm that I was with your mother. That I, not Clive Maitland, am your father."

"My—" Clive let out a loud laugh. "You? I don't think so. You... you were evil."

"My son, remember what you have read in your books. History is written—*re*written, in fact—by the victors, is it not?" De Falaise eased forward even more on the throne. "And I am not around, not able to defend myself against such heinous accusations."

Your dad might not even be *your dad.*

"But—"

"If your mother had been allowed to stay with me, as she'd wished, then your life would have been very different right now. You would have been heir to my kingdom. Together, who knows what we might have accomplished!"

Clive thought about this for a moment, then shook his head. None of it was real, it was just a dream—brought on by talk of his parents, the loss of his history books. His longing for greatness someday. But not like this, he wouldn't have wanted this.

Would he?

"It is much to take in, n'est-ce pas? Yet I swear to you I speak only the truth." He clicked his fingers. "I can prove it. Being dead offers you a certain... clarity. The past, the present, the future." De Falaise wafted his hand like he was batting away a bothersome insect. "There are no boundaries. And I can see what your future might be. There is still a chance for you to gain your birthright, my son—with a little help from a few friends of mine."

"I—I don't understand," said Clive.

"Of course not. Not yet. But you will. Someone is going visit you, Clive—oh, how that name sticks in my throat!" He coughed loudly for emphasis. "Your name is *De Falaise!* No matter... Someone will come to you, someone who also loved your mother, in his own way, and has been keeping an eye on you. Do not be alarmed at the sight of him. He will have the answers. Answers to all of your questions. And he is someone who can offer you the assistance you require to get where you need to be. So that one day you can reclaim what should have been yours in the first place. Only then will you be able to avenge Tanek, myself and your sister."

"My—" Clive began, but there was a tapping at one of the windows. He looked over, and as soon as he did so he started to drift towards it. Another tap, louder this time. Clive looked back at the Sheriff and the throne, at Tanek, but they were gone, the dream itself breaking up around him. He pressed his hands against the glass of the window, but that too was melting, becoming like smoke.

He fell through, into nothingness. Clive attempted to fly, or glide, as he had done before in the dream, but just kept plummeting. Down and down, into darkness.

Until—

HE JERKED AWAKE, almost banging his head on the back of the wall he was leaning against. It was dark, but only because it had clouded over outside and the day was wearing on.

Clive shook himself, took slow, deep breaths to calm down. "Just a dream," he whispered. "Only a dream."

Then the tapping came again. A single tap, on the glass of his bedroom window. Clive rose, started to walk across the room. Another tap, which made him jump this time.

He hesitated at the window itself, jumping one final time when a tiny stone struck it. Keeping to one side, Clive peered down the side of the house.

There was a figure below, standing on the grass. At first Clive thought it was the Hooded Man himself, a carry over, a hallucination caused by the dream. But this man was real. And while it was true he had a hood, it was part of some kind of robe he was wearing (which was the same colour as the curtains and carpet from the dream).

Then he looked up and Clive let out a gasp. The man's face was just a skull.

Someone will come... Do not be alarmed at the sight of him... He also loved your mother, in his own way.

But this person wasn't even human, surely? What the fuck was going on? He should call for Darryl and Karen, let them know there was a monster outside, before it got *in*.

Then Clive noticed the person's hands. These weren't skeletal at all, they had flesh on them: they were real hands. Just the face, then, that was—

No, wait. It was paint. Either that or some kind of weird tattoo. Why would anyone do that to themselves?

He was still scared, how could he not be? But if the guy had meant him harm, why would he have alerted Clive to his presence? It just didn't make any sense.

The skull-faced man smiled, and it was the strangest thing Clive had ever seen. Yet somehow he found it comforting. The man placed a finger to his lips, urging Clive to stay quiet.

To his surprise, Clive was now standing fully in front of the window. And when the man crooked that same finger, beckoning Clive to climb down and join him, the boy was equally surprised to find himself opening the catch. It wasn't hypnosis—not that Clive would know if it was—it just felt like the right thing to do.

And, in his head, Clive heard the voice of De Falaise again: *He will have the answers.*

Answers to all your questions.

CHAPTER FIVE

IT WAS A town like so many others he'd seen grow and develop over the years since the Cull.

A place he'd seen thrive since they'd got the market system up and running once more, making the trade routes as secure as they could between communities—thanks in no small part to the Rangers.

And to him.

All right, there was still the odd incident with bandits, but generally they were few and far between. Not like they had been when the Dragon and the Widow had been around. Back then, you could virtually guarantee your load would get 'jacked—in fact it had almost put paid to the trade routes altogether. It gave him no small satisfaction to know they'd kicked both of those maniacs' arses, kick-starting a new era of trade in the process. They'd definitely come a long way since those sporadic, ad-hoc markets near Nottingham he'd overseen, that was for damned sure. The ones the Sheriff's men had loved to tear into. That was how he'd met Robert Stokes in the first place, when the Hooded Man had intervened during one of those attacks. Mark had been there too, just a boy back then. And look at him now.

Progress, thought Bill Locke as he watched the hustle and bustle of the stalls in the square. It was good in one way, and he was certainly proud of all their achievements in this respect, just as Robert was rightly proud of his Rangers. But it had taken such a long time, and before you knew it, you were getting on a bit in years. Next thing you'd be "Ready for the knackers' yard" as his dad used to say.

"Not bloody yet, though," Bill mumbled under his breath, taking another long draught of the pint he was enjoying. Real ale, brewed right here in town. You couldn't beat it.

He was standing in the doorway of the Pig & Whistle, which had been totally renovated a few years ago, courtesy of the new owner Arnold Brant, who'd been a landlord all his life. Bill had helped organise the labour and facilitated the procurement of any bits and bobs Arnold needed, all of which meant that he never had to pay for another beer ever again. Not that anyone paid for anything in the old sense, since they went back to the barter system. Every now and again there was talk of a monetary system, talk of the banks starting up again—usually at one of those terminally dull council meetings he'd had the misfortune to attend once or twice himself. Or the King might say something about it. But it would get forgotten about just as quickly. This worked, for now—might even be better than going back to having those fat cats, creaming money off people. At least it was all up front and honest this way. Any disputes over the worth of items were usually settled by having local Rangers step in.

He'd often been accused—though never to his face—of being like those fat cats of years gone by. That Bill was using the marketing systems to cream things off for himself. Those kinds of people obviously didn't know him that well, didn't realise what he'd done in the past to battle bastards, and bitches, like that. This was all the reward he needed: a busy market; a fine brew in his hand; and maybe, just maybe, to find a good woman he might share it all with.

He'd been thinking about that more and more lately, how he'd sidelined that kind of thing while he'd been so busy. Or maybe it was the other way around, kept himself busy so he wouldn't have to think about all that. How he'd been doing the same thing since he was twenty-five and Connie had broken his heart, leaving him standing there at the altar like an idiot in front of all their friends and family. Only to be told later that she'd run off with someone else, that she'd never really loved him in the first place. He'd vowed after that to leave love well enough alone, that it was a mug's game. And yet... This was a new world after all, and time was ticking on. Perhaps—

Bill shook his head; such thoughts were more dangerous than a whole gang of bandits. He took another gulp of his drink instead.

It was then that he noticed them, on the main road heading into town. This town, the real name of which had been lost in time and was now only referred to by its nickname; a joke that had stuck: 'Bartertown.' In the distance were several men on horseback. Several hooded men. The hooves were kicking up dirt on the track, making it look like they were riding in on a dust storm. Rangers...

Now what were *they* doing here? Bill wasn't aware of any patrols that were due, nor that there were any disputes that needed attending to—and he liked to keep track of these things. Which usually meant there was trouble. Maybe they were coming to fetch him? Wouldn't be the first time he'd been called on since he'd left Nottingham Castle and branched out on his own. Somehow his and Robert Stokes' paths always kept crossing, and you could almost always guarantee bloodshed in the wake of it.

The riders brought their horses up short on the edge of the town square, prompting the people at the market to look over in their direction. One of the Rangers trotted his horse forward, obviously the captain of the group. He kept his hood on, though, which Bill found strange. Rangers were taught the value of letting the people they were dealing with—or protecting—see their faces. After all, *they* were people as well; peacekeepers, not soldiers. "Your attention!" he shouted from under the hood. He had most of the crowd's attention already, but now all the townsfolk gathered were looking directly at him.

No "please can I have your attention," no common courtesy. Whoever was in charge of training them at the castle these days needed tearing off a strip or two, Bill decided, and he'd be more than happy to oblige.

"We have reason to believe that illegal weapons are being hidden in this town," the man's booming voice continued. By *illegal*, he probably meant guns—the kind that had been banned by the Rangers to make their jobs safer and easier. Bill's reaction when he'd heard about the law had been "Bollocks to that!" Same as it had been in all those 'discussions' with Robert over the use of them by Rangers. 'Course, now they had the NRI, which carried and used modern weaponry, so it made more sense. The police hadn't used guns in the world before the Virus, apart from in emergencies, and had banned them on the streets: why not now? After kicking up such a stink, though, and in light of the things that he'd done in support of the Rangers in the past, Bill had been given a special licence to carry his beloved twelve-bore. There was no way he was going to be parted from that after everything they'd been through together. It wasn't some kind of toy, like those stuck-up twits used to have at their country retreats back in the day; it was functional, practical. And it was the closest thing he had to a best friend.

"These weapons, we believe, are being kept here with a view to aiding and abetting the organisation known as the Defiants," the Ranger added. "Everyone remain exactly where they are. We're here to search this place from top to bottom, to search everyone present. And if we find anything suspicious, then..." He deliberately let the sentence tail off.

There were murmurs from the townspeople, concern etched on their faces. One minute they were enjoying looking round the markets, making a few deals, the next they were being accused of assisting terrorists. Oh, Bill knew all about the Defiants and their methods, their wild accusations against both Rangers and the new monarchy alike. Sadly, they were growing in number, but surely it hadn't come to this? Bullyboy tactics and what had to be unsanctioned searches? Were Robert's people so spooked by this group they'd lost all sense of proportion? Bill doubted it. Even if there was a cache of weapons here, and anything was possible, this wasn't the way to go about dealing with it. By putting fear into ordinary folk.

Gritting his teeth, Bill slammed his pint down on the nearest table, sending a crack up the side of the glass. "Oi!" he shouted back to the mounted man. The hooded Ranger looked across towards him. "Hold up, there."

When the Ranger didn't answer him, Bill continued. "On whose orders are ye doing this? I'm pretty sure it's not gonna be Robert Stokes. Or Jack Finlayson's, fer that matter."

Again, nothing. Bill was starting to get a really bad feeling about this.

"We don't need to tell you anything, scumbag." This was from one of the other Rangers behind.

"Izzat so?" Bill cocked his head, jabbing a finger in his direction. "Well, let me tell *you* something, *scumbag*. I—"

A couple of the Rangers had readied their bows and were training arrows in his direction. "Aye. So it's like that, is it?" said Bill to himself.

Several things happened all at once then. The first was, somebody broke free from the market crowd and ran for it; Bill didn't know why, and probably never would. Maybe they were worried the Rangers would search them and find something else, maybe they *were* armed illegally. Whatever the case, the man—who was dressed in jeans and a white shirt—darted like a hunted deer, away from the Rangers. One of the men turned and let his arrow fly. It struck the fleeing man in the back, hard. Not in the shoulder or thigh, or anywhere else a Ranger would be trained to target just to take someone down, but slap-bang in the middle of his back. The man spun, blood staining the front of his shirt and spraying from his mouth. A girl nearby, not much older than Robert's lass, April—Bill's god-daughter—screamed loudly.

Understandably, the crowd panicked.

As the Ranger was turning and firing, Bill saw the handle of an automatic pistol slip out from under the man's top, the rest of it tucked into his trousers. If the killing wasn't enough to tell him these weren't Rangers, then that definitely was. No way any of them would be armed with guns; it went against everything they stood for.

More arrows were loosed into the crowd, piercing chests, arms, legs. One poor soul was even staggering around with an arrow in the face, like some kind of warped recreation of King Harold's death.

You could almost always guarantee bloodshed in the wake of it...

But not like this, not a massacre. And it had absolutely nothing to do with Bill and Robert's paths crossing, he knew that. This was cold-blooded murder, pure and simple.

Bill ducked back inside the doorway and an arrow hit the jamb, inches away from his head. "Judas Priest!" he exclaimed, rummaging around under his seat for the bag he'd brought in with him.

When Bill emerged again from the Pig & Whistle, it was with his shotgun in his hands. He was already moving forwards when a couple more arrows flew past him. Then something caught his eye.

Turning, he saw a dozen small fires had sprung up, the pub included. *Flaming arrows!* The gun was up and at his shoulder even as he was arcing back in the direction of the 'Rangers.'

Blam!

The one just to the left and behind the lead Ranger was blown clean off his horse. The man in charge growled something, then pulled out a gun of his own—abandoning any pretence of legitimacy now. He fired a couple of bullets at Bill, who stepped sideways, letting them splinter off the frame of a market stall.

"Damn and blast it!" growled Bill, as the other Rangers began firing as well—not just at him, but at the people escaping. He leaned on the stall, tipping over a stack of cheeses, but creating cover he could hide behind. Bill rose and emptied another barrel in the Rangers' direction. It went wide, but caused one of the horses to rear up. The Ranger astride it had a hard time trying to wrestle the animal under control again.

More of the incendiary arrows were loosed, this time into the market itself. Awnings quickly caught fire, the wood of stalls doing the same moments later. A couple of the projectiles slammed into Bill's makeshift shield, sending a wave of heat up and over the top. He had to break cover. Bill primed his shot-gun again and half-ducked, half-stumbled out from the stall, firing another round as he did so.

Something landed a few metres away from him, small and black.

He barely had time to register the fact it was a hand grenade—let alone think again that this was definitely not the kind of weapon a Ranger would use—when it went off. Bill was carried upwards and sideways across more falling market stalls. He blinked once, twice: taking in the sight of the flames engulfing not just the market, but the entire town. All reds and yellows and oranges. In their own way, they looked beautiful.

Then, as his eyelids grew heavier, all Bill could see was blackness: total and overwhelming.

CHAPTER SIX

THERE WAS NO point in asking how things had taken such a turn for the worse, this quickly.

They had, and not for the first time, so that was that. Now it was simply a case of dealing with them. Though how this was ever going to be resolved was anyone's guess.

"Why don't they just make their goddamn move?" asked Jack, standing next to him on the battlements of the outpost, looking out at the forest ahead, then looking up and seeing the sky was growing dark. It would be night soon; they'd probably come then.

The monsters.

Of course, there were no such things. Robert used to tell Stevie that, when he swore blind there were goblins and all kinds of hideous creatures hiding in his wardrobes, or under his bed. Humans were bad enough—the things they did to each other—without anything supernatural adding to the mix.

He cast his mind back to when they'd arrived at the fort, hours ago. To when that local Ranger had also sworn he'd seen monsters. That is, until he'd passed out from blood loss.

Medic Cole had tried to stabilise him as best he could—which wasn't easy, as what passed for a med-bay at the outpost had also been trashed—but the man needed urgent medical attention.

Nobody asked the obvious question: what had happened to the rest of the contingent? Nobody really wanted to know.

"Get on the radio, we need to call this in," said Robert to a young female Ranger called Poynter. And that's when they'd encountered their first problem. None of the radios in the vehicles they'd been travelling in worked, she reported. And the same went for the battered jeeps they'd found in the yard, the radios in them still strangely intact.

"Could be just a problem with the signal out here," suggested Lagorio once more; they were, after all, surrounded by hills. But Robert, Jack and Azhar thought otherwise.

"They have... *had* a radio," said Robert. "But something tells me it wasn't working even before it was busted up."

"Some kind of jamming?" said Jack, scratching his chin. "You're thinking whoever struck this place knocked out communications first, right?"

"It's definitely a possibility," Robert replied. "And way too much of a coincidence."

That didn't help the poor local Ranger, however. So Robert suggested sending him off with Cole and an armed guard, to get the medical attention he needed and to alert the authorities. For all they knew, those people were still working under the assumption that there had been some kind of communications breakdown rather than an enforced blackout.

So, a handful of Italian troops accompanied Cole as they loaded the dying man into the back of one of the Lince vehicles. They trundled off out of the gate, towards the one way to and from this outpost—through the forest.

The rest watched as it entered, Jack nodding in satisfaction. But only a few minutes later the sound of gunfire reached them. "What in the Sam Hill...?" said Jack, opened-mouthed, as he saw the Lince backing up again, skidding on the grass as the driver attempted a handbrake turn—which wasn't a good idea in a vehicle that size. The sides of the green and black camouflaged brute were covered in dents, the glass of the windscreen and side windows splintered or smashed completely, and the thick wheels looked like they'd been clawed at by wild animals. Even from this distance, they could hear the screams and cries of panic as the Lince suddenly pitched over onto its side, parallel to the treeline.

One of the Italian troopers emerged from the back, firing off a machine gun into the forest. Then suddenly he was gone again, spirited away into the foliage before anyone could see what had happened. More of their party began to clamber out, but were meeting the same fate. One minute they were there, the next they were gone.

A couple managed to make it away from the Lince, running in the opposite direction. With them was Cole, easily recognisable by his tattoos. He had a handgun and was firing indiscriminately back into the trees. They began to sprint then, as if their lives depended on it.

"We have to help them!" Robert called out, signalling for Lagorio to come with him and directing him to the Thesis state car they'd ridden there in. The man hesitated, then saw the look in Robert's eye and did as he was told, climbing in and gunning the engine as Robert climbed into the back with his bow and arrows. The car had no sunroof, so Robert ground the back window down and clambered out with his weapon— arrow pointing beyond the soldiers in case whatever was inside the forest should think of pursuing them. Lagorio pulled up alongside the men, who gladly clambered into the car. "What the hell's going on?" asked Robert, as Cole climbed into the back. He didn't get a reply.

Robert kept his weapon trained on the trees, but nothing emerged. The car did a u-turn, throwing up clumps of grass, then Lagorio sped up—heading towards the fort. Still nothing followed.

Once they'd got the trio of men back to the outpost, they sat them down and asked what exactly had attacked them. The Italian troopers were gabbling, speaking faster than Robert could keep up with even if it had been in English. But he did catch that word again: "Monstri!"

"Cole, help me out here. What did you see?"

The medic just shook his head. "It all happened pretty quickly, but... I don't know, suddenly there were these... these *things* all over the vehicle. Clambering all over it, trying to get in."

"Things? What kind of things?" Jack demanded, turning Cole's chair round to face him.

"Feral, all teeth and hair and—they were quick, I can tell you that. I just got flashes of them. But I did see what they did to the wounded man from the outpost. Practically dragged him out through the window, like they had unfinished business with him." Cole hung his head, and one of the Rangers gave him a mug of steaming black coffee, a jar of which they'd manage to salvage from the wrecked office. "And there were a lot of them. I mean *a lot*." Cole looked up. "I think maybe those woods are full of the fuckers."

Robert frowned. "So why didn't they attack when we first arrived?"

"Maybe they've only just come back?" offered the Ranger who'd made the coffee, a man with pinched features Robert knew as Hurst.

"Maybe," said Robert rubbing his chin. "But why not follow these men out and attack them as well?"

"Perhaps they like the cover of the forest," Jack mused. "You of all people should be able to relate to that."

Or perhaps they've been trained, thought Robert. *Perhaps they're following some sort of orders?*

"Monstri, monstri," one of the Italian men was shouting again.

Monsters? It was the most ridiculous thing Robert had ever heard. "Is that what you think as well?" he asked Cole. "That these things are... are monsters?"

Cole shrugged. "Hard to say without taking a closer look at one, and I'm not fucking going back in there to do that."

"Then I guess there's only one thing for it," Robert said, turning.

Jack grabbed his arm. "I hope you're not thinking what I think you are."

"I'm going to get Cole here his closer look," Robert informed him without missing a beat.

"You can't be... Robbie, you saw what they did to the Lince!"

"My eyesight's not what it once was, but I'm not blind yet, Jack."

"Then—"

Robert placed a hand on his shoulder. "Stay here, and shore up the defences. We need to know we can keep them out if they try again."

"They didn't have much luck with that the first time around," his friend said, knowing it was no use arguing with Robert once his mind was made up.

Robert clapped Jack's shoulder. "I've done my fair share of hunting in my time," he said with a smirk. "I'll be fine." Although he was far from convinced.

THERE'D BEEN NO way of hiding his approach, so Robert hadn't even bothered trying. No sneaking in, no ninja-style tactics. If they hadn't followed the men up to the outpost, then chances were they wouldn't go for him. Yet.

So he just walked up to the edge of the forest. Robert stood there for a moment or two, glancing sideways at what remained of the Italian personnel carrier. They'd certainly done a number on it, and this close it looked even worse. Robert pulled up his hood, stared at the treeline from under it, then took an arrow from his quiver and slid it into position.

"Now you see me," he muttered under his breath, briefly looking down at his sword on one hip, the bag that linked him to his own forest back home hanging from the other. Then he prayed that this place would embrace him in the same way Sherwood had done.

And he was gone, away into the trees.

He kept his breathing low, his muscles flexed, and his tread light. Here, amongst the foliage, he blended in, became invisible. Robert pressed himself up against a trunk, peering around it. He could sense the presence of those things before he even saw what came next. Cole had been right, there *were* a lot of them. And they seemed to be everywhere.

Then they opened their eyes. Red in the darkness, they almost glowed. Dozens of pairs of crimson orbs, all searching for him. For this intruder who had so casually strolled up and knocked on their door, then snuck inside like a thief. For a moment it made him think: about all those times he'd said to Stevie that those monsters of his weren't real, then looked under the bed, in the closet, to reassure the kid.

Had he just been reassuring himself all along?

There was no such luxury this time, not now he was being confronted with those eyes. Robert couldn't deny the existence of *these* monsters. He heard the faintest of movement from above, and looked up. One was clambering through the branches. It was a move he'd employed many times in the past, keeping above ground so you could see your enemies. Robert tilted his bow, following the outline of the figure. What was it, some kind of ape? A trained ape? Like Poe's orang-utan, or something out of an old sci-fi movie he'd seen as a child?

But if they were monkeys, then where was the organ-grinder? Robert wondered. It stopped directly above him, and he leaned back into a crouch so he could shoot.

Crack!

Robert cursed the bones in his knee, letting out a "Shit!" as the thing hurled itself at him, plummeting through the branches. There was neither the time nor distance to shoot, so Robert improvised. He fell backwards onto the ground, lifted both his legs—bringing them back and bracing for the thing to land on the soles of his boots. As it did, Robert flipped it over his head and straightened his legs.

His position had been given away. He scrambled to his feet, aware that there were figures behind him as well as in front. Robert turned and loosed three arrows in quick succession, which he knew hit their mark. Nevertheless, the figures didn't go down. They just kept on coming.

"What now, old man?" he asked himself, as they surrounded him.

He let off a couple more arrows, in various directions, but again they didn't slow the creatures down one bit. Hell, if machine-guns and pistols hadn't done anything, what had made him think his arrows—which he'd relied on all these years—would be any different? If he'd been in Sherwood, then maybe. But the pouch at his belt just wasn't going to cut it this time, he feared.

Almost on him, coming from all sides. This was it, he was never going to see Mary or April again—

He felt hands on him, tugging him backwards.

"Come on! *Move!*" It was an American accent, his old friend's. Jack was pulling him out of harm's way, having broken through the ring, smacking the creatures left and right with his staff. You couldn't argue with brute force and leverage. By his side was Azhar, cutting a swathe with his razor-sharp scimitars. "Didn't think we'd let you have all the fun, did you?" shouted Jack.

Robert remembered his own blade now, shouldered his bow and pulled the broadsword free of its sheath. He flung it left and right, punching another one of the creatures in the side of the head. "Look out!" warned Jack, and Robert spun—just in time to impale one of them on the end of his sword. It slid up the length of it, still squirming. *Christ these things are strong,* thought Robert. Then it shuddered, and finally fell still. *So, they* can *be killed!*

He was about to kick it off, when Jack stopped him. "Cole never said his sample had to be alive, did he?"

He hadn't.

"Let's leave this party, shall we?" Robert suggested, withdrawing with his friends on either side of him, dragging the body—their prize—along with them. Once they were a few feet away from the things, they turned and ran as quickly as they could—hoping that their pursuers wouldn't follow them out. If they were wrong, though, they were screwed. Jack took the body and hefted it across his broad shoulders with a grunt, after handing Robert his staff.

They'd guessed rightly; the creatures were now pulling back. Robert risked one last glance backwards into the forest and thought he saw something else apart from the 'monstri.' A robed figure, wearing a hood.

"The organ-grinder," he spat through clenched teeth.

"What are you jabbering about?" asked Jack, as they spilled out into the light again, tumbling forward and ensuring they were out of reach.

Jack dumped the hairy body in the back of the waiting truck they'd used to reach the forest, then climbed in himself. Azhar was next, followed by Robert. "Drive!" Robert called to Ranger Poynter in the front.

Jack repeated his question as they set off: "What do you mean?"

"I mean I reckon I know who's behind the attack on this outpost," he told his friend gravely. "And if I'm right, we're all in a lot more trouble than I thought."

APART FROM THE Rangers and NRI keeping watch at the walls—the remaining Lince had been used to barricade the broken gates—the rest of them gathered around the table the dead beast had been laid out on. In total, there were something like a dozen of their number left, not including Robert, Jack and Azhar.

Stretched out, the thing looked less ape-like and more human. Still naked but covered in hair, it more closely resembled some kind of deformed caveman than anything else. Muscles bulged abnormally as well, like they'd been inflated with a bicycle pump.

"If you're saying that the Morningstars might be behind this, then yeah, we're definitely in trouble," Jack had said when Robert told him what he'd seen.

"Morningstars?" Lagorio had asked, voice rising. "We have heard of these people. They are in league with the Devil himself!"

"They're just men," Robert said. "We've fought them before... *I've* fought them before, one-on-one. Actually, one-on-several. They're incredibly strong and are driven—most fanatics are—but they're still just men."

"They have raised demons!" This came from one of the Italian soldiers who'd made it out with Cole.

Robert turned to the medic. "What do *you* think, doctor? Is that what they've done?"

Cole, who had been busy examining the corpse—lifting the hands to study the sharp, elongated nails, peeling back lips to reveal ragged teeth, peering at the bloodshot eyes—stood back and rubbed the top of his head again. "No, he's human enough."

There was an audible and collective exhalation of breath, including—Robert was surprised to find—his own. "So what—?" he asked.

"He's been experimented upon. If I had access to a lab, I could draw some bloods and tell you exactly what this poor sod had been given. There were all kinds of Chembrews knocking around after the Cull, that did all kinds of things to you: gave you enhanced vision—if it didn't send you blind— altered your perceptions. Some were developed by the military, like the Perf-Es or Meg-Grade PCP."

"English, doc," said Jack.

Cole sighed wearily. "There was a lot of stuff going on behind closed doors, gentlemen. You heard rumours but... When the shit hit the fan, people who shouldn't have had access to it suddenly did. And that's not including DIY drugs off the streets. Dealers are like cockroaches, not even an apocalypse can get rid of them."

Robert was familiar with some of the crap that had been around after the Cull. While Bill was busy setting up his legal trading systems, there was a whole underground that relied on the fact that people wanted to forget their lives before, or at least make this one tolerable. They'd done their best to try and stamp it out, but there was only so much the Rangers could cope with.

"But this... I think we're dealing with something else here. Maybe an extrapolation of some of those, a refinement? Some kind of animal DNA mixed in there? It's hard to say without looking through a microscope, without being able to run the proper tests."

Robert folded his arms. "The effect is clear enough, though. It's made them wild, stronger even than the Morningstars. And they don't appear to feel any pain."

"But they're under the control of those bastards?" Jack spat.

"That'd be my guess," said Robert. "Or maybe they're just in the process of training them?"

"You mean this is some kind of trial run or something?" Jack said. "And we've wandered slap bang into the middle of it."

"The location's definitely remote enough for something like

that." Robert pointed to those red eyes. "Is it possible that whatever drug concoction they were given could also enhance their sight, even give them night vision?"

"Like I said," Cole answered with a nod, "even back then, some of the shit could do all kinds of things to you."

Jack leaned against the wall, adjusting the baseball cap he wore, though somehow it always ended up in the same place on his head. "Would certainly explain why they'd stop at the treeline. If they're sensitive to it, there'd be too much light out in that field for them."

"At the moment," Robert said. "But it'll be night soon enough."

"And our only way out is through that forest path," Cole reminded them, though it hardly needed saying. "Fuck doing that again!"

Robert shook his head. "Doesn't look like we've got any options left then. We batten down the hatches and wait for them to come to us, maybe pick them off as they do."

"But you said..." Lagorio began. "It's just that there are so many of them, signore. And they got in here already once."

"That's when these guys were caught with their pants down," said Jack. "Probably overnight or early morning. *We* know they're coming."

Robert wasn't sure if that was a blessing or a curse.

Which was why he was so twitchy as they stood and watched that forest right now on the battlements, the sky growing increasingly dark.

"Why don't they just make their goddamn move?" Jack had asked not long ago. Now here they were and how the big man must have wished he could take those words back.

Because that's when they'd seen them again: the eyes, glowing at the treeline. More than ever before. Advancing now across the field. So many that Robert lost count.

The monsters. The human monsters that someone, somewhere had created, according to Cole. Here they were, and Robert knew.

Knew that nothing, absolutely nothing, would ever be the same again.

CHAPTER SEVEN

THINGS WOULD NEVER be the same again, Mary knew that.

How could they be after what she'd found out? After what she'd stumbled upon that late afternoon? April was seeing a friend after school that day, so Mary had decided to go and have a chat with Sophie. Maybe she could help, get Sophie's take on what was happening between her and Mark. She'd never been one for interfering, in fact she liked to think she had a pretty good mother-in-law relationship with the girl, but she hated seeing them like this. Hated seeing *Mark* like this. Yes, he needed to get a handle on his jealousy, but at the same time Sophie needed to realise that some of her actions were a little... unwise. She was a friendly girl, nothing wrong with that—but some men saw that as a green light. Mary had witnessed this kind of thing for herself.

So, knowing Mark was away for a while, she'd knocked on their door and waited. No-one in. Mary checked the rest of the castle, but couldn't find her anywhere. Next she looked in the grounds, curious as to where Sophie might be, more than anything. She even asked at the gate to see if the girl had left—they'd have logged her out, provided an armed escort to wherever she might be going. None of them left the castle without one of those in tow. Sophie hadn't gone anywhere that they knew of.

She did a bit of asking around, in the hopes that someone had seen her at some point. If they hadn't, then Mary needed to report it. People going missing at the castle always set alarm bells ringing because of what had happened to Mark a few years ago: kidnapped by Shadow and taken to Sherwood to be exchanged for Robert. And with the place on alert anyway...

Then she bumped into Ranger Abney, who was up and about again today, though still looking a bit peaky. Mary asked him how he was feeling. "Okay now, thanks. I guess it must have been something I ate."

"I don't suppose you've come across Sophie on your travels, have you?" asked Mary. "Only I can't seem to find her anywhere."

Abney smiled. "Oh, I saw her not long ago up near the stables. I assumed she'd been seeing Mark off."

Mary uttered her thanks, not mentioning the fact that Mark had taken a horse and gone around midday. She headed off in the direction of the stables—it was at least a place to start looking. Sophie had probably decided to go for a walk or something around the grounds; it was a nice day after all, and they'd been cooped up inside the castle most of the winter. Any excuse to get out into the Spring sunshine after months of darkness and snow. At least there had been a sighting of her, which meant that she hadn't been captured—thank God.

She reached the stables, not actually intending to go in herself, just to use it as a starting point, but then she'd heard the giggling from inside. It sounded girlish, childish even, and for a moment Mary wondered if April and her friend were playing where they shouldn't be again. She'd been told on several occasions how dangerous it was in the stables, that a horse could kick out and seriously hurt someone, if they were spooked.

She imagined the voice of her late brother David in her head, although she hadn't heard him for such a long time now. *I really don't like the looks of this, Moo-Moo.*

Tentatively, Mary stepped inside.

There were only a couple of horses around at the moment, making the place look quite bare. It had been re-designed a few years ago to accommodate more animals, though even then they'd had to convert a house near to the castle to keep more as an overspill. Today, most of the horses from here had been taken. There was hay everywhere, extending into the shadows at the back... and that was where the giggling was coming from.

"April!" Mary called out, effecting her stern 'mum' voice—which actually also worked on Robert, she'd found. "April, if that's you—"

The giggling stopped.

"Don't make me come in there and fetch you!"

Mary heard a man's voice then, followed by shuffling noises. She frowned, a different kind of alarm going off now, then marched through the hay to the back of the stables. It was hard to see at first, but as her eyes grew accustomed to the dimness, she caught sight of a familiar face. One she'd spent the past hour looking for.

"Sophie?" she said.

The girl was on her feet now, stepping forward fully out of the shadows. She was adjusting and smoothing out the yellow, knee-length dress she had on. Pulling it *down* to knee-length, where it had been hitched up.

No, I don't like the looks of this one little bit, Moo-Moo.

"Sophie, what—" But even as she was saying it, Mary knew exactly what was going on. Her mind grasped for other explanations, but none came. So she just asked in an even tone: "Who's back there with you? Booth?"

Sophie look puzzled then, almost outraged that Mary could think such a thing. "This isn't how it looks," the girl replied.

"How it... I asked you a question," Mary snarled. Then the man joined them, stepping into the half-light himself, and her mouth fell open. Mary almost couldn't get the name out: "*Chillcott!*" Bloody Chillcott and that sour bloody face.

He said nothing, looking everywhere but at Mary.

"I wish April had bitten you somewhere else now," she said.

Told you, said David in her head.

"It... it isn't—" Sophie began, but was cut off by Mary raising her finger. Nevertheless, she persisted. "We... we weren't doing anything. Nothing happened. It was just a bit of fun. A game."

"You," Mary said, aiming that finger at Chillcott like it was one of her Peacekeeper pistols, part of her wishing it was. "Out of my sight."

Chillcott nodded, skirting round Mary and giving her a wide berth. Sophie made to leave as well, but Mary barred her way. "A *game?*"

"No, I mean—"

"A roll in the hay, Sophie? Classy. You're a walking bloody cliché."

You tell her, Moo-Moo!

"Look, you don't know how it's been. With Mark the way he is, the way he..." There were tears in Sophie's eyes now. "He doesn't trust me."

Mary couldn't believe what she was hearing. "*Trust you?* I can't imagine why!"

"This... it's the first time we... Nothing happened, I swear. It's just, well, Mark's never around, and... I needed someone to talk to and..."

And if you believe that, you'll believe anything.

Mary couldn't help herself. Suddenly she'd delivered a hard slap to Sophie's face, rocking the girl's head sideways and leaving white imprints on the skin.

Nice one, sis!

"I can't believe we let you into this family. Can't believe we loved you, took care of you. You don't deserve Mark."

Mary turned her back on the girl. She felt a hand on her arm, attempting to pull her back. "P-Please," Sophie burbled through the tears, "please don't tell Mark. Please, I can't be on my own again." Mary didn't know whether she meant *single*—which would inevitably happen when Mark found out—or cut off from the people here at the castle, back where she started out, aged fifteen, when Mark had found her; but then, Mary didn't really care anymore. Sophie's first thought was for herself, rather than what this would do to her devoted husband—and that said a lot about how she'd changed. Or maybe she'd had this in her all along, but none of them had seen it?

"Let go of me," Mary said and the hand was promptly removed. It didn't stop Sophie from following Mary out of the stables, though, blubbering all the way. What did stop her, stopped them both, was the sight of a hooded Mark on horseback arriving home. He trotted his brown and white steed up towards them, then dismounted.

He didn't ask what was going on, didn't want to know why his wife was crying, why she was following his mother out of the stables in such a state. He just pulled down his hood to reveal eyes that had also shed tears.

Then he walked up to them, looked over at Sophie and said: "Pack your things and get out."

She stared at him, then at Mary, bewildered. Nobody had told him anything; how could he possibly know? Mary had that answer: "You knew he'd gone out, but you didn't know where, did you? He's been to Sherwood, Sophie. He's been at Sherwood."

Mary didn't have to explain any more than that. The girl knew, though probably didn't fully understand—who of them did, including Robert?—the power of that place. The visions, the knowledge it provided.

Mark had been asking for the Forest's guidance since his father had allowed him to go on trips with him there, and it still gave it. He'd seen *something* there, at any rate, and hadn't needed her to tell him about Sophie.

"Mark, no. Let's talk about this. I—"

"I said: *go!*" Mark bellowed, loud enough to draw looks from Rangers up near the castle itself.

Sophie opened her mouth once, twice, then closed it again. "Fine," she said, turning and striding off to do as he'd asked. To remove all traces of herself from the room they shared.

Mary gaped at her son. She wanted to say she was sorry, that everything would be okay. But she knew that it wouldn't be. And she heard her brother's voice again, one last time:

Nothing will ever be the same again now, Moo-Moo, he told her. It was only what she knew already.

So, she did the one thing she could do. She opened her arms and let Mark collapse into them, feeling each wracking sob with him.

Trying, but failing, to lessen the hurt and pain he was feeling.

CHAPTER EIGHT

The outpost was surrounded.

Those inside looked out, made increasingly anxious by the mounting numbers. They'd soon be cut off, if they weren't already. It was only a small place, which probably made the crowds seem that much larger. Or maybe there really were that many outside, crowding in.

Either way, it was bad news.

Captain Jane Francis bit her lip as she looked out of the window of what had once been Matlock's police station, now requisitioned as a Ranger outpost. The people had been gathering since early that morning, at first one or two, then over a dozen, then suddenly hordes of them. More, surely, than could ever live in this small community just down the road from Ashover.

Jane knew why, of course. They'd heard the chatter over the radio, news of that incident in Bartertown spreading like... well, like wildfire. She didn't know all the ins and outs of what had happened yet, but folks were up in arms about the heavy-handedness of the Rangers. There had been injuries, fatalities, and damage to property, she did know that. All she could think was that an incident had gotten out of hand, but none of the Rangers under her command would ever have acted like that unless they'd felt seriously threatened. In fact, up until now, she'd prided herself in the relationship they'd developed with this community—that they'd gone to great lengths to foster—especially since her posting here the previous October.

Now they were marching on the Ranger HQ with placards that had slogans painted on them like *BULLIES OUT* and *NO TO STRONG-ARM TACTICS* and *DON'T LET THE BASTARDS GRIND YOU UNDERFOOT*. Some of them were chanting too, like hooligans at one of the old football matches she used to have to watch; her late husband had been so rabid about the game. Maybe some of them had had relatives in that town, maybe they were just bored. In any event, by midday, Jane knew she needed to do something. There were only a handful of Rangers stationed out here, and they were massively outnumbered if things got out of hand again. They'd radioed the town of Chesterfield for backup, but it seemed they were experiencing their own problems with protestors.

Just what had gotten into these people?

It was time to find out; to talk to them, at least. "Are you sure you want to do this, boss?" asked her Lieutenant, a bearded guy called Kelvin Tuttle. "Looks a bit hairy out there."

"What choice do we have? Someone's got to try and calm things down," she'd told him.

Jane tentatively opened the front door of the stationhouse, stepping out and holding her hands up to show she wasn't armed, looking down the steps at the crowd. "Could I have your attention, please!" she said, raising her voice. In the time before, Jane had been a gym instructor, used to raising her voice and dealing with awkward clients; this was no different, she thought to herself. They just needed a firm hand, someone who'd defuse the situation. The noise died down a little. "Thank you, I appreciate it," said Jane. "Now, I know why you're here and—"

"Piss off back inside your sty, pig!" someone shouted. Jane scanned the crowd but couldn't identify the speaker. There were quite a few people she didn't recognise, actually, mixed in amongst a smattering of villagers who—it had to be said—were starting to look quite uncomfortable.

"There's no need for that. I'm sure we can straighten out any—"

There was a shattering sound, a glass bottle smashing against the doorframe just inches away from her head. Jane flinched, recoiling. "*Hey!*" she said, "who threw that?" Jesus, she sounded like she was dealing with school kids. What did she actually have to threaten them with? Their cells didn't have enough room for *all* these people here.

Another smash, quite a distance from her, along the side of the building. Jane turned and looked, saw that where the bottle had exploded this time, there were flames. A Molotov cocktail.

Bloody hell, this is Matlock, for Heaven's sake! This kind of stuff just doesn't happen here, thought Jane. It hadn't even before the A-B Virus. But it *was* happening, and she needed to get back inside quick.

She retreated, backing through the doorway again and slamming it closed. "So what now?" asked Kelvin, concern etched on his face.

Jane wished to God she knew.

SO WHAT NOW?

Dale wished he knew what to say, but just couldn't find the words.

Hadn't been able to since he'd heard the news yesterday. He certainly hadn't said what he'd been on his way to find Mark to tell him, about him and Sian. About the baby. He couldn't do that to the poor guy, not after all the crap with Sophie. Dale still felt bad sometimes about what had happened back when he'd first come to the castle, about the way he'd been with Sophie—basically just messing with her, like he had done with a lot of girls up to that point. Seeing it as a challenge, enjoying the way she'd responded to his chat, the way they always did. Not thinking—not caring—about the effect it was having on Mark, especially as the couple hadn't even got together properly by then.

They'd all come through that little misunderstanding though, and if anything it had made them firmer friends... in the end. Could all have gone very differently, however. He could have ended up like Chillcott, having his arse handed to him by Mark—not that he would have been able to take Dale back then, as young and inexperienced as he was. Who knows, Dale might just have let him out of guilt—although Dale hadn't really felt regret in those days, either. But now, placing himself in Mark's shoes, imaging Sian with someone else... It put things in a slightly different light. He'd probably have pounded the guy into the dirt, too. Would probably have been grateful later that someone had stopped him, mind.

As Dale had done, when Mark had caught up with the Ranger that had been messing with Sophie. It had certainly been no training exercise, no game this time. Chillcott had raised his hands, almost in surrender, backing off and trying to get out of Mark's way. But Mark was having none of it. He'd pushed the Ranger, got in his face until Chillcott had retaliated. Then Mark had gone to town on him.

It was the first time Dale had really seen Mark fight like this, like he meant it. In the past, he'd always felt like the lad had been holding something back. But not on this occasion. Chillcott had been fighting for his life, blocking blows, managing to get a lucky punch or two in. But Dale could see it in Mark's eyes as he finally kicked out the man's legs from under him, then straddled him, raining blows down on his head...

He'd been ready to kill him.

Dale had dragged Mark off just in time, and for a moment there he wasn't sure whether his friend was going to start in on him too. As it was, he'd wrestled himself out of Dale's grip and made to return to the stricken Ranger, to finish the job. It had taken Dale and two other Rangers to restrain Mark.

"Clean him up," Dale had ordered, nodding to Chillcott. "Then get him away from here—for his own safety." Sophie had already gone by this point, hadn't even said goodbye to Dale or Sian. Why she'd done what she'd done, Dale didn't have a clue. He'd thought Mark and Sophie were tight as could be. Had never picked up on anything like that on her part.

Once Mark had calmed down a little, Dale had taken him back to the castle, assuring Mary he was in safe hands. That he'd look after Mark. And, though Dale hadn't known what to say, he'd known exactly what to *do* and what this called for. Single malt, lots of it.

They sat and drank in silence for a while, in one of the private rooms of the castle, furnished with easy chairs. Then Dale had listened as Mark talked, drunkenly slurring, pouring everything out, as more whiskey was poured into his glass. About how it felt like someone had stabbed him in the heart. No, not stabbed: had shot an arrow—a flaming hot arrow— into his chest. Dale had murmured "I know" and "Yeah, that's right" every now and again, silently thanking his lucky stars that he had Sian—and now the little one on the way. They'd fallen asleep sometime in the early hours of the morning, Dale knowing that Mary would have filled in his wife and told her not to worry if he didn't make it to bed that night.

When Dale woke around noon the next day, bleary-eyed and more than a little hung-over, he'd realised that actually it hadn't been such a great idea after all. Not because he felt like seven different kinds of shit (he very rarely drank these days, and never to excess like this) but because if an attempt had been made on the people they cared about last night, two of the best fighters in the whole place would have been pretty much useless. Pissed as farts and wallowing in self-pity.

There was also no sign of Mark.

Frantic, Dale roused himself, slapping his own face, trying to clear his head. He stood, feeling dizzy and more than a little sick. But he ran from the room, calling Mark's name as he made his way through the castle.

Passing a window, he saw the armoured jeep just inside the side gates of the castle. And there was Mark, standing and talking to two men in NRI uniforms.

As Dale made his way downstairs, he was joined by Mary. "What's going on?" he asked her, but she didn't know. What she did know was that Robert hadn't been in touch in well over a day, that they hadn't been able to raise him and nobody over in Italy seemed to know where he was.

"I haven't said anything to April yet," she warned Dale. And as they walked out into the sunlight, they were both hoping that the NRI hadn't brought bad news about the man who'd brought them all together so long ago.

From the grave look on Mark's face, they feared the worst. It wasn't until they reached him that they discovered the real problem, though.

"Sergeant Allen," said the first soldier, saluting to Dale and Mary on their approach, "and this is Private Potter. As we were just saying, the situation down south is turning grim. There's rioting on the streets of London, and it's growing ever closer to the palace." This was where King Jack was based most of the time. When they asked what had started this, the men quickly filled them in about what had happened at Bartertown, about the fight between the townspeople and the Rangers.

"We're getting calls from various Ranger outposts and main stations around the country, reporting volatile protests," Mark added, having seemingly bounced back a lot quicker than Dale from the previous night's session. He appeared more together, at least, which was good, thought Dale. The situation had seemingly focussed him. "I'll bet anything that the Defiants are helping to stir up this unrest."

"His Majesty is requesting assistance from the Rangers," Potter chimed in.

"How much assistance are we talking here?" asked Dale.

"Anything you can spare basically, in the interests of both the safety of the United Kingdom and our future alliance."

Dale wasn't sure, but the last bit sounded very much like a veiled threat: *if you're not there for us now, we won't be there for you in the future.*

"And the advice that's being given is the use of extreme force to quell the threat," said Mark.

"Fight fire with fire, if you like," stated Potter.

"The advice?" asked Mary. "Whose advice?"

"It comes from the very top, ma'am." Allen pronounced it *marm*. Mary didn't bother asking what it was the top of, probably because she knew she wouldn't get an answer.

"We can't afford for all this to escalate," Potter pressed, "or everything we've worked so hard to build together could start to unravel."

Mark nodded. "You can count on our support."

"Mark, wait a second," said Mary.

"And the word'll be put across the wire about how to handle any mobs," he added.

"Mark, are you sure about this, mate?" asked Dale. "Maybe we should wait till we can get a hold of Robert and—"

"Dad—Robert left *me* in charge," said Mark, voice rising.

"I'm not questioning that," Dale replied, shaking his head. "I just think we need to take a bit of time to think about—"

"What's to think about? Our people are in trouble, they're getting hurt. And the King needs our help."

"It's not as simple as—" Mary began, but Mark held up his hand to silence her. She stepped back, mouth open. Dale couldn't believe what he'd just seen. This really wasn't Mark; or not Mark in his right mind, at any rate.

"Listen—"

"It's done, Dale! Sergeant, I'll make arrangements for the support you need."

Allen nodded. "Thank you sir, you won't regret this."

He will, you know, thought Dale to himself as Mary stormed off, arms folded across her chest. *And probably sooner rather than later.*

But what would happen now was anyone's guess.

CAPTAIN JANE FRANCIS had been agonising over what to do, when the decision had been taken out of her hands. Things were growing worse by the minute out there, with more Molotovs being thrown at the building and railings, spreading fire across their line of vision, rocks and bricks being thrown at windows already weakened by time and vandalism. She was loathe to retaliate—they were meant to be a peacekeeping force after all—and when the use of extreme measures had come down the wire she hadn't exactly felt comfortable about that. But it had made the decision to fight back a little easier.

Maybe they'd back off with a few warning shots, Jane reasoned. So she'd given the order to shoot a couple of arrows across their bows from the upstairs windows. All that seemed to do was antagonise them, whip up those who seemed intent on a scrap into a veritable frenzy. More projectiles were hurled, and—though she couldn't be sure—it even sounded like a gun was fired at the station.

That was it, time to end this. "Tuttle, Fletcher, with me... Simpson and Hodges, cover us." Bows raised, hoods up, they opened the door and braved the angry crowds. "Stick close together," Jane said to her companions. Then to the protestors: "If you do not disperse, we will fight back!"

A large stone struck Tuttle on the shoulder, sending him reeling backwards. Fletcher shot first, aiming down at the direction the stone had come from. Then a couple of people, wearing scarves pulled up to cover their lower faces, rushed up the steps at Jane and she hit the first in the thigh, the second in the arm. She'd specifically said they needed to bring people down with as little damage to their person as possible: wound, nothing more, if they could help it.

Three more people came at them, closing the gap too quickly for Jane to use her bow effectively. Hodges winged one of them from above, and another arrow—presumably from Simpson— missed its target completely, bouncing uselessly off the steps. Then Jane was being struck with a piece of wood, which knocked her bow out of her hands anyway. Using the defensive techniques she'd been taught at Nottingham Castle, she blocked the next strike with her forearm, delivering a blow to her attacker's sternum that pitched him into two more behind. A knot of them went down then, like pins in a bowling alley.

More arrows were shot into the crowd and it was only now that Jane heard a high pitched cry. It was coming from the back, and the crowds parted then to reveal a body on the floor with an arrow sticking out of her. A middle-aged woman with long, silvery-blonde hair, blood pooling at her chest. There was another, younger woman—teenaged even—with short hair beside her. A daughter maybe, thought Jane, and she was the one who was screaming.

"Help! *Help her!*" the younger woman was yelling to anyone who'd listen. "Please help her!"

Jane tried to swallow, but couldn't. Time seemed to slow down, neither side fighting now, just standing there. Then the younger girl turned and glared at Jane.

"You! You did this! She only came out to see what was going on."

All eyes were on the Ranger Captain now, boring into her. It didn't matter that this lot had started the riot.

And, as much regret as Jane felt right now, she knew she wouldn't be the only Ranger leader who would have to carry such a burden before this day was out.

CHAPTER NINE

IT WAS THE dream of a forest on fire again.

Except, was it a dream? He couldn't remember. He recalled the run up to it well enough. The waiting—for something. Now what was it? Ah yes, night-time. No, not the night specifically, but what it would bring.

Monsters. Moving like a wave over that field, towards the fort. There had to be at least three times as many as them: sixty, maybe even seventy. Robert and Jack had watched them carefully, studying their movements. Watching how they bounded, some even using their arms and hands to propel them forwards. The Rangers were on the wall, including Hurst and Poynter. Robert knew from talking to her earlier that it would be her first time in a proper battle—and she'd certainly picked a peach to start off with. Looking over, Robert couldn't help imagining April at that age, what she might be like—maybe a lot like Poynter. "It'll be okay. You'll be fine," he'd said to her, not really knowing how much comfort his words would be. She'd given him the best smile she could muster.

"Here they come," Jack had said, preparing himself as much as the rest of them.

Lagorio, holding a Socimi Type 821 submachine gun in front of him like it was about to come alive, began praying loudly in his native tongue. In the courtyard were a mixture of NRI and the Italians that were left. They were there to hold the gate in case any should get through, the second Lince turned sideways and propped against the already mangled doors.

Cole, who was also on the wall with them and armed with an HK53 rifle—a little way over to Robert's right—called out, either in response to Jack's line or the praying: "God help us all!"

They could certainly use the help of some kind of deity right now, Robert remembered thinking, touching that bag again on his belt.

Then the horde was just metres away, splitting off into different packs—some tackling the sides of the fort, others heading straight for the gates. "Pick your targets, everyone," said Robert. "Aim for the heads."

Several were scaling the walls of the outpost, clawed fingers and feet finding purchase. It should have been agony, but of course they felt nothing. Robert bent over the side and loosed two arrows in one shot. The creature he'd been aiming for swung away from the wall on one arm, dodging the projectiles, then swung back again and carried on climbing. Whatever else they were, they had fantastic reflexes.

There was the sound of gunfire, both on the wall and from down at the entrance, where Robert could see the beasts were making headway breaking in. For their part, the defenders of the fort weren't making a dent in the enemy's numbers. In fact, Robert didn't think they'd taken one solitary creature out yet. It was time for Phase Two.

"Okay," said Robert. "Let's lighten things up around here a little."

He bent and grabbed one of the arrows he'd made earlier; all the Rangers had them—with strips of cloth tied around the ends, doused in petrol taken from the jeeps they'd found in the courtyard, and the truck. Robert lit it with a match, aimed, and shot it at the monster he'd missed. It tried to dodge again, but this time Robert hadn't been trying to hit it. He'd been aiming for a spot just to the side of the creature: difficult at this angle, but never impossible for him. The arrow struck, spreading the flames outward and across to the beast, who recoiled and lost his grip on the wall, then tumbled back and into more of his kind just below him. Robert followed it up with another flaming arrow, this time hitting the bodies that had fallen and setting them all alight. The hair covering them went up like a bush-fire.

He allowed himself a satisfied grunt, but soon regretted it when he saw that more creatures to the left and right had reached the top of the fort's wall. Hurst was ripped to shreds almost immediately, letting out an ear-piercing shriek. Cole was firing at one of them, which had perched on the ledge like a bird, before springing off and leaping at the medic. There were sparks as the bullets hit the wall, but inevitably the man was carried backwards and fell off the battlements, dropping into the courtyard where his prolonged cries were suddenly cut off.

"We all going to die!" Lagorio was yelling at the top of his voice.

"Get a grip, pal!" Jack shouted, before turning his attention to a creature clambering over the wall. He thrust his staff into its face, sending it back where it had come from with a growl.

Another had got onto the battlements near the Italian, and he grabbed Poynter, spinning her around and using her as a human shield.

"For the love of..." Before it could reach either of them, Robert lit another arrow and loosed it at the beast, striking it in the back. The creature stumbled around, a living torch, reaching out to snag anyone close enough and take them with it. It found Poynter and pulled her over the side. Robert covered the distance quickly, though not as quickly as he would have done a decade ago—more's the pity—but he did get there in time to grab the girl's wrist. The monster was still hanging on to her by the legs, and Robert was struggling to keep hold of them both, to take their weight. He looked over for Jack, but the man was busy going toe-to-toe with another beast that had made it over. He turned his head the other way, looking to Lagorio for assistance. "Help me, man!"

The Italian stood frozen, still holding his weapon as if he didn't know what its purpose was. Then, to Robert's amazement, he turned and ran—off along the battlements, heading for the steps to take him downwards.

"Bloody coward!" Robert let go of his own weapon to cling on to Poynter with both hands. The girl's eyes were pleading with him.

You'll be fine... It'll be okay. It's all going to be okay, April.

"Y—You're going have to work with me here," Robert told her, but she didn't understand what he meant. Then the penny appeared to drop and she kicked out, dislodging the creature hanging on to her with the third attempt. "Good girl!" Robert began dragging her up the side, puffing a little as he did so.

"Look out," she said, pulling a knife and lunging past Robert—plunging it in the skull of one of the monstri. Its eyes rolled back into its head and it fell over the wall with a whine.

Robert gave her a grateful nod, and she smiled back, only now remembering to put out the fire that had spread from the monster to her cargos. He looked around him, pleased to see that the men were now employing another one of his ideas. Robert had seen this plenty of times on prison visits when he was a copper. Boiling water, mixed with the sugar from the kitchens. Not only did it burn, it also stuck to the skin—or fur, in this instance. They had heated pans of the stuff up here, for use in close quarter combat, and so they could tip it over the side and douse the creatures still climbing up.

Were things actually turning in their favour? he wondered.

Apparently not, because it was then that he heard a noise from beneath him: the unmistakable sound of the gates giving way yet again, of the brutes climbing through over the Lince. Robert glanced down into the courtyard, only to see those red-eyed bastards leaping onto members of the NRI and Italian guard, a smattering of gunfire all they had time to let loose. One poor sod was torn limb from limb, blood spraying everywhere at once.

Robert shook his head. Now they were inside the fort once more, streaming inside even though the gap at the gate was relatively small.

Then, like a miracle, there was Azhar. His blades whipped

left and right, so fast they were like helicopter blades. If the beasts thought their claws were savage, then they hadn't seen this man in action. He was tearing through the mob that came at him, never once letting them get more than a foot or two inside his reach.

Good old Azhar! thought Robert, snatching up his bow once more and slotting one of the petrol-soaked arrows into it. Maybe there was still a chance after all then...

Who was he kidding? These guys were still flooding over the tops of the walls, relentless and unstoppable. There were just too damned many.

It was then that Robert heard an engine above all the confusion. Only this was on the outside of the fort rather than inside. He looked over, to see the Thesis revving up. Bloody Lagorio! Somehow, the man had made it to the state car and was attempting a getaway, leaving them to it.

But the monstri had heard the noise too, were gravitating towards it. In a panic, the Italian flashed on the lights, momentarily blinding those closest. Then he set off, mowing a few over and attempting to cut a swathe through the beasts.

Robert barely had time to register the development, when he was suddenly barrelled into. Three of the creatures were on him, clawing at him. It felt like he'd been fed to the lions.

"Robbie!" came a cry and Jack was suddenly by his side, attempting to bat them off with little success. Poynter was on the other side, doing the same.

Robert was struggling to balance, and he was beginning to feel not only the weight of the creatures latched on to him, but also of the years. The next thing he knew, he was falling. With nobody there to catch him, as he'd done with Poynter, he plummeted from the wall of the battlements.

It seemed like a long drop. Long enough for him to try and position himself so that the beasts bore the brunt of the landing.

Still hurt like hell when he struck, though—like being hit by a train. Two of the monstri popped on impact, or at least that's what it felt like. Certainly something inside them popped, as indeed it did in Robert himself. One survived, rolling off him—but instead of attacking again, it limped away.

Robert's head was fuzzy. He tried to straighten his left leg, but found he couldn't. Found himself in excruciating pain, actually, looking up and seeing a hooded figure. A reflection of himself, perhaps? And a dead version of himself at that, because this figure had a skull for a face.

Or Death itself, finally here to tell Robert that his time was up. It was holding a machete in one hand. "G-Go on then. Do it," Robert managed, recognising the Morningstar Servitor he'd seen earlier on in the forest. "G-Get it over with."

But instead of raising the machetè, the man raised something in his other hand, and blew into it.

A whistle, thought Robert. *Like the kind they use to train attack dogs.* This man was calling back his pets, those that were left, so they could fight again another day. He nodded at Robert on the ground, then began striding away, joining the monsters flocking to him from the fort. As swiftly as they'd arrived, they began departing again.

Robert got on to his side, then his front. He hauled himself up, bracing himself on his good knee, and squinted. In the distance, he could make out the Thesis with its lights still on, inside and out now. The door was open, the driver's seat empty. Lagorio had apparently been dragged out to meet his fate, leaving the car to carry on driverless. It had struck a tree at the forest's edge, not far from where the Lince had overturned.

The Mornigstar and its monstri soon caught it up, heading inside the trees themselves.

"Oh... oh, no you don't," Robert managed through clenched teeth. He picked up his bow, knocked another arrow, and lit the end. "I... I can still see well enough for this."

And the arrow was away, travelling the length of the field as only one of Robert's could. It found its home, slamming into the state car's tank with a force it shouldn't really have had. Seconds later it went up, and with it the trees closest.

The fire spread, finding the Lince and devouring that too—until its own tank erupted. Soon the entire front of the forest was ablaze, the flames leaping from tree to tree, branch to branch.

Even at this distance, he could hear the howling from inside, the things in agony as they burned alive. Some even staggered out into the field, blazing...

Robert winced. Not because of his own pain, but because although it had been the only way to ensure the creatures didn't get away, burning that forest down made him incredibly uncomfortable. And he felt sure one day it would come back, as Jack might say, to bite him on the ass.

But for now he was done. Spent. Could no longer even hold himself upright. His vision, which had been clear enough momentarily as he took the shot, was now blurring again. His head hurt; his *everything* hurt.

As he collapsed, blacking out—as he'd done so many times before—he wondered if this really was the end for him.

And he wondered if the real Death was on its way now to claim him.

HE BLINKED ONCE, twice, then opened his eyes.

It wasn't Death's face he saw hovering over him, but Cole's. Last seen falling from the battlements, being attacked by one of the creatures. So, this was Heaven then? They'd sent someone familiar to greet him, to ease his transition?

Only, as Robert blinked a few more times and the misty halo disappeared from around the heavily-tattooed man, he saw that the medic's left arm and upper body was in plaster. His face and other arm had also been stitched, where the beast's claws had slashed him. But nevertheless, Cole smiled.

"Back in the land of the living, then?"

Am I? thought Robert.

"It was touch and go for a while there, so I'm told," the doctor continued, trying to shrug under his injuries. "Professional curiosity. I have to say they're very good here. Patched us both up nicely."

Robert looked past the man, looked around him to see a couple of beds, a large window at the far end, taps and a sink. It smelt of disinfectant in here; he was definitely in some kind of hospital. Robert ached, inside and out. Tentatively, he moved his right arm and found there was a drip attached. Then he tried to hitch himself up the bed so he could see down the length of it. His left leg was elevated, and there was a similar white cast encasing it.

"Oh," said Cole when he saw Robert pulling a face, "Broken in a couple of places, I'm afraid, though they were clean breaks; didn't have to be pinned or anything. You should be back on your feet fairly soon."

Robert pulled down his covers a little, saw that he was wearing torn pyjama bottoms, that his upper half was bandaged tight. Where there was flesh exposed, he'd also been stitched up. "Broken collar-bone and a couple of ribs as well. Still, you were lucky. We both were, when you think about it, compared with..." The medic's eyes dipped.

Robert's eyes caught sight of something on the bed with him, resting beside him. His pouch.

"Yeah, Jack wouldn't let them take that away, said you weren't to be separated. That it would help. Medicinal herbs or some bullshit. That right?"

"Some... something like that," said Robert. It could *definitely* have been a lot worse if his link to Sherwood had been severed.

"Speak of the Devil," said Cole, waving with his one good hand. "He's never been far away these past few days while you've been out of it."

Robert craned his neck to see his best friend standing in the doorway. The giant took his cap off as he entered, nodding a greeting. "Howdy," he said.

"It's good to see you," said Robert.

"Same," his friend replied, pulling up a chair. "How're you feeling?"

"Like I've just gone ten rounds with the Hammer," Robert said with a dry laugh, and started coughing. Jack was there immediately with a glass of water, urging Robert to take a few sips. How he felt was old. *Very* old. "How... How did they find us?" he asked eventually.

"Bit hard to miss the forest fire." This was Cole. "Might as well have sent up a flare."

"How... how many..." They knew what he was asking, who had survived the night? Both men's eyes brushed the floor this time, but it was Jack who answered.

"Not many, aside from the three of us—and Azhar, of course. He'd survive anything, that guy. Barely a scratch on him, in fact. One of the NRI is still in a bad way, one of the locals is looking like he won't make it through the next hour."

"Fort Vittoria," Cole whispered. "Some victory."

"Poynter?" asked Robert, suddenly.

Jack looked up and smiled. "Oh, yeah, the girl's all right. A few burns, but she'll live to fight another day."

Robert was glad about that. Then he thought about April, about Mary.

"Don't worry," said Jack, as if reading his mind. "I've been keeping in touch with home. I downplayed how serious things were, but you know how Mary is. If you feel strong enough to talk to them..."

Robert said that he was, so Jack arranged for the radio to be brought in. "Hi, sweetheart," was the first thing he said to his wife. "Told you I'd be in touch whenever I could. Love you."

"Oh, Robert, you have no idea," she said, and he could tell she was crying. "I've... we've been worried about you."

"Hey," he said. "It's me."

She laughed then. He spoke to her for a good half hour, then to April for the same amount of time. As usual, nothing much of importance was discussed, it was just lovely to chat to them, to hear their voices.

"You be a good girl now for Mum, okay?" Robert finished. "And Daddy'll be home as quickly as he can."

"'Kay, Dad. Love you," said the girl, and he repeated it back to her.

There was silence then, and he'd been expecting Mary to come back on. Instead, it was a man's voice he heard next. No, not quite a man's voice; it sounded too young for that. Sounded almost like a boy. "Hey."

"Mark?" asked Robert, not quite sure himself for a moment.

"Dad. I need to talk to you. I've messed things up, here. *Really* messed things up. Mum said she'd give me the chance to explain, so... Well, I'll try, but—"

"Mark, what is it, son?"

"I didn't know, you see. Not until we heard from Bill. He was there when it went down, in Bartertown. But he was injured, so we didn't... We didn't know they were behind it and... Then there was Sophie and—"

"Son, slow down. Slow down," Robert said. Then he

listened to what had happened, Mark's voice becoming more and more childlike as he went on, younger even than when they'd first met. As if he was confessing to stealing apples from an orchard.

When he'd done, and had apologised profusely, Robert simply sighed. Now he felt even older. Felt the weight on his shoulders of all this, because it *was* his fault. He'd been the one who left Mark in charge when he clearly hadn't been ready.

He was responsible, it was all on him. Whatever happened next.

And whatever that was, Robert knew one thing for sure. As Jack might say: It would not be good.

It would not be good at all.

CHAPTER TEN

HE WATCHED HER from his window, from his room—where he was still being 'held captive.'

Clive Jr peeped out, just as he had done the night *she* arrived. When he'd climbed out through that same window, climbed down the side of the house, and had that very interesting conversation with the man in the robes.

The man with the skull for a face.

He had indeed held the answers to so many of Clive's questions, and so many more the boy hadn't even thought of. But that was just the start, the man had promised him. There was so much more to discuss.

It was after the conversation had ended and he'd climbed back up to his room that she'd arrived. He could see the gate of New Hope from his bedroom, the only way through their walls—walls that his mother had put up to keep out invaders (a little late for his father... no, not his father... that still took some getting used to). Saw the commotion as people gathered and Tate had been called for. The gate had opened, and a visitor welcomed inside.

She was beautiful, that girl. Older than him, much older, but that didn't bother Clive. The girls his own age were immature, and some of them incredibly mean. This one, in the yellow dress, the girl with the freckles, was something else.

He'd learned later on that her name was Sophie, that she'd been cast out from the castle at Nottingham and sought refuge—sanctuary—here. An outcast, an outsider. Just like he was, at heart. Nobody would tell him why she'd been thrown out, but that didn't matter. They'd rejected her, and he felt sure that she'd feel the same as he did: cheated.

As Clive watched her now in the town, pumping water into a bucket, wearing a shirt and trousers but looking no less appealing—bending over first one way, then turning and bending the other—he felt feelings he'd never really experienced before. A longing, a burning inside him.

The man with a skull for a face had promised him he could have everything he'd ever wanted, could have the world. So maybe that included a queen to share it with? It would be a very lonely existence without someone by his side.

Yes, that's definitely what he wanted. As well as the rest... He'd return this girl to the castle, if that's what *she* wanted. She'd sit by his side, and they'd rule together.

But first there was something he had to do, the man had said. And Clive had agreed, even felt kind of okay about doing it.

First, the man had said to him, first he must get rid of his adoptive parents.

Kill them, and then in time...

Kill the Reverend Tate.

Somewhere near Lake Geneva

He had welcomed her back with open arms.

And why wouldn't he? She was his lover, after all. That was something Virgil hadn't known, or maybe he had and just didn't care. Well, the fool cared now. After trying it on when she stayed over at his country retreat, she'd given him something to think about. A few bruises, a split lip and a kick in the balls, to be precise.

Though that was nothing compared to what Mark had done to Chillcott, Virgil's man on the inside. He was still undergoing treatment, as far as she knew, the head Ranger having all but killed the man. Still, nothing he wouldn't have done for the cause anyway, for the charismatic Virgil—though his 'charms' had been wasted on her. Talk about an ego! But he was useful, a tool. A pawn in their game.

"Uschi," Schaefer'd said, planting a hard kiss on her lips. Now this man, her man, he had power. *Real* power. Schaefer, the head of the Neo-Nazis in charge of the German armed forces, driven underground—in more ways than one. But, instead of dwindling as many might have imagined, they'd flourished in hiding, and were stronger than ever. Had their fingers in more pies even than before. And they'd spread out into other countries, like this one: Switzerland. It was the base of operations for someone they had been keen to work with, a doctor who was not averse to testing his home-grown concoctions on human test-subjects. His labs were down here, in this system of tunnels they had taken over for their own purposes. A very secret set of tunnels that also housed one of their most prized acquisitions. "It's good to see you," Schaefer told her in even tones, breaking off the embrace.

"You also!" Uschi replied, with just a little too much fervour. She couldn't help it. Because of her mission—the one he'd give her personally—she hadn't seen him in several days. And she knew what that meant, where he'd take her once the formalities of the report were over and done with. What they'd do when they got there.

"All went well I trust?"

She nodded curtly. "Operation Flaming Arrow was a total success, on both fronts: Hood's inner circle has been destabilised, and support has been raised for Virgil's group. In fact, it worked better than we ever could have hoped." Right from the start, with Chillcott infiltrating the Rangers, they'd had the upper hand. It hadn't taken much effort to seduce Hood's daughter-in-law, making it a simple case of co-ordinating when they struck: both the market town and at the castle. It was a risk, certainly, but from what they'd gleaned about Mark and his jealous behaviour, they could pretty much predict he'd not be thinking clearly. Even the tour to get Hood out of the way had been their idea, planted by people they had on the inside. They knew that with their figurehead elsewhere, Mark would be left to hold the fort. It had only taken a nudge to get the young man to fall to pieces. "More successful, it would seem, than the good Doctor's pets and our other... associates." She said the word like it was venom she'd just sucked from a snakebite and was trying to spit out. The Morningstars were no friends of hers. But, again, they were useful at the moment. More pawns.

"On the contrary, I think it proved without a shadow of a doubt that those... pets, as you call them, are more than combat ready. Proved it to that fucking cult, at any rate."

"But Hood destroyed them, didn't he?"

Schaefer waved a hand. "Casualties of war. There are more, as you well know, where they came from."

"A shame they did not take out Hood first, though," Uschi commented. "Why was that again? How were there *any* survivors left?"

"My sweet, you know the answer to that question as well as I do."

She did, though she didn't agree with it. Schaefer had his own particular axe to grind with Hood, wanted to make him suffer rather than just putting him down like the dog he was. It was a long-term plan that could backfire on them spectacularly, if he wasn't careful. Not that she would ever say this to his face. He would probably have her executed.

So, having reported back, she waited as Schaefer dismissed the armed men surrounding them. Then the pair walked together down the long, man-made tunnels. Uschi was trembling with anticipation, both anxious to reach the place and wanting to stave off the moment so she could relish the excitement.

She remembered the first time Schaefer had taken her there, not that long into their relationship. Had he known how much of an aphrodisiac it would be to her, that thing? Maybe, maybe not. But he was certainly aware of it now.

As they rounded the final corner, making their way along the circular platform encircling it—high up, almost at its nose—

their metallic footsteps echoing throughout this cavernous space, she couldn't help smirking.

Uschi rushed to the rail, gripping it with both hands. Taking in the sight of the massive pointed cone in front of her, she let out a gasp. Another moan came, though, when she felt Schaefer behind her, hands reaching around to undo her camouflage jacket; then her belt; then the buttons of her cargos, which fell to the ground.

That was power. She was looking at it right now. Just the threat of it, let alone its use. The ultimate flaming arrow! She shivered with delight, which urged Schaefer on.

And, as he took her by those rails, she continued to stare at the huge rocket in front of her, knowing its potential.

Thinking about what would happen if—*when*—it was launched.

EPILOGUE

"...WELL?"

"Well what?" asked the storyteller.

Mouse was leaning so far forward on the stump, he was in danger of losing his balance and toppling off. "What happened after that?"

The storyteller pointed upwards. "The sky grows dark—or even darker, I should say. It will be night-time soon and I don't have to tell you what dangers await if you linger in these parts too long."

"But—"

The storyteller held up a finger, though it didn't stop Mouse from continuing.

"But that can't be the end of the story!"

"The end?" said the old man, smiling and revealing those rotten teeth. "Oh, my young friend, stories never end. They have happened before, many times—and *will* happen again."

"What?" Mouse was confused. "What do you mean?"

The old man said nothing.

"Look, I just want to know what happens next!"

"I'll tell you what, if you return this time tomorrow, I promise I will continue the story. Is that acceptable to you?"

Mouse thought about it for a moment or so. It seemed fair enough, and the sky was getting quite dark. He *should* probably find somewhere to sleep... to hide overnight. "Okay," he said. "If you promise."

"I just did, did I not?"

Mouse got up off the stump. "So I'll see you tomorrow, then?"

The old man nodded.

Mouse was turning to leave, when he thought suddenly. Something he couldn't wait for, something he had to know. "The... rocket thing, as you called it; was that what caused—" He began, but realised there was nobody around. The old man, the storyteller, was gone—as quickly and mysteriously as he had appeared in the first place.

Mouse looked about him, but all he could see were the blackened stumps.

There was no time to think about that now; Mouse had to get out of there. Find cover before night really did fall.

But he *would* return tomorrow, because he wanted to know. Whether or not the old man would keep his promise, Mouse couldn't be certain. Trust was a hard thing to come by these days.

Yet as he wandered off to lose himself, to get to safety, he began to hope. And that seemed strange, after its absence all these years.

In the end, though, he realised—as well as the story—that was something else the storyteller had given him.

Hope, where once there had been none.

And trust, in a world without faith.

BONUS STORY
A DREAM
OF SHERWOOD
PAUL KANE

IT STARTED, AS most dreams of his beloved Sherwood inevitably did, with the stag.

Older now than it once was, it still had power; still had strength. It was not to be underestimated. And it moved through the undergrowth like it owned this place... which, really, it did. In fact, it was more accurate to call the stag its caretaker, though as much as the creature looked after the forest, Sherwood also looked after it... after *him*. For he had worked out long ago what the stag was. It was a representation of him, the Hooded Man—in turn a symbol of something else. Of justice, of truth and right, in a land that had none.

Or *hadn't*, until he'd come along; now it was a very different story. He, the stag, could hold his head high, knowing he'd done all he could for the people. That he'd brought them safety and security, of a kind. Although in these perilous times you could never be sure that anything would last. Indeed, there was a battle coming that would change everything again. In spite of all he'd been through, there was still more to come.

That's what the forest had told him.

Today the stag he'd become was standing in a clearing,

flanked by foliage and trees. It was warm there, basking in a ray of sunlight. He closed his eyes, turned his face towards it: illuminated. Hopefully soon in more ways than one.

He felt—when he opened his eyes again—the heat shifting, coming from another source. Something that whipped over his head: an arrow, with a flaming tip, making its way through the forest. A guide of sorts, he realised, and as such he was compelled to follow it. Chase it, as fast as his ageing legs would carry him.

As he did so, he risked a look left and right, and saw visions: on one side was a big black snake curling itself around a golden throne, while a brutish bull-creature stood guard next to it like the mythical Minotaur. The snake showed its crooked and yellow fangs as it began hissing at him—the symbol of all evil since the Garden of Eden—and then shifted position to reveal a second snake. It looked exactly like the first one, only smaller; its child, perhaps? It hissed at the stag like its father. Somehow he had the feeling that, once fully grown, the smaller serpent would be infinitely more dangerous than the one who had sired it.

On the other side was a bear, which immediately reared up and stood on its back legs. Its fur was red, as if dyed, and its growl was loud when it finally came. As he continued to watch, the animal split into two, producing a perfect duplicate in every respect apart from one: it had a curved blade in place of one of its front paws. The new bear also growled, as its twin disappeared in the trees, and then began slashing with the blade, cutting through the air. Suddenly, the Minotaur was there, too, and the pair were fighting. Locked in combat, struggling against each other, the Minotaur holding the bear's front legs as it gored its opponent with its own horns, staining the bear's fur with blood.

Though he was still in motion, the stag somehow saw all of this and more. The forest was trying to tell him things, and he'd learned long ago to take notice. As well as healing him when he was wounded, it also showed him the past, the present... and the future. Sometimes it was hard to work out which was which, especially as time seemed to curl around in circles, some events apparently destined to happen again and again.

He looked back across at the throne and saw that the first snake was now gone, replaced by its successor—and he'd been right. As it grew, it spat its venom at the stag's feet. The liquid hissed as it ate into the floor.

By the time he cast his gaze back to the fight, it was all over and the bear was standing, victorious, over the body of the Minotaur. But its celebrations didn't last very long before it was struck in the back of the head by something metallic which the stag couldn't quite make out. Something that went on ahead, racing in front of the arrow and disappearing out of sight. He felt sure he hadn't seen the last of it, though.

On and on, and when the stag looked to the side once more there were bones in the woodland. The skeletal remains of something huge, which looked at first glance to be a bird—for it had wings—but which he saw now was dragon. On the opposite side, the stag saw a large cauldron that had been upturned, its contents spilling out onto the ground. More bones, *human* remains this time that had been boiling away inside the pot. Cards were scattered around the grass there as well, the kind used by fortune tellers to try and predict the future. Their owner wasn't far behind, also skeletal but still moving, a giant spider which climbed over the cauldron and began to gather up the cards. It kicked one across, close enough for the stag to bend and see. Elaborately illustrated, the card portrayed a colourfully-dressed man dancing along a path, with a bindle over his shoulder. The man was casually dancing along towards the edge of a cliff, unaware of the mortal danger.

The card, and the man it depicted, was THE FOOL.

Was that what *he* was doing? Was he rushing headlong towards his doom without knowing it, chasing the arrow still burning so brightly ahead of him? Or was it what he was doing in that other place? The *real* world he'd come from, where there were no symbols or warnings, where things just happened and you had to deal with them.

The stag couldn't really stop anyway, his legs propelling him forward whether he wanted to go or not. And he'd suddenly been joined by another animal that ran alongside him, light brown in colour with a mane: a majestic lion, roaring to announce its presence. To offer its company. That was a comforting thing at the moment, because the forest was darkening. He felt like *he* was the one being watched now. Studied.

Then he *saw* that he was being observed. By dozens... no, tens of dozens of eyes. That was all he could see, in the darkness between trees: *things* scrutinising him, because he was sure they weren't people. Or not really people anyway, not the way their eyes glowed red like that. The stag looked around for the lion, but it was gone, leaving him wondering whether it had been friend or foe—or even something in-between. He was safe enough, though, here in the middle, his way lit by the flaming arrow ahead of him.

Leading him on, finally, to his destination.

Before he reached it, he caught sight of the metal thing from earlier, now flapping its wings. A large bird of what looked like iron, hanging in the air ahead of him, above another clearing. It opened its wings wide and then transformed into something else, a cross of sorts—though all of its four 'arms' were bent. The stag stared at it, wondering what it meant, lit up by the arrow it had overtaken.

When he looked back down again, he saw what had been waiting for him at the end of this journey.

Death.

Not his own, no precipices to walk over while he wasn't looking. This was much, much worse. The people he cared about, the people he *loved* so much were laying there covered in blood. He wanted to go to them—especially his beloved wife, his child, his brothers—but realised that he could not. Here he was not a man at all, he was an animal. He was only what the dream forest would let him be; all he could do was take in those bodies, those faces. All he could do was mourn them. Then came the anger—and the questions. How had this happened? Who was responsible?

He really *had* been a fool, hadn't he? While he'd been bounding along, his family was being slaughtered by unknown hands. But if he hadn't been able to save them, he could at least avenge them. The stag, teeth gritted, looked up again at the strange iron cross in the sky, saw the flaming arrow strike its centre. Knew, in his heart, that he'd been the one who'd shot it.

Yet he felt a compulsion to look back, look behind him over his shoulder. It was only at this point that he saw the damage done by the arrow, a forest alight. Burning brightly one minute, burnt to the ground the next, leaving behind only blackened stumps.

More tears came then, because not only had he lost his kin, he had also lost his home.

This dream of Sherwood had become a nightmare.

THE HOODED MAN woke, sitting bolt upright, looking around, a hand automatically on his bow.

He had to make sure they were still safe. For a moment he panicked; they were all prone, laid out like they had been in the dreamscape. But they were far from dead. He picked up soft breathing, even snoring, as they slumbered. And now a couple of them stirred, though only long enough to roll over and continue sleeping. He let out the breath he'd been holding, looked down and across to see his wife beside him, her dark hair splayed out beneath her like some beauty from a painting. Reaching out, he placed his hand on the swell of her stomach then wished he hadn't, because she was instantly awake.

"Robin?" she said, on seeing his face. "Robin, what is it? What is amiss?"

He shook his head. "It is nothing, Marian. A troubling dream." Now she looked concerned as well. Marian knew as well as he that a dream in Sherwood, probably *of* Sherwood if she knew her Robin well, did not mean nothing. Moreover, his dreams—the warnings the forest spirits gave to him—had saved them all on more than one occasion.

"Tell me," she insisted, and he did... or as much as he felt comfortable saying. Robin did not—could not—share the image of her and his men, murdered where they lay: Much, who was like a son to him; Little John, his brother; Friar Tuck, a brother in more ways than one; and Will, who he was forever clashing with but loved all the same. Once more, he cast his eyes around their camp to check they were all right. For one thing, any intruder on this night would have to get past Alan and the Saracen, on lookout in either direction.

"There is more, is there not?" Marian was far from stupid, Robin knew that.

"Aye," he told her wearily. "This dream was different from the others I have had in the past. It did not feel as if I was dreaming about us, about our conflict... That is to say, the Sheriff was definitely there—in the form of a snake as before—but it was not him. For one thing, he remains childless, as far as I know. And those others... The red bears, the dragon, the spider-witch. Enemies yet to be encountered, perhaps, but I do not think they are ours. I did not even feel like *I* was truly myself. I was the stag again, yet..."

Marian's brow creased and she shook her head. "I do not understand, my love."

"Neither do I," Robin admitted. "But I did get the sense that what we are doing here, today, will affect what happens after this. Maybe even long after we are gone ourselves, leaving the struggle to those who follow." He patted her belly again, rearranged the moss and leaves around her to make her more comfortable. It was a balmy night, this one, so they'd chosen to bed down outside under the stars. "Now sleep, Marian. We will speak of this again tomorrow."

Before she could say another word, Robin placed a finger on her lips, then took her head and rested it on his chest, leaning back with her. Though he knew it would be a long time before sleep visited him once more.

Thoughts and wonderings about what was to come flitted and whirled around inside his head. Wonderings that would bother him from that day forward, until he took his dying breath. About the possibility of another Hooded Man.

A man whose dreams he may have accidentally stolen upon.

ACKNOWLEDGEMENTS

My thanks to the team at Abaddon for letting me loose with the characters in the *Hooded Man* world once again and allowing me to catch up with them down the line. I was just as surprised to see what they were doing as readers will be, I think. In particular my heartfelt thanks to David Thomas Moore and Ben Smith for their support. My thanks also to Jonathan Oliver who commissioned those first three novels, which I had so much fun with—as indeed I did with this one. To all my mates in the writing world, you know who you are and how important you are to me. And to my other family, the one that keeps me going, especially my lovely daughter and *Arrowhead* fan Jen, and ever-loving wife. My very own Mary and my inspiration: Marie.

ABOUT THE AUTHOR

Paul Kane is an award-winning writer and editor based in Derbyshire, UK. His short story collections include *Alone (In the Dark)*, *Touching the Flame*, *FunnyBones*, *Peripheral Visions*, *Shadow Writer*, *The Adventures of Dalton Quayle*, *The Butterfly Man and Other Stories*, *The Spaces Between* and GHOSTS. His novellas include *Signs of Life*, *The Lazarus Condition*, RED and *Pain Cages*. He is the author of such novels as *Of Darkness and Light*, *The Gemini Factor* and the bestselling *Arrowhead* trilogy (*Arrowhead*, *Broken Arrow* and *Arrowland*, gathered together in the sellout omnibus edition *Hooded Man*), a post-apocalyptic reworking of the Robin Hood mythology. His latest novels are *Lunar* (which is set to be turned into a feature film), *Sleeper(s)* (a modern, horror version of *Sleeping Beauty*) and the short Y.A. novel *The Rainbow Man* (as P.B. Kane).

He has also written for comics, most notably for the *Dead Roots* zombie anthology alongside writers such as James Moran (*Torchwood*, *Cockneys vs. Zombies*) and Jason Arnopp (*Dr Who*, *Friday The 13th*). Paul is co-editor of the anthology *Hellbound Hearts* (Simon & Schuster)—stories based around the Clive Barker mythology that spawned *Hellraiser—The Mammoth Book of Body Horror* (Constable & Robinson/Running Press), featuring the likes of Stephen King and James Herbert, *A Carnivàle of Horror* (PS) featuring Ray Bradbury and Joe Hill, and *Beyond Rue Morgue* from Titan, stories based around Poe's detective, Dupin.

His non-fiction books are *The Hellraiser Films and Their Legacy*, *Voices in the Dark* and *Shadow Writer—The Non-Fiction. Vol. 1 & 2*, and his genre journalism has appeared in the likes of *SFX*, *Fangoria*, *Dreamwatch*, *Gorezone*, *Rue Morgue* and *DeathRay*. He has been a Guest at Alt.Fiction five times, was a Guest at the first SFX Weekender, at Thought Bubble in 2011, Derbyshire Literary Festival, Edge-Lit and Off the Shelf in 2012, plus Monster Mash and Event Horizon in 2013, as well as being a panellist at FantasyCon and the World Fantasy Convention.

His work has been optioned for film and television, and his zombie story "Dead Time" was turned into an episode of the Lionsgate/NBC TV series *Fear Itself*, adapted by Steve Niles (*30 Days of Night*) and directed by Darren Lynn Bousman (*SAW II-IV*). He also scripted *The Opportunity*, which premiered at the Cannes Film Festival, *Wind Chimes* (directed by Brad '7th Dimension' Watson and sold to TV) and *The Weeping Woman*—filmed by award-winning director Mark Steensland and starring Tony-nominated actor Stephen Geoffreys (*Fright Night*). You can find out more at his website www.shadow-writer.co.uk which has featured Guest Writers such as Dean Koontz, Robert Kirkman, Charlaine Harris and Guillermo del Toro.

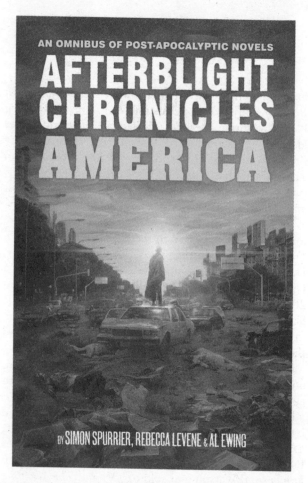

AN OMNIBUS OF POST-APOCALYPTIC NOVELS

AFTERBLIGHT CHRONICLES AMERICA

BY SIMON SPURRIER, REBECCA LEVENE & AL EWING

It swept across the world like the end of times, a killer virus that spared only those with one rare blood type. Now, in the ruined cities, cannibalism and casual murder are the rule, and religious fervour vies with cynical self-interest. The few who hope to make a difference, to rise above the monsters, must sometimes become monsters themselves.

An English soldier, killing his way across America to find the one hope he has of regaining his humanity, which he'd thought lost in the Cull; a doctor at the precipice of madness, who'd taken a Cure, in the last days, that may prove worse than the illness; a maniac who'd never had cause to care about anyone or go to any lengths to help them, until now.

Three stories. Three damned heroes.

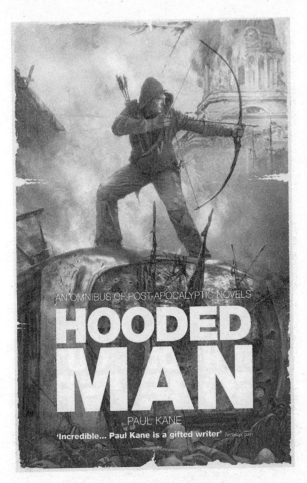

AN OMNIBUS OF POST-APOCALYPTIC NOVELS

HOODED MAN

PAUL KANE

'Incredible... Paul Kane is a gifted writer' *Terror.com*

After the world died, the Legend was reborn

When civilisation shuddered and died, Robert Stokes lost everything, including his wife and his son. The ex-cop retreated into the woods near Nottingham, to live off the land and wait to join his family. As the world descended into a new Dark Age, he turned his back on it all. The foreign mercenary and arms dealer De Falaise sees England is ripe for conquest. He works his way up the country, forging an army and pillaging as he goes. When De Falaise arrives at Nottingham and sets up his new dominion, Robert is drawn reluctantly into the resistance. From Sherwood he leads the fight and takes on the mantle of the world's greatest folk hero. The Hooded Man and his allies will become a symbol of freedom, a shining light in the horror of a blighted world, but he can never rest: De Falaise is only the first of his kind.

 WWW.ABADDONBOOKS.COM
Follow us on Twitter! www.twitter.com/abaddonbooks

AN OMNIBUS OF POST-APOCALYPTIC NOVELS

SCHOOL'S OUT
FOREVER

SCOTT K. ANDREWS

'The twists and turns keep you reading.' *SFX on School's Out*

**"After the world died we all sort of drifted back to school.
After all, where else was there for us to go?"**

Lee Keegan's fifteen. If most of the population of the world hadn't just died choking on their own blood, he might be worrying about acne, body odour and girls. As it is, he and the young Matron of his boarding school, Jane Crowther, have to try and protect their charges from cannibalistic gangs, religious fanatics, a bullying prefect experimenting with crucifixion and even the surviving might of the US Army.

Welcome to St. Mark's School for Boys and Girls...